THE DRAGON'S DESIRE

Almost desperately, Annice tried to twist away from him, but he held her much too easily.

"Do not force me, my lord," she said between angry breaths. " 'Twill go hardly with you when the king and my overlord learn what you have done."

"I had thought to hear more convincing arguments from such a fierce adversary," le Draca mocked without releasing his grip the slightest bit. "Do you not have a better reasoning than that?"

"Aye!" She glared up at him. "If you take that which I do not willingly yield, I will see you spitted for it like a wild boar."

His teeth flashed. "Ah, 'tis a violent nature you possess, sweet vixen. Like the fox, you bare your teeth and snarl a threat that you cannot sustain." One hand shifted to tangle in the loose twist of her hair. He lifted it slowly, letting it slide over his palm. "I am not a hare," he murmured, "that will fear the red fox."

Lifting his gaze to her face, he said softly, "And I can make you yield all to me willingly enough, milady. . . ."

Her breath came more quickly as he bent his head. . . .

The
QUEST

Juliana Garnett

BANTAM BOOKS
New York Toronto London Sydney Auckland

THE QUEST

A Bantam Fanfare Book / November 1995

FANFARE and the portrayal of a boxed "ff" are trademarks of Bantam Books, a division of Bantam Doubleday Dell Publishing Group, Inc.

ISBN 0-553-56861-2

Published simultaneously in the United States and Canada

Bantam Books are published by Bantam Books, a division of Bantam Doubleday Dell Publishing Group, Inc. Its trademark, consisting of the words "Bantam Books" and the portrayal of a rooster, is Registered in U.S. Patent and Trademark Office and in other countries. Marca Registrada. Bantam Books, 1540 Broadway, New York, New York 10036.

PRINTED IN THE UNITED STATES OF AMERICA
RAD   0 9 8 7 6 5 4 3 2 1

To

Walter Eugene McKinney,

who fought the dragon all twenty-two years
of his life—I think you won, after all.

THE QUEST

PART I

England
March 1214

CHAPTER 1

Mist curled softly around high stone walls, tattered trails shrouding the turrets of Stoneham Castle. A light wind blew, sifting through mist and the tree branches burgeoning with fresh green buds of new life. A cock crowed sleepily to herald the approaching dawn. The faint clatter of awakening inhabitants inside the castle could be heard in the thick woods stretching beyond the moat that encircled Stoneham.

Waiting with ill-concealed impatience for the sun to rise, Rolf of Dragonwyck quieted his restless destrier with a gentle rein and softly spoken word. He did it absently, his mind already on the anticipated meeting with the Earl of Seabrook. It was long overdue, as was a visit with Rolf's son, Justin. Only recently returned from France, Rolf had hoped to see Justin by now, but Lord Thurston had delayed.

A surge of anger tightened his mailed hands upon the reins, and the black destrier gave a startled snort, shaking his head with a harsh jangle of bit and curb chain.

Leaning forward, Edmund de Molay said softly, "Patience, my liege. Mayhap this time Lord Thurston will relinquish the boy."

Rolf did not reply for a moment. Edmund meant well. But both men knew that the likelihood of Thurston of Seabrook giving up custody of his nephew was slim. If it would not endanger Justin, Rolf would have risked the king's wrath by razing Stoneham to the ground to get his son. 'Twould not be the first castle he'd reduced to a pile of rubble; but if he acted without King John's sanction, he'd soon find himself one of the outlaw barons. He had worked too hard, endured too much, to lose it all now.

This time, with a letter from the Church pressing his suit to recover his only son and heir, he hoped for success. It had taken two years and many petitions and bribes to get even this politely worded letter from the cardinal. It was a slim chance at best. Even John ignored the Church when it was expedient. John's quarrel with the pope over the appointment of a new Archbishop of Canterbury had resulted in the king's excommunication from the Church. Only the year before had the rift been mended, so now it was doubtful the letter he had worked so hard to secure would matter to Seabrook.

Yet Edmund de Molay's hopeful words still rang in his ears, and Rolf managed a slight smile. "Mayhap he will, Edmund. I have heard that Thurston is not high in the king's estimation at the moment." His smile twisted into a sardonic curl. "Something to do with the debauchery of a young lady-in-waiting who had also caught John's eye, I understand."

Edmund laughed softly, his brown eyes gleaming with humor. "It has never been said that Thurston of Seabrook has either restraint or foresight." He paused, then added as a curse, "Bloody swine."

"Aye." Rolf stared at the forbidding stone walls of the keep that held his son hostage. "But that swine had foresight enough to take my son from me. I have been held hostage as well as Justin and would have it done. If I must, I will pursue Seabrook to the death to take back that which is mine."

Edmund lapsed into silence, and both men gazed at the

mist-shrouded castle. One of the men-at-arms coughed, and a horse whickered softly. There was the muffled sound of hooves against dirt, mingling with the metallic clank of weapons and chain mail. They had brought only a small band of men, just enough to make a show of force without being a threat. Rolf wanted only his son, and he would take whatever means he could to move Seabrook to consent.

But it was not in his nature to plead, even for that which he desired most. Nay, Edmund had oft made the remark that Rolf was as his ancestors of old, the daring Northmen who had mingled with Saxons to produce valiant warriors much more accustomed to storming castle walls with fire and sword than with letters and words. And it was true. Jésu, but nothing truer had ever been spoken of him. He had not earned his fierce reputation by offering up flowery phrases and stilted speeches. Since he'd been a boy barely strong enough to lift a sword, he had been used to taking what he wanted by force. Always large for his age, he had learned early and by necessity that the weak were quickly vanquished, while only the strong survived. Yea, he had learned it at his father's knee and, in so doing, had accumulated keeps and wealth.

But he would yield it all to have again one small boy. . . .

"Have you heard who awaits without the keep?"

Annice d'Arcy turned at her cousin's soft murmur. Gray shafts of early light streamed through a high window in hazy ribbons, picking out the pale glints in Alais's hair as she leaned closer. Nearby, sleepy-eyed ladies huddled close to a large brazier, warming hands and bare toes at the glowing red coals. Alais beckoned one of them come to her to do her hair, then turned back to Annice with an expectant expression.

Annice was working a long strand of her hair into a neat twist, carefully winding a thin blue silk ribbon around the coil. As she tied the ends in a long bow, she looked up with a faint smile. Alais loved to gossip and usually prefaced her choicest bits with "Have you heard . . . ?" If Alais wasn't such a sweet-natured person who normally wouldn't harm anyone, her fondness for gossip would have been more than Annice could bear.

"No," Annice asked dutifully, "who is outside the keep on such a chill morning?"

"A dragon," Alais whispered with a dramatic lilt in her tone. She glanced over her shoulder at the girl binding her hair, then added, "I long to view the ravening beast my husband says is the most vicious warrior in the land."

Frowning, Annice said slowly, "Do you mean Rolf, Lord of Dragonwyck? The man they call le Draca?"

Alais nodded. "Aye. Have you heard of him?"

"Yea. I have heard a little." Annice paused. "His reputation is grim, even for one of the king's warring barons. 'Tis said that he is ruthless with his enemies, and a stark man even with those of his close acquaintance. 'Twas le Draca who burned the entire keep of one of John's enemies, giving no quarter to any inside." She drew in a deep breath. "What does he here?"

"Thurston does not discuss business with me, but I know that he is guardian to le Draca's son." Alais smiled at her cousin's surprise. "You have been here only a short time, so you could not know. Rolf was wed to my husband's sister. She died in childbed, and Thurston was made guardian of their child. I do not understand myself why the king would name him guardian to Dragonwyck's son, save that it does keep the Dragon on a short leash. Rather like a tame bear, Thurston once said."

"I hardly think one could compare a man of le Draca's brutish nature to a poor bear," Annice murmured. "P'raps the title of dragon is more suited to him, after all."

Alais laughed and gave her a quick hug. "Yea, and a comely dragon he is, I hear. Shall we see for ourselves how comely he is?"

"Of course. I am never averse to viewing a man said to be comely, even one also said to wage war as savagely as the Welsh."

"I am so glad you came to stay with me. All the other ladies in residence are dull creatures, and much too dreary. I do hope your stay is lengthy."

"No more than I do," Annice replied. It was true.

Though there were times when Alais could try her patience greatly, she was grateful she was there instead of imprisoned. Circumstances had rendered it impossible for Annice to remain in her own keep after her husband had been executed. Luc d'Arcy had been all that stood between her and disaster; even he had failed her in the end.

"Here," Annice said when Alais sharply reproved her serving maid for pulling her hair, "let me bind it for you. I'm much faster."

"Aye," Alais muttered in relief. She waved the girl away with an impatient hand. "I vow I shall go mad if Thurston insists upon putting one more of these slatternly girls in my care. Do I look like a nursemaid?"

"Nay, sweet cousin." Annice hid a smile. It was unusual to find Alais interested in her own two daughters, much less the young girls Thurston seemed to favor as serving maids. Annice was the one who often visited the nursery, not Alais. She tied the last ribbon in her cousin's hair, neatly binding the willful blond tresses. "There, Alais. 'Tis done."

Alais peered into a small mirror and nodded with satisfaction. "I think the scarlet ribbons look best in my hair, don't you? Your hair is such a dark red that the blue ribbons look best on you. Now, come. We shall be late for Mass if we do not hurry. You know how ill-tempered Père Francois becomes if we arrive late."

"It seems to me," Annice murmured as she tucked her hair beneath the folds of an ermine-lined hood, "that Père Francois is much too fond of being ill-tempered."

Alais broke into a peal of laughter. "Yea, but he enjoys it so. One should suffer the whims of the elderly, I suppose."

Annice smiled faintly and went to warm her hands at the fire while Alais began to scold the ladies still gathered around it. A quick, hard slap or two was administered; then the group left the main chamber for the small chapel in the bailey.

Gray light filtered through the mist in shifting patches. Early-morning chill was still in the air. Even in her mantle of wool and ermine she was cold, and Annice slid her hands beneath the long cuffs attached to the sleeves of her cotte to keep them warm. Her lamb's wool gloves had been lost recently, and she suspected that one of the girls Thurston had sent as attendants for his young wife was responsible for their loss. Poor Alais. She pretended not to know why her husband sent her the girls, when everyone else was well aware of Thurston's penchant for casually tumbling serving wenches. It wasn't that Alais wasn't pretty, for she was; her complexion was fair and unblemished, her hair a golden blond that men seemed to favor, and her body pleasingly rounded. Yet Thurston of Seabrook favored lowborn sluts and common serfs in his bed instead of his wife. Why, Annice often wondered, were men such rutting beasts?

Père Francois was already waiting impatiently on them and cast a severe glance at the group of giggling girls with Annice and Alais. Alais gave the nearest girl a harsh pinch, and the giggling ceased at once as they entered the chapel.

It was so cold in the chapel that Annice's breath formed frost clouds as she knelt to pray. First she prayed for the repose of the souls of her parents, then, more dutifully, for her husband. Candlelight flickered over gray stone walls, embroidered hangings, and the gilt threads in the elderly priest's surplice. His voice seemed to drone on forever. The responses Annice made were reflexive, learned by rote and spoken by rote. As usual lately, her thoughts turned to her situation instead of to the priest's homily.

These were perilous times for her. She had pleaded with Luc not to listen to the discontented barons mouthing treason, but her husband had refused to hearken to her. When the plot against King John had been discovered, some barons involved had been fortunate enough to escape to France. Luc had been one of the less fortunate. He'd lost his life, and his wife had lost her home. And her freedom.

Good fortune, however, had rescued Annice. Her father had been one of the few who had kindly tolerated the child John. Even after Hugh's death ten years before, the king had not forgotten the kindnesses shown to a prince. It was a stroke of sheer whimsy that John had recalled Hugh de Beauchamp's daughter, but that recollection had saved Annice from prison or worse.

It was at the king's order that she had come to Seabrook to stay with her cousin. Luc d'Arcy had been the Earl of

Seabrook's vassal, and his death had left her Thurston's responsibility. The earl had appointed a steward to care for her lands until he settled a suitable husband on her. *Husband.*

Annice hoped that it would be a long time before a husband was found. She had been betrothed in her cradle and wed at the age of thirteen to a man she'd never seen before; though Luc d'Arcy had not been an overly cruel man, neither had he been a good husband. Her first reaction to Luc's death had been fear for her own safety, then irritation that he had so foolishly cast his own life away. Annice had observed the proper period of mourning with little emotion.

She blew warm breath over her icy fingers. In the eleven years she'd been wed to Luc d'Arcy, she had spent many hours in prayer. Not, perhaps, as she should. How many times had she knelt on cold stones to pray that she might have a child? More times than she could count, yet she had never conceived. That she was barren had always been a bitter draft to swallow, yet now she hoped it might dissuade at least some suitors for her hand in marriage. She had seen enough of men and marriage to last her an entire lifetime. If possible, she would rule her own lands and spend the rest of her years in happy solitude.

But that, she knew, was not likely to happen. Luc's treason had wrested his lands from her grasp but left intact her inheritance. Though not a great fortune, it was substantial. Her only kin, a half brother raised in Normandy, would not dare interfere with the English king who was also his Norman overlord. As her overlord, Seabrook earned a tidy sum from her estates. She was a valuable pawn to the earl. With her dowry lands as prize, more than one man would press his suit.

When, finally, Mass was ended, Annice followed Alais and the others outside. The sun was higher now, burning off the mist. New green buds sprouted in the garden beyond the small fence, and she could hear the faint bleating of lambs. Spring at last, when everything was new and promising after the cold, bleak winter.

"Annice," Alais said, nudging close to her, "let us hurry to the hall to break our fast. Mayhap we will actually see this grim Dragon who haunts our forest. . . ."

The hall was chaotic, as always. A fire burned huge logs in the center of the room, smoke spiraling up to blacken the rafters. Well-trained birds of prey perched on the blackened beams, and an occasional feather drifted downward. Huge tapestries hung on the walls and fluttered slightly in elusive drafts. High windows filtered gray light. Torches sputtered in wall sconces, and branched candle holders glimmered at intervals on the long tables. The lord's table was placed at the head, with more tables set up at right angles down the length of the hall to accommodate knights and guests. Servants scurried back and forth from the kitchens to the tables, bearing massive platters of food that was usually cold by the time it reached those crowded at the tables.

Lord Seabrook favored a substantial morning meal; with the usual bowls of porridge and milk, he required meat when it was not Lent, eggs, and large quantities of white bread. Annice ate sparingly. Seated at the lord's table with Alais and her husband, she had the vantage point of viewing the entire hall. It was always interesting to her to observe the others who gathered of a morn. Some of them were knights in Seabrook's service, and she recognized one or two of his vassals, as well as one of her own vassals. She knew few men seated below the saltcellars. There was no sign of the Dragon.

Dogs quarreled beneath the long tables, fighting among the rushes for scraps of food. An occasional yelp was heard when a booted foot made contact with a particularly quarrelsome dog. The hum of conversation ebbed and flowed around her.

It was a relief to Annice when the morning meal was over. Knights and vassals departed, and servants began to clear the tables. She started to rise. Alais quickly grabbed the trailing cuff of her sleeve and gave a sharp tug.

"Stay," she whispered. "Don't you want to see the Dragon?"

Annice hesitated. Curiosity prompted her to linger, but prudence bade her flee to her chambers. The less she knew of Thurston's affairs, the better she liked it. The little she'd heard since she had been at Stoneham Castle was more than enough to convince her that she did not truly care for the earl's method of dealing with his villeins or the barons loyal to him. But this meeting did hold interesting promise. As a matter of courtesy, Rolf le Draca should have been invited inside the castle to break his fast with the earl. That he had been kept waiting outside until the meal was over was an open insult.

"Aye," she murmured, sitting back down on her stool, "p'raps I shall stay."

Alais smiled and squeezed her arm. It was a conspiratorial gesture; if Annice had departed the hall, Thurston would have probably sent his wife away with her. As it was, he seemed not to notice either of them as he gave the signal for business to begin. Tall, thin, and with the sharp face of a hawk, Seabrook took his seat in the high-backed chair behind a small table and waited. Torchlight flickered over his dark head as he drummed his fingers impatiently. A scribe stood just behind him, holding a ledger and quill.

Trestle tables were being removed and stacked against the walls until the next meal, and only a few benches were left scattered among the rushes. At the far end of the hall, the massive wooden doors were guarded by men-at-arms. Annice noticed that some of the knights had returned to the hall wearing chain mail and bearing weapons. They lounged with studied indifference against walls and in small groups. There was an air of expectation in their stances, almost of eagerness. 'Twas plain they anticipated trouble.

Annice's hands tightened in her lap when the double doors swung open at last and the Lord of Dragonwyck was announced. The atmosphere in the hall was charged as if with summer lightning when he stepped into the vast chamber. Alais muttered something under her breath that sounded like a prayer, and even Annice fought the pressing desire to cross herself as if to ward off a demon.

Framed in the open doorway and quite alone, the Dragon paused to survey the hall before approaching. Annice's first impression was of a much larger man than she'd supposed him to be. P'raps it was the armor he wore—or his demeanor. It was rumored that he descended from the fierce, huge Northmen who had raged along England's shores at one time. The resemblance, it was said, was especially notable in battle, when he fought as one of the wild berserkers feared for their savagery and strength.

Annice thought now that the rumors must hold much truth. Despite the intimidation of the earl's armed men in the chamber, the Dragon's manner was casual, almost indifferent. Even, she thought with growing amazement, slightly amused as he looked around the hall.

He did not wait to be beckoned nearer. Rolf le Draca strode forward with the arrogant bearing of a king, ignoring the stir he made amongst those watching. There was none of the air of a humble petitioner about him, as one might have supposed. Nay, this man had the insolence to approach the table where Seabrook waited without performing the courtesy of a formal address.

"You know why I have come," le Draca announced without preamble, and Annice shivered at the hostility in his rasping tone.

There was an odd unsettling in her stomach, as though she had eaten too many green apples. The Dragon was not at all what she'd expected; his massive shoulders were covered with chain mail and a surcoat that bore a rampant gold dragon against a field of black. A scarlet mantle swung from his shoulders, and a sword was belted at his side. He had removed his gauntlets and held them loosely in his hands. He wore no helmet, and his hair was a blaze of golden blond cut short over the ears and on his neck. His dark brown beard was neatly trimmed. Instead of the brutish, coarse man she had anticipated seeing, this man projected a leashed ferocity and aristocratic bearing that was startling. There was none of the butcher in his appearance; nay, he could have stepped from the verses of a romantic tale of knightly love. High cheekbones and a straight nose, large eyes beneath dark-blond brows, and a well-chiseled mouth that was now set in a taut line gave him the look of an archangel more than of a savage barbarian. Could this be the same Rolf le Draca whose name had been coupled with whispers of murder and vile excesses? It seemed unlikely, yet there could be no mistake.

The Dragon shifted impatiently when Seabrook did not reply; his spurs clinked. "Well, my lord?"

At last Thurston reacted, his voice light and faintly amused. "You have a novel method of begging a boon, Lord Rolf. 'Tis not my wont to discourse on such things in so terse a manner."

A dark-blond brow rose abruptly. "Nay? 'Twas my thought that you would prefer not to discuss this at all, Seabrook. Yet I have brought you a recommendation from the cardinal that you release my son to me."

"Have you?" Thurston leaned forward, clasping his hands on the surface of the table and smiling blandly. "Which cardinal, may I ask? As you know, there has been some contention as to who is the proper ecumenical authority in England."

"Robert Curson," was the growling reply, and Seabrook's smile broadened.

"Ah. He is now the legate in France, is he not?" Thurston gave a careless shrug. "Though Curson may negotiate with kings, he has little power to sway me."

"He is English born, and an ecclesiastical power. I have proved my oath of fealty to the king. Now I would have my son returned to me." Dragonwyck drew in a deep breath, and Annice studied him more closely.

Tension cut deep grooves in his face, and his eyes were slightly narrowed and intense. Beneath thick brown lashes, his eyes glittered a hot green that revealed tightly held fury. Yet there was something else there that intrigued her, a look almost of pain. His hands twisted his gauntlets into a tight coil as he waited for Seabrook's response, and Annice was suddenly, inexplicably, sympathetic.

"I would see the document signed by the cardinal," Thurston said after a moment, and le Draca withdrew a sheaf of folded parchment from a pouch on his belt. He stepped forward to place it on the table before Seabrook. There was an immediate reaction from the armed knights, a faint clink of swords and chain mail as they stirred. The Dragon paid them as much attention as he would have one of the huge hounds lurking under the tables. He stood impassively while Seabrook unfolded and read the missive.

Only Dragonwyck's eyes moved, registering those around him with an alertness bred into well-trained knights.

When his gaze shifted to her, Annice caught her breath. There was a faint flicker in his eyes; then he looked past her to the others at the table and beyond. She felt herself flush at his casual dismissal. There had been no interest in his gaze, only the recording of her presence as unimportant. It had been a long time since she had been so summarily dismissed.

For some reason his reaction rankled. Though she had no idea why she should care, Annice took affront. Few men looked at her without interest; even those infrequent visitors who had not yet been made aware of her status as heiress had appreciated her looks. She was not vain about her appearance, but she would have been utterly ignorant not to realize the effect she had on men at times. Too many men had stammered out paeans of praise for her "fair, beauteous face." It had never mattered to her before, yet it was oddly disturbing that the Lord of Dragonwyck did not seem to have the same opinion.

A crisp rustle of parchment drew le Draca's immediate attention, as well as everyone else's. Seabrook crumpled the document in one hand, his dark eyes narrowing into thin slits as he studied the man before him.

Annice was not at all surprised to hear Thurston murmur, "I regret that I must refuse your petition. Until King John returns from his sojourn in France, I have no authority to release the boy to you. It is at John's request, after all, that I have been named protector for your son." A faint, derisive smile curled Seabrook's mouth. "Something to do with doubts about your loyalty to the crown, I warrant."

"My loyalty to the crown and to England has never been in question," was the sharp, snarling reply.

"P'raps I have heard wrongly, then. Forgive me. Alas, the outcome is the same. My decision is still no." Seabrook's smile grew a bit weaker when le Draca took an abrupt step forward, one hand dropping to the hilt of his sword. There was the metallic whisk of swords being drawn along the sides of the hall. No one else moved, though someone in the chamber gave a nervous cough.

Dragonwyck, however, seemed to recall his situation and paused, eyes still glittering with fury. There was a brief, siz-

zling silence when even the great hounds seemed to hold
their breath; then le Draca inclined his head in a terse acceptance of Seabrook's edict. "As you will, my lord. When
the king returns, I expect to see you again."

"When King John returns from his foray into France,
perhaps you should offer your petition to him."

Holding out his hand, le Draca said evenly, "So I shall.
Return it to me."

There was a brief hesitation as Thurston clenched the
document in his fist. His eyes clashed with le Draca's; then,
slowly, he held out the crumpled sheaf of parchment; le
Draca took it from him. He gently smoothed it before re-
folding it and placing it back in a leather pouch. Then he
looked up at Seabrook with a cool stare that made the earl
shift uneasily in his chair.

Lip curling, le Draca asked curtly, "May I at least visit
with my son? It has been over a year since I have seen him."

"Of course. He is being held hostage, not prisoner."
Seabrook gave an airy wave of his hand. "I will have an escort accompany you to a private chamber for a visit." He
paused, then added, "You will understand, of course, if I insist that you leave your weapons with my bailiff."

"From you, my lord, I would expect nothing else."

Annice realized she was holding her breath when le
Draca pivoted on his booted heel and strode from the hall.
She let it out slowly and heard Alais do the same. A curious
silence lengthened; there was only the sound of the scribe's
pen furiously scribbling notes. The hush was broken when
the earl cleared his throat and gave the order for the Lord
of Dragonwyck's son to be taken to an antechamber.

Turning to his wife, Seabrook commanded, "Go with
them." He did not give a reason, but Annice knew that the
earl expected Alais to report upon everything said between
father and son. If he had sent one of his men, it would have
been too obvious. A gentlewoman, however, would not be
as suspect.

"Come with me," Alais murmured as she obediently rose
from her stool, and Annice assented. Curiosity as much as
compassion prompted her to attend her cousin. No small
child should be forced to confront a man of le Draca's fierce

temperament alone, but Annice could not help but wonder what such a man would have to say to a son he had seen only a few times in five years.

And, she could not help but muse, it would give her the chance to study him at closer distance. For some reason she could not explain, Rolf le Draca intrigued her.

CHAPTER 2

―――――――――

$\mathbf{A}$ high window allowed in dusty streamers of light that fell in a square across the stone floor. Rolf stood stiffly in the center of the room, hands curled into fists around his gauntlets as he stared blindly at the furnishings. He could feel the slight warmth of sunlight on his face, but his gaze was trained on the open door through which his son would soon enter. He hoped. Thurston of Seabrook was not a man to be trusted, even with so small a courtesy.

By now he knew that only too well. Aye, he had been overfoolish before in trusting Seabrook, and it had cost him dear. How could he have ever allowed Margerie to remain at Seabrook's castle for the lying-in of their son? It was a mystery to him why he had succumbed to his wife's wheedling. Guilt over his extended absences, mayhap, had led him to yield to her pleas. She had wanted to be at her family home for the birth of their first child, and he had agreed. If not for the small fracas over a disputed tract of land that had taken him away at a crucial time, he could have stopped Seabrook's machinations. Alas, by the time news reached him of his son's birth, Margerie was dead and their babe held in guardianship by his uncle.

And now he was reduced to this, disarmed and pleading like a ragged beggar for even a few moments with his own child and heir. Justin was never far from his thoughts. Jésu, but there were moments when he wanted to surrender to the driving urge to lay waste to Stoneham and all those in it who would keep his son away from him. It was a constant weight in his belly, as if he had swallowed a stone.

A small sound in the hallway outside the chamber brought him to the present with a jerk, and his muscles tensed when he heard the light chatter of a child. Not until Justin entered the room did Rolf realize just how stiff he'd become; it was difficult even to move forward, harder still to force his lips into a smile that felt more like a grimace.

"Son," he said, and was embarrassed by the hoarseness of his voice. The boy was accompanied by two women; he recognized Seabrook's wife, but 'twas the other who had a gentle hand on the boy's shoulder. Justin hung back shyly, and Rolf's throat tightened with suppressed emotion. How could he expect a child to understand a father who was never there for him, when he didn't understand it himself? His hands clenched into fists, and he gazed helplessly at his son.

" 'Tis your father," the woman bent to say softly beside Justin's ear. Rolf tore his gaze from his son to glance at her. It was the woman from the lord's table in the hall. He'd not seen her before today, for if he had, he would never have forgotten her. She was not a woman who would be quickly forgotten. Though she wore a simple cotte hardie of blue velvet, it was temptingly fitted at the bust, skirts widening only below a slender waist. Two thick strands of reddish-brown hair that was intertwined with blue ribbons hung down her back to her slim hips. The brilliant color of her hair alone would have been memorable, but 'twas her face that commanded the most interest. Yea, she was fair indeed.

Glancing back at him, the woman knelt beside Justin and smiled into his face. "Your father has come a great distance to see you," she said, "and he has waited a long time."

"I know," Justin said simply. His eyes turned to Rolf with a steady, assessing gaze. "I remember him."

Still, the boy did not move toward him, and Rolf hesitated. He did not wish to frighten him, but dear God, he wanted to touch him, to ruffle the pale-blond hair and see the winsome smile he had held close to his heart for so long.

Clearing his throat, he muttered, "I brought you a gift."

Justin's eyes widened, and a tremulous smile touched the corners of his lips. "A gift? For me?"

"Aye." Feeling clumsy, and as if his hand bore five thumbs instead of fingers that were adept with a sword and battle-ax, Rolf dug into the leather pouch hanging from his belt. He drew out a carved wooden horse the size of his hand. He had hoped to give it to the boy on the journey home but had been practical enough to realize that it might be just another gift in another brief visit.

Delighted, Justin stepped close and took the horse from his father's hand. Just the brush of those small fingers against his palm made Rolf's heart lurch, and he found himself kneeling on the floor on one knee so that his face was level with the boy's. The tip of his empty scabbard scraped loudly against the stones.

"See here," he said, and pointed to the carved saddle and trappings on the horse. " 'Tis my—our—family crest. Look closely, for it is not easy to see . . . aye, there. See the dragon? It stands for valor and courage against one's enemies. My destrier carries the same charges on his armor. Because you are my son, I have added a cadency mark to your device. See this? It's called a label, because you are the eldest son. I carved it very small, but you can still see it."

Justin examined the horse eagerly, face alight. "I see it! Did you really carve this for me?"

"Aye. Just for you. 'Tis a horse like my own. I have even given him the same wild look in his eye as Wulfsige." He smiled when Justin leaned casually against his bent knee, and put an arm trembling with strain around the lad. He was so small, yet so sturdy. Beneath the short tunic he wore, Justin had the wiry muscles that would one day make him a strong man. His hose were slightly baggy and twisted, his shoes scuffed as if he was used to rough play. Yea, one day Justin would be a man full-grown, a son to be proud of. What would he say to his father then?

"Can you make more horses?" Justin was asking. "Some with my mother's charges, perhaps?" Long lashes shadowed his childish cheeks as he clutched his horse to his chest, then looked up. Green eyes gazed trustingly at him, and Rolf could only nod silently while he struggled for control.

"Aye," he finally whispered. "I can carve more horses. This winter past I carved several knights and another destrier for you. I thought p'raps you could play with them."

Brightening, Justin exclaimed, "I can have my own lists, can't I? Just like a real tournament. Did you bring them with you?"

Rolf shook his head. "Nay, lad. Not this time. If I am able, I will bring them to you soon."

Disbelief was frankly reflected in his expression as he regarded his father for a long moment. "Aye," he said flatly, "bring them the next year you come."

At a loss Rolf floundered, wanting to tell his son that 'twas not his fault he could not come more often, but not wanting to burden the boy with troubles that might be too adult for him to comprehend. Angry and feeling helpless, his hands curled into tight fists as he stared silently at Justin.

It was the russet-haired woman who intervened. "May I see your gift?" she asked, kneeling beside Justin. She admired the horse for a moment, remarking on the exquisite craftsmanship and love that had gone into the carving. Slowly, as she talked of how thoughtful a gift it was, and how much time it must have taken to carve it, some of the disappointment faded from Justin's eyes and expression. A faint smile curved his mouth again.

"Tell your father about your new pony," the woman urged, and Justin hesitated.

" 'Tis just a pony," he said in a small voice. "Not as big or fierce as my father's destrier."

"I'm certain your father had a pony long before he ever rode a destrier," the woman said, and gave Rolf a pointed stare. He returned it for a moment blankly, then realized what she was about.

"Aye," he said hurriedly, "my first mount was a fat pony named Bramble. It didn't take me long to discover how he had earned that name. 'Twas his wont to toss me into the brambles every chance he got, until I was covered with weals and scratches."

Justin laughed delightedly and said, "My pony threw me, too! I named him Spiteful. But I truly like him. Next week, if my riding is better, I can ride outside the bailey walls. Montrose promised, and he always keeps his promises. He's the head ostler in the stables—oh, you should see the horses in my lord Seabrook's stables. Some are as big as three ponies. . . ."

As the boy chattered, Rolf looked up at the woman with a rush of gratitude. He did not know why she had done it— 'twas obvious to even a complete lackwit that the women had been sent with the boy to report anything of note he might say—but he was grateful she had come to his aid. Visits with Justin were so few and precious that any constraint between them would be devastating.

At his glance the woman flushed slightly. Color made her blue eyes seem brighter, and he noted distractedly that she needed no enhancement to her considerable beauty. He wondered who she was. One of Seabrook's multitude of conquests, mayhap? Nay, that could not be so, or she would not have been seated next to the earl's wife in her obvious high favor. Most likely a family member, or some visiting lord's wife.

Justin's hand on his knee drew his attention back to his son, and Rolf smiled. Yielding to his earlier compulsion, he ruffled the lad's blond hair so that it stuck up in wisps like straws. It was coarse like his own, without the fineness of his mother's, but he had Margerie's pale skin. A complex blending of two families into one small child that should have united them had somehow gone awry. The struggle for power was never ending, and he was as guilty in his way as Seabrook.

". . . you come back for the May Day celebration?" Justin was asking, and Rolf shook his head.

"Nay, lad. I would like to join you, but 'twould not be possible this year. P'raps next year, if the king allows it, you will be living with me at Dragonwyck. Would you like that?"

"I don't know." When Rolf smiled wryly at the boy's honesty, Justin added, "I have never seen it. Is your keep as big as Stoneham?"

Rolf hesitated. He was much too aware of Seabrook's wife hovering nearby and listening very carefully to the conversation. Even a small admission of strength could be dangerous.

Slowly, he shook his head. "Nay, not near as large. I have only a few men, and much of the keep is in disrepair. Most of my gold has gone into warfare of late. But soon I hope to turn the tide of our family fortunes," he couldn't resist adding when he saw Justin's disappointment.

"Oh." Justin looked crestfallen for a moment, then said, "You must do better. If I am your heir, I do not wish to inherit a pile of stones."

Surprised by the mature response, Rolf looked up when he heard a smothered laugh. His gaze met feminine blue eyes sparkling with amusement, and he couldn't help a faint laugh himself.

"I shall strive to do much better," he promised, and clasped Justin so tightly, the boy squeaked with alarm. He loosened his hold, not wishing for his mail to scrape the boy's tender skin. Gripping him on the shoulder, he looked into Justin's eyes for a moment. "Know this, my son," he said softly, "that even though I may not be here with you in body, I will always be with you in spirit. What I do, I do not for just myself, but for you. Do you understand?"

"Aye, Father."

It was the first time Justin had called him that, and Rolf could not speak for the lump in his throat. He ruffled the boy's hair affectionately, then rose to his feet. A mailed soldier stood in the open doorway, and he knew his brief time with Justin had ended. 'Twas just as well, he thought, for if he endured much more, he might unman himself with tears. He touched his son lightly on the head in farewell.

"God be with you, my son," he said gruffly.

Justin gazed up at him, eyes wide beneath lashes spiked

with tears. "God be with you, my lord," he replied dutifully, his voice small and shaky. Then he turned away.

Seabrook's wife stood by the doorway, and the russet-haired lady took Justin by the hand. He turned to go with her, then tore away and flung his small body at his father. Rolf caught him and hugged him fiercely. He could feel the tiny heart thumping even through his surcoat and mail, and he briefly closed his eyes. Then, gently, he set Justin on his feet. This time the boy left without a backward glance, small back held stiff and straight, the carved wooden horse tightly clutched in one hand.

Looking up, Rolf saw tears in the feminine blue eyes glancing back at him and wondered again who she was. Whoever she was, her heart was compassionate. It was not a common trait in the women he had known.

He walked to the door when they had departed, and the armed soldier standing guard gave him a wary glance. Rolf looked at him. "My lady of Seabrook's companion is her sister, is she not?" he asked casually, and the soldier shook his head.

"Nay, she is the lady's cousin."

Her cousin. There was a certain similarity, he supposed, though Lady Alais seemed more petulant than reserved like her cousin. And there had been no compassion in the cold brown eyes regarding them with suspicion. But he should not be surprised by the dissimilar natures of family members. Hadn't he served under King Richard? Didn't he know well the contradictions between that warrior king and the craven man who now ruled England? Aye, well he knew and regretted those differences. Richard might not have been the most politic ruler, but neither had he been as devious as John.

And neither would he have resented rendering unto his loyal vassal that which he had earned, as John did. Yea, one day John would rue his harsh tax laws and the autocratic seizures of lawfully owned property.

As would one day Thurston of Seabrook regret keeping his son away from him. Rolf's hands closed into empty fists at his sides.

"Come with me, my lord," the guard was saying, and

Rolf swung his attention back to the moment at hand. He lifted up his gauntlets from the floor where he had dropped them and followed the guard.

"I thought to make the moment more comfortable is all," Annice said in response to her cousin's query. "The boy should not be made afraid of his father."

"God's grace, but what do you care?" Alais opened her brown eyes wider. "He's only a hostage here, held against the Dragon's good behavior. It matters not if the child or the father is content. To allow them communication is dangerous."

Annice frowned. "You begin to sound like your husband."

"And so? Thurston may not be the most equitable of men at times, but he is often right about such matters. Think on't—near all of Lincolnshire is said to be in rebellion. Richmond Castle is under attack in Yorkshire, barely held by rebels. If le Draca is allowed even the smallest concession, he will soon be at our gates with an army. Is that what you desire?"

"I think," Annice said slowly, "that the Lord of Dragonwyck wants only his son. He did not strike me as a man who would break an oath, if one could force him to give it." She toyed with the end of her hair, brushing the loose tips against her palm. The scene she had witnessed earlier had left a vivid impression upon her. Though she conceded that her tender heart could misconstrue words, there had been no doubt of the father's love and devotion. It had been plain enough in the small carved horse. How many hours it must have taken him to detail so painstakingly the family crest, the mane and tail, the flared nostrils and wild eyes of his own destrier. There was more intent than just a plaything in his gift; he had included a sense of family in the carving of the horse, the legacy from father to son. Each time young Justin played with the horse, he would grow more familiar with his familial heritage. And he would remember that 'twas his father who had given him the toy.

Alais snorted. "I think you've read more into the Dragon's actions than there truly is. Once he has his son back, he would feel free to make war again. Haven't you heard of his past exploits?"

Impatiently, Annice said, "Aye, 'twould be hard not to have heard of them. But I recall my own father saying that all war is brutal, and men ofttimes grow ruthless."

"That does not excuse le Draca. Have you heard that he allowed his wife to die for lack of care after her lying-in?" Alais punched her needle through the square of linen she was embroidering, then looked back up at her cousin. " 'Tis why Thurston removed the boy from le Draca's care. After all, 'twas his sister's child he sought to save from harm. If a man would not see to his own wife's welfare, would he do more for a helpless child?"

It occurred to Annice that from what she knew of Thurston, he would be much more interested in claiming his dead sister's revenues from the dower lands left her son than in seeing to the boy's welfare, but she did not say that aloud.

"Lord Rolf seems extremely fond of his son," Annice said instead. "I do not think he would harm him."

Alais shook her head. "I do not trust him. 'Tis good that his fortunes are so slim of late, else we might find the Dragon at our gates with his army, loyalist or no. I told Thurston what he said about his keep being in ruins and his gold spent on warring." Her needle flashed in and out of the embroidery linen stretched upon a hoop. " 'Twas useless sending me to listen. All le Draca could do was gaze at that silly boy."

Annice looked away, staring blindly at the tapestry she had been working earlier. 'Twas for the vestry. It still hung on the frame, a scene from Christ's life depicting his first miracle. She wondered if she should pray for guidance.

Confused by conflicting emotions, she questioned her first instincts. Alais was so certain of her facts, and in truth, Annice had heard nothing to contradict her. Dragonwyck's reputation had long preceded this day and, she was certain, was founded in a great deal of truth. Yet could there be underlying circumstances? Could the decency she had sensed

in him be only a masquerade? Certainly his capacity for ferocity was not exaggerated. She knew she was not mistaken
about the hostility in his eyes when he had regarded
Thurston of Seabrook.

But, then, she could well understand his animosity for
the earl. Her own dislike of the man grew apace with her fa-
miliarity with his mind and methods. Seabrook used his
nephew as a pawn, but no more so than the king would do.
It had not been so long ago that King John had ordered the
hanging of twenty-eight Welsh children—some of them no
more than five years old—held as hostages against their fa-
thers' good behavior. It had a dilatory effect on Welsh upris-
ings, to be certain, though she was appalled at the king's
brutality.

It was not necessarily true that one became inured to in-
humane actions if continually exposed to them. Alais often
chided her for being too tenderhearted, and p'raps she was.
Few seemed to regard such actions in the same light. She
thought again of the tender scene between Dragonwyck and
his son. Could a brutal warrior have the capacity for such
love?

"Are you even listening to me?" Alais demanded loudly,
and Annice turned to look at her.

"Forgive me. I was thinking of something else."

"I can well imagine." Alais pursed her mouth. "Have you
heard that Robert FitzWalter's eldest daughter, Matilda, wed
to Geoffrey de Mandeville, is rumored to have been poi-
soned by the king for her refusal of him? He sent her a poi-
soned egg. 'Tis said also that Robert was forced to flee to
France after the king caused his Castle Baynard to be pulled
down. . . ."

Relieved that Alais had turned her attention to other
matters at last, Annice picked up her needle and thread and
pretended to focus on her tapestry and gossip. For the present she would do her best to offer what comfort she could
to a small boy without mother or father to aid him. She
missed her own parents dreadfully, and p'raps she could
ease that loss for a tiny hostage. Her visits to the nursery
would increase slowly, so that none would suspect what she

was about. Yea, if nothing else, she could brighten the days of a child.

Edmund de Molay shifted in his saddle and glanced again at his lord. A patch of sunlight sifting through overhead branches illuminated his face beneath the helm and noseguard as he gazed at Rolf. "If they do not come this day either, my liege? Do we wait again on the morrow?"

"We wait. They will come, whether this day or no, I cannot say." Rolf's hands tightened on his reins. "But they will come, of that I am certain, Edmund. I am committed to the quest, and this may well be my only chance to retrieve my son."

Nodding, Edmund lifted slightly in his stirrups; age made his joints stiff when he sat too long, Rolf knew, but there was little other choice. Edmund had been too obstinate to remain at Dragonwyck, insisting upon joining his overlord. They had been waiting in the woods lining the main road leading from Stoneham Castle each morning for the past week. Rain had scoured them two days, but the last three had been bright and sunny. Rolf was certain that the ride Justin had been promised beyond fortified walls would be soon. The boy had been too confident of the promise not to regard it as truth. It was difficult to deceive a child accustomed to deceit. And the fact that he had been so skeptical of his father's return was proof enough that he was not a child easily fooled.

Rolf was grateful for the intervention of a lovely lady in his behalf. It had been Edmund who had revealed the mysterious lady's identity to him.

"Ah, a russet-haired lady, you say?" Edmund had chuckled. "I vow, 'twould be none other than Lady Annice, who was wed to that lackwit, Luc d'Arcy. 'Tis true she is Lady of Seabrook's cousin. She was recently sent to Stoneham by the king for her husband's foolish actions. Aye, and a lovely widow she is, I hear."

Frowning, Rolf had regarded his old friend for a long moment. "Can you recite the family history of every English citizen?" he'd asked finally, amused by Edmund's vast knowledge.

Nodding, Edmund replied, " 'Tis likely. Lady Annice's father was Hugh de Beauchamp, a noble gentleman who was loyal to King Henry and then Richard."

"Ah. Hugh de Beauchamp. I recall his being with King Richard at Châlus when he was given the fatal wound, was he not? His was one of the clearest heads in the aftermath, as I recall." Lapsing into silence, he'd considered a moment, recalling those turbulent times. He'd been a youth still, having just acquired his knight's spurs. It had been the leadership of men like Hugh de Beauchamp that had impressed him most.

It was not surprising that Hugh de Beauchamp's daughter possessed the same clear vision. Lady Annice's quick wit had aided him with Justin in a very difficult moment.

Swatting at an annoying insect buzzing round his head, Rolf glanced again up the wooded road leading to Stoneham Castle. He had adopted a method used by the Welsh, of having his men blend into the woods like shadows to wait. So had the Welsh done in his wars with them, seeming part of the forest itself at times. Pray God that it worked as well for him as it did the crafty Welsh barons.

Time seemed to crawl, and it grew warmer. Insects swarmed with tiny glistening bodies to torment the waiting troop. Despite the brisk chill in the air, sweat dampened bodies beneath hauberks and helmets as the sun rose high into the sky. Shifting patches of light filtered through the thick tree limbs and new green leaves overhead, and the forest was quiet.

Rolf shifted in his saddle, and his destrier gave a shake of its head to dislodge an annoying fly. The sound of rattling bit and curb chains were overloud in the gloom. He leaned forward to soothe his mount with a quieting hand. A faint glimpse of motion caught his attention, and he had just stood up in his stirrups when a forward guard he had posted came to him through the deep, murky gloom of the woods.

"My lord," the guard said softly, "they come. There are a dozen soldiers guarding six children and three women."

Patience, Rolf thought exultantly as he spurred forward, was sometimes rewarded. In the distance, riding at a leisurely pace into the woods, came the small group. Armed men rode ahead and behind, but in the center he could see the women and children as they drew nearer. Sunlight reflected from helmets and chain mail in patches and splinters; among the group he recognized the lady Annice. Justin, he was certain, would be close to her.

His men knew what to do and had fanned out in two flanks. One would wait until the riders had passed to come in behind, attacking at the same moment that the group would be assaulted from the front. The element of surprise should add greatly to their advantage, and Rolf hoped for a swiftly executed maneuver that would gain him his son. The road was narrow at the spot he had chosen for the attack; thick woods lined the route, which would inhibit Seabrook's men in their retaliation.

Curbing his impatience, he waited in a copse for the riders to come abreast. They were hidden from view again by a bend in the road, but he could hear feminine laughter and the light chatter of children above the sound of hooves striking the dry roadbed. As they came into sight around a shadowed curve, he gave the signal to the forward flank.

Bursting from the woods onto the road, Rolf's men cut down the first two of Seabrook's soldiers. Women screamed shrilly, almost indistinguishable from the high-pitched squeals of startled horses. Swords clanged and men cursed, and there was the heavy thud of clashing man and beast.

Rolf forged into the midst of the group and saw Justin struggling to keep his seat. His pony reared and plunged, eyes wild with fright. For the moment he was unprotected. Leaning forward, Rolf scooped the boy from his saddle. He was momentarily startled by Justin's fierce resistance until he realized that the boy would not know him with a noseguard and helmet covering most of his face.

"Be still," he said as he struggled to hold the frantically thrashing child. " 'Tis your father who holds you."

Justin's struggles ceased, and he glanced up at Rolf with an anxious frown. There was no time to reassure him; the fight had escalated with the charge of the rear flank. Wheeling his destrier around, Rolf forced his way through the combatants to where Edmund awaited him. He thrust the boy into the hold of his master-at-arms with a terse command to ride hard.

"Get him to safety at all costs," he added, and reined his mount around to reenter the fray. He must occupy the knights until Edmund had time enough to escape with Justin. His sword flashed in glittering arcs. There was little time to think; his body acted of its own accord. Battle was an accustomed habit, the furious thrust and parry of weapons familiar to a man who had spent over half his life at it.

Efforts were made to avoid the women and other children caught in the fight. Seabrook's men-at-arms had managed to form a tight circle around them as a protective barrier. Once Edmund had been able to escape with Justin, Rolf would call back his men at the earliest possible moment for retreat. He had no desire to risk the lives of women and children once his aim had been accomplished. Recovering Justin would be triumph and vengeance enough.

Deflecting a blade with his shield, Rolf kneed his huge destrier forward, bringing his sword up and around in a wicked slice. It bit deeply into his assailant. He heard a hoarse cry and glimpsed a fallen opponent as he pressed on. A brief assessment of the situation was reassuring. Of the dozen mounted soldiers sent out from Stoneham, only half remained.

Rolf was about to give the signal for retreat, when one of his men struck down a soldier guarding the women and children. Spurring forward with an angry shout, Rolf saw the wounded man fall, still holding on to his mount's reins. The panic-stricken beast reared, hooves thrashing wildly as it toppled over backward into the midst of the women and children. Another scream rent the air.

In a blur of flashing hooves and flailing bodies, another horse and rider went down. It was Lady Annice; her bright hair was unmistakable. Rolf saw her fall from her horse and scramble to her feet, but the surge of frantic horses raged around her in an overwhelming tide, and he lost sight of her. Even as he put spurs to his horse, he knew he was taking a great risk to help an enemy. Yet none of her own seemed inclined to assist her as they battled Rolf's seasoned knights.

He urged his mount closer. Despite the chaotic blend of churning horses, flashing blades, and terrified, screaming women, he managed to reach Lady Annice. She looked up, eyes registering fright and trust at the same time, and held out her hand. At that moment another horse lurched sideways and reared. A glancing blow from a hoof struck her in the head, and she collapsed just as Rolf reached for her. He swore. Bending from his saddle, he managed to scoop her up before she was trampled. She hung limp and unconscious, bumping against his horse with every movement. Rolf's mail and weapons combined with this new burden put him off balance. Sweating from the effort, he did his best to recover. Lady Annice was a heavy weight on his arm; worse, it was his sword arm, which left him vulnerable to attack. Only his shield arm was free. He had to rid himself of her at the first opportunity, or risk all.

Wheeling his great destrier out of the battle, Rolf looked up for a safe spot to place her. Then he heard a high, thin cry that jerked him around.

"Father!"

His blood chilled. Far down the road Edmund de Molay was waging a desperate struggle. One of Seabrook's knights had engaged him in a fierce battle for Justin. Even as he spurred his mount forward, Rolf saw that he was too late.

A sword lifted high, then sliced down into the curve of Edmund's neck and shoulder. As Edmund fell from the saddle, the earl's man plucked Justin from his dying grasp.

Not to be easily vanquished, Justin kicked out, crying again, "Father!"

The knight gave the boy a quick cuff to quiet him and spurred his horse through an opening in the thinning line of trees and into a hard canter across a meadow. Rolf glanced at Lady Annice draped over his arm and made a quick decision. He barely reined in to drop her onto a hillock of grass at the roadside, then continued his pursuit.

Hooves thundered as he pursued them, tearing up chunks of thick grass from the earth and sending it skyward. He could feel his destrier's muscles strain as he stretched out across the broad meadow in pursuit, and Rolf urged him faster. But Seabrook's man rode as if the devil were after him. As he topped a knoll thick with new green grass, Rolf saw reinforcements riding out from Stoneham. Apparently, one of the men had managed to sound an alarm.

Unwilling to yield even in the face of such great force, Rolf urged his destrier to a greater pace. Sunlight skittered along the stained blade of his drawn sword as he lifted it high. If he could come within a sword's length of man or beast, the fight would be won. All he needed was the slimmest of chances. . . .

Bellowing his war cry, Rolf saw the knight glance back over his shoulder, a look of desperation in his eyes. He must know that he had to reach the reinforcements to gain safety, and that the Dragon was drawing much too close. Could he make it in time? Rolf put spurs to Wulfsige, just as desperate to apprehend the knight and retrieve his son.

But good fortune was on Seabrook's side this day, for even as the huge destrier lunged forward with greater speed, a contingent of men-at-arms crested a grassy knoll within a wagon span of their comrade. Now, instead of one knight, there were a half dozen or more. A fight would only endanger Justin, not guarantee success.

"God's teeth," Rolf swore softly, fighting despair as he was forced to rein his mount to a halt. He paused for only an instant as his destrier tossed his head and snorted, prancing restlessly in the grass. Sunlight glinted from armor and Justin's fair head. Rolf caught a glimpse of the boy's frightened face peering over his captor's shoulder; then they disappeared down the side of the crest.

Defeat was bitter in his throat. All for nothing. Now Thurston would be doubly on his guard, and there would be little chance for another attempt. Wheeling around, Rolf rode back the way he had come with all haste. By now the battle had ended. The dead lay strewn on the ground, and the road was empty. Wounded were attempting to stagger to their feet, clutching bloody arms and legs. The faint thunder of approaching enemy troops could be heard in the distance. He looked down at one of his men.

"We tried, my lord." It was Guy FitzHugh, panting for

breath and bloodied. Sweat plastered his dark hair to his head. Unhorsed, he stood in the middle of the road and gestured toward a crumpled form. "Edmund de Molay is dead."

"Aye." Rolf's throat was tight. "Gather the wounded. We will have to leave our dead for now." At Guy FitzHugh's startled glance, he added tersely, "Reinforcements approach. Did they escape with all the women and children?"

Sir Guy nodded. "Aye. But for that one." He pointed, and Rolf turned to look.

Lady Annice still lay in a heap of skirts on the tussock where he'd left her. Rage burned hot and bright. If not for coming to the aid of the lady, he would have seen Edmund struggling with the soldier. If not for the lady Annice, Edmund might still be alive—and he would have his son with him.

Rolf looked back at Guy FitzHugh. "Bring her," he commanded harshly. "P'raps Seabrook will be interested in an exchange of hostages."

CHAPTER 3

────────────

𝕴t was the constant motion that jarred her most. Annice shut her eyes to stem the throbbing in her skull. Pain had settled in hot, piercing waves behind her eyes, and the left side of her head was tender to the touch. But discomfort was the least of her worries.

Opening her eyes, she stared ahead at the straight back of Rolf le Draca. He rode at the head of his men, setting a hard pace that was grueling. Since she had awakened, held in front of a mail-clad knight smelling of blood and sweat, apprehension had gripped her more than the aching throb in her head.

She had realized at once what must have happened while she had lain unconscious. It did not take a great intellect to discern that she was prisoner. The band of mailed knights had struck their colors so as to go unrecognized, and carried no banner. To the casual eye they could well appear as outlaws. And she one of them.

Never having traveled in any manner but in a litter for a long journey, and atop a dainty palfrey for sport, Annice found the hard gallop of the destrier painful. She gasped out a plea for respite, and the knight who held her in front of him called out to his lord.

Reining his mount, le Draca turned back to them, his gaze hard beneath the helm and noseguard. A curve of sunlight streamed through the heavy branches overhead, slipping over his face. "Yea, Sir Guy? Is there aught amiss?"

"Nay, lord, but that the lady must rest."

Piercing her with a cold gaze from eyes an icy green, le Draca swiftly banished her first impression of him as a gentle knight caught in a difficult situation. "There is no time for female frailties. We ride hard."

"Then leave me here," she got out, caught between outrage and throbbing pain, "for I cannot continue."

"You will remain with me until I have decided your fate, my lady," he snapped. "Pray God that your overlord feels sufficiently moved to barter for your life."

"And if he does not?" she snapped back.

He stared at her while his lathered destrier tossed its head in a spray of foam and jangle of bridle. "Then you shall rue the day you made the unwise decision to seek harbor with him."

Annice lapsed into silence. This was the Dragon of ballad and nightmare, the hard-faced man whose savagery was legend.

"My lord," Sir Guy began, but le Draca had already wheeled his great horse around, leaving her more shaken than she would have liked to admit. No words were exchanged as the knight nudged his mount forward again.

Nothing in her life had truly prepared her for this sort of circumstance. Leaving the shelter of her girlhood home had been simple, as she had done so at an early age, receiving her training in wifely arts in the castle of Walter de Montmorency. When she'd married, war often raged and though she was accustomed to her husband's absences, she had never been in immediate danger.

Once, at Montmorency, she had endured a siege by a warring vassal, but it had been short, and she had not been inconvenienced in any way but the tending of the wounded. This was vastly different and terrifying. Not even Luc d'Arcy's frequent rages could compare to the icy ferocity of Rolf le Draca.

The day became an unending blur of jarring motion and thick silence broken only by the changing thud of hooves from hard roadbed to leaf-cushioned forest floor. There was a curious crackle of dried leaves and twigs snapping, the labored breathing of the horses, and the clink and clank of harness and armor. Trees crowded close around them at times, tangled brush snaking across narrow paths. The woods were dark and hushed, huge oaks rising like specters in the gloomy shadows, seeming to peer out with faces older than time in the twisted trunks and branches.

Shuddering, the lady clasped her arms around her body as if chilled. A faint tremor shook her limbs.

"Are you cold, my lady?" Sir Guy asked close to her ear, not daring to speak loudly enough to alert Rolf. He could feel the lady's quivering even beneath his mail, and worried.

She shook her head, but that action must have brought stabbing pain, for she gave a soft cry. Immediately Guy reined in his mount. The horse's sides heaved with strain and exhaustion, and the lady's skirts were damp from the lathered hide. Steam rose, thick with the pungent smell of horse. Shifting position slightly, the lady glanced over her shoulder at him.

Her breath frosted the air in front of her face, her words giving the lie to her actions. "I am but slightly chilled, Sir Knight."

Sympathy prompted him to remove his cloak from the saddlebow to sling around her shoulders. "Shall I ask again for a halt?"

"Nay. I would not have your lord chastise us for being laggard." A faint smile twisted her lips. "Though I could wish for a more even-gaited palfrey."

Grinning, Guy nudged his destrier forward. "A frail horse such as that could not bear our weight, milady. But I shall endeavor to keep a more even pace."

After a moment of silence broken only by the clopping of hooves against roadbed, the lady shifted again to look at him over her shoulder. "Sir Knight," she whispered softly, and there was a quiver in her voice that betrayed her fear,

"I do beg a boon of you. I can pay well for a moment of in-attention and a horse. . . ."

Guy was half expecting it and had already begun to shake his head when the lady tugged at one of her long, slim fingers and removed a ring. She held it up so that it caught the light in a sparkle of blue glitter. Quickly he closed his first around ring and hand to hide it.

"Nay, milady," he said harshly. "Do not ask of me what I fear you will—I am sworn to yon knight and would be ever loyal."

Her lashes cast long shadows on her pale cheek. The sapphire-and-diamond ring in her palm and his fist would have bought an entire suit of armor, a horse, and p'raps a year's lodging. But even if he were inclined to betray Rolf, the dishonor of it would have killed him ere that fierce warrior could do so. He shook his head again, his voice kinder.

"I understand your desire to flee, but have more faith in my lord's honor."

As he released her hand and she slid the ring back onto a shaking finger, she said in a bitter tone, "I understand well the honor of most men and have found nothing to recommend it."

"I am sorry, milady."

She didn't say anything for a moment but finally inclined her head and turned around to face forward. "Aye, Sir Knight. As am I."

As the lady settled back against him, the woolen cloak snug around her form and cushioning his chest, Guy had the thought that she was much stronger than she appeared. Few females of his acquaintance would have suffered the rigors of the day without loud complaints and wailing, yet beyond her first protests, this lady had made no other murmurs. She had to be uncomfortable. The clime had grown chill and damp, and the road was hard. Yet she bore her discomfort more silently than she did her indignation at being taken hostage.

He hid a grin. It occurred to him that Rolf of Dragon-wyck might have met his match in this one small female. She possessed a stubborn streak to match that of the Dragon's, and he anticipated most interesting days ahead. How would Lord Rolf react to a woman who dared say him nay? It should be most entertaining to observe. . . .

Their pause had not gone unnoticed. The Lord of Dragonwyck waited until they had ridden abreast of him, then kept apace.

"Is there trouble, Sir Guy?" His words were directed at his knight, but his gaze shifted to Annice. She met it steadily. Nay, not for her the cowering prisoner. Rolf le Draca would soon discover that he had no meek maiden in his care, but a woman full-grown and well versed in defiance. Not for nothing had she endured the beatings and rages of her husband with an unbowed head. It was that, she had often thought, that had enraged Luc most. 'Twas a small victory, to be certain, and had often cost her dear in bruises and stripes, but her inner spirit had taken great satisfaction in the triumph.

"Nay, lord," Sir Guy said, taking Annice by surprise. He shifted her slightly in the saddle, one arm holding her to him. "I but paused to situate myself more comfortably."

"We do not stop until nightfall." Dragonwyck gestured toward the east. "Then we shall rest only a short time. If we ride hard, we will reach our destination before Seabrook's knights can find us."

The past hours had not been spent on any road, but riding over thicketed vales that had no more than sheep tracks as lanes. Avoiding villages and scattered cottages, le Draca clearly intended to reach Dragonwyck with none to mark his passage.

Annice clutched at the high pommel of the saddle with both hands, her voice steady. "And do you think you can withstand both Seabrook and the king's combined forces, my lord?"

"John is in Poitou," he said abruptly. "When I left, he was at Geoffrey's castle of Mervant, with no intention of leaving France too quickly."

"When he learns of this outrage against a ward he safely placed, he will hasten to send troops to lay siege at your gates."

"Let them come." A merciless smile curled his mouth. "If they think to effect a rescue, I shall send out a portion of you at a time until they have the whole. Do you think, my lady, that would satisfy them?"

She stared at him. A chill settled in her internal organs that rendered her speechless. There was no doubt in her mind that Rolf le Draca would do what he threatened. Frozen with fear and horror, she watched as he gave her another mirthless smile and wheeled his horse. He rode away without a backward glance.

Shivering, she barely heard Sir Guy's murmured words; they made no sense to her anyway. All she could hear was le Draca's mocking voice sounding her doom.

God help her. And she had once thought, however naively, that the Dragon possessed a soul.

Light from sputtering torches placed in sconces on the castle walls were all that illuminated the dark night when the small band came to a halt at Dragonwyck's fortifications. True to his word, Rolf had paused for only brief rests. Haste had earned him safe passage to his castle. Tilting back his head, he bellowed out his name to the sentry in the barbican, though 'twas hardly necessary. Dragonwyck thrust up from a hilltop, commanding a view of the surrounding countryside for five leagues or more on a clear day. They would have been seen an hour before, when light still lay on the land.

A dark shape appeared in an arrow slit, silhouetted against the fitful light of a torch. Recognizing his lord, the sentry withdrew immediately and called an order to lower the bridge. Sensing rest and fodder, the horses stamped and blew impatiently, harness bits jangling in the night. There was the crisp smell of newly plowed earth in the air beyond the castle walls, familiar and reassuring. He was home.

Accompanied by a loud, rasping rattle of chains, the drawbridge slowly lowered. It came to rest with a heavy thud, and Rolf nudged his destrier forward. Hooves sounded overloud on the wooden bridge as they passed beneath the teeth of the portcullis. Moving slowly along angled passages pocked with murder holes in the high walls, the weary band passed through five more doors and under six portcullises before crossing a second drawbridge and moat. This sluggish ribbon of water was just as dank and murky as the first, and a light mist hovered above its surface.

After traversing walls twenty feet thick, they finally entered the inner bailey. Topped by runways, the walls bore crenellated battlements as protection for defending archers; faint shadows moved along them, posted guards to keep Dragonwyck secure. At regular intervals bastions swelled the walls. 'Twas unlikely indeed that any enemy fortunate enough to penetrate this far would be victorious.

More torches flared, shedding pools of light into the deep shadows of the inner bailey. Liveried squires and servants scurried toward them, yawning sleepily as they greeted their lord. Hounds bayed a deep-throated welcome. The familiar humps of the outbuildings were dark outlines in the night. Rolf dismounted and turned to his squire.

"See to Wulfsige," he ordered, thrusting the destrier's reins into the youth's hand. "Give him an extra measure of grain, for he has earned it well this day, as have the others."

Turning, Rolf strode to Guy FitzHugh, who was still mounted and holding Lady Annice. She was pale, even in the murky orange-and-rose light of the torches. Her dark-red hair fell past her hips; the bound strands had loosened, wisps framing her delicate face in loose tendrils. Without speaking he reached up to take her down, his hands firm around her waist. She was lighter than he'd thought she would be as he lowered her to her feet. And smaller than he recalled. The top of her head rose only to his chest.

Though she gave a slight gasp, she did not offer resistance at his handling of her. 'Twas just as well. His temper was none too sweet, and he would not have borne opposition with good grace.

Sir Guy's cloak hung off her shoulders to drag on the ground. Keeping his hands on her waist, Rolf said mockingly, "Welcome to Dragonwyck, milady."

She glanced around her at the well-tended buildings and dense fortifications, then up at him. " 'Tis not so needy of repair as you would have Seabrook believe, I think."

" 'Tis my hope that the earl presumes my keep is crumbling into ruins. 'Twould give me great pleasure to have him at my gate for a change."

"You may well get that desire fulfilled, my lord."

She trembled slightly, and he realized that it was as much with weariness as it was with chill. Faint bluish shadows like bruises marked her eyes, and her shoulders drooped. Yet she held her head high, refusing to cower. He felt a certain grudging respect. His hands fell away and he took a step back.

"On the morrow you shall make your mark upon a letter to send to Seabrook, milady."

He lifted his hand to beckon a servant forward, then gave a start of anger when Lady Annice said coolly, "I have no intention of signing any missive to him. Do what you will. I'll have no part of it."

"You," he said with soft menace, "have no choice. I care not whether I dip my quill in ink or blood, so be forewarned—I am in no mood to quibble with a woman."

He'd not thought her face could grow any paler; he saw now that he was wrong. All color leached from her complexion, and her lips looked almost bloodless as she tightened them. Deep-blue eyes fringed with dark lashes regarded him for a long moment.

"That is twice you have threatened me with grave harm, milord," she said quietly. "Is it your wont to war on women now?"

"I do what I must to achieve my ends. If it includes making war on women, then so be it. I've not noticed any lack of restraint on Seabrook's part for using children to further his ambitions. Should I be more squeamish?"

"Nay, not the Dragon," she retorted. " 'Tis said that you have few scruples at gaining your ends."

Fury narrowed his eyes and stoked his temper to a blaze. His hand flashed out, grasping her by the chin to hold her head up and still. "Yea," he ground out, " 'tis true enough that I do what I must without regard for those who would gainsay me. Yet hear this, my lady—those who have been foolish enough to thwart me swiftly bemoan that decision."

"I have seen no sign of lament in my lord Seabrook's manner," she shot back at him. Her thick words were forced out between lips crushed by the grip of his fingers against her jaw.

Rolf stared down at her, half-amazed, half-angered by her temerity. A brindle hound whined as if sensing disaster. Around them he could hear the shuffle of feet and sputter of torches, while all else was still and waiting. Few men dared defy him so openly, much less a lady of small stature and great foolishness. He drew in a deep breath to dampen his flaring temper.

"You shall," he said softly, and released her chin. Marks from his gauntlets splotched her face, and he felt a moment's sorrow at marring such beauty. He had forgotten he still wore them and had not considered the effect of rough mail against tender skin. He stared at her. "You shall soon see more than regret in Seabrook's manner, I vow."

Turning, he beckoned his steward, Vachel, forward. "See that the lady Annice is taken to a chamber," he commanded. "And bring me the key once she is secured inside."

From the corner of his eye he saw Sir Guy's head snap up and a faint frown crowd his brow. But the knight said nothing, merely glanced from Rolf to the lady, then toward the steward.

"Aye, milord." Vachel hesitated, then asked, "Shall I ready a chamber in the east wing, seigneur?"

Rolf paused. It was Vachel's delicate way, he supposed wryly, of asking if the lady was to be given a chamber due her status or cast into a damp cell. He nodded. "Aye, Vachel. A small chamber in the east wing will be most sufficient."

'Twas immediately plain that Lady Annice had well understood this small play, for she said with rich contempt lacing her words, "How noble a captor you are, my lord. I shall pray daily for the repose of your immortal soul. . . ."

Wheeling around, he said softly, " 'Twould be well-advised that you pray for your own soul in these times, milady. You stand much closer to heaven's gates than you know."

It gave him much less satisfaction than he'd thought to see her eyes widen and her mouth tremble with barely suppressed fear. He should have been fiercely pleased at her re-action. Yet he was not. Instead he began to feel more like the savage beast she obviously thought him, and it was not a pleasant sensation.

Alone in a small, dimly lit chamber that smelled of burning oil and musty stone, Annice was able to yield to the exhaustion and fear that had been weighing heavily on her since before dusk. Long hours of mental and physical torment had taken their toll. She removed Sir Guy's cloak, then sagged onto the bleak comfort of a straw-stuffed rope bed and put her face into her palms. At least she was alone with her suffering.

Passing through the great hall to the staircase that wended upward in a full circle, she'd had a brief impression of curious faces and stone dragons. It was the last that had unnerved her most. The walls seemed full of dragons, cut into corners and over doorways, grinning, slathering beasts with bared fangs and drooling tongues to guard the halls. Even windowsills bore squatting scaled beasts carved into stone. The vast hall of Dragonwyck had seemed full of grotesquely staring faces as she had been escorted past, and she'd dreaded confrontation when she felt so drained.

But Vachel, who seemed to have a kind heart despite his service to le Draca, had buffered the few hostile queries thrown at them with his casual replies. The slightly built steward had been gentle in word and deed, shielding her from the unfriendly glances and muttered words of her armed guard sent with them.

That she had been thought dangerous enough to require an armed escort had been ludicrous; for one enemy to think it necessary to protect her from another had been added insult.

Yet now she was alone, locked into this evil chamber that was furnished with only a bed, table, stool, and chamber pot. A tattered velvet wall hanging fluttered in a draft; the lamp was a crude bowl filled with fish oil and lit with a wick of reed pith. Better, she thought, than the smoky, foul-smelling torches that lit Dragonwyck's wide corridors.

The resinous wood gave off dangerous sparks that could set fire to clothes in an instant. Not that her garments had survived the day's ordeal in decent shape. Her ermine-lined cloak had been torn from her, she supposed, in the confusion of the fight. Her blue velvet cotte was a simple one, donned for an expedition into the meadows beyond Seabrook's castle and not for endurance. The vee-shaped neck of the outer garment was edged with gilt embroidery that was repeated on the sleeves. Somehow it had been torn during the day and hung now in a frayed loop from one long cuff. She tugged at it idly, reflecting on her options.

Despair battled with weariness, and Annice wondered if le Draca would truly be cruel enough to hold her hostage. Negotiations could take years, given her cousin-by-law's stubborn temperament and the Dragon's unyielding tenacity. Who would prove to be the more valuable hostage in this game of wits?

It was not especially comforting to realize that to Rolf le Draca, nothing was as important as his son. A man who dared hide in Seabrook's own woods to snatch the boy from under the earl's well-armed nose would have little compunction about harsh retaliation in order to gain his own ends. Or to exact vengeance.

Closing her eyes, she shuddered. Aye, she was well and truly a pawn in this game. And there was naught she could do to deliver herself, save keep her wits about her. That, she thought with another shiver, would be much easier done if the Dragon did not terrify her at times.

Where was the humanity she'd thought she'd glimpsed in him that day at Stoneham Castle? He had exhibited tenderness and love to his child, a gentleness that few knights she knew had ever possessed. Was it, as Alais had suggested, merely a masquerade for the benefit of those watching? Nay, there had been no disguising his true emotion that day. She had not been wrong in that. No man could so readily duplicate his hoarseness of voice or the slight sheen of tears that had been present when she had taken Justin away.

Yea, 'twas the same man who had risked his life to save her from thrashing hooves, when Seabrook's men had fought to save themselves. It was mystifying to her why he had done so. 'Twould have been much more in keeping with his reputation to risk nothing for an enemy.

Rolf le Draca was a complete enigma to her. He was a complex man of vast contradictions. And he held her life in his hands. She opened her eyes and stared across the chamber at the flickering lamp on the table. If he chose, he could snuff out her life as easily as he would a lamp. Who would stop him—the king? Nay, John had his own enemies, and though he would evoke a fine on one of his barons for such a deed, he would be more interested in the provinces of Anjou or Aquitaine than in a dead heiress whose lands would revert to the crown. Yea, John would probably be pleased at such news.

A sound at the locked door startled her, and Annice heard the scrape of a key in the lock. Her hands curled into fists and she rose to her feet, legs trembling as she waited.

It was not surprising to see Rolf le Draca fill the portal. He studied her for a moment, then stepped inside and flung the door shut with a mighty crash. His mail was gone, as was the dust and mud of the day's travel. A long ebony tunic covered his broad frame and was belted at the waist. Gilt threads formed a rampant dragon on the tunic's front. Lamplight made his hair shine with the color of ripe wheat and picked out gold hairs sprinkled through the dark beard.

A smile lifted one side of his mouth but did not reach his eyes as he folded his arms across his chest and leaned against the closed door. "I see that you are expecting me, milady. P'raps you know why I have come."

She didn't reply. Her heart thumped so hard against her rib cage that she was surprised he did not remark upon the noise. Surely he could hear it. 'Twas all she could hear clearly, the loud beating that heralded her fear.

Over the rapid, throbbing clamor in her ears, Annice heard him say, "You have had time to reconsider your impulsive refusal of earlier. My scribe will be here at first light, and you will sign a plea to Seabrook for an exchange of hostages." A hard light glittered in his eyes, making them gleam like bits of green stone. " 'Tis for your own comfort that I suggest you yield the day. Life here can be pleasant enough, given the proper circumstances."

Pride pricked her into flinging le Draca's demands back into his teeth, no matter the outcome of her defiance. 'Twas not a thing done consciously, but instinctively. She met his gaze with a proudly lifted chin.

"I have experienced discomfort aplenty, my lord. 'Tis nothing new to me. Dishonor, however, is more your wont than mine. I will sign nothing."

She wasn't certain just why she defied him, save the fact that craven surrender was alien to her nature. Never had she cried for mercy before, even when Luc was wont to beat her most harshly. Nay, she had not done so even to save herself bruises; her pride had not allowed it.

Yet she wondered in the next instant if she had not gone too far this time. Though her husband had only beaten her, this man held her life in his hands. And he was furious.

Stepping forward, he growled, "Do not be fooled by my gentle words, milady. I will brook no resistance. You will sign what is put before you or suffer the consequences."

"And would you kill me?" she flung at him, curling her hands into the grimy folds of her gown to hide their trembling. " 'Twould make my use as a hostage of little worth then, my lord. Seabrook would hardly want a cold body in exchange for a warm one."

The smile that curled his lips was more a snarl. "I am not fool enough to slay you outright, milady. There are many methods of coercion available to me, as you should well know."

Aye, she knew that well enough. Observations of the king's methods of persuasion were amply chilling. Imprisonment was King John's kindest method of dealing with recalcitrant ladies; starvation and torture were the most effective.

Now, faced with over six feet of glowering, hostile male, she felt the first pangs of surrender raking at her. Could she withstand him for mere principles? After all, she had thought more than once that his son should be returned to him. Even understanding the reason for holding the boy hostage had not tempered her sympathy. As long as Seabrook held the child, he was certain of le Draca's behavior. It was as if he held the Dragon on a leash and could jerk him to heel with just the suggestion of harm to his son. Yea, she understood well the reasoning behind holding Justin hostage, and the same applied to her situation now.

She drew in a shaky breath, wishing she were not too weary to think clearly. If only le Draca had waited till the morrow to press his demands. Then she could have met him with a clear head and solid arguments. As he must have well known.

"Well, milady?"

His brusque reminder frayed her already tattered composure. He was standing too close; the proximity of his height and breadth was intimidating enough without his growling reminder. She took a step back and felt the hard pressure of the bed against her knees. To her dismay, le Draca stepped even closer. He was almost touching her now, so close that she could count the gilt threads of the embroidered dragon on his tunic.

"I will not yield," she heard herself saying in a breathless voice, and saw his dark-blond brows snap down over his eyes.

"Yea, milady," he grated, "you will yet yield the day, I assure you." His hand flashed out to grab her arm, fingers biting into flesh already bruised by the day's travails. Jerking her close, he thrust his other hand into the tangled mass of hair on the nape of her neck, curling his fingers into a painful fist that held her still.

Annice felt the sharp pressure of his belt buckle against her chest, and her hands flung out to brace herself against him. She encountered the hard, unyielding muscles of his chest beneath her palms and fought a spurt of unbridled fear. There would be no mercy from this seasoned knight, only retribution for her defiance. The fingers of her right hand brushed against the hilt of the dagger in his belt and immediately closed around it. Before the Dragon could guess her intent, she had drawn his dagger from its sheath.

Holding it against his belly, she stared up at him with more boldness than she felt. Tension and fear made her hand quiver, but her voice was steady. "And now, my lord? Would you loose me ere I carve my name into your belly?"

For a brief, sizzling instant he stared down at her with as much surprise as fury. 'Twas plain he had not considered her reckless enough to draw a weapon on him. There was a flicker of something like admiration in his green eyes before they narrowed to cold, glittering slits.

Not loosening his grip on her, he said softly, "Your folly is like to cost you dear, milady."

Annice had no time to react before he jerked harshly on her hair, snapping her head back at the same time that his other hand closed around the wrist of the hand holding his dagger. Hard fingers bit into the tendons, and she dropped the dagger with a cry of pain.

"Release me," she gasped out, unable to stop the plea before it escaped her lips. He had her bent backward, his grip tight on her hair while his other hand caught up the dagger.

"Nay," he said, " 'twill not be at your whim that I release you, little vixen. 'Twill be at my own. And I find myself intrigued by a woman with such a willful nature that she would dare attack a knight in his own keep. Are you that brave? Or merely that foolish? 'Tis an interesting puzzle, I vow."

Pressing her slowly back, le Draca forced her harder against the unyielding bed frame, until she found herself sinking backward. Panic flared hotly in her as she felt the straw-stuffed mattress cushion her shoulders. Surely he did not mean to—

"Nay, lord!" she blurted, struggling against his grip and the hot intent she read in his eyes. "I warn you, do not do this. . . ."

A muscled thigh settled over her, effectively pinning her flailing legs to the mattress. He still gripped her hair to hold her still, his other arm braced against the mattress beside her head. There was no sign of mercy in the mocking green eyes gazing down at her.

"Do not do what, milady? Dishonor you? But 'twas you who pointed out that honor was one of my shortcomings, was it not? I merely behave as a man of my breed would do." One hand shifted to stroke lightly over the curve of her cheek, then settled on her throat with suggested menace. "Mayhap I should reap the rewards of such a ferocious reputation. You are very fair, after all, and it has been some time since I have bedded a noblewoman."

He deflected the blows she aimed at his head and caught her arms in a harsh grip. Deliberately, holding her gaze, he wedged a knee between her legs and thrust them wide apart. Only pride stifled a cry of protest. She knew his intent. She was no maiden and had done her wifely duty to Luc without complaint. Though her husband had been rough at times, taking his pleasure with little regard for her needs, he had rarely subjected her to force. Nor had he ever stirred in her any feelings of desire, save that it be over with quickly. Luc had not seemed to deem passion necessary.

Rolf le Draca, however, seemed determined to wrest a response from her, willing or no. He shifted his grip on her wrists to one hand, and with his other began a leisurely exploration of her body. Even through the velvet gown, she could feel the heat of his hand. Shaping her breast with his palm and fingers, he kneaded it in gentle, circular motions that sent shivering sparks through her nerve endings. She tried to bring up a knee to kick him, but he easily evaded it by gripping her leg between his thighs.

"Nay, lady," he said softly, "you will not escape me so easily till I am done."

Frustrated, Annice squeezed her eyes shut and tensed her muscles, willing her mind elsewhere as she had done so often with Luc. But that was not so easily managed, either. He seemed to know just where to touch to arouse the most unusual sensations. Closing his thumb and finger on her nipple, he rolled it between them. That act sparked an immediate dull, aching throb in her belly that spread lower, pulsating between her thighs. To her horror and dismay, the scalding heat of response made her moan aloud.

Her eyes snapped open to see him watching her through the bristle of his lashes. A faint smile curled his mouth.

"Cease that at once," she managed to gasp out, and he shook his head.

"You are no maiden. You've played this game before. 'Twould be to your advantage to play it well, for then I might be persuaded to be lenient with you."

How could she tell him she had no idea what he was talking about? Almost desperately she tried to twist away from him, but he held her much too easily. The iron-hard muscles beneath his long-sleeved tunic and tight chausses were evidence enough that she waged a losing battle, but she could not yield without a struggle. It was not in her nature to surrender so easily.

"Do not force me, my lord," she said between angry breaths. " 'Twill go hardly with you when the king and my overlord learn what you have done."

"I had thought to hear more convincing arguments from such a fierce adversary," he mocked without releasing his grip the slightest bit. "Do you not have a better reasoning than that?"

"Aye!" She glared up at him. "If you take that which I do not willingly yield, I will see you spitted for it like a wild boar."

His teeth flashed white in the dark, bearded face. "Ah, 'tis a violent nature you possess, sweet vixen. Like the fox, you bare your teeth and snarl a threat that you cannot sustain." One hand shifted to tangle in the loose twist of her hair. He lifted it slowly, letting it slide over his palm. "I am not a hare," he murmured, "that will fear the red fox."

Lifting his gaze to her face, he said softly, "And I can make you yield all to me willingly enough, milady. . . ."

Her breath came more quickly in lungs starved for air, and she shuddered. Then her stomach gave an unfamiliar lurch when he bent his head to place his lips where his hand had been. She felt the damp heat of his tongue against her breast, wetting the material of her cotte as he drew her nipple into his mouth. A flash of heat ignited in her belly and lower, making her ache most strangely. It was like nothing she had ever felt before, a peculiar, hot writhing inside that made her breath shorten and her face feel flushed.

"My . . . my lord," she said in a strangled gasp, "please. . . ."

His head lifted. The lamplight behind emblazoned his hair with bright gold yet left his face shadowed. He gazed down at her for a long moment. A thoughtful smile curled his lips. With his knee still between her thighs, he settled his body closer, so that she could feel the thrust of his arousal against her belly. That evidence of his resolve shook her more than she had thought possible. She could not still the sudden tremors that made her quake like an untried maiden.

"Nay," she said in a broken plea, "do not . . ." She bit her lower lip to still a spate of words that would surely shame her yet still not sway this grim knight from his purpose. There was determination in the touch of his hand and the burning light in his eyes.

"Let us see," he murmured, "what you hide beneath your gown, lady fair."

Annice closed her eyes as his fingers caught in the neck of her gown and gave a sharp jerk. The velvet parted with a ripping sound of thread and fabric. She wore nothing beneath her gown but a sleeveless tunic of loose-woven linen and white stockings tied at the knees with silk garters.

It took him only a moment to divest her of the outer garment, tossing the shreds carelessly to the floor. She lay shivering in her knee-length tunic, eyes tightly shut. The air was cool on her bared flesh. She felt helpless and exposed, completely at the mercy of this angry baron.

"Yea," he muttered thickly, "you are most fair indeed. P'raps I shall delay sending a message to my lord of Seabrook."

Still shivering, she opened her eyes to look up at him. There was an intense expression on his face as he gazed down at her. Thick, long lashes hid his eyes, but when he finally looked up, she recognized the hot glitter in his gaze. Just so had Luc looked at times, the same narrowed, intent light in his eyes that would precede his most amorous efforts. Yet this knight cared naught for her yea or nay in the matter, but did what he was wont to do without regard for her agreement.

"Nay," she whispered, hating the way her voice sounded more pleading than defiant. "Do not delay my release. . . ."

Sitting back on his heels, he lifted a brow. His weight was still heavy on her legs, pinning her to the mattress. A mocking smile touched the corners of his mouth. "What do I hear, my lady? Do you wish to sign the letter I would send, then? Is that what you signify?"

Annice swallowed a too-hasty reply. If she agreed, she was well and truly defeated. He would know the best way to force her to his ends, whatever they might be. And would her signing of the letter save her from him? Nay, she knew better than that. It would be only the first step up the scaffold of her destruction.

Drawing in a deep breath, she said simply, "Nay, 'tis not what I meant at all."

For a moment he just stared at her, then gave a light shrug of his broad shoulders. The movement made the gilt dragon on his tunic appear alive, with gold and green-gilt scales shimmering in the faint light. Releasing her wrists, le Draca's hands went to the belt at his waist.

Instinctively, Annice threw up her hands. She had received too many beatings with Luc's belt not to know what came next, and she would protect her face if possible.

To her surprise le Draca's hands stilled. He scowled. "I do not mean to beat you, Lady Annice, so do not cower like a whipped cur."

Not quite believing him, she kept her arms up over her face. Then her heart gave a sudden thump as she saw lamplight skitter off the blade of his dagger. Holy Mary, but he meant to do much worse than beat her. . . . She should have gutted him when she had the chance instead of hesitate as she had done. . . . Now he would kill her for certain.

She couldn't help a soft cry when she felt the cold steel of the dagger slide over the shrinking flesh of her belly as he sliced her undertunic from neck to hem. It fell apart, baring her body, and she clenched her teeth, expecting at any moment to feel the thrust of the blade in her heart.

Instead she heard le Draca curse softly, his lips curling back from his teeth. "Jésu, but you still cower. Do you think I would harm my only hostage just for the sake of murder? Aye, 'tis plain that you think just that. Be still, or I will truly cut you by mistake. And a sin it would be, to mark this lovely body . . . nay, lady, do not move."

In three quick slices he'd cut away the rest of her tunic and left her naked and shivering on the straw mattress. He rose and gathered up the shreds of her garments, balling them into a tight bundle. He gazed down at her with a tight smile.

"As you refuse to make your mark upon a letter, I shall

send your garments to Seabrook in your stead. Your cousin will recognize them, and I vow that the earl will understand the message I send with this shredded clothing."

Annice could not respond. She lay staring up at him, not even daring to attempt covering her nudity. The Dragon gave a harsh laugh. He stepped forward again, bending a knee on the mattress and making the ropes squeak a protest. Once more the dagger flashed. She felt a sharp tug on her head, and when he lifted his hand, he held a length of her hair.

" 'Twill be enough to convince him I do indeed have you, don't you think, milady?"

She nodded mutely. It was not until he had carelessly tossed Sir Guy's cloak over her and shut the door behind him, locking it, that she realized he meant her no more harm. By the Holy Virgin, he had swept her from terror to anger and back again in but a few short moments. She shuddered. Rolf le Draca was a devil, indeed, just as so many had named him.

CHAPTER 4

Sir Guy FitzHugh stared up at his liege with a troubled frown. Light reflecting from the hall's fire flickered over his face and made his hazel eyes glisten. He held the ruins of Annice's garments in his hands. 'Twas plain to see where a blade had sliced through linen, and he did not speak for a moment. When he did, his words were cautious. "Am I to assure Lord Thurston that the lady is unharmed, seigneur?"

"Nay. Assure him of nothing save that she is my hostage. He may read into those rent garments what he wishes." Rolf tilted his cup, eying Guy's furrowed brow with a scowl. Not even wine could wash away the sour taste in his mouth; Lady Annice's fear had rankled. It should have pleased him. Aye, he should be well pleased that he had left her quaking on the bed. Mayhap it would bring her to her senses. Draining the last of his wine, he slammed his cup to the table.

The noise made Sir Guy jump slightly. His hands tightened on the ruined garments until the knuckles were white. "I shall give the message as you wish, my lord," he murmured. He hesitated, and 'twas plain he wanted to say more.

"Speak, Sir Guy," Rolf finally said impatiently. "You have the doleful countenance of a whipped hound. What is it?"

"The lady." He drew a deep breath. "Is she well?"

"Well enough." Rolf's eyes narrowed on his knight. "Albeit she is defiant and stubborn and probably deserves a sound beating. Rest easy on that score. Even if 'twas my wont to abuse women, I remember too well Hugh de Beauchamp."

Guy's head snapped up; his hands stilled on the pouch into which he was stuffing the ruined garments. "Beauchamp?" he echoed in an odd tone. "What has he to do with the lady?"

"The old lord was her father. He has been dead over ten years now, but I would not harm his daughter."

He did not miss the look of disbelief on Sir Guy's honest face and smiled wryly. 'Twould seem that even one of his most trusted men was uncertain of his reaction to this woman. Aye, and well he felt like doing someone harm. The loss of Edmund de Molay was as bitter as his failure to retrieve his son. The old master-at-arms had been with him since he'd been a squire in training for knighthood, and he felt his loss keenly. Leaving the body behind had been equally difficult. He could only hope that Edmund would receive a decent burial, as would the other bodies he'd been forced to abandon. If such had happened at Dragonwyck, he would have sent a priest to tend the matter, but he had no assurance that Seabrook would do the same.

"Milord," Guy murmured, "do I have your leave to go now? I maun make haste if I am to negotiate the lady's ransom."

"Aye, ride swiftly and safely. And see what you can learn about those we left behind." He passed a hand over his face and snarled an oath. A sleeping mastiff at his feet woke with a startled bark, and he soothed it before muttering, "Would that matters had ended differently, Guy. It weighs heavily on me that I abandoned our dead."

"There was no other choice, my lord." Guy's face bore lines of strain. "There was still the living to consider."

"Aye. 'Tis true enough. As now. Watch to your safety." Rolf dismissed Sir Guy and sank into a high-backed wooden chair near the fire. He put an absent hand upon the great mastiff's head when the dog rested a muzzle on his knee. The day's events were sorrowful, indeed. Now Seabrook would be ever more watchful and probably would send word to the king of Rolf's attempt. Not that he cared a whit for that. John rarely involved himself in his barons' squabbles, except where it would benefit him.

Rolf had sworn fealty and paid homage to John in 1199, though it had galled him to do so. But King Richard, on his deathbed in Châlus, had commanded that his brother John be king instead of Arthur of Brittany, their nephew. It had been the wisest choice, for few Englishmen wished a foreign king, and Arthur had been brought up in France under Philip. With him as king, the English would have been subject to Philip before long. William the Marshal had urged the barons to accept John, and they did, though most barons misliked it as much as did Rolf. John Lackland, he was called behind his back.

Rolf smiled faintly. How that appellation must irritate the king. His older brother had been respected by all; even the greediest barons had been reluctant to incur Richard's wrath for fear that he would be at their gates with his troops. Yet John frightened few with his military prowess. Nay, this king's skills were more political, with his intrigues and convoluted plots that even the most seasoned courtier found alarming. With Richard a man had known just where he'd stood in the king's favor. John would smile into a man's face even while sharpening the dagger for his back.

Worse, not even the king's sworn oath could be trusted. 'Twas common for him to rescind an agreement at his slightest whim. His court was a pit of lies and intrigue, while he busied himself trying to recapture French provinces. Before, it had been Ireland and Wales. For months John had been absent from England. England was left in the tyrannical hands of the Bishop of Winchester, Peter des Roches, who ruled with an iron fist. And that, too, created new problems with many of the barons.

God's mercy, William the Marshal and the Earl of Salisbury were able to temper the worst of the bishop's acts, as well as John's. If not for those men—as well as a mere handful of other earls who stood high in the king's interests, if not his favor—England would be even more chaotic. Laws were erratic, or worse—deliberately ignored.

Not the least of which was the matter of dishonest sheriffs appointed by the king to collect fees from the barons and their tenants. Aye, Rolf had clashed more than once with Sir Ralf of Ridel, a sheriff of Lincolnshire. Corrupt and greedy, Sir Ralf had raised the fees to an exorbitant amount, claiming that the value of land had increased extensively. Bluntly refusing to pay, Rolf had appealed the fees. He had not truly expected John to listen, as it was well-known the king took his share of the increased fees, but he had hoped to force him into a public position of either admitting his hand in the extortion, or conceding the fees were too high. It had not worked.

In retribution the sheriff had accused two of Rolf's knights of offenses they had not committed, then condemned them to trial by ordeal. It was in direct defiance of King Henry's ordinance limiting the employment of that mode of trial instead of a sworn jury.

Yet the more Rolf protested to the crown, the more vengeful Sir Ralf became. If not for the fact that the king needed his barons and their trained knights in his service, Sir Ralf would have been allowed even more freedom in his depredations. But John did need his barons. Without them he could not wage war. If they chose not to send men, they were required to pay a scutage, or fine, in their place. With those fines John could afford to hire mercenaries to fight for the crown.

Foreign mercenaries in England. . . . It chilled the blood to think of those men loosed on English subjects. John did not consider what would happen if ever those mercenaries decided to turn on him should he be unable to pay. Even a dog would fight for food, more loyal to his stomach than to a hated master.

Rolf looked down at his favored mastiff, curled up on the floor next to him with the tip of its tail touching its nose. Stretching out his legs to the fire, Rolf rubbed absently at his thigh. An old wound ofttimes pained him, a reminder of a battle long past. There were many such old scars on his body, yea, and new ones as well. 'Twas the legacy of men trained up to fight.

Yet the wounds that had left no scars still pained him most. His hand tightened into a fist, and he saw in the dancing flames the face of a small boy gazing back at him over a mailed shoulder. Would Justin ever forget that his father had failed him? Nay, 'twas unlikely. Time stretched endlessly for children, until it became a blur of vague impressions. Only a few memories stood out, and it was those sharpest that pained the most.

He should know. Hadn't his own father left behind painful memories of abandonment and betrayal? Rolf could recall few times he had felt safe or loved. After the death of his mother there had been only long days of fear and misery. It wasn't until he had come of age to be a page in the service of the Earl of Whiteville that he had begun to feel as if he had any control of his life. His father had taken an interest in him again when he had shown exceptional ability as a squire, and thence become a knight.

Now he could better understand his father's position. With two older sons as heirs, there had been little reason to shower a small boy with attention. A third son inherited little enough as it was, but as a knight of some consequence, he'd finally gained his sire's notice. Little matter that it had come so late; he had reveled in it. As he had reveled in the honors he'd earned on the battlefield and in the tournament lists. Until he had earned a title, he'd carried on his standards the image of a dragon, which he still wore. It had seemed more fitting to bear that standard, the snarling beast of legend that his ancestors had carved upon their shields and weapons. The sign of the dragon had long meant yielding no quarter, as when the dragon-ships bringing Northmen of old had stormed England's shores with no mercy.

King Richard had thought the standard fitting as well when he had granted Rolf the earldom of Dragonwyck. For loyal service in the thwarting of a plot against him by the French king, Philip, Richard had given him English lands and title, and even a wife. Rolf had found himself betrothed to an eight-year-old English heiress. Never mind that he was reluctant to wed, Rolf had done as his liege lord bade him, knowing his duty. 'Twas only after Richard had died at Châlus and he had returned to England from France that Rolf had actually wed fourteen-year-old Margerie.

Though he had not loved her at first, they had dwelt together pleasantly enough for a time. After several years passed and she did not conceive, he'd thought her barren. But, at last, she'd borne Justin. And died of it.

One hand clenched into a fist. A grieving midwife had claimed that the child fair tore her body asunder being born. 'Twas said that frail, tiny Margerie had died cursing Rolf's name for putting such a big babe in her. He had borne that guilt in silence for the five years past, but it frequently came to mind. As penance, he had vowed not to slay another wife with his child. Nay, he would remain unwed for his remaining years. Justin would be his only heir.

Not that he had vowed celibacy; far from it. He often took his pleasure with the looser ladies of the court. One thing that could be said of John's court was that licentiousness was winked at by all but the Church. Rolf had found no lack of feminine companionship, even with his fierce reputation. Or p'raps because of it. There were those ladies who found intriguing the notion of lying with a man said to crush his enemies without mercy. Many a noble lady had pranced before him with shining eyes and parted lips, offering a challenge with bared bosom and ill-concealed excitement.

At first he had been insulted by the realization that he was merely a conquest, a tidbit of gossip to be relished among the court ladies. Then he had decided 'twas to his advantage to benefit himself of their favors. There were those highborn ladies who overheard much in the beds they frequented, and he was not averse to learning information from whatever source was presented. Aye, on more than one occasion he had learned of fortifications and plans some unwise, loose-lipped baron had divulged to the lady in his arms.

Which brought to mind the lady in his possession. Lady Annice d'Arcy was widowed these eight months past. He had met her husband once, several years before. Luc d'Arcy had been a weak man, a vessel to be used by those stronger

than he and more used to intrigue. Rolf pondered Hugh
de Beauchamp's motives in wedding Annice to him. Just as
it had prompted Rolf's marriage, most like, loyalty to the
king had prompted Hugh de Beauchamp's decision.

Staring into crimson flames of the fire by his feet, Rolf
thought of the lady's brilliant-hued hair, the dark red of a
winter fox. Aye, and like the fox, she bared her teeth in useless defiance. Though 'twas true she was widowed only a
few months, he was vaguely surprised that she was not yet
betrothed to another. Seabrook's slow plotting, no doubt.
That earl would dangle her before one vassal, then another,
as a carrot before a cart horse, weighing promises of fealty
and homage should he yield the lady as wife. He would be
frothing at the mouth like a rabid dog that she was hostage
to Rolf le Draca instead of available for his disposal.

Rolf smiled mirthlessly. Yea, 'twas vengeance of a sort
against the earl for holding Justin hostage. They might well
come to terms with the lady as lure. Her lands would be
worth much to the man she wed, as well as to her overlord.
Hugh de Beauchamp would have settled a fair dowry on his
only daughter. Unless Rolf was very much amiss in his
thinking, the Beauchamp lands in Normandy would have
been inherited by Hugh's son and heir, leaving the less important lands in England to fall to his daughter. He tried to
recall what he knew about the earl's holdings but could remember little. On the morrow he would seek more information.

It was important that he learn how valuable the Lady
Annice would be to a brother. If her brother took offense at
the lady's being held hostage by Rolf, that could be another
army he would find at the gates of Dragonwyck, or one of
his other keeps. Frowning, Rolf decided to send messages of
caution to the bailiffs at his other holdings. 'Twould not hurt
to be wary. Not only relatives, but others, might seek to do
him harm for having taken the lady.

There were times his reputation would stay an assault,
but a matter of honor demanded an attempt at restitution.
If Lady Annice's brother came from Normandy to avenge the
insult and recover his sister's person, Rolf would be required
to yield her or pay a fine. Or both, depending upon the

king's mood. John would not be delighted to discover foreign troops on his soil. Too often men could be distracted by greater temptations.

As was he. The memory of Lady Annice beneath him on the hard bed was a scalding one. Though his intention had been to frighten her into making her mark on the letter to Seabrook, he had been too easily distracted by the silky feel of her skin beneath his hands, and the tempting curves of her body. For an instant he had almost yielded to the pressing urges of his body to take her. There had been a moment when he'd been ready to cast honor and caution to the winds and lose himself in the sweetness between her thighs. Yea, if not for her heated reaction, he might have done just that.

But he had realized, if the lady had not, that her body had turned traitor to her will. It had been that which had stayed him from doing what he wanted, not any sense of honor. Despite her physical response, she was unwilling. While he had yet to take an unwilling woman, it had been a fierce struggle with himself to keep from taking Annice d'Arcy. The aching fullness in his body still reminded him of his frustrated needs.

The brindle mastiff lifted its head and growled a warning that Rolf quelled with the touch of his hand. "My lord," a voice just behind him prompted, and Rolf turned to see Vachel.

He nodded at his steward. "Aye, Vachel?"

Vachel approached his lord, his face clearly showing signs of weariness. He would not seek his straw pallet until his lord had retired, that Rolf knew well from experience. Though still young, Vachel regarded his position with gravity and responsibility. His father had been in Rolf's service as steward until his death the year before, and Vachel recognized the honor he'd been given by inheriting the post.

"My lord, I have seen to the comfort of the lady as you requested me to do and would know if you also require comfort."

"Aye, but not the kind you can provide," Rolf muttered under his breath, and saw from Vachel's expression that he had not heard. 'Twas well that he hadn't. He had no desire to make public that the lady had aroused an unwilling fire in him. "For now," he said aloud, "I require only my bed and sleep. We rise early on the morrow, for there is much to be done. I will need to send messages to the bailiffs of all my keeps and ascertain that they are well provisioned. Do you see that the stores here are victualed in case of siege."

It would not have been the first time they had endured siege, and Vachel nodded. "I took the liberty of sending men to the village to procure what might be needed and warn the mayor of possible attack," he said. "By night's fall tomorrow we should be most ready to withstand whatever may come."

Rising to his feet, Rolf stretched his weary muscles. "You are invaluable, Vachel. I am blessed, indeed, to have you. Now, come. Let us seek our rest, for there will be much still left to do on the morrow. I may have to call up my vassals if Seabrook decides to fight."

Vachel snorted. "I doubt very much that worthy knight will be at our gates. His wont is more to mouth empty threats and whine to the king than to ride boldly forth. Aye," he continued with obvious pride, " 'tis few men who dare challenge the Dragon at his own gates."

"Do not count too vastly on that," Rolf said dryly. "There are more than a few who would love to lay me low. Even my own brother would not mislike seeing me fall."

It was true enough. His eldest brother, though possessed of lands in France and Normandy, had long regarded Rolf as an insolent upstart. Not once had he offered assistance to him in battle or word, and Rolf had long ceased to care. Theirs had never been a close kinship, as William was much older and gone before Rolf had left the nursery. Geoffrey, however, was closer in age and more of a like nature. P'raps it had to do with the fact that Geoffrey's lands all lay in England, as did Rolf's. The difference was that his had come by inheritance, while Rolf had fought hard for what he now owned. More than once Geoffrey had remarked upon that fact with blatant admiration. There was a bond of sorts between them, and Rolf was careful not to abuse it.

Genuine affection was more precious than gold and jewels, rarer than a unicorn, he'd once remarked cynically to

Edmund. His views had oft distressed the faithful master-at-arms, who rarely missed an opportunity to point out the best in people. Yea, Edmund would be sorely missed at Dragonwyck.

As Rolf mounted the winding stairs to his chamber, he thought again of the lady locked in his east wing. He felt an unusual burst of sympathy. It must be frightening to be a pawn between powerful barons, yet she had exhibited little frailty of spirit. Nay, she had resisted submission most courageously. For all the good it would do her in the end. It was a woman's lot in life to be ever yielding to the strength and will of a man, however she might wish it otherwise. Just as it was a vassal's lot in life to yield to his overlord, no matter the integrity—or lack of it. And it was much wiser to submit when the outcome was inevitable. As he would convince Lady Annice.

The first hazy fingers of dawn's light poked through the high window across from her bed, slanting over Annice's face and waking her. She blinked, wondering vaguely why Alais had allowed her to sleep so late.

Then her memory returned with a rush. Jerking upright, she clutched Sir Guy's cloak tightly around her, shuddering. The Dragon had stolen her. . . . Her skin still tingled where he had touched her, and as if he were still in front of her, she could see the burning of his eyes, green as the scales of the beast whence he'd taken his name. Yea, like that ravening beast, he had no mercy or soul.

There had been only ruthless determination in his gaze when he'd sliced her garments from her, leaving her naked and shivering with chill and fear. Shame flushed her cheeks when she recalled how she had responded with frightened gasps; more shame burned brightly at the memory of how her body had turned traitor beneath his hands. He was a sorcerer, indeed, that he should be able to coax such exquisite sensations from mere flesh.

Annice tucked the cloak around her bare feet to warm her toes. Taking a deep breath, she calmed her wild thoughts and tried to make sense of her predicament. She had to think, had to sort through all the implications of le Draca's actions to the real purpose beneath.

In the prosaic light of day, the chamber that had seemed evil the night before now seemed merely bare and stark. Only a thin curl of smoke drifted up from the oil lamp. Light from the high window did not quite reach the shadowed corners on one wall but fell across the woven tapestry over her bed. The tattered wall covering depicted St. George battling the dragon, a most appropriate subject, though it appeared as if the dragon was winning the battle. Most likely le Draca had chosen the hanging himself, she thought irritably.

Sighing, she reflected on the night before. She had overreacted to him, mayhap. After all, his demands were logical enough, in retrospect. She would have demanded the same of a hostage, were she to take one. In defending her husband's keep, she had never been put in that position, though women frequently were required to oversee the defenses in their husband's absences. Fortunately, it had never fallen to her to do so. Now she wished it had, so she would have some experience of what to expect as a hostage.

And now, with the Lord of Dragonwyck at a distance, she could view his actions with a clear head. He had intended to terrify her into submission, of course. She should have seen that at once, and might have, had not she been so exhausted and aching from the day's ordeal. Even so, faced with his raging temper, she might still have been reduced to quivering fear. Lord Rolf in a fury was formidable, indeed. She would not be foolish enough to forget his icy ferocity or what he was capable of doing if he chose.

That he had succeeded so easily in giving her fright she put down to her mental instability at the moment. He would not find it so easy the next time he chose to intimidate her. She sensed that any capitulation would only increase his intention to have all, but that he would— grudgingly, of course—respect an able adversary.

Yet what could she do against him? She had no support, only her wits to keep her safe. Pray God she could outwit him long enough to see her safe. She was certain that he would meet with her ere the day was gone.

Yet two weeks passed in slow tedium without word or sign of Rolf le Draca. The delay gave her a great deal of time to think. Her first impression of him returned again and again, doing battle with what she had recently experienced. Despite his cold anger of late, she could not help but recall the gentle knight tenderly holding a small boy to his knee, his soft words and almost shy reaction to the child. Yea, 'twas true that the child was his only son and heir, but most men of her acquaintance were not so enamored of their children. Fond of them, certainly, but not besotted. Could it be that the evil knight, said to slay unmercifully, possessed a tender spot? Or was he a fierce, unrelenting man without tenderness? 'Twas a great puzzle that turned around and around in her mind.

When the summons finally came, daylight streaming through the high window had grown dim and faint, barely brightening the chamber. Food had been brought to her twice that day, along with another lamp and clean garments. Slowly rising from the bed where she had been silently contemplating the list of sins that had led her to this moment, Annice nodded at the steward garbed in the black-and-gold livery of Dragonwyck. Then she drew in a shaky breath.

"Give me but a moment to compose myself."

"Of course, milady." He hesitated, then said, "Should I wait for you in the corridor?"

"Nay, I am ready. I needed but a moment to collect my thoughts." She smiled and indicated the fading square of light from the unshuttered window. "I had thought 'twould be another fortnight before I was summoned."

"There has been much to do, or the lord would have summoned you sooner, I am certain."

Wryly, she murmured, "Yea, I am certain he is overanxious to speak with me again."

The steward, Vachel, had the grace to flush and look down at the floor. He had to be aware of his lord's ploy, as was Annice. The wait was only to make her more edgy and fray her nerves so that she would be eager to come to an agreement.

But he had misjudged his quarry this time, she vowed as she followed Vachel down the wide corridors and winding stone steps. Torches sputtered and hissed in metal holders on the walls, casting flickering pools of light and making the carved stone dragons seem almost alive.

As they drew near the hall, Annice could hear the familiar chaos of an evening meal. 'Twas the same in every hall, the clatter of feet and voice vying for space, the laughter and occasional sharp word, the growling of dogs beneath long trestle tables. Someone was playing a lute, teasing a light melody from the instrument that was almost drowned out by the hum of conversation. The smell of fish pasties and honeyed treats made her stomach clench, for she had eaten nothing but bread and hard cheese for the past two days.

Stepping off the bottom step, Vachel paused, still holding her hand upon his forearm. Annice gazed about the hall. It was not as rustic and crude as she'd remembered, that due in part, no doubt, to her fear and exhaustion upon her arrival. Rich tapestries and wall hangings embroidered with hunting scenes lined the stone walls. The overhead beams had been painted in bright colors with signs of the zodiac. Trestle tables had been set up at right angles to the high table on the dais, with benches for the guests.

Behind the high table hung a tapestry woven with Rolf's crest. Golden gilt threads formed a dragon that seemed almost alive as the cloth shifted in a draft. Seated in a high-backed chair at the table, Rolf looked up, his gaze riveting on Annice and Vachel.

"Be of strong heart," Vachel murmured, and urged her forward.

Vachel stayed close to her side as they traversed the hall, and Annice was painfully aware of the stares she received as they crossed to the lord's table at the far end. Her ears burned at the loud whispers she was meant to overhear, and her chin lifted in defiance. If they thought to shame her because she was held hostage, 'twould not be made easy for them. The shame was not hers to bear.

Holding her head high, she traversed the crowded hall at Vachel's side. Seated at the high table, Sir Guy watched her progress and gave her a smile of encouragement. Though the knight had refused to allow her to escape, she could understand well enough his reasons and did not bear him ill will. His steady gaze and the supporting hand Vachel kept on her arm bolstered her courage.

Refusing to hurry, she walked slowly and with dignity until she reached the table where Rolf sprawled in his chair watching her progress. There was a gleam in his eyes that she could not interpret. A huge brindle mastiff lay on the floor at his side, and she recalled the dog from the night she had arrived. Its tongue lolled from one side of the huge muzzle, but its eyes were bright and alert. She had such dogs at her own keeps. 'Twas said that the massive animals had first been brought to England by the Romans to hunt down the resisting Celts. They were still useful, guarding keeps and possessions with a loyal ferocity that had unmanned more than one brigand.

"Bordet." Rolf spoke the single word in a low tone, yet the dog immediately snapped to its feet, watchful and tense. A faint smile curled the baron's mouth when Annice shifted her gaze from the bristling mastiff to him. "He obeys readily, does he not, milady?"

"Yea, lord. Most dogs do."

Her inference was apparently not lost on le Draca. A dark-blond brow lifted in cynical acknowledgment. The knuckles of his curled hand brushed idly against his bearded jaw as he studied her for a moment. Conversation close around them had ceased, though there was still the rumble of talk in the rear of the hall. Annice refused to look away, keeping her chin held high as befitted a wellborn lady.

"Dogs are not born knowing obedience," le Draca said. "They must be schooled in it. Some are exceedingly willful. Yet even the most stubborn bitch is brought to heel eventually."

Anger flared at his obvious comparison, but Annice quelled it with an effort. " 'Tis said," she murmured, "that the most loyal dogs are those kindly treated. Given harsh handling, even an obedient dog will ofttimes turn on its master and bite."

Sir Guy muffled a snort of laughter that earned him a glancing frown from his lord, and he suddenly became intrigued by the wine in his goblet. Rolf shifted in his chair, eyes narrowing at her. "Those dogs who bite the hand offering food are always destroyed. No man will long bear treachery without retaliation."

"Should there be a lesson in that for the king's loyal barons?" Annice asked boldly.

A shocked silence fell. Though her gaze remained on Rolf, she saw the swift upward glance from Sir Guy and recognized his open distress. At one of the lower tables someone tittered nervously. Annice held her breath. She wished she could recall her impulsive words, but 'twas done. The likening of her to a bitch had rendered her foolish enough to strike back at him, and now she regretted it. Should her words be repeated—as they surely would be—there could be grave repercussions for her. No matter how she had meant them, a misinterpretation might see her brought to grief.

Apparently, not even Rolf le Draca wished to witness such a swift downfall. Leaning forward, he growled in English, "Curb thy foolish tongue, milady. Else thou be brought to task for it."

"Aye, lord," she said, bowing her head. With her head meekly bowed, she could glance around her at the avid faces. Some would be swift to carry tales to the king, she was certain; others merely looked aghast at her temerity.

"Vachel," le Draca said, signaling to his steward, "see that the lady Annice is made comfortable on a stool. She will take her evening meal with us."

Uneasy at his seeming indifference to her presence, Annice made no protest or comment when Vachel brought her a stool and seated her between Sir Guy and le Draca. The high table was at a right angle to the other tables lining two sides of the hall, giving an excellent vantage point. A fire burned in the middle. Supper was usually a light meal, coming as it did after evensong and sunset. It was still the Lenten season, so platters of meat were replaced with broiled fish and trenchers of fish stew. Cheeses and white bread made up for the lack of meat. There was no lack of spiced wine, with cups readily refilled. Intricate subtleties were brought out for admiration and inspection of the delighted guests. One subtlety was constructed of towering pastry and glazed honey in the shape of a castle complete with jellied moat.

'Twas obvious that the Lord of Dragonwyck was not close or mean with his food, as if he did not suspect a siege might soon be laid at his walls. Any other lord might be frugal at such a time, fearing long abstinence from ready supplies.

Even the beggars common in every hall were being doled out fresh foods along with scraps; Annice saw servants burdened with huge baskets leave the hall. Frowning, she toyed with her spoon instead of eating. Was this show of abundance supposed to impress her with the lord's indifference? Or had he already received an answer to his proposal and knew he would not have to wage war.

Looking up hopefully, Annice noted le Draca's gaze resting on her. Thick lashes shadowed his eyes, hiding any possible clue, though a faint smile tugged at the corners of his mouth. He was too serene, too confident. He must know something. A courier could well have traveled to Seabrook and come back with a reply in a fortnight.

Her heart gave an erratic thump. P'raps she was about to be released. . . . Had negotiations been completed to that end?

She had her answer in the next moment, when he leaned close to her to say, "I trust you will enjoy your stay with us, milady, for it seems that it will be an extended one."

The breath caught in her throat. One hand rose as of its own accord, fingers going to her mouth to still any impulsive reply. She stared at him. His lashes lifted, and she saw in the banked green fires of his eyes that he was furious. Dismay choked her, and she was barely aware of the intent, curious gazes fixed on them as she half rose from her stool.

Catching her arm, he pulled her back down none too gently. "Nay, do not think to flee. You are well and truly snared, little fox. It seems that your overlord prefers the hostage he has for the one I have. Or so he claims. Will he be so satisfied with his decision in the future? I wonder. Though I will not harm you for concern that he might think it politic to do harm to my son, there are varying degrees of subjugation."

His hand stroked up her arm, brushing the green velvet of her gown in a slow, languorous caress that made her stiffen. One of her long strands of hair had fallen over her shoulder to drape her breast, and the backs of his fingers rubbed against her as he lifted the heavy rope of hair in his palm. He did not move his hand but allowed it to remain pressed against her breast as he twisted the strands of hair entwined with ribbons between his thumb and fingers. Staring at her with a thoughtful expression, he slowly began to wind the bound hair around his hand to bring her even closer to him.

Annice wanted to resist but knew that 'twas useless, even in front of the assemblage. None would stay their overlord. Helpless, she found herself almost in his lap, her face mere inches from his and her hands braced against his chest.

"It seems," Rolf murmured softly, his words obviously intended for her ears alone, "that your overlord regards me in the role of abductor rather than captor. Though there may seem to be little difference 'tween the two, there is a significant one. As abductor of a widowed female, I will be required to pay penance as well as a fine for taking you." An unpleasant smile slanted his mouth and curdled her blood. "Unless, of course, I receive permission from your next of kin—in this case, your brother."

"My . . . my brother?" Annice struggled for words. "But I have not corresponded with Aubert in years. We barely know one another, and—permission for what?"

Still holding her hair so that her face was unnervingly close, he grasped her chin in his other hand, fingers cradling her in a loose grip. P'raps she should have been better prepared. After all, abduction was not unheard of, though times had passed when it was common.

Yet, still, Annice was totally taken aback when le Draca said in a rolling growl, "Permission to wed you, milady."

CHAPTER 5

As all the color drained from Lady Annice's face and she began to tremble, Rolf added harshly, "Do not be misled by my proposal, sweet lady, for I promise you I will make a very bad husband."

As she pushed away from him, a surge of color returned to her cheeks, making her eyes look an even brighter blue. Lines of strain marked each side of her mouth, and her voice was tight.

" 'Tis a poor jest, my lord. Of all the men in England, you are the one I would least consider as a husband. And my brother will never agree to a marriage between us."

"Your brother," Rolf said coldly, "has already indicated his willingness to negotiate the terms of an agreement. He requests a portion of your inheritance for his assent, of course. 'Twas not unexpected. Yet the king dictates the terms. He has even generously excused me from serving him in France and bade me remain in England to wed you properly. Only your overlord sees our union as damaging, for 'twill yield your estates to me."

Her lower lip began to tremble, and she caught it between her small white teeth to still it. Staring at him with eyes so wide and blue that he was reminded of a summer sky, Annice whispered, "But can you not refuse to wed me?"

"Aye." He released his tight grip on the heavy rope of her hair, though he held the silky strands in his palm. It seemed the lady was no more pleased about the situation than he, but he had far more to gain. He held her gaze and said softly, "But I won't refuse. Make no mistake—you will wed me."

When he relinquished his hold on her hair, she sat back on her stool, white-faced and trembling. It was hardly complimentary that she viewed their union with such horror, but he was in no sweeter a temper than she. St. Jerome! but he was caught in a trap of his own making, and it infuriated him.

Rolf did not speak to Lady Annice again during the course of the evening meal. This was not a situation he had considered when he had taken her from Seabrook, yet that foolish earl had swiftly invoked the aid of the Church as well as the king.

Would John allow one of his most powerful barons to flout the Church's authority? Especially after just mending Pope Innocent III's edict of excommunication? Did he dare risk Rome's displeasure? Canon law required the king to pursue abductors. . . .

Thus Seabrook had presented matters to the king, a dismayed Sir Guy had informed him. It left Rolf in a precarious situation, indeed, and his own fault. If his temper had not been so flayed by Edmund de Molay's loss and the failure to retrieve his son, he might not have yielded to the temptation to abduct the lady.

Though furious, Rolf could almost appreciate the fact that Seabrook had unwittingly done himself more damage than he had Rolf. Because he was too cowardly to come with troops to storm the walls of Dragonwyck, Seabrook's appeal to Church and king had manipulated Rolf into a position that was difficult, but not unmanageable. That was little compensation. For two days Rolf had considered actual armed rebellion. It would have been easy enough to fall in with other Lincolnshire rebels. Yet he had sworn an oath to

John that not even excommunication had absolved. Never had he broken a sworn oath. Would he do so now, even though he detested the king and his manipulations?

The king's messenger obviously vacillated between fear and curiosity and had looked relieved when Rolf had snarled that he would abide by the king's command. 'Twas an untenable position, indeed. Already a courier had been sent to Normandy to secure permission from the lady's brother to wed. From what he learned of Aubert, that worthy would be pleased to deprive his half sister of part of her inheritance. Though he was her closest male relative, his permission was merely a formality; still, it would seal the negotiations most neatly.

Rolf could, of course, refuse to wed Lady Annice. That had been his first inclination when the king's messenger had given him the parchment stating the terms. It was the king's sworn duty to pursue abductors with the same fervor as he would a thief. Yet since Lady Annice was not already betrothed to another man, John might have accepted a hefty fine in lieu of agreement; then the lady would have been returned to Seabrook, and matters would have been as before. Nothing would have been lost but time, a few thousand marks, the king's good graces—and the lady's honor.

Already rumors and gossip were rife. The court of Isabella reveled in lewd talk, and nothing was more delicious than the downfall of a highborn lady. It would be said, of course, that Lady Annice had been his mistress. Probably that she had even connived with him to be taken thusly in order to circumvent more tedious methods of surrender. He was more than familiar with the queen's tendency to make much of nothing. Normally, he did not care.

Yet for some reason he could not fathom, he found himself reluctant to see Lady Annice branded a whore before the entire kingdom. Guy FitzHugh had pointed out the advantages of his liege's accepting the king's offer of marriage to Lady Annice.

"Seabrook hopes, my lord, that you will refuse. 'Tis what he wants you to do." Sir Guy's voice had risen to be heard over Rolf's snarling oaths. "All know that the taking of hostages is common. John has too many score of them even to count. If you refuse to wed her, however, John would be easily persuaded to name your capture of Lady Annice as abduction. It fits in perfectly with his claims to the Church that his barons have run amok since allowed to repudiate their oaths to him. Though you are one of those who did not do so when he was excommunicated, he would not mind deseisining your lands and those of the lady's in reprisal for this deed. I vow, 'tis Seabrook who would ultimately lose most if you agree."

"Do you not think I have already considered that?" Rolf had asked, his voice so dangerously soft that even Sir Guy had hesitated. "Staying in the king's good graces may yet win my son back from Seabrook, whether that lord wills it or no."

"Yea, lord," Sir Guy agreed. " 'Twill gain you much more than open rebellion. John may order the earl to return Justin to you. And once the lady is wed to you, petitions can be made to claim her lands as dower. Your obedience to the king can only strengthen your position at court. 'Tis well-known that you are one of the few in Lincolnshire who have not openly reviled John or broken your oath of fealty. The taking of Lady Annice in marriage can be explained as an excess of passion."

Here Guy had grinned, and Rolf had stared at him for several moments before yielding to amusement. "How would you explain my marriage," he'd asked Guy dryly, "if the lady bore warts and wattles? I do not think any would believe me swept away by passion on that score."

"Yeah, but the lady, fortunately, has no warts or wattles. She is uncommon lovely, and 'twould be quite believable that a man could be consumed by desire for her. . . ."

That explanation had left Rolf less than comfortable, though he saw the sense in it. P'raps he could escape his precipitate actions relatively unscathed, after all. Though he had no desire to wed, neither did he find Lady Annice undesirable.

The memory of her first night at Dragonwyck had left him lying awake on more than one night since she'd arrived. So much so, that he had deliberately avoided seeing her. Few women had gained his interest for longer than a few hours of bed sport, and that the lady Annice had managed to remain in his thoughts for so long was cause for concern.

It had occurred to him that p'raps the lady's courage and fire were what piqued his interest most. She would not be a meek, placid mate that would leave a man restless and yearning for livelier company, 'twas certain. Yea, there were definite advantages to the marriage, far outweighing his reluctance ever to wed again.

Yea, the idea had merit. It would enrage Seabrook to see his ploy turned about on him, and an outwardly compliant agreement would only place Rolf more firmly in the king's camp. A letter had been composed and sent by swift courier, and the deed done.

But now that he had made his decision evident to the lady and his assembled knights and vassals, he fretted against the invisible chains that bound him. And, perversely, he put the blame on Lady Annice's shoulders.

When the meal neared an end, he signaled for Vachel to escort the lady back to her chamber; she rose from her chair and walked across the rush-strewn stones of the hall with her head held high. She still did not cower, though he had given her ample reason. Unwilling admiration tinged his resentment of her.

Though she was not overtall, her carriage was graceful, her body slim and firm beneath the green velvet gown. He could well recall the thrust of her breast against his palm, and the silky softness of her skin. The memory sparked interest anew, and his hand closed around the stem of his goblet. The dark fire of her hair reflected glimmering lights in the bound strands that brushed against her hips, and for an instant he visualized it loose and spread beneath her. There was an implicit invitation in the way it swayed when she walked, beckoning a man to bury his face in the soft waves and lose himself for a time. Even her eyes seemed to entice beneath the curved fringe of her lashes, though the glances she'd given him of late had been more hostile than beguiling.

When she disappeared through the far archway, Sir Guy leaned forward, gazing at his liege over the rim of his goblet. "She is fair, indeed, my lord."

Rolf flicked a glance at him. "Aye." His voice betrayed him with a huskiness he had not intended, and he took an angry swallow of his wine. "And as stubborn and willful as she is fair."

"Yea, p'raps so. But 'tis said of her that she has a sweet nature at times. The words I heard spoken of Lady Annice were most often kind and gentle. Those in her own keep spoke well of her and, if not for Seabrook's cowardly refusal, would have mounted troops to send to her aid."

"Would they." Rolf grunted irritably. " 'Twould have done them little good. With the king's gracious permission for me to wed their lady, they would soon be under my hand."

Sir Guy could not have missed the heavy irony in Rolf's use of the word "permission" in reference to the thinly veiled command to wed Lady Annice or suffer consequences. Wisely, he did not expand on the subject but said instead, "Once John has your consent in hand, he will most like release a portion of her lands to you as dower. After all, he would not dare to distress unduly one of his most powerful barons unless he stood to gain much from it."

"John dares whatever he likes," Rolf said heavily. A thrum of melody from a minstrel sounded, almost drowning him out. He paused, then said, "Have you not noticed how blatantly he wields power? He does not care that he alienates his barons. He thinks himself invincible."

"There are those," Sir Guy said softly, "who wish to prove him wrong on that score. Eustace de Vesci and Robert FitzWalter curry favor on one hand and backbite at every opportunity. 'Tis said they rally the northern barons to their cause, even while mouthing oaths of loyalty to the king."

Rolf's smile was bitter. "Eustace de Vesci is a fool. He has wed King William of Scotland's bastard daughter, and that monarch seeks to use Eustace as a tool to best John. Make no mistake about it, I foresee trouble from that quarter."

"But Robert FitzWalter and Eustace de Vesci stand in the king's favor. . . ."

"Nay, Guy. John reinstated their lands to them last year, but he is not fool enough to trust either man. Do you not recall the plot of two years ago to hand over the king to the Welsh? Other men died for it—Luc d'Arcy among them—

but those worthy knaves fled to France. Both have proved to be traitors and cowards. 'Tis merely expedient for the moment to allow them free rein. Neither has the king forgiven those northern barons who refused to follow him to France. If not for the archbishop reminding him that he would bring contempt upon his sworn oath for making war upon men without legal sentence, John would have sought to bring them low."

Sir Guy nodded. "Yea, I fear you are right. 'Tis well that you have managed to stay this high in the king's favor."

Rolling the stem of his goblet between his fingers, Rolf said slowly, "Yet I cannot help but think I will not always be able to keep my sworn oath. There are times the king goes too far." He looked up at Sir Guy. "I do not know what I will do on the day that John forces me to the choice between personal honor and my oath. And the day will come, Sir Guy, whether I will it or not."

There was nothing Guy could say to that. It was true, and both sensed the time would not be far off. Wedding Lady Annice just might be the first fraying of the bond he had sworn to his king. Yet Rolf found himself impatient to have it done.

It did not sweeten his temper to realize that the lady herself was the lure that might be his undoing.

Annice paced the small confines of her room with quick, angry steps. That braying ass of a baron—did he think her so meek that she would yield to him without protest? Surely he was not that big a fool. Where was Seabrook and his sly schemes when she needed them? Fool indeed—Thurston had only played into le Draca's hands with his appeal to the king. Would John pass by an opportunity to bind Dragonwyck even closer to him? And her marriage to the baron would surely do so, whether she willed it or not. Her father had been Richard's man and had sworn fealty to John, though reluctantly. His death soon after that oath had left Aubert as heir. Aubert, too, had sworn fealty to John, though he remained in Normandy. With her marriage to Luc d'Arcy, Annice had also been bound to the king. Until Luc had turned traitor and met his death for it.

Now, if she wed le Draca, she would be bound even tighter to the king and forced to his bidding. Her vassals and knights would be at John's disposal for his interminable wars in Wales, Ireland, and France, as well as against his own barons. 'Twas no wonder the king was surely smacking his lips with glee at the prospect. If she had remained with Seabrook and wed a vassal of lesser lands and reputation, 'twould not have been nearly as profitable for John. How he must have been delighted at le Draca's taking of her and Seabrook's unwise petition for aid!

But 'twas she who was left to face the Dragon.

Shuddering, Annice recalled the fury in those green eyes staring at her with naked hostility. 'Twas plain he was being forced into the marriage, but that was hardly compensation for her own position. Marriage was a matter of choice, but not for the bride nor the groom. The bride's relatives had the final decision, and she could only hope that Aubert would consult with her before giving permission.

Even that hope was slim. Her correspondence with her half brother had always been sparse. He had left home when she'd been yet a child in the nursery. No sibling affection had ever existed between them. And even if it had, 'twas unlikely that it would have prevented his accepting the king's thinly veiled command that his sister wed le Draca.

If the king had decreed that she wed him, there would be no possibility of buying her freedom with fines. She was caught in this struggle between powerful men. It made little difference to either of them that she was unwilling.

Annice moved to the bed. Smoothing the coverlet with one hand, she lay down and stared up at the ceiling high overhead. Little light reached the corners. Gauzy nets of cobwebs looped in silky drifts, shifting in the breeze that wafted through the uncovered window. The flame in the lamp danced erratically, casting wild shadows on the stone walls. Darkness lay on the land, but the faint glimmer of moonlight threaded into the chamber. Distant noises could be heard, reminding her of long-ago days as a girl when she had lain in her bed and dreamed of the future.

Had she known what lay ahead, would she have acted differently? She had not protested the marriage to Luc, knowing her duty as a daughter and wishing to please her parents. Yet if she had known him for what he was, she might have pleaded for another suitor. A faint smile touched her lips. Yea, and many a wife might do the same, she supposed.

Now she was faced with the prospect of Rolf le Draca as her husband, a fact that left her trembling with emotion. More than just his reputation and harshness frightened her. She recalled only too well her reaction to his caresses the night she had been brought to Dragonwyck. Never had she expected to feel such a response, and certainly not to such a man. It was appalling that he had reduced her to the level of a willing wanton with just the touch of his hands and lips. How could she have been so base as to yield? And worse, he had known of her surrender. There had been a triumphant gleam in his eyes when he'd mocked her, then rejected her.

To him it had been a meaningless encounter. No doubt just one among many. But to her it had been a shattering awakening of a desire that haunted her nights and dreams. More than once she had awakened in this crude bed from a dream of him, his golden hair and green eyes as real as if only a hand span from her. She'd tried to ignore the hot, restless feeling he'd sparked in her, the nameless yearning that twisted her at times.

But it was always there, lurking in the back of her mind like a constant shadow, waiting to claim her dreams. Rolling over, Annice pulled the coverlet around her and faced the wall. She would sleep, and this night there would be no dreams.

A noise awoke her, and she turned slowly to see Rolf enter the chamber. He was smiling, a lazy smile that gave him the appearance of a confident predator. There was a sensual quality to his heavy-lashed gaze that unnerved her, and words froze in her throat. She could not move nor speak when he came to her bed, could only gaze at him helplessly as he began to remove her garments. With slow, casual movements he undressed her completely. She closed her eyes, opening them only when he was over her, his weight pressing into her, holding her down on the mattress. He was as naked as she; she could feel the slide of his bare skin over hers, feel the press of his heavy arousal against her inner thigh.

But it was his hands that tormented her, touching her breasts, her belly, that aching moistness between her thighs. She shuddered when his mouth found the rigid bud of her nipple and covered it. The pulsing pressure between her legs grew greater, and she arched against him in a wordless plea. His eyes narrowed slightly, hot and green beneath dark lashes tipped with gold, staring down at her with an expression she could not fathom. It was as if he asked for something, wanted something from her. But what?

Her hands clenched and unclenched at her sides. She lifted her arms to put them around him, let her fingers slide down his broad, muscled back in a leisurely glide. His breathing was harsh and rasping in her ear, his body curiously heavy, restricting her movements. Empty and aching, she tried to pull him even closer, yearned for the release only he could give her. But he resisted, teasing her with more caresses until she was panting for breath. She stared up at his face in the dim light, saw the deep green of his eyes grow darker and darker beneath the thick brush of his lashes. He was muttering something she couldn't hear, the words hoarse and blurred. Then his body slid lower, and she felt him brush against the damp, aching need between her thighs. His hardness slid over the place of throbbing torment in a heated glide that made her shudder with pleasure. She wanted more, but her squirming efforts gained her nothing as he seemed to move farther away. Annice moaned. Release was just beyond her reach.

He was breathing deeply, the dark fringe of his lashes shadowing his face as his head bent to look down at what his hands were doing to her. With his head bent she could see only the thick gold of his hair and his broad shoulders rising and falling in an erotic rhythm. Her hands lifted to touch his face and he looked up at her, eyes a vivid, glittering green that seemed to sear her soul. His lips were drawn back from his teeth, his nostrils flared, and she had the sharp impression of a dragon about to devour her. She cried out, but he did not respond nor loose his hold on her, however much she tried to get away. She was caught.

Quivering beneath his weight, she tried to draw a deep breath, but it was impossible. The air was suffocatingly close around her, and she grew frantic. Lashing out, her hand hit the wall in a painful smash of knuckle and stone.

The sharp, searing pain jerked her upright. . . .

Annice clawed blindly at the folds of blanket over her head. They confined her arms, twisted around them in a clinging tangle. Finally she was free, and she sucked in a deep breath of cool, fresh air that smelled of rain and fish oil. A dream. It had been just another dream.

She looked down at her aching hand. Her knuckles were scraped and bleeding from where she'd struck the wall. The sound of rain was a light patter against the stone ledge of her unshuttered window. The flame in the lamp was dim now, barely sputtering. Shadows flirted with the pale light. Only a dream, she told herself again.

Yet instead of relief, she still ached with an unfulfilled yearning that seemed to fill her entire body. It seemed that Rolf le Draca had invaded even her dreams. Was this her destiny—to be so completely consumed by him that she had no free will left? Yea, and so now she knew how it must feel for those knights of lore who had gone out seeking dragons to slay. She had her own fire-eating dragon of emerald and gold, looming in her future to devour her as surely as the scaled beasts were said to sate their appetites upon maidens.

Yet she was no maiden, and her dragon was very, very real. Emerald eyes and golden hair, beautiful to behold and deadly to be near. Aye, she was well snared. . . .

Despairing, she buried her face in her palms.

CHAPTER 6

$\mathfrak{I}$ do not believe you." Annice faced Rolf with a steady blue gaze that did not waver. Her chin lifted defiantly, and she gave a shrug of her shoulders that shifted the heavy weight of a ribboned rope of hair to her back. Light from the central fire played over her face, gilding the high curve of her cheek with a rosy glow. "Aubert would not be so greedy as to demand half my lands in payment for his signature."

Rolf tossed the parchment to the table between them. Only the brindle mastiff was witness to their discussion. They were alone in the hall, save for a few servants spreading clean, pungent rushes at the far end from the dais, where they stood by the high table. Rolf shrugged.

"Yet he did. Not that it did him much good. The king refused, and in the end your brother will receive a small keep or two that will leave most of the revenue still in John's purse." He smiled. "Are you surprised? John is a shrewd bargainer, and he would not yield much. It is to your brother's advantage that he allowed him any lands at all. If John chose, he could name you a prisoner, and your dower lands forfeit for your late husband's unwise part in the plot to overthrow him."

Annice turned away, her hands trembling. She slid them inside the wide, trailing cuffs of her sleeves and stood with her back to Rolf, staring into the fire. He felt an unaccustomed burst of sympathy. It was difficult being a pawn. Though it had been a long time since he had felt that same helplessness, the emotions were easily recalled. As a page, he'd been thrust about unmercifully, victim to the whims of those older and in command. He'd hated every moment and rebelled so often that he'd worn constant stripes upon his back for flagrant disobedience.

But he had finally realized that one must learn to obey in order to command. Without self-discipline, how could he discipline others? It was that self-discipline that kept him from offering sympathy now. 'Twould not help the lady Annice, save to salve her wounded pride. Best that she learn quickly who could be trusted with her interests and who could not. 'Twas obvious Aubert had only his interests in mind, not those of the woman standing stiffly before the fire.

Moving forward, Rolf slung one leg over the corner of the table and sat quietly while Annice composed herself. He recognized in her rigidly held spine and taut stance that she was struggling with her emotions. When she turned finally, only her eyes betrayed any sign of inner conflict.

"So," she said quietly. " 'Tis done, then. The king is agreed and our marriage is at hand." Her brow lifted. "Am I allowed out of my prison for the ceremony, or is it to be conducted under guard?"

His mouth tightened against a flare of anger. "That depends upon your behavior," he said calmly. "If you think to make a public spectacle by refusing your vows at the altar, you'd best consider the consequences of your actions to those who depend upon your gentle hand as guidance."

Knitting her fine brows, Annice stared at him. Her cheeks were flushed, eyes so frosty a blue beneath the dark fringe of her lashes that he was reminded of winter ice.

"Pardon me," she said coldly, "but I fail to see your

meaning. Who depends upon my guiding hand, save those in my keeps that I am no longer able to command?"

" 'Tis those I speak of." Rolf let that sink in, then added, "You know that as holder of demesnes, keeps, and vassals, you have but to beckon and they will honor their oaths to you. Should you do so, however, it will not please the king."

"I am well aware of that," she said in so bitter a tone that he knew she had already thought of that alternative. "With me as virtual prisoner, my vassals would be doomed should I attempt such a mad scheme. They could not fight both the king and you, and I would not ask it of them. If the black brush of treason had not touched me, I would never yield. But I know, as do my vassals, that I could well end up as Lady Maud de Braose did for her courage in speaking out against John—starved to death in a dungeon. Nay, my lord, you need not fear that I will repudiate any vows at the altar. I have no choice."

With her hands still tucked into her trailing sleeve cuffs, she indicated with a nod of her head the parchment on the table. "Is this the terms of our marriage?"

"Yea." Rolf reached for it. "Shall I read it to you, or do you prefer a scribe to do so?"

Annice removed one hand from the embroidered cuff and held it out palm up. "I will read it myself, if you please."

Skeptical, Rolf did not give it to her immediately. " 'Tis written in Latin," he said, and she gave an impatient nod.

"Many legal documents are. My last wedding documents were also written in Latin. May I?"

Slowly, he held it out and watched as she read it. At some points in the terms her brows lowered ominously and her mouth tightened, a certain sign that she understood what she read. He could not blame her for anger over some of the terms. He would have felt the same. What surprised him most, however, was her ability to read. Many well-bred ladies were taught the rudiments of reading as well as some writing, but the ability to read Latin was rare for a woman of his acquaintance.

After several minutes she lowered the parchment and

looked up at him. "So I am virtually deseisined of all I have."

"Nay, not at all. Can you not understand what you profess to read?" He reached for the parchment, but she held it up against her breast, eyes flaming with anger.

"It states that my lands will be under your control after we wed," she replied, "which is expected. But also, should there be a child born of our union, my lands will become his for life by the courtesy of England." Her lips twisted. "That clause can be omitted, for there will be no child."

His brows rose. "If I did not believe that, milady, I would not wed you."

Her eyes widened with surprise, then darkened in confusion. "What say you—that you wish for no child?"

Shaking his head, Rolf said softly, "I have a child and heir that I cannot have with me. I wish for no other child of mine to be born, for there is no certainty that another would not be somehow held as hostage also. Times are perilous. One hostage is enough."

"I agree." Her hands shook slightly, and the parchment rustled loudly. " 'Tis just as well you wish no more children. I have no intention of providing them for you."

Though he should have told her he knew she was barren, her cold avowal that she would not bear his child angered Rolf. He found himself scowling. "If I wished more children and you were able to provide them, rest assured that you would, indeed, bear them." He stepped forward when she shot him a look of contempt. "Do not think to fight me at every turn, milady. I will not tolerate it. You are but a woman. Once we are wed, you will quickly learn your place."

Annice took a step back, lip curling. "Will I? Will I quickly be brought to heel, milord? You overrate your skills. I am not a dog to be whistled to the chase, nor a hawk to be brought to the lure. Nay, I am a woman, and I have rights." She held up the parchment, crumpled now in her fist. "There is mention of alienating my rights to my property for the duration of our marriage or for your lifetime, as customary. Do you seek to do so in perpetuity? I warn you—my signature is needed to make such a deed permanent. I will not willingly transfer my property to you for-ever."

Rolf gazed at her angry face. Though tempted to tell her bluntly that she would do whatever the king willed her to do—just as he would—he forbore to do so. It would only lengthen an argument he considered already decided. If he told her he understood her need to make angry snarls like a chained hound, that would only infuriate her as well. No, 'twas best he make no comment to her tirade.

When he rose silently, intending to bid her good day and allow her to return to her chamber, Annice took three quick steps away from him. Thrusting the parchment over the licking flames of the fire, she caught the loop of her cuff in her other hand to keep it free, then turned to face him boldly.

"Shall I show you what I think of the king's decree and this document, milord?"

Rolf paused, eyes narrowing as the dangling edges of the parchment began to curl from the heat of the fire. "Do you think more copies cannot be made, milady?" he snapped. " 'Twill only delay matters and anger the king."

"Delay would be most welcome. I cannot displease the king any more than he is already displeased with me, so 'twould be to my advantage to do as I please for a change. I have been thrust about without regard for near a year, and I am weary of it. No one asks if I have done such, or if I wish such, or even if I have anything to say about matters. Nay, I am bandied about like a caged bird."

Her hand and voice were shaking, and the curled edges of the parchment began to blacken. Rolf looked from it to her face. "The pages blaze," he said calmly, and when she glanced away from him toward the document, he lunged swiftly forward.

Grasping her wrist and jerking, he snatched her away from the fire. She loosed the document, and it fluttered with a crackle toward the greedy flames. Rolf shoved Annice to the floor with a hard hand, then grabbed at the document. Flames seared his hand, but he managed to retrieve the parchment and smother the blazing edges with his sleeve. There was the stink of burning velvet and parchment, but he'd saved the document from being devoured by fire. Only some of the words were gone, obliterated by charred ash.

Still crouched on the floor, Rolf pivoted on his heels to look at Annice. Sprawled on her side, propped up on one elbow, she faced him defiantly, eyes glittering with reflected flame. The hem of her gown was twisted beneath her, midway up her legs. Silk garters held up white hose, and her silk undertunic wadded between her knees in a tangle, restricting her movements. A bound rope of hair snaked across the stone hearth, dark-red strands glowing in the light like a line of fire. The tip of her hair was within a handsbreadth of the toe of his boot.

Nothing was said as they stared at each other, he furious, she as poised and tense as a she-wolf. Tension vibrated between them like the taut string of a lute. Beneath the shadowed fringe of her lashes, Annice's eyes were a clear, calculating blue that regarded him with speculation.

Meeting her gaze, Rolf read her intention and reacted swiftly. He dropped the parchment to the floor, one hand shooting out to grasp the end of her hair just as she moved to leap to her feet. He began to draw her toward him by the simple expedient of using her hair as he would a rope.

Slowly he wound it around his fist, forcing her to come to him on her hands and knees when the pressure grew too great to resist. There was fire in her eyes and in the epithets she flung at him, but in a moment she was at his feet. Still kneeling on the stones of the hearth, Rolf stared down at her. There was little pleasure to be gained from crushing a foe already vanquished, yet this woman seemed not to know of her defeat.

Battle lights sparked in her eyes, and a hot flush stained her cheeks with anger. Though the long, trailing cuff of one sleeve had somehow become entangled with the free rope of her hair, she still resisted his effort to draw her up to her knees.

"Jésu," he muttered, "have you so little sense that you would still fight me?"

" 'Tis not a question of sense," she shot back as she jerked at the offending hair and snarled cuff, "but of pride. If you must wed me, so be it. But I shall not yield to you easily, my lord of Dragonwyck, no matter how you try to force me."

A faint smile tugged at his mouth. "I have always enjoyed the contest more than the victory, milady. 'Tis sweeter, indeed, when the prize is hard-won."

"But is it so sweet to lose?" she mocked, freeing at last the cuff from the loosened strands of her hair. "I think not. For you, anyway. Those men more confident of their prowess know that even the best man can ofttimes be conquered if the circumstances dictate."

Rolf still held the other rope of hair in his fist. As if she were in her own chamber before a mirror, Annice began to comb her fingers through the flowing locks of her free hair. The ribbon wound through the loose tresses was a brilliant green silk; calmly twining it back around the thick strands, she rebound her hair as if he were not there.

Flipping it over her shoulder to fall down her back, she looked up at Rolf with a bold gaze. "Do you fear I will escape you, my lord? I am but a woman, by your own words. I can fight such a fierce warrior as yourself with but pitiable weapons. My tongue and my wits are all I have as resources—would you deny me those?"

"At times," he said tightly, " 'twould be advisable to silence that waspish tongue before I am tempted to remove it for you. And the wits you boast of would be better used to contemplate ways to keep me in a better humor with you, rather than seek ways to annoy me. Even a caged bird sings sweetly for its supper."

Her lashes lowered, and he saw a faint shudder pass through her body. He did not allow sympathy for her plight to move him. It would be kinder in the end to accustom her now to accepting him as lord and master.

Tightening his hand in the hair he still held, he slowly pulled her head back until her face was tilted up to his. He could hear the harsh rasp of breath filling her lungs, see her eyes dilate to wide pools as he gave another tug on her hair. Her nostrils flared slightly, and her lips parted. Half-sitting, half-reclining, Annice was propped with one hand against the floor, leaving her unstable and vulnerable.

Rolf slowly rose to his feet, drawing her up with him;

one hand held the hair at her nape so that she could look only at him. Lifting her slowly so that her toes barely brushed against the stone, he held her suspended. He felt a quiver in her muscles as the arm he bent behind her back pressed her more tightly against him. The soft pressure of her breasts against his chest and thighs, trembling against his groin, sparked an immediate reaction in him that was vaguely surprising.

Jésu, she should not be able to affect him so swiftly. Long ago he'd vowed not to allow a woman to cause him any emotion, beyond a certain distant sympathy or generous impulse. That this woman could send the blood coursing through his veins in a raging tide was more than enough evidence that he should avoid her. She squirmed in his grasp, feet banging against his shins. He held her more closely, one arm shifting down to press her hips tightly against him. Then his gaze focused on her face.

There was a sly, catlike smirk curving her mouth, and Rolf's eyes narrowed. Apparently she had felt his desire and would mock him for it. Yea, but he would show her how little she affected him.

Deliberately, slowly, he bent his head, smothering her startled gasp as his mouth captured hers. She did not try to avoid it—could not have, with his hand holding tight to the hair at her neck. As his lips slanted over hers, softly at first, then with growing pressure, her breath came more quickly. He kissed her until she went limp in his hold and he heard a soft moan beneath his lips. But it was not until her arm lifted to clasp him tentatively to her that he released her.

Setting her back from him abruptly, he gazed down at her. Uneven breaths lifted her chest, and her eyes were wide and moist. She put up a hand to touch her lips, which were slightly swollen from his kisses.

"Ah, milady," he said lightly, "do not become too captivated with me. Desire is ofttimes fleeting in a man. . . ."

She looked first flustered, then angry as comprehension flooded her face with color. "Swine!" she hissed. "Do not dare touch me again!"

"This is my keep. I dare anything." Rolf smiled slightly.

"As you will soon learn when you are my wife, Lady Annice."

Even with hate and anger darkening her eyes and marking her face, she was beautiful. But he had known many beautiful women. Why should this one make a difference? There was nothing special about her, other than the fact that she was his hostage and soon to be his wife. He could not allow her to affect him. The memory of the sleepless nights he'd spent since visiting her chamber still rankled.

And though he would not admit it to her, his body raged with frustrated need. Years had taught him the value of schooling his reactions, and he had long ago mastered the art of disciplining his breathing so that he did not appear like a panting youth dangling after his first woman. But there was no hope of schooling his body's response to her, and he was grateful for the long tunic that hid his most obvious reaction.

Releasing her hair, he took a step back and called for his steward. Vachel must have been hovering nearby, for he was there before the loud echoes had done more than disturb a few small birds nesting in the rafters.

"Aye, seigneur?" Vachel said, his eyes darting from Rolf to the lady with practiced impassivity.

"Escort the lady Annice back to her chamber. And see that she has all she requires for our coming nuptials. Within reason, of course. Should there be any requirements that are—questionable—bring them to me to approve."

"Yea, lord," Vachel said with a slight bow. He turned to Annice and hesitated, but she had composed herself enough to nod slightly.

They had gone only a few feet before Annice turned back, so abruptly that poor Vachel almost collided with her. She looked at Rolf, chin held at a haughty angle.

"Tell me, my lord, how soon are we to be wed?"

"In a fortnight. The week after Easter Day and the new year, as they fall close." A mocking smile curved his mouth. "Are you so anxious to seek our conjugal bed, milady?"

"God's grace, but you are a vain dreamer," she said sharply. "I have but a sensible reason for asking. I will have need of my own trunks from Seabrook, if you will. Send for them." She paused, then asked, "Does the king plan to attend?"

"John sends his regrets, but he is at La Souterraine in Berry and cannot be present at our nuptials."

"How unfortunate," she said demurely. " 'Tis even more unfortunate that you are not with him. If I would be prepared in such short order, I needs have a woman to assist me in readying myself. 'Tis not that Vachel is unreliable, for he is most reliable, but I fear it would be too great a burden on him with all his other duties. And I desire a person of my own sex, who will understand my needs."

It seemed a reasonable enough request, and Rolf instructed Vachel to find a suitable woman to attend Annice. "And move her to a chamber in the west wing," he added. "One more suitable for the new Countess of Dragonwyck." When Vachel hesitated, Rolf continued dryly, "But do not relax your guard for a moment. Set a man by her door at all times."

"God's mercy, my lord," Annice said caustically, "for your generosity and concern." Wheeling about, she stalked from the hall with Vachel scurrying at her side.

Rolf watched until she had disappeared from view up the winding flight of stairs. A faint whine distracted him from his musings, and he glanced down to see Bordet at his side. He put a light hand on the huge mastiff's head.

"Would that a woman could be as faithful and easy to understand as a dog," he muttered, and received for his compliment a wet tongue across his hand. He winced at the stinging reminder of the burns he had suffered snatching the parchment from the flames. It still lay on the floor, charred at the edges but perfectly legible save for a few words on the edge. No matter. It would suffice. And the lady Annice would be his wife whether she willed it or no.

Yet he found it vaguely disquieting that she fought so hard against it. 'Twas not that he thought himself a grand prize, but he knew that many a maid and matron had sought his eye with eagerness and hope. Why did Lady Annice loathe him so? He'd thought—nay, he was certain—he had seen a gleam of sympathy in her eyes that day at Stoneham Castle. Yea, she would not have shed tears were she not in sympathy with his plight over Justin.

She must be still angry over the manner of her abduction, then his necessary attempts to frighten her into signing a letter. St. Jerome, but did she not know how cruel he could have been? He'd thought his restraint rather admirable under the circumstances. Losing Edmund and his son in one day had been almost more than his temper could bear. Holy Mary and Joseph, even women would react violently when faced with similar situations. Annice was just being stubborn. And childish. If not, she'd realize that he was being as gentle as he could be with her.

Muttering an oath, Rolf retrieved the parchment and rolled it carefully, binding it with the ribbon and seals. In so doing, he scraped the burned flesh of his hand and flinched. He'd better see it tended, and soon. The thought of being a one-armed knight should the injury become inflamed was not very appealing.

Furious, Annice paced the floor of her new chamber with quick, hard steps. This room was larger, and much more comfortable, but she took no pleasure in it. A huge bed dominated one side of the chamber complete with embroidered hangings and a thick mattress stuffed with goose feathers. Pillows and coverlet matched. Rich hangings covered the walls and looped from the ceiling. In the center of the chamber a large brass brazier filled with glowing coals provided warmth for the still chill evenings. Tall branched candlestands held tapers that gave off steady light, and there was a large table as well as a small writing desk. Several chairs and stools were scattered about on carpets as if awaiting guests for a cozy chat. There were even panes of precious glass in latticed windows that looked out over a steep decline falling away from the castle to a village nestled below. Thick Lincolnshire forest stretched beyond the village, treetops easily visible from the window.

Annice swept it all with a contemptuous glance. Did the beastly knave think to set all aright with the return of comforts that were the norm? Did he think removing her from her small, dank chamber would earn him praise? He had best reconsider, she thought darkly. 'Twould take much more than he had shown her to raise her opinion of him to even the bottom level of the deepest moat. Nay, that black knight could not earn her high regard despite what he might do.

Yet even while she raged silently, pacing until her legs ached, Annice could not help but unwillingly recall things best forgotten. The touch of his mouth on hers had been unsettling, renewing sensations that she'd tried hard to ignore. That he had been so unmoved by what to her was a searing kiss was humiliating enough. But the fact that he had the effrontery to mock her for it made her cringe with shame. How could she have been so foolish as to yield for even one instant? She'd thought herself immune to him, thought herself so well armed against his arrogance and insolence that she could withstand anything he said.

She had not considered that he would taunt her for what she could not help. Ah, that her body had so betrayed her with even the slightest of responses to his touch was bad enough—that her dreams were haunted by him was even worse. God's mercy that he did not know of that, or she was certain he would use it against her as well.

Tugging at the trailing cuffs of her sleeves, she ceased her pacing when she heard a knock at the door. Her heart leaped into her throat. She turned slowly as the door swung open, and her heart dropped back down to normal again. It was a dark-haired woman; from her dress and manner it must be the serving woman Rolf had promised.

"My name is Belle, milady," she murmured in English, and Annice saw that she was little more than a girl. "I have been sent to thee."

Smiling, she moved forward to greet the girl, who was staring shyly at the floor. She answered in English, "I am Lady Annice, Belle. I am pleased thou will be here to help me."

Still shy, Belle wadded her hands in a fold of her skirt and mumbled, " 'Tis said thou art to wed the lord soon. I can sew a fine seam, milady."

"That talent will be sorely needed if I am to ready a

proper gown before the set day. Dost thou have any suggestions, Belle? I would gladly hear them, as I do not know what will be available to me."

Looking rather startled, Belle nodded. "Aye, milady. From what Vachel said, thou art to have anything thou wish. I am but to fetch it for thee when thou bade me do so."

"I see. Did Vachel also say how I am to know what there is to choose from?" When Belle shook her head, Annice sighed. "P'raps that is a problem we can solve on the morrow. For now, I am weary, and thou must be also. Tell Vachel that I will require thee to stay in my chambers with me, and prepare thee a pallet in my chamber. Doth that suit thee?"

"Aye, milady. It suits me very well." Belle glanced around the chamber. " 'Tis fortunate I am to be in Lord Rolf's keep. He is ever the fairest lord . . . all strive for a place here. Afore, I worked in the kitchens. I am honored to be thy maidservant. I'll try my best to please thee."

"I'm certain thou will, Belle. There will be much to do in the coming days. When my own belongings arrive, I will need thee to assist me. I am well pleased to have such pleasant company and willing hands."

"God's mercy, milady," Belle said, bending slightly in a small courtesy. "I shall do what I can to make thy days pleasant."

As the girl looked up with a smile and soft brown eyes, Annice felt for an instant as if she was finally being made welcome in the dark Castle of Dragonwyck. P'raps 'twould not be as evil a place to dwell as she'd feared.

"Then please begin with a small task, Belle," she said. "Remove those candlesticks from the chamber. The less I see of dragons, the better I will like it."

Slanting her a curious glance, Belle moved toward the candlesticks Annice indicated. Shaped to the forms of rampant dragons, fangs bared and wings outspread, the cast-pewter candlesticks reminded her too greatly of her betrothed. Her dreams were filled enough with all things dragon—must she bear daily reminders?

When Belle returned from removing the candlesticks, Annice said with a wide smile, "Now, we shall deal quite well together, I think. There is little enough to do in my days, and I am glad to have thee with me."

Belle's eyes shone with pleasure. " 'Tis my honor, milady, to serve thee. Sir Guy hath told me thou wert a great and noble lady, and I maun do nothing to distress thee."

"Did he?" Annice looked at the girl in surprise. "And what else did Sir Guy say?"

Belle looked away shyly. She fidgeted for a moment, then said to a spot on the floor, "Only that thou maun naught be made to feel unwelcome here, for 'twill be difficult enow for thee in the days to come."

That was true enough. It did not take a soothsayer to predict turbulent times ahead for all of them. But did Sir Guy mean for England, or for the Dragon's wife?

CHAPTER 7

Rolf paused at the closed door of Annice's chamber. He could feel the eyes of the guard flick nervously toward him, then away again, and knew that the man must be wondering what ailed his lord to make him prowl like an enraged wolf. Lifting his hand, Rolf jerked at the door latch, then swung it open with a hard shove.

The heavy oak door must have recently oiled hinges, for it flew back with a loud crash against the stone wall buttressing the doorjamb, drawing a scream from the maidservant attending Annice. The lady, however, was more composed. She sat in stiff, wide-eyed silence, a mass of amber silk material draped over her lap. In one hand she clutched a needle and length of thread poised over the silk.

Calmly, she punched the needle into the silk and set it aside, rising to her feet to face him. "I am honored to have you visit my chamber," she said as if he had not just burst into the room. "May I offer you wine?"

He drew in a deep breath to calm his mounting anger.

Holding up a crumpled sheaf of parchment, he demanded, "Explain this, if you will, madam."

Annice eyed the parchment with a faint expression of unease creasing her lovely face. "Ex-explain? I don't know what you mean, my lord. . . ."

Taking a step forward, Rolf snarled, "The devil you say—do not think to play me for a fool. I am well aware of all that takes place in my keep. Did you think to slip this from my hall without my knowing about it? My people here are very loyal to me, little though you may credit it."

Her chin lifted. "Do you truly think me witless, my lord? I have faults aplenty, God knows, but I would have to be blind and deaf not to have witnessed how you command loyalty from those who serve you. While you may not like the nature of my letter to my brother, I did not think you petty enough to deny me a last plea for clemency."

Crumpling the letter in his hand, Rolf tried to stem his rising fury. "*Clemency?* P'raps you are confusing marriage with execution, milady."

Annice's eyes lowered, and she clasped her hands in front of her. At her feet the wide-eyed maidservant cowered like a hound afraid of a storm, and Rolf fought the urge to send her from the chamber with a few well-chosen words. It did not ease his temper when Annice murmured, "In this case I view marriage and execution in the same light, milord."

"I see." His voice cracked like a whip, and he saw the maidservant flinch as if struck. "You. Girl. Leave us," he commanded, jerking his head toward the door when the maid raised wide eyes to his face. She did not wait for further commands but scrambled to her feet and fled without looking back.

Rolf waited until the door had slammed behind the girl to look back at Annice. Though white-faced, she did not quiver or utter a sound. Standing very still, she met his gaze with calm regard, blue eyes bright beneath the curve of her dark lashes.

"Madam," he forced out in as civil a tone as he could manage, "you try my patience. Do you think me joyous at the prospect of marriage to you? If so, you are much mistaken."

"Yet you stand to gain, and I do not," she interrupted in a frosty tone that should have left icicles hanging from the ceiling.

"I gain naught but a shrewish wife, it seems," he shot back, infuriated by her cool regard. "Do you think I care for the lands you bring? I do not. But my king has decreed that we shall wed, and so we shall, whether either of us likes it or no."

Her head tilted slightly to one side, and a faint frown puckered her brow. "Do you always agree with the king?"

"Nay. Rarely do I agree with the king," Rolf said bluntly. "What has agreement to do with John? He does what he wishes even against strong advisement from those around him. But he is the king."

"I find that attitude remarkable."

"How so? Do you not find it more politic to keep your head? Wait—I forgot that you do not mind tweaking the nose of any man."

Smiling faintly, Annice said, "Not quite true, my lord. 'Tis only your nose that I do not mind tweaking."

Stung by her apparent disregard for him, Rolf took two steps forward. He grabbed her by the shoulders when she would have stepped back. His fingers tightened to hold her, bunching the material of her gown. He loosened his grip only slightly when he saw her wince.

"You sorely test me, madam. Do you think me so poor a man that I would allow you to taunt me?"

Shaking her head, Annice whispered, "Nay, lord. But neither am I so poor-spirited a woman that I would allow you to subdue me without a struggle. I have a mind and a will, and I have never yet given up control of either."

"I do not demand control of your mind. I demand your respect."

"Respect must be earned." She looked up at him, eyes a deep, solemn blue that seemed to penetrate to his marrow. "One cannot command the sun to rise, nor the moon to shine. It comes as the natural order of things. So does my respect for a man. If ever I give you my respect, my lord, you will have earned it, have no doubts."

His fingers curled into the silk of her cotte. A wave of frustration washed over him. "If you think I will consider disobeying my king, do not be misled. Though I rarely agree with John, neither will I break a sworn oath. I paid him homage and swore fealty, and 'twill take an act of God to force me to break my oath."

"An act of God?" Annice's mouth twisted into a bitter smile. "More like an act of godlessness will turn men against the king. I have seen much, have had the king take my husband and my lands from me, and now you think that I wish for you to repudiate him? Nay, my lord, you completely misunderstand me. I do not care if you love the king or hate him. That has naught to do with me. What matters to me is the merit of a man. 'Tis shown in his deeds, not his words."

"And my deeds are so few and shallow that I merit no respect?"

Rolf snarled the question at her and saw her eyes widen. It wasn't what he'd meant to say. God only knew what he should have said—but he saw from her expression that he'd at least succeeded in frightening her again. That wasn't the reaction he wanted. It galled him to know that the reaction he most wanted from her was one she would refuse to give.

Lowering her gaze, Annice was silent for a moment before saying softly, "Your valor and skill as a warrior have never been questioned. While those deeds command the respect I would give any brave knight of the realm, 'tis not those qualities that I admire most in a man."

His grip tightened on her shoulders. "No? 'Twould fascinate me to learn what you do admire."

"I hardly think so—"

"Yea, my lady. Humor me. Tell me what you admire most in a man."

Stiffening beneath his hands, she said, "Honor."

"And how do you define 'honor,' my lady? 'Tis different, I have learned, for a woman than it is for a man. Men tend to regard it as personal integrity that is not required by law or oath, but by nature. Women, however"—he paused, let-

ting the silence lengthen for a moment before finishing—
"women tend to regard honor as a thing to be won or pur-
chased, not inherent."

She stared up at him. "P'raps the women you know have
done so, milord, but not I."

Rolf smiled slightly and shifted one hand from her
shoulder to touch her cheek in a light caress. The skin was
smooth and soft beneath the backs of his fingers, heated
with her anger. "No?" he murmured. "I trow you would sell
your honor quickly enough if offered the right price, milady."

"There's not enough gold in all of England to buy my
honor," she said shortly.

Rolf's smile deepened. "Gold is not always the price required. Ofttimes it is vows of love, or worthless promises."

"Love is worthless to you?" She turned her face slightly
away from his caressing hand, and he let it drop to his side.

"Yea, more or less. No woman's love has ever been worth
more than the breath it takes for her to profess it. 'Twas the
most difficult lesson I've learned, but I learned it well at an
early age."

"Then I pity you, my lord." Annice looked back at him,
eyes bright with some emotion he couldn't define. "For if
you have never loved a woman, you have never known what
it is to be loved by a woman."

"Nay, but I've seen the damage done to those who have,"
he said harshly. "What I've seen was enough to warn me not
to lose my head long enough to barter my heart for my soul.
And that is what it would be to be fool enough to love a
woman."

Tossing her head so that one of her bound ropes of hair
shifted to her back, Annice said with a lifted brow, "I am
certain your son will be glad to hear that you never loved
his mother."

For an instant Rolf could not speak. The arrow was so
swift and accurate, it left him floundering. Of course he
could never tell Justin such a thing. There would be no
point in it, nor would it do more than hurt him.

Drawing in a deep breath, he said, "I would never tell
him that. Surely," he added to quench the flash of triumph

in her eyes, "he will draw his own conclusions on the merits of a woman's love once I tell him all I know."

"That should be a short discussion indeed, milord!"

"Are you saying I know little about a woman's love, chérie?" he asked incredulously. "One does not have to subscribe to a certain theory to know about it. I have knowledge of history, but I was not there. Shall I tell you of the ancient Greeks, or would you believe nothing I have to say because I was not there when Alexander the Great fought his battles?"

"One can hardly compare the two, milord," she said stiffly. "Men who were there have written of the battles fought by Alexander, and 'tis those accounts we read. You are here now. Can you correctly tell your son about a matter of which you know little?"

"Since you seem to know so much, p'raps I should send him to you should the occasion ever arise. What will you tell him? Tales of knightly chivalry and poetic love? I do not think even a child will be much impressed with those."

"I suppose you mean like Tristan and Iseult?" Annice pulled free of his grip, and he did not try to keep her. She stepped back warily, as if afraid he would grab her again. " 'Tis a romantic tale that has little to do with the truth, I'm afraid."

"My point exactly, milady."

Lifting her chin, she said indignantly, "But that does not mean love is only a mythical tale. True love between a man and a woman is special and pure and should be viewed as sacred. I know this."

Rolf fought a wave of unnatural jealousy and couldn't keep from asking sharply, "As you truly loved your husband, I suppose?"

"Luc?" Her eyes widened. "If you had but known him, you would not doubt for a moment how I felt—" She stopped, voice trembling, then said softly, "P'raps this is my penance for feeling as I did when he died—for not being able to stop it."

Penance? Rolf's throat tightened with fury and frustration. So she viewed him as penance for losing her beloved husband? By all the saints, he would not stand for that. Nay, he was no substitute for any man, much less a cowardly traitor who had forsworn his oath to his king and courted treason and death for his treachery.

Before he even thought about it—before her quick gasp and recoil were more than an instant's reaction—Rolf had snatched Annice to him and covered her mouth with his. The driving urge to wipe any thoughts of another man from her mind prodded him into harsh retaliation. His lips seared across hers in a burning kiss, hot need welling up inside him the moment he touched her. Drawing one hand down through the twined rope of her hair, he paused in the luscious curve of her back, spreading his fingers. He held her to him while he kissed her, felt her short gasps for breath push her breasts against his chest.

With warmer weather had come looser garments, and the thin blue silk she wore did not buffer the lush feel of her breasts, their shapes cushioning his hold. It made no difference to him in that moment who she was, or why she was with him—all reasoning was cast away in the sense of urgency that flooded him. He could feel the silky strands of her hair beneath his fingers, the strain of her breasts a bruising pressure against his chest, and her softly trembling lips a sweet agony beneath his questing mouth.

Almost feverishly, his hands moved to explore her, softness beneath his fingers wherever he touched—silk-shaped breasts and velvety skin shaping to his finger pads in luxurious torment. Lush curves and tempting hollows beckoned invitingly. She drew back from him, inhaling deeply, eyes wide and dark with shadows. Slowly, he drew her toward him again, hands moving down the narrow line of her body to mold against her hips, bringing her even closer.

Her hands lay lightly on his forearms, not quite pushing him away, but offering silent resistance. She breathed heavily, and each indrawn breath made the silk stretched tautly over her breasts shiver with the movement. His gaze riveted on the play of light and shadow, the enticing glimpse of creamy skin beneath the vee-shaped neck of her bodice a teasing temptation. The sweet promise of her body's secrets drove him past the last scrap of restraint that he possessed, catapulting him into determination. It was madness and stupidity, but at the moment he didn't care. Nothing mattered but the woman in his arms and his possession of her.

Crushing her to him, he bent to kiss the base of her throat, forcing her head back. The heavy rope of her hair swung free, and he caught it in one hand and spread his fingers through it, loosening the ribbon that bound it. His hand combed through the silky tresses as he'd thought of doing so many times, freeing it to tumble down her back in a dark, fiery mass. He cradled a twist of it in his palm.

"Your hair is beautiful," he muttered thickly. She braced against the slow pull of his hand through her hair, but he would not let her free. Exerting a steady force, he tilted back her head until her lips were once more lifted to his. He kissed her lightly, barely grazing each side of her mouth before taking her lips fully. Softly, more gently than he'd thought himself capable of, considering the force of his desire, he coaxed her lips apart with his tongue until she yielded.

It was honeyed warmth and softness when he touched his tongue to hers, and he shuddered at the immediate need that almost consumed him. His arms trembled with strain as he held her, and when he lifted his head, his lungs ached for air. He drew in a deep, unsteady breath that did nothing to still the rapidly beating drum of blood through his veins. More shaken by his response than he'd considered possible, he looked down at Annice's flushed face. Her eyes were closed, lashes making spiky shadows on her cheeks. A rapid pulse beat in the hollow of her throat, mimicking his own rapid heartbeat. Then she seemed to melt into his arms, boneless and yielding.

Any control he might have had over his body's pressing urges evaporated in the heat of desire that enveloped him. Without pausing to consider the consequences, he lifted Annice in his arms and strode to her wide bed, deftly avoiding the hanging bed curtains as he placed her on the mattress. She made a murmur of protest, but whether it was against him or against the disregard of her clothing as his hands worked at stubborn laces, he did not know. Nor care.

Nothing mattered but that he sate himself in her body, in the sweet, perfumed flesh that had haunted him since her first night in Dragonwyck. Yea, he wanted her. And she made no protest after that first whimper when he'd rent her gown. Instead she lay pliantly beneath him, one leg bent at the knee, her hands palms up beside her head in the tangle of russet hair spread on the pillows beneath her.

The press of desire was hot and heavy, made more urgent by her silent acquiescence. By all that was holy, he would have her. . . .

Silk and velvet garments were cast aside, baring her to his eyes, making him groan aloud. He bent forward and kissed her mouth, her closed eyelids, the slope of her cheek where silent tears made wet paths. She made not a sound. Sitting back, he stared down at his prize, his palms upon the flat mound of her belly. Yea, she was as lovely as he'd remembered. Creamy pale skin, flawless and firm, deep rose nipples tightening into buds on breasts that were high and proud—he swallowed heavily and moved his hands to cup them.

She shuddered, a ripple through her body as his thumbs raked across the taut nipples, and slowly he bent to capture a tight peak with his mouth. His tongue teased and tasted, explored the luscious shape beneath his lips, moved to the scented valley between. Annice was making soft sounds in her throat. He moved lower, trailing a damp path with his tongue down the center of her body, dipping into the small indention of her navel. She cried out softly and gripped the arms he'd bent on each side of her, her fingers curling into the material of his tunic.

"Nay, lord," she said in a panting breath, "I cannot! Do not dishonor me before our wedding, I beg of you."

He looked up at her imploring face, then down at the slender body beneath him, the red-gold curls crowning her mount, the quivering thighs that still hid her femininity. His body urged him to action, to ignore common sense and decency and take what would soon be his anyway. Already he'd loosened the laces that held up his breeches, and his shaft strained against the linen in raging need.

Shifting, he pressed his body between her thighs and shuddered with pleasure. Even through the cloth of his breeches he could feel her warmth; muttering hoarsely, he shoved forward, restrained from his goal only by the thin barrier of cloth. His hand moved between them to remove that obstacle, and Annice caught him by the wrist.

"Please, milord," she begged softly, and Rolf took a deep breath. *Jésu*. Where was his resolve not to allow this woman to affect him?

Gone, obviously, in the heat of the moment.

With a great effort Rolf sat back on his heels, common sense battling with raging passion, and barely winning. There would be the right time for this, but if he yielded to his need and took her now, it could cause more complications than he wished to combat.

Glancing down, he yanked viciously at the laces of his breeches, tying them back up over the obvious bulge in front. Annice shuddered, and he moved from the bed to retrieve her discarded garments. He gave them to her silently. Her gaze lifted to his, and he saw her lips trembling. A faint wave of bitter satisfaction washed over him.

"P'raps, milady," he said in an admirably steady voice, "you will not miss your late husband's attentions so much once we are wed."

Annice laughed softly. It did not sound like disdain—as he might have expected—but more like surprise. Her eyes widened.

"Nay, lord," she said, "p'raps I shall not miss him then."

It was not the most satisfying response, nor one that left him feeling a sense of victory. In fact, it left him with even more questions than before.

The slamming of the door echoed in the room. Shivering, Annice folded her arms across her chest and sat slowly down in the chair she'd vacated when Rolf had entered. God's mercy, he was gone. As usual, he'd left her shaken and in turmoil. How did he accomplish it so easily? It didn't seem fair, that he should be able to possess such a command of her thoughts and emotions.

But he did.

Just his presence was usually enough to cast her into a turmoil, and his touch made her lose all her wits. He must know it. Why else did he deliberately force her to accept the touch of his hand and mouth? He sought to discompose her, to addle her wits so that she could not think properly.

Pressing her fingertips to her temples, she bent to rest her elbows on her thighs, still trembling with reaction. For a moment she had thought he would pursue his assault of her senses without regard for her protests. That he had halted when his body was so obviously ready gave her much thought. P'raps he possessed a decency she had first seen in him, after all. Not many a man would listen at such a moment, especially when she had not protested more vigorously. But Rolf had, though his muttered curses had burned her ears while she'd dressed.

Had she revealed anything to him that she had not intended? She wished she could recall all that had been said and done, but the memory most vivid in her mind was of his hands moving over her body and the sensations he'd provoked. Holy Mary—that was enough.

Her throat tightened. Why did he have the power to affect her so drastically? He didn't even have to touch her— the sound of his deep voice sent shivers up her spine and sharpened her senses to the slightest nuance of his words. Just knowing he was near was enough to set her nerves to tingling.

With such physical confusion, it was a wonder she could even recall anything that was said. Things became a jumble of fragmented thoughts and impressions when she reflected on them.

One thing did stand out in her mind—his statement that though he did not agree with John, he would stand by his sworn oath. In these perilous times, when barons betrayed their own kin as well as their king, that stance could cost Dragonwyck all if he was not cautious.

It also made her reconsider her suspicion that he was as false as Seabrook. If Rolf le Draca refused to betray King John even when that monarch deserved betrayal, he had more honor than she had first thought. Few men would stand by their principles in the face of the seething rebellion that now infested the king's court. She may not have been privy to state secrets, but Alais's penchant for ready gossip had kept her well abreast of the latest news. Yea, many loyalists were already retreating from John's ranks as slyly and stealthily as possible, ready at a moment's notice to cast their lots with the side most likely to be victorious. It was a risky business, choosing between monarch and survival, when the wrong choice could mean death.

Another shiver shook her, and she lifted her head to gaze at the closed door. Dragons were carved into the heavy oak, a constant reminder of the Lord of Dragonwyck—as if she needed a reminder. Not even the presence of her own things about her—a silver hairbrush and mirror, familiar perfumes and powders and trinkets from her trunks—could ease the knowledge that she was still hostage in a strange castle, still held powerless by the Dragon.

Her gaze fell upon the length of amber silk lying in a puddle on the floor. Bending, Annice picked up the shimmering silk. Her nuptial gown. She rubbed the tunic against her cheek. A cloth-of-gold cotte was to be worn over it, side lacings and low neckline providing ample glimpses of the amber silk beneath. Though Belle did most of the sewing, 'twas her own hands that did the delicate working of jewels in intricate patterns on bodice and skirt. This gown was finer than any of those brought from Seabrook in her trunks. With Belle's cheerful assistance the cotte hardie was almost done. Only the gilt trimming needed to be added once the sleeves were set in and the hem sewn. It would be a beautiful gown to be wed in, though this wedding would be much different from her first. As would the husband. Her throat tightened.

Marriage. What would it be like to be married to the Lord of Dragonwyck? He was nothing like what she'd thought he would be—neither as cruel as she'd feared, nor as gentle as she'd hoped. His reputation portrayed him as a brutal warlord with little regard for human life. She didn't find that to be true. But neither did she find much comfort in her earlier impression of him as a man who possessed gentle strength. He'd shown her no sign of the tenderness she'd glimpsed that day with his son. In truth, he'd made it plain that he thought little enough of women. Or of love.

Though she did sense honor in him, she did not know

him well enough to predict his reaction to the perilous times ahead of them. Too much could happen—too much could be lost by the simple saying of yea instead of nay. Hadn't she learned her lesson before? Luc had been foolish and too quick to be swayed. He had almost ruined her with his failed plotting.

But something told her Rolf le Draca would never take that chance. Nay, he had sworn an oath he meant to keep, and if the barons rose and dragged the king from his throne, all those loyal to John would forfeit everything. Even life. . . .

A soft, bitter laugh spilled from her mouth. What a farce. She had almost lost all because of a plot against the king and might do so again, for the opposite cause. But there was nothing she could do about either. It was too late for one, and out of her control for the other. She hated the feeling of helplessness, of her fate being left to the whim of a man. Luc had almost ruined her; Rolf might still do so. And there was nothing she could do. 'Twas ridiculous, that in these enlightened times, a woman had so little power over her own life.

Oh, there were women who wielded power through their husbands, or even as managers of their own estates, it was true. But it was so easily wrested away from them if they did not watch every step. It wasn't only young maids who were married off without a say in the matter; grown women could be summarily married off unless able to purchase freedom from their overlord or the king. In her case, of course, this last option had been rendered impossible by her tenuous position as the widow of a condemned traitor.

In the normal course of things, as a young widow she could have been wooed and won again, perhaps, by a man she would respect and love. Fate had not been that kind. Now she was to wed a man who inspired more fear than love.

But it was the unsettling dreams he inspired that distressed her most . . . the vague longings for something as yet unknown to her. . . . The memories of his caresses and kisses left her seething with unfamiliar emotions. How could she contend with a demon she could not identify?

Equally disturbing was Rolf's apparent belief that she had loved her husband greatly. It had been too ludicrous a statement for her to deny—especially when she saw how it plagued him.

But perhaps that might be to her benefit. A slow smile curved her mouth. Yea, she might have unwittingly found a weapon to use against the Dragon. . . .

After visiting the chapel for morning services, fast was broken in the great hall. Annice, with her ever-present guard, took her seat at the high table with Rolf, occasionally giving him wary glances. For his part, he seemed content to ignore her.

Unreasonably annoyed by his indifference, Annice studied her trencher of oat pottage with fierce dislike. Though her stomach was empty, she could not bring herself to taste the thick concoction. It was unlike what she was accustomed to in Thurston's castle, nor was it what she would have served to break the fast if she'd been supervising the kitchens. There would have been white bread, cheeses from France, fruit in season, and in absence of meat during Lent, coddled eggs.

Lifting her gaze, she chanced to meet Rolf's amused gaze. He indicated her untouched trencher with a nod of his head. "Do you mislike it, my lady?"

"Yea." She shrugged lightly. "But I have not been offered tempting food to break my fast since I have come to Dragonwyck."

Rolf leaned back in his chair, studying her for a moment. "Have you not?"

She flushed slightly. It was the height of rudeness to remark upon the lack of suitable fare. Had she not viewed the lavish display of food prepared for other meals, she would have thought him master of a poor castle.

Still staring at her with a faintly amused smile, Rolf said, "You have my leave to repair to the kitchen and speak with the cooks."

When she stared back in surprise, he added, "Tostig will accompany you, of course."

Tostig. Her constant guard. He even slept outside her door at night, presumably to safeguard her, but in fact, to keep her from attempting escape. Annice glared at Rolf.

"God's mercy on you, milord, for such generosity of spirit."

He grinned. "Your words are sweet, but your eyes gleam like daggers, fair lady."

She lowered her lashes. "Daggers ... 'Tis naught but your own fevered imaginings, milord."

"Fevered?" His brow lifted. "If I am fevered, 'tis naught of my imaginings, but of memory. P'raps you have already forgot last night, but I have not."

A flush heated her face, and she turned away from him so that she did not have to see his knowing gaze. Nay, she had not forgotten the past eve for an instant. Just sitting beside him awakened strange, heated tremblings in her body that she strove to ignore. It did not help that he seemed to know it.

When the morning meal was ended and the servants attended to the removal of tables and benches to stack against the walls, Rolf's scribe arrived with quill and ledgers. Business was to be conducted, and Annice debated rising immediately. P'raps there would be a hint of events outside Dragonwyck to warn her against future mishaps. A chance word might give her some indication beyond the little that Rolf had told her.

No one seemed inclined to force her departure, and she retreated to a stool near the fire as if to warm herself. Rolf took his place by the scribe, conversing in low tones as to the day's roster.

The doors at the far end of the hall were opened to reveal a crowd of petitioners, barred entrance by men-at-arms. Allowed in one at a time to plead their cases, a vassal came first to offer reason why he had not yet paid the fines due Rolf as his overlord. As an excuse, he protested the king's forest law enacted upon his land.

"I've no recourse, milord," he said indignantly when asked to explain, "but to purchase wood from another, when there are thickly wooded forests already upon my demesne. I am not even allowed to hunt game for my table, yet when traveling through my forest, I see stags grazing the meadows like sheep. They fear no man but gaze contemptuously about as if challenging a hungry hunter to snatch them from under the protection of the king's gamekeeper."

"Those forests are protected by the king," Rolf replied. "John has amerced those foolish enough to poach wood or game he regards as his. If you would protest, you should petition the king. I have no authority to grant permission to take what is not mine nor yours."

"Nay, but nor do I wish to come to the same end as Thomas of Moulton," was the bitter retort. "He ended in prison, deprived of his shrievalty and freedom."

" 'Twas for failing to meet the terms of his proffer and accounting to the crown, not for poaching wood or game," Rolf said with a frown. "I see no connection between Thomas and you, Sir Roger, for Thomas was a sheriff."

"Yea, and backed by Lincolnshire gentry he dared not anger," Sir Roger spat. "Had he been able, he could have collected the shire debts from nobles such as you and remained free."

"That was six years ago." Rolf stared at the angry man. "Though I did render my debt to Thomas, I sense more here than just grievances with the king's forest laws, Sir Roger."

Taking a deep breath, the vassal looked down at his feet for a moment, then back up. "Yea, lord. Thomas of Moulton was my cousin. And now I am under the burden of a new sheriff, who has increased my fines threefold. The sheriff's men range through my lands like ravening wolves! They take wood from my villeins, plunder my serfs' few belongings, hunt my sparse game, and even steal fish from my ponds! My villeins cannot even pay me what I am owed upon pain of starvation. Dead millers and farmers are of no use to me. Not even the heriot and mortuary derived from their deaths would alleviate my expenses. Am I allowed no recourse? Will I end as my cousin, because I am unable to pay what the sheriff now demands?"

Annice glanced from the vassal to Rolf and saw frustration flicker in his features. It was obvious from the taut set of his mouth and the fist he clenched upon the surface of the table that his vassal's plight affected him.

After a moment of thick silence he said heavily, "I cannot repudiate the king's law."

Sir Roger gave an angry oath, and Rolf held up his hand, piercing the man with a frowning stare. "But this I will do, in recognition of your unjust plight. Render unto the king what is his, but delay an accounting to me until Michaelmas of next year. If there is a bountiful harvest this year, p'raps you can retrieve some of the debts owed to you by your own villeins and serfs. I do not absolve you from rendering unto me what is owed, but I will accept your oath that you shall give me an honest accounting of receipts and debts for my perusal."

For a moment Sir Roger just stared at Rolf. Then he inhaled deeply and nodded. "God's mercy, milord. I swear upon my honor that I will give you a just accounting. God willing, John will send a new sheriff to replace this one before next Michaelmas, and he will levy an honest amount on my lands."

"Do not dwell too long on that dream," Rolf said dryly. " 'Tis unlikely to happen."

While Sir Roger moved aside to the scribe to give the accounting of his debts, another petitioner was called. Annice looked over her shoulder at Rolf, who sat at a table with a grave expression. Was this the man regarded by many in England as a ravening beast? What she had just witnessed gave the lie to those reports. But was it a common thing, to delay the debts owed him? If so, he would have to dig deep into his own coffers in order to pay the king the fines he levied freely upon his barons and nobles. Nay, it could not be. Few men would subject themselves to such a burden just to ease the plight of their vassals.

Yet before the morning's business was concluded, Annice was witness to several such acts. These mostly involved villeins come to complain about grievances done to them by the king's men, and Rolf did what he could to alleviate their hardships. One of the cases brought before him was a dispute over a pig.

Claiming that 'twas his pig and his neighbor stole it one night, Walter of Pinchbeck, a freeman, insisted that the animal be returned to him at once. Rolf deliberated, hearing both sides, and learned that the sow was pregnant. Unable to determine which man truly owned the pig, he ended by decreeing that the sow be left at Dragonwyck until delivered of her progeny, and those be equally divided between the squabbling petitioners. Then ownership of the pig would be determined by drawing lots.

Annice smothered her laughter as both men quit the hall, still squabbling over ownership of the sow and only slightly mollified by their lord's decision. When she glanced back at Rolf, she saw his gaze on her, and her heart lurched. He was smiling ruefully and shaking his head.

"For a moment I was tempted to react as King Solomon of old, and order that the pig be cut in half and divided between them. But that would most like deprive their families of needed meat for the winter."

"There are times," Annice murmured, "when you must wish for the wisdom of Solomon."

Rolf looked away from her, his smile fading. "Yea. More than you know, lady fair. More than you know."

Annice gazed at him, her eyes lingering on him long after the next petitioner approached. Sunlight from a high window lit his hair with pale streaks that gleamed with all the brilliance of a gold halo. Almost like a halo, she mused with a twinge of self-derision. Nay, no saint this, but a man. Yet a man who showed infinite patience at times, when she would have been tempted to irritation.

Rolf of Dragonwyck was a contradiction, an enigma that she had yet to understand. What manner of man was this that she was to wed in such a short time? Dragon—or saint?

CHAPTER 8

Guests had been arriving for days to attend the betrothal feast. Dragonwyck keep was filled to bursting with retinues of servants and a surplus of baggage. It seemed that every noble who wasn't in France with the king had decided to witness the Dragon's marriage to a traitor's widow.

Rolf was torn between cynical amusement at the king's obvious machinations, and annoyance that his loyalty was suspect. Not that he had expected any different from John. 'Twas more than expected that he would wrest assurance from one of his most powerful barons. Though Rolf had supplied men and money for the king's war, his private battle with Seabrook had been reason enough to return to England. He'd known his failure to stay in France would anger John. Now he knew how much the king was annoyed with him. *Jésu*, but he hoped it did not affect his battle to regain Justin. . . .

"Milord."

Rolf looked up to see Vachel in the open door of his bedchamber. A harried expression carved the young man's face. It was an expression Rolf was growing increasingly accustomed to seeing on his servants.

Buckling his belt, he said, "I take it that you're having difficulty finding room for all the guests and their attendants."

Vachel nodded. "I did not wish to burden you, seigneur, but Lord Henry de Sauvain is here, and I have no chamber for him or room for his attendants."

"Lord Henry can sleep on a cot in someone else's chamber, and the servants can stay in the hall or the stables."

Looking distressed, Vachel protested, "But all the chambers are filled, and Lord Henry says he will not stay in the same room as Lord Georges de Beaufont, and——"

"Then put Sauvain in my room, and I'll sleep with Beaufont," Rolf snapped. He raked a hand through his hair and took a deep breath. "I care not, Vachel. Shift them about any way you please. If any man should have complaints, he may bring them to me to settle. For all I care, they can all sleep in the stables. Or the sties. I'm weary of this chaos and bickering barons."

"Aye, milord." Vachel hesitated. "I admit that the barons seem to be a testy lot. And there are few wives in attendance."

Rolf shrugged. "Are you surprised? With such short notice I'm amazed John was able to get this many barons to do his bidding. He thinks to deplete my purse with all these mouths to feed, but I am not unprepared. I feel no compunction to be overgenerous with my food or my hospitality when I know the reason behind their presence in my hall."

"The reason, milord?"

Rolf stamped his foot down into his boot and looked up. "Aye. The only reason for all these barons' presence is to ensure that I am properly wed as John wishes. Did you think his suggestion less than a command, Vachel? 'Twas not. A honey-coated command, certes, but no less of one. He will be most satisfied to hear that the wedding is just as he wished. 'Tis a grand way to begin the new year, do you not think?"

Looking confused, Vachel muttered, "Does he think you a traitor, milord?"

"Aye. That's just what he thinks." Rolf smiled grimly at Vachel's shocked expression. "John thinks every man a traitor if given the opportunity. 'Tis probably wise of him in most instances. Hand me my poniard, if you please."

Vachel lifted the jeweled dagger from a table and brought it to Rolf, still frowning. "But, milord, surely the king should know by now that you are one of his most loyal barons. Haven't you proved it time and again?"

"What is that to John? Have not Eustace de Vesci and Robert FitzWalter proved their loyalty on occasion? And then gone posthaste to the other side when it grew more profitable . . . aye, Vachel. 'Tis wise of the king to be chary of those who profess loyalty. My refusal to stay with him in France for this latest war against King Philip did not set well with John. He will continue to test me for some time, I fear."

Vachel sighed. " 'Tis most disagreeable and vexing."

Smiling, Rolf nodded. "Aye, for certain. But at least we know where we stand in John's estimation at the moment. There are those unfortunate barons who must bide and wonder."

Vachel's answering smile was a bit weak. " 'Tis true, lord, but I cannot be as blithe as you about the king. The winds of fate oft blow evil, and I truly pray that you pass the king's test."

"I will." Rolf frowned down at the jeweled poniard in his hand. "My marriage to the lady Annice will seal his approval quick enough."

This time Vachel's smile was broad. "She is lovely, indeed. And with a sweet nature."

"Sweet?" Rolf gazed at him with mocking disbelief. "I've not seen this sweet nature I've heard spoken of, in truth. The nature I've most often witnessed is as prickly as nettles."

"Aye, lord, you do seem to bring out the fight in her," Vachel observed with a faint sigh. " 'Tis not an easy thing, being a hostage. 'Twill be good to have this wedding over, so that the two of you can be easy with each other."

"I doubt a few words spoken by a priest will do that," Rolf muttered as he sheathed the poniard in a scabbard. " 'Twill take a full miracle to accomplish amity between us, I fear."

"P'raps not. I've seen you charm more formidable court ladies in scant time. If you would but attempt the same cajolery with the lady Annice, I believe she would soon cease all thoughts of enmity toward you, milord."

"You dream, Vachel. There is much more to the lady's anger than minor irritation." He put up a hand to forestall any well-meaning advice from the beardless young man. "But once we are wed, she will curb her sharp tongue whether she wills it or no. I do not intend to endure insults."

Lapsing into silence, Vachel nodded and turned to leave. At the door he paused and looked back. A faint frown puckered his brow as he said, "The lady is not sharp-tongued with others, milord. P'raps she fears you too well to be otherwise."

"And so she should."

There didn't seem to be anything Vachel wished to say to that, and he closed the door gently behind him. Rolf stared at the dragon carved into the heavy oak for a long moment. Did all in his keep feel the need to come to the lady's defense? Even Guy had done so, despite long years of loyalty to his lord. That meek little Belle flashed him a glance of defiance upon occasion was an astounding fact, considering that almost everyone made her squeak with alarm. Except Lady Annice.

Irritated, Rolf raked a hand through his hair. She had been at Dragonwyck less than a month, yet had managed to earn the respect of his own servants and companions. He felt a grudging admiration that she had done it so easily. She would make a fine lady for his keep. Yea, Lady Annice was well suited to be some lord's wife. If he had chosen a wife himself, he might well have considered her as a bride.

The thought faintly shocked him. It had been so long since he had thought of a woman in that way, he'd not dwelled upon the virtues he would seek should he wish for a wife. And he'd not realized that he'd noticed her virtues.

A faint grin tugged at his mouth. Nay, that was not true. He had dwelled at length upon her physical virtues despite earnest attempts to think of other things. Always her winsome face and pleasing curves came to mind, even inhabiting his dreams at night so that he woke thinking of her. . . .

Peste! What was he doing standing in the midst of his chamber thinking of her when he should be in the hall entertaining his illustrious guests? Madness, indeed, that had infected him. Once they were wed, he would soon be cured of it. On that score he was confident. The passion he'd felt for Margerie had faded quickly enough after they'd been wed. The marriage bed had soon lost its allure for him when faced with her whims and malaise. It would be the same with Annice.

Smoke rose from the central fire and wended upward to the smoke hole in the roof, curling in drifts. Revelers crowded trestle tables and meandered over rushes that had been fresh that morning but now held the remains of food and other refuse that did not bear thinking about. Serving wenches bearing heavy platters deftly dodged groping hands.

Annice paused at the foot of the steps, as yet unnoticed by any save Tostig, a constant guard at her heels. Blinking, she surveyed the crowded hall with a feeling of trepidation. Some of the knights and barons she recognized, but others were complete strangers to her. They were to witness her vows to Rolf of Dragonwyck and report to the king, she knew. It would be done and her fate sealed, will she nill she.

But—and this was the oddest to her—she found herself thinking of their marriage with a thrum of anticipation. Rolf was a man such as she had never known before, and though she might not agree with him on many things, she felt a growing respect for his sense of justice, as well as for his loyalty and courage. Few men in these troublesome days dared say nay to the king, yet Guy FitzHugh had told her how Rolf had refused to stay with John in France. Once he'd received the document from the Church giving permission to retrieve Justin, he had left his troops with an able lieutenant of John's service. John had viewed this defection of one of his most able barons with disfavor. Hence, she supposed, his determination to bind Rolf closer to him with this marriage to his ward.

It would certainly do that. She was as much a pawn as ever. Only the masters had changed, and that was the basis of her resentment. If not for that—aye, if not for that, she would have viewed this marriage more favorably. Long had she yearned for a strong man in her life, a man she could respect and love. Luc had never been that man. Her father had been such a man, and she had despaired of ever finding another of his ilk.

Until Rolf.

A flutter of movement at her right distracted Annice, and she felt a moment's gratitude when she saw the smiling countenance of Sir Guy FitzHugh at her side. The knight was clad in courtly garb that made him look quite handsome. His pleasure in seeing her was obvious. They had enjoyed many an hour conversing in the hall lately, and she appreciated his company. He was ever willing to allow her to talk of impartial subjects and even encouraged her to reminisce about her childhood and her parents. Few men would relish that, yet Guy did.

"My lady," Guy said, admiration lighting his hazel eyes, "you are more radiant than ever. I had not thought it possible."

Annice laughed. "Do you wish a boon, Sir Knight? Fie on you for being such a base flatterer, when I thought you a man of truth."

"And 'tis the truth I speak." He caught up her hand and bent over it with a graceful flourish, pressing his lips to her skin in a brief gesture. When he straightened, he still held her hand in a light clasp. "You are the most beautiful woman in all of England—nay, in all of Christendom, I vow. My liege lord is the most fortunate of men."

Gently withdrawing her hand, Annice murmured, "He would argue that point with you most vigorously, I think."

"Nay, not even a stubborn man such as le Draca could argue with that." Guy's smile was warming, and as if he sensed her discomfort at his teasing flattery, he took her hand and tucked it over his forearm, saying, " 'Tis my fortune to be your escort to the high table, my lady. I beg your pardon for not greeting you when you first entered the hall, but I was unavoidably detained by a baron whose eye outpaces his stomach when it comes to wine."

"There seem to be quite a few of those in attendance," she said, as she had already observed more than one or two men stumbling in the awkward steps of the inebriated.

"Yea." Guy's smile was a bit rueful. "I earnestly pray that there will be no hot tempers flashing steel this eve, for 'twill put a damper upon the morrow's festivities should tempers fray and blood be shed."

"At the very least." Annice's gaze had already swept the hall and not discovered Rolf, but she hesitated to ask his whereabouts. For the past sennight she had made her usual appearance in the hall after evensong. Nervous as the wedding day drew closer, she had delayed as long as possible this night, and now the visiting barons had imbibed much too freely. There had been few of them in the chapel for evensong, she'd noted, and the Lord of Dragonwyck had been absent as well. Nor was the earl now in his hall.

Forcing her attention back to Sir Guy, she saw him watching her keenly and flushed. There was a knowing light in his eyes, as if he had guessed the reason behind her distraction. Embarrassment warmed her cheeks.

"Please come with me, my lady," Guy said, guiding her through the crowded hall toward the high table. "The seigneur has been detained by a small problem and wished for me to attend you until his arrival."

Rolf's chair was empty, and to her surprise there was a matching high-backed chair placed beside it. Plush bolsters cushioned the carved wooden seat, and the back and side-arms were hung with not only the sable and or of Dragonwyck, but the gules and argent of her father's colors. Black and gold, red and silver—her throat tightened. He had honored the house of Beauchamp, and her, by displaying those colors.

Saying nothing, she allowed Sir Guy to seat her, though her hands trembled slightly with emotion. Ever was the Lord of Dragonwyck taking her by surprise, even with so grand a gesture when none would remark it but her. Few would recall her father's colors, or think it exceptional that they were displayed thusly.

Moreover, any who thought upon it would have expected her to wear Luc d'Arcy's standards. With a still faintly trembling hand, she lifted up one corner of the argent silk upon her chair and saw tiny emblems embroidered along the hem. The Beauchamp device. She brushed a fingertip lovingly over the threads. Yea, Rolf of Dragonwyck had somehow discovered what lay dearest to her heart.

It softened her toward him, so that when she saw him wending his way through jongleurs and tumblers and drunken knights, she was glad instead of apprehensive. There was an odd tightening in her chest as she watched his approach. Lord Rolf stood a full head taller than any other man in the hall, but he would have been imposing in any company. His broad shoulders filled out the sable velvet of his surcoat with strong assurance, and the gilt dragon on his chest glittered as brightly as his gold hair. Yea, he was comely, indeed, and had shown her a rare kindness in remembering her father's house.

"Good eventide, milady," he said courteously when he drew near, and she murmured a reply. She put her hands in her lap so that he would not see the way her fingers trembled. She felt his presence as keenly as if he had reached out to touch her, though he did not so much as greet her with a kiss upon her hand. For a moment he stood behind her chair, conversing softly with Tostig.

When he took his seat beside her, she did not speak but waited for him to indicate his readiness for conversation. Around them the noisy merriment of the hall was a steady, familiar hum. 'Twas all so familiar to her, the broken chords of music from lute and harp and flute, the laughter of knights and maids, and the occasional outburst from a hound, yet she felt as if she existed in a strange dream. The solid presence of the man beside her was real, though she could scarce credit it. Nothing in the past month seemed truly real, save for her fear and apprehension.

And the dreams. . . .

A faint flush warmed her cheeks, and her hands tightened around the carved wooden curve of her chair arm, fingers bunching the silk that bore her father's device. Mary and Joseph! that she should even think on such a thing when Rolf sat so near her and all were crowded about them. Yet if she was honest with herself, she would freely admit that the night dreams haunted even her days.

Why else would she look at him and recall the rough scrape of his beard against her breast, the heated caress of his palm upon her thigh, and the searing excitement of his kisses? Their last encounter had left her with a restless yearning that extended even into her soul. Yea, he haunted her well, this dream-dragon of the night. And the solid substance of the man was no less haunting, no less disturbing.

Turning, Rolf settled his gaze lightly on her. Beneath the dark, gold-tipped bristle of his lashes, the green eyes studied her for a moment. "Do the accoutrements please you, milady?" he asked in a low tone, startling her.

"Yea, lord," she replied softly, "they please me full well. I am most flattered."

He smiled slightly and turned away again, his attention bent toward the knight on his left, a baron from Nottinghamshire. Sir Guy sat on Annice's right side, and she felt him stir.

Offering a honeyed sweetmeat as if it were dipped in gold, Guy murmured softly, "Take only a bit, milady. 'Tis sweet upon the tongue, like honeyed words."

She looked up at Sir Guy's face but saw no hint of double meaning in the guileless hazel eyes. There was only a faintly questioning lift to his brows. Slowly, she took the proffered sweet.

"My thanks, Sir Knight. Honeyed treats are usually sweet, though ofttimes cloying, I think."

Guy smiled. "Yea, and 'tis a wise woman who recognizes it. It has been said that you are very wise, fair lady. P'raps even wise enough to enchant fierce dragons. . . ."

Her brow arched. This sort of conversation was common enough in royal courts and keeps, but she had not expected it in le Draca's remote castle. Here there had been little of the thrust and parry that passed for normal speech; most talk was plain enough. For Sir Guy to engage in the roundabout prattle slightly surprised her.

Forcing a smile, she said easily, " 'Tis said that dragons pursue only maidens, and that attribute is long in my past. Fie, that I should consider enchantment when I have been treated most gently."

Guy's hazel eyes were half-hidden by the lowering of his dark lashes, and a faint, worldly smile touched the corners of his mouth. "Thou dost naught need to bandy words with such as me, milady. I well ken thy predicament," he said in English.

His words caught her by surprise. Never had she expected frank speech in a familiar tongue spoken by so few nobles. Most did not bother to learn the native speech of the land but preferred the more courtly French most oft spoken.

Lowering her eyes, she said softly, "I do not understand your meaning, Sir Guy."

"Nay, but I think thou understands full well. Hast thou ever thought that it maun be lonely being a dragon?" Sir Guy drew back a bit, studying her before he turned away to the man on his right.

Rather bemused by this byplay, Annice frowned down at the silver cup holding her wine. Sir Guy had not been in the hall enough for her to know him well; she had only instincts to guide her. Duplicity was considered a necessary virtue in royal courts, as well as the ability to parry sly words and innuendos. Somehow she did not think Guy FitzHugh was making idle conversation, but attempting to ease her fears. Or warn her.

She shifted slightly, glancing toward Rolf. He was bent toward his neighbor, talking softly about falconry and the merits of hunting around his keep. There was to be a hunt on the morrow in celebration of the betrothal and to add to the feast. Any game brought in would be added to that already brought in by the huntsmen, and be cooked to appear at the table. Already delicious and varied scents emanated from the kitchens, wafting on vagrant breezes. It seemed that though the marriage was not of his choice, the Dragon intended that it be a merry occasion.

This should have pleased Annice. So why did she have this unsettled feeling, as if she were about to embark on a perilous journey?

Reaching for her wine, Annice curled her fingers tightly around the slender stem to still the sudden shaking of her hand. Jewels studded the cup, blinking red and green and gold in the light of fire and candle and torch. Wrought of silver, the cup bore carved dragons with tiny emeralds for eyes, slavering tongues of ruby, and gold-tinged scales. Everywhere she looked, everything she touched, all around her bore the mark of the dragon.

Including her dreams.

"*Hast thou ever thought that it maun be lonely being a dragon?*" Guy's words rang in her ears, and she slanted another glance toward Rolf. Lonely? The dread Lord of Dragonwyck? It did not seem possible.

She drew in a deep breath and took a swallow of wine. It was rich, potent, heavy with spices on her tongue. A warm path from mouth to stomach gave mute testimony to the strength of the wine. P'raps that was what gave her the courage to lean forward and capture the attention of the man she would wed in two days' time.

"Milord." She lifted her goblet when he turned. "My thanks for your generosity."

An amused smile touched the hard lines of his mouth, making him seem less fierce and more cavalier. "Do you thank me for the wine, milady?"

She shook her head. "Nay, 'tis your generosity of spirit that earns my gratitude. The Beauchamp colors are most dear to me, and I would not have thought any man had guessed."

For a moment Rolf studied her face, dark lashes shadowing his eyes. "I well remember finding precious the colors of my father's house, especially after a long absence. I thought you might feel the same," he said slowly.

Their eyes met, and Annice caught her breath at the intensity of his gaze. Gold specked the green of his eyes, tiny striations that radiated from the dark centers. She could not say what she saw there—wariness or curiosity—for it quickly vanished, hidden from her by the swift lowering of thick lashes. Gone was the brief glimpse of emotion, and in its place the casual indifference she was more used to seeing.

Rolf stretched out a lazy hand to lightly clasp her wrist. He drew her arm to him to sip from her cup, shadowed eyes watching her.

"Much sweeter from your own lips, I would think," he murmured when he released her wrist and cup.

"You are ever the gallant courtier," Annice responded in a light tone to match his.

"Nay, never think it." Rolf's smile did not reach his eyes. "I say only what I mean, lady fair."

"Always, milord?" She arched a brow, determined not to let him best her at this game of verbal chess. "I think you jest."

A faint grin squared his mouth, teeth white against his dark beard. "I would be amiss if I were to say an untruth, would I not? Why do you think differently?"

Having neatly put her again into a defensive position, Rolf gazed at her with an innocent expression. Annice glanced down at the cup she still held, then looked up at him through her lashes, forcing her lips into a demure smile.

"Fie, milord, 'tis only by your words that I may judge. If you say that you would be amiss to tell me an untruth, then I must agree."

Genuine amusement laced his low laughter. "Aptly done, milady. You are adept at jousting with words, I see."

"I may only credit my short stay in my cousin's company for anything I have learned. I am but a poor player compared to a man of your vast reputation, my lord." Annice caught and held Rolf's gaze. Her heart lurched when he put his hand atop hers. She had meant to tease him a bit, to match his insouciance, but the expression in his eyes had grown intent. Light-tricked, the green of his eyes had taken on a subtle golden glow like that of a flame. She looked down again, focusing her gaze on the jeweled goblet in the curve of her hand and his. She could not bear that gaze resting upon her too closely.

"Most times," Rolf said, "I do not play games."

The sudden seriousness of his tone, coupled with the intensity of his gaze, threw her into confusion. She looked up at him wordlessly. Gone was the ready reply on the tip of her tongue.

On her other side Guy FitzHugh leaned close. "My lord," he said drawing Rolf's attention to him, "Lord Henry de Sauvain tells me that you intend to use your lanner falcon on the morrow's hunt. Do we expect to flush wood ducks or herons?"

Annice pressed her spine against the back of her chair while Sir Guy and Rolf spoke of the merits of hunting birds and prey. The conversation washed around her like tidal currents, ebbing and flowing in a ceaseless roar. She was grateful for Sir Guy's intervention. Most likely, he had done it a'purpose to give her time to recover. Was she that obvious? Or had he been eavesdropping?

Probably both, she answered her own questions. But this one time she would forgive, for he had rescued her from floundering in helpless reaction to le Draca's mercurial changes of mood. 'Twas that swiftness in moods that still caught her off guard, and she determined to be better prepared the next time.

Drawing in a deep breath that smelled of wood smoke and roast meat, Annice politely turned her head toward the men discussing the morrow's hunt. The talk had changed from the virtues of a lanner falcon over a lanneret, to the choice of game to be pursued.

"Two of the pages brought in fewmets," Sir Guy was saying, "so I understood we were to hunt boar tomorrow." He idly turned his empty goblet of wine upon its footed stem, twisting it between his fingers as he divided his attention between Lord Rolf and the lady. He had heard the talk between them and known the instant Lady Annice had foundered. Well aware of his liege's moods, he had prepared to rescue her.

It didn't help that le Draca must be aware of his intent. There was a faintly amused tilt to Rolf's mouth that let Guy know he comprehended his intercession. He must be wondering why. But as Guy had no inclination to reveal his reasons for helping Lady Annice, he launched into a lengthy argument for hunting boars instead of birds.

"Some of the barons are grown restless, and a vigorous

hunt for a dangerous prey would take the edge from their quarrelsome natures," Guy pointed out. "Hawking is too tame a sport for men after a long winter. 'Tis the new year, and boars are growing fat in the forests."

"Boars are still lean after the winter months, Sir Guy. And the dogs are too fresh and eager. 'Twould be a disaster."

A squire paused to replenish the empty goblets of wine, and Guy waited until Rolf had sipped from his cup before he said with a sigh, " 'Tis only the dogs that are fresh and eager, I see. Some of us have grown lazy of late."

Rolf's frowning gaze rested on him for a moment. He toyed with the stem of his goblet, blunt fingertips grazing the jewels with quick, restless motions.

"Do I detect a challenge in that observation, Sir Guy? Or do you think to lesson me on the choice of game for our hunt?"

For an instant Guy thought he had gone too far. Then he met Rolf's uplifted gaze and saw the gleam of interest in his eyes. He relaxed slightly, smiling.

"A challenge, of course," he said promptly. "I have grown lazy with inaction these past winter months. The new year finds me chafing for a new sport."

"I would think last month's failed quest would be enough sport for any man," Rolf muttered, then gave a shrug. "But you do have a point. The visiting barons are much too rowdy and should be given an opportunity to exhaust themselves."

Satisfied, Guy took another sip of wine. 'Twas his thought exactly. The barons should all exhaust themselves into a stupor, including his liege lord. Weariness was the best antidote he knew for lust.

"Yea, milord," he merely said blandly, "I agree."

He would have added more, especially as Rolf was gazing at him with a narrowed stare that portended a sharp question, but at that moment a noisy clamor at the doors of the hall gained his attention as well as the Dragon's. Men were struggling, and there was a flash of silver and red amidst the sable and gold colors of Dragonwyck. A muffled oath rose above the chaos of the hall, delivered in rough English, and Guy rose to his feet.

Rolf was already standing, his hand upon the hilt of the

dagger in his belt. Alarmed, Guy put out a restraining arm at almost the same instant that he heard Lady Annice's soft cry.

Between them, she still managed to gain her feet, her protest sharp and loud. "Do them no harm! 'Tis my vassals who have come to pay me honor, and I will not have them stayed."

Turning toward le Draca, Annice demanded, "Would you forbid my own vassals entry, milord? Fie, I think it would commend you well to greet them with open arms, for as you will be my husband, they must now swear to you as overlord."

Anger sparked her blue eyes, making them glow with the hard sheen of deep-hued sapphires. Guy subdued his admiration, the savage expression on Rolf's face taking immediate precedence.

"My lord," he intervened smoothly, " 'twas I who sent word of your impending marriage to the lady's vassals. With time so short, I knew you would want as many of them present as witnesses as could arrive in time. Pray, forgive me for failing to mention it earlier, but with my travels between Seabrook and here, I fear that I did not think to tell you of my presumption."

"Presumptive, indeed," Rolf said so coldly that Guy felt a moment's misgiving. His heart thumped hard. Had he earned his lord's enmity for his daring? He prayed not, for he fervently wished to do him no ill.

Sliding a glance toward the end of the hall where Dragonwyck men-at-arms still barred entry for the northern barons, Guy waited for what seemed an eternity until le Draca gave a sharp jerk of his head. "Bid them enter and well come," he said shortly. "They have traveled long and hard to reach Dragonwyck and, as my lady's vassals, should be greeted with due respect."

His voice had lifted to be heard down the length of the crowded hall, now quiet at this new and interesting event. The men-at-arms lowered their weapons and stepped back, and the ruffled vassals gave them a brief, hard look before coming forward.

Guy felt Annice's sigh of relief more than heard it in the

rising murmur and looked down at her. A faint smile curved her mouth upward, and he could detect a slight trembling in her rigid stance.

Only when the four vassals had reached the dais and gone to one knee, heads bowed in obeisance as they greeted their lady and overlord, did she speak.

"Rise, messires. I am well pleased to see thee before me, as it has been overlong," she said in English.

Each man came forward to take her outstretched hand, touching his forehead to the backs of her fingers and murmuring allegiance. Only one man dared look up at the towering frame of le Draca, a swift glance that bore neither enmity nor acceptance. Guy suffered an instant's doubt. Had he erred in sending for these men? He had thought to please the lady, and that he had plainly done. Mary, but he could only hope that these men would not fail to see the advantages in swearing fealty to le Draca. Even though most northern barons hated the king, and it was well-known that the Dragon gave John unswerving loyalty if not love, Guy had hoped that his act would bind them together. He still hoped to see his plan come to fruition, but 'twas plain it would take more than a few smooth words.

Fortunately, Rolf obviously realized the advantages to having these northern barons' allegiance. With a solemn expression he moved forward to stand beside Annice, who had come from behind the high table to greet her barons. At seeing the tall earl standing beside his sworn overlord, the foremost baron hesitated, then dropped to one knee again.

"My lord of Dragonwyck," he acknowledged in clumsy French.

"Rise, sir," Rolf said in English, "and name thyself as I maun greet thee properly."

A look of startlement flickered for an instant upon the baron's face before he hid it well and rose to his feet. "I am Cleit of Wulfcot, in Durham. Long have I served the house of Beauchamp, and fain have served Lord Hugh's daughter."

"Sir Cleit, thy service is well-known to me, and spoken of most proudly by those who know of thee. I commend thee for thy loyalty."

Guy noted well the pleased expression on the baron's

face and relaxed. Yea, Rolf of Dragonwyck would swiftly comprehend the need to bind these men to him in faithful service and had the facile wit to accomplish it.

A glance at the lady Annice revealed that she was well pleased by her betrothed's greeting to her vassals, and Guy drew in a deep breath of relief. There were times that even the best-planned acts could go awry by a chance word or deed, and he spared a moment's prayer of gratitude that his daring had caused no grief. It could easily have gone the other way, which would have done his eventual plans no good at all. Nay, 'twould have truly harmed all if the barons had taken offense, or if the Dragon had not the wit to see their use.

They came in turn, Rannulf of Melton Mowbray in Leicestershire, and Richard de Whitby in North Riding, followed by Simon de Roget, the eldest and wariest of the northern barons sworn to fealty by the house of Beauchamp. Sir Simon was a pleasant surprise, for Guy had not summoned him. Yet here he was, accompanying Sir Cleit. All had sworn to John, though 'twas said now that William de Mowbray, who was Sir Rannulf's overlord, was in rebellion. Sir Rannulf had apparently come to align himself with a barony loyal to John, which bore great reflection.

Yea, Guy mused, 'twas a varied and noble company, and well worth the risks he had taken to insure Annice's safety, as well as Lord Rolf's future. If her vassals swore fealty to their new liege, all might be well, after all.

CHAPTER 9

'Tis no sport for ladies," Rolf said gruffly, gazing down at Annice's upturned face. A patch of pale sunlight streamed through a square niche in the bailey wall to fall across her cheek. "Boars are vicious, evil beasts with unpredictable natures."

A faint smile curved the full line of Annice's lips. "Yea, so I understand. I did not ask to accompany you, milord, only when you would return. 'Tis customary to have food prepared for the returning hunters." She indicated men, horses, and dogs in the bailey with a wave of her hand and slight turn of her head.

"A squire will announce our return in time to set the servants to work," Rolf replied. He tugged impatiently at his gauntlets, wondering about her show of wifely concern. Light gilded the high curve of her cheek on one side, while shadows haunted the other. There were moments he thought her a changeling or sorceress, for she seemed to transform with the passage of time. From haughty lady to frightened maid, to tempting seductress—aye, she had encompassed all those visages and now presented him with yet another.

"The cooks even now prepare for the wedding feast," she said, "as they have these four days past. Shall I have them await your success?"

Horses and riders milled amongst excitedly yapping hounds, while morning mist curled around them in gauzy shrouds. Rolf shrugged. "My people know what to do," he said shortly, and saw the lift of her brows at his arrogant reply. There were moments he forgot that she was accustomed to commanding her own household, as now. He schooled his rising impatience into a semblance of courtesy and said through his teeth, "If you wish to oversee them, Vachel will be of aid. God's grace, but he is harried enough with details and will welcome your assistance."

Hunting stags or fowl would have been much better to his liking this day. Boar hunting was too arduous and lengthy, though he had to agree with Guy that it would blunt the edgy tempers of the visiting barons. As well as his own. He had not missed that knight's attempt to abate his lord's surly temper of late and knew it was on the lady's behalf that he did so. As was Guy's summoning of her vassals.

What he could not guess was why.

"Go with God, milord," Annice murmured, dropping into a slight courtesy before turning away.

Rolf resisted the urge to reach out and halt her. He dared not touch her, for fear he would not release her if he put a hand upon her. She haunted his every hour, waking and sleeping, until his frustration was almost overpowering.

God's teeth, but if the morrow did not come—and with it the wedding eve and nuptial bed—he might lose his tenuous grip on any control he could claim. It must show in his every move, every glance at Annice. He could feel it, as if he wore a heavy mantle of desire slung round his shoulders for all to see.

It came to him then with a suddenness, Guy's possible motives for the lengthy hunt. 'Twas more than just an outlet for an excess of temper—he meant to keep his lord distanced from Annice. But was the knight's determination to remove Rolf from the lady's side due to concern for her virtue, or to allow her easy access to her newly arrived vassals? Only one of them joined the hunt this morn; the others pleaded weariness from their journey.

Lifting his head from his perusal of the gauntlets clutched tight in one fist, his gaze sought and found Sir Guy a short distance away. The knight stood beneath the heavy shadow of a wall where sunlight did not yet touch. He was conversing quietly with a huntsman dressed in the livery of Dragonwyck.

For a moment Rolf considered what he knew of Guy. He had come to Dragonwyck a landless squire—bastard son of a nobleman, it was said—and had been raised in a Norman monastery before being sent to a wealthy English household as page. His parentage was not known for obscure reasons, and Guy had never divulged it, if even he knew. None of that had mattered to Rolf, for he had divined integrity and worth in the young man during a fierce battle with the Welsh several years before. When the knight Guy served had been killed, Rolf had taken the young page to his own household, where the boy had soon earned his spurs and knighthood.

Being of like natures, both men had dealt well with each other, and Rolf had never had cause to regret taking Guy into his keep. Yet in the past five years he still knew very little about the man. Talk centered on many things, but rarely on the young knight's past.

Now Rolf began to wonder if he had been hasty in placing his trust. Boar hunts were dangerous, and he had not missed the light in Sir Guy's eyes whenever Annice entered the hall. Should he be wary? 'Twould not be the first time a man had been killed in a hunt and murder suspected.

As if sensing that Rolf was thinking about him, Guy chose that moment to look up from his conversation with the huntsman, and there was a vaguely startled expression on his face. After a swift glance at the huntsman and a sharply spoken comment, Guy stepped from the shadows. Sunlight broke over the bailey in a glittering wash, shining on his dark hair as Guy strode to Rolf and stopped.

"Milord, Gowain informs me that fresh fewmets and spoor have been found in the forest beyond the village to mark the recent passage of several boars. Shall I send some of the men in that direction?"

"Certes," Rolf replied casually. "Let the beaters find the game as they will, while the barons rumble and growl with aching heads. I thought the purpose of the hunt was to soothe restless tempers."

"And so it is, milord." Guy's smile was fleeting. "But the pursuit of fleeing game will soon rouse them to sweet natures, mark me on't."

Rolf's gaze met the hazel eyes staring back at him. "I shall, Sir Guy. By day's end I expect all tempers to be well mended."

Catching up the reins to his mount, Rolf stepped into the saddle with a mutter of caution to the squire who handed him his lance. When he was settled, Bordet barking joyously about the snorting horse's hooves, he glanced up to see Annice watching him from the top step of the guard-house. A faint smile curved her mouth, and a light breeze tugged at the hem of her skirts. She lifted a hand in a farewell gesture that caught him by surprise.

Returning the gesture, he found himself wondering if 'twas only his surly nature that made him suspicious of all. Yet it had long been his good fortune to trust his instincts, and he did not dare grow lax now.

Rolf wheeled his mount around and rode over the bridge spanning the moat. The clatter of horses and men was close behind him, dogs straining and barking at their fetters. Guy was not far from him but kept a discreet distance, as if sensing the constraint. It did not sweeten Rolf's mood. Not even the hunt could do that.

Pale sunlight scattered once they reached the forest. Mist rose thickly over the Welland River, drifting through high water weeds into the dense growth of ancient trees and clumps of brush. It shifted in tattered strands that glided eerily in vague fingers creeping along the low earth. Every sound seemed magnified a hundredfold, as if an entire troop of hunters roamed the wood instead of only a score. The beaters spread out to flush the game, disembodied voices muffled as they were swallowed by the mist.

One of the barons made the sign of the cross to ward off

evil at the ghostly sound of voices without form whispering in the trees. Edgy men gazed around them with uncertain glances. Rolf exchanged a glance with Guy, then spurred forward to take charge.

" 'Tis best that we separate into small groups. Horns will sound the flushing of game quick enough," he said firmly, and began to designate the groups. He assigned leaders for each group of men, ignoring their startled glances.

Lord Henry de Sauvain began a protest, but the excited barking of dogs in the distance distracted them. Horns blared the call that their prey had been sighted. Putting spurs to horses, the hunters rode off eagerly, bunching together in the groups Rolf had assigned them.

Avoiding Guy's questioning gaze, Rolf followed the sound of dogs and horns. Thick brush barred his way at times, fallen logs lying across snaking trails webbed with hanging vines. Then his lance caught on a low-hanging branch that he had not seen for ducking a tangle of vines and was knocked from his hand. Swearing, Rolf reined in and dismounted to retrieve his lance.

He had it in hand examining it for breaks when he realized that he was alone. The others had followed the baying of the hounds, and the horns had grown faint. Mist still clung to the ground in places, though with the passage of time and the sun's slow rise, it had mostly dissipated. The deep woods of Kesteven stretched about him, dark and mysterious, eerily silent. Rolf looked about, thoughtfully balancing the lance in one hand.

Steam blew from his mount's flared nostrils and rose from the heated hide in clear waves. Pungent and familiar, the smell of horse was vaguely pleasant. There was another scent in the air, of waxy leaves and decomposing wood, of dank forest and misty breezes rife with the slight tang of salt. The North Sea lay several leagues distant, and he imagined he could almost hear the rushing sound of breaking waves upon the rocks.

The fading clamor of the hunt could be heard far away, muffled by the forest. Reluctant to follow too quickly, Rolf propped a booted foot upon a fallen log. Thick silence enveloped him, broken only by the warble of birds and jangling of his horse's bridle as it foraged among dead leaves and branches for succulent shoots of new grass. This silence was unusual. He was too used to hearing the noise of the hall and castle, of people surrounding him. This serenity was blessed, indeed, and he savored it for several long moments.

P'raps solitude was what he needed most. Certes, he had much to think about lately. Paramount in his mind was his marriage to Lady Annice. Of late she was ever on his mind. Natural, he supposed, as he was to wed her. Yet he knew there was more to it than that. When he thought of her, he did not consider her importance to him in political terms or as a means of retrieving his son, but as a woman. And a woman that he desired. Thick russet hair, blue eyes that could sparkle with amusement or grow fiery with anger, and a fair face with creamy skin—yea, his desire for her grew with every passing hour. 'Twas most difficult for him to conceal or control. As she well knew.

There were moments, as this morn before the hunt, when he was certain he saw the knowledge in her eyes. She knew that he wanted her. That he thought of her when he knew he should not. But when he finally took her, would she be thinking of him, or of her beloved husband? Would there be a ghost in their nuptial bed, the memory of another man between them? Aye, 'twas a bitter draft to swallow, this need for one particular woman. . . .

Rolf roused himself from thoughts of Annice. 'Twas foolish to linger too long alone during a hunt. Glancing down at the lance in his hand, he removed his gauntlet and ran his palm along the length of the wooden shaft. It appeared whole and unharmed from the mishap, and the gleaming iron blade was unbroken. A damaged lance could well mean a man's life if he was careless.

He took a step and heard the sharp snap of a twig beneath his booted foot. A rustle of dry leaves sounded behind him. Not far away a limb suddenly dropped from a tree to plummet earthward, landing in a shower of leaves and loud crackling. A shrill whinny slashed the air, and he turned to look at his horse. Its eyes rolled to show the whites. He lunged for the bridle, anticipating the animal's reaction, but it was too late.

Half rearing, the horse lashed out. Rolf jerked his arm, barely getting the lance out of the way, while still grabbing at the bridle. Panicked, the horse evaded capture.

"Curse you," Rolf muttered in a panting growl. He wished he had ridden Wulfsige. The well-trained warhorse was too smart to be spooked by forest noises and obeyed instantly. Not this cursed nag, who looked as if it thought the fiends of hell were coming. He would have been glad to deliver the animal to them if they had been; now he found himself caught between tossing aside his lance or losing his mount, neither a very appealing prospect. He could well imagine the hoots and howls of the others should he be unhorsed.

Skillfully dodging Rolf's attempts to capture it, the horse backed into a snarl of briars. Thorny branches dug into its hide, causing more panic. Rearing, the hooves lashed out and kept Rolf from grabbing the trailing ends of the bridle. If he did not manage to grab the leather straps, the cursed animal would end up hopelessly entangled in the brush.

Rolf reluctantly jabbed the end of his lance into the ground in a swift move, freeing both hands. Fortunately, he wore only a leather aketon over his breeches and tunic, so he had little restriction. Thus unimpeded, he was able to seize the dangling ends of the bridle before the horse could do itself more harm.

He stood a moment to calm the animal, one hand lightly stroking the sweat-dampened neck as he held it close. But it would not be soothed, eyes rolling to show the whites and nostrils flaring. Rolf frowned as the horse trembled and plunged, and turned to look behind him.

The hair on the nape of his neck prickled, and he froze. In the midst of a thicket only a scant distance away, a long-tusked boar had paused. Its sides heaved in and out as if it had been running hard, and the small, beady eyes were riveted on the man and horse. It was huge—p'raps twenty-five stone or more. Despite the gray light of mist and deep forest, the long, curved tusks gleamed white and deadly.

Rolf's muscles tightened. His lance was just out of reach,

between him and the boar. Wild boars were unpredictable at best. Should he chance losing the horse and possibly enraging the boar to snatch his lance? It was doubtful that he would have time to throw it before the boar reached him. At best the horse would be gored. At worst the beast would catch one of those long, deadly tusks in human prey. More than one man of his acquaintance had met an untimely end in such a way, and a cold sweat beaded his forehead at the memory.

Holding tight to the horse's reins, Rolf knew that at any moment the boar would be goaded into action by the frantic neighing of the horse. It was all he could do to keep hold of the animal while gauging his chances at reaching his weapon in time to fend off the boar.

A shrill squeal rent the air, and the boar pawed the ground with cloven hooves, its red eyes glaring at Rolf. Slowly, Rolf released his grip on the reins. Feeling the restraint gone, the horse jerked back with a terrified whinny. A breath of wind passed close by Rolf's cheek as flailing hooves cut the air where he had just been.

Diving forward, Rolf grabbed at his lance even as he saw the huge boar spring toward him with astonishing speed.

Annice frowned at the closed doors of the hall, as if her impatience would open them. 'Twas long past the hour for the hunters' return. The cooks were probably frantic with the effort to keep food warm and tasty in the kitchens. All in the hall had been made ready.

"Milady."

Turning, she met the questioning gaze of Sir Rannulf, who had remained behind. He sat on a stool near the fire, his earnest face reflecting flame and concern. She schooled her features into a pleasant smile. "Yea, milord?"

"I can see thou art sore troubled. Shall I—"

Whatever he had been about to offer was drowned out by a sudden commotion at the doors. Half rising from her chair, Annice felt a thump of alarm tighten her throat as the doors swung open with a loud clatter. Men scurried forward, garments askew, excitement bubbling from their lips as they entered the hall in a wash of confusion and loud voices.

Sir Rannulf had already risen also and stood before Annice as if he would protect her from the rush of men into the hall. Though he wore no armor, his sword was securely belted at his waist, a certain sign that he did not feel wholly comfortable within Dragonwyck's stone walls.

"Delay, milady," he said when Annice took several steps forward, "until we discern what has happened."

But Annice had seen a litter brought into the hall and did not wait. If it was one of the huntsmen who had been wounded, he would have been taken to one of the chambers near the granary, mayhap, or even near the chapel. That a wounded man was being borne into the hall could mean only that it was someone of some consequence—such as Rolf.

She could not explain the cloud of conflicting emotions that enveloped her. Paramount was the driving necessity to reach the man lying on the litter. Frantic, she pushed past Sir Rannulf and fought her way through the press of men and women crowding close together.

A faint cry escaped her when she saw the muscular form draped on the litter, one hand dragging through the rushes as he was brought near the fire. But when she reached the litter's side, she saw that it was not Rolf of Dragonwyck who lay limply.

Sir Guy stretched upon the litter and gave a moan when it was slowly lowered to the rush-strewn floor. His eyes opened slightly to focus on her as she bent over him, and a faint smile wobbled on his lips.

"Mary, but 'twas a foul demon . . . that bade me suggest . . . hunting the boar," he got out in a raspy voice. His attempt at humor ended in a rending groan when one of the huntsmen accidentally trod upon Guy's trailing arm.

Annice clutched his hand and placed it atop his chest. Long rips rent the leather of his tunic, and there was a deep gash in one thigh that needed immediate attention. She had seen wounds like these before and forced her attention to the mending of them.

"Hush now," she said softly, "while I send for a bag of

herbs." She looked up at the men crowded near and saw the frightened face of Rolf's young squire peering down at the fallen knight. "Corbet," she ordered, "fetch proper herbs. And clean cloths and hot water. Some of you men lift up the litter and carry it—*gently*—into the next chamber. I will need a fire built. Are there more injuries?"

No one answered for a moment, and dread welled inside her. It seemed to her they looked away, as if unable to tell her. Was he dead, then? The lord of the castle? On the day before their wedding. . . . Holy Mary have mercy, should she grieve or be glad?

Kneeling there beside Sir Guy, looking up at the sea of faces leaning near, Annice knew in that instant that if aught had happened to Rolf, she could not bear it. 'Twould not be for fear of what might happen to her, but fear for him.

The blinding revelation was at once both terrifying and illuminating.

Fumbling with his good hand, Guy reached out to her and took her by the long, trailing cuff of her sleeve. His grip left streaks of dirt upon the gold-colored cloth.

"Nay . . . nay, milady. 'Twas my own . . . feckless act that . . . brought this mishap . . . upon me. None else . . . are much hurt."

His hand fell away, and she stared at him numbly for a moment. Rolf was not harmed. Relief flooded her. She managed a smile of comfort and put a tender hand upon Guy's dirt-streaked brow.

"God's mercy," she said. "Now, here—suffer these men to bear you hence, where I may tend your hurts in a more private chamber."

Rising, she looked up to meet Rolf's steady green gaze. Her heart lurched. He stood only a few feet opposite, arms folded across his chest. Dead leaves clung to the long sleeves of his linen shirt, and there was a jagged rip in his leather tunic. Dirt matted his hair and beard, and there was a strip of cloth wound round his left hand.

But he was alive and well, seeming whole and hale. He held her eyes for a long moment, while around her all seemed to recede into the distance, the babble of voices and flurry of action fading as Guy was lifted and borne away. All her attention was focused upon this one man, this one golden knight with blazing green eyes and the look of dragon-fire in his gaze.

"Milord," she said finally, slightly breathless, the words feeling as if torn from her soul. "Do you . . . have hurts that need tending?" She indicated the cloth on his hand, but he shook his head.

"Nay. No hurts that my own squire cannot tend for me."

"How does it come that Sir Guy was injured?"

Rolf's eyes narrowed slightly. "I am still wondering that. The boar circled back, 'tis said. It came upon me when I was unhorsed and my weapon disabled." He shrugged slightly. "I am still uncertain as to how Sir Guy came between us, for the last I was aware, my lance had broken when the boar first charged."

Pausing, he drew in a deep breath. Annice sensed tension beneath the casual words and frowned. Did he think Sir Guy somehow responsible for the outcome of the hunt? Was he angry that his knight had been injured? She recalled that Rolf had been reluctant to hunt boars; p'raps that was behind his tension.

"Milord," she began, but he was shaking his head and taking a step back.

"Nay. Do not think on it now. Sir Guy needs your attention. I am certain he would much prefer gentle hands on him rather than those of his squire or mine. I will see to the guests."

Pivoting on his booted heel, Rolf made his way through those around them without glancing back at her. Annice stood still for an instant and stared after him. Then she realized that Sir Simon was staring at her, as well as others. She hastily composed herself.

"Corbet, show me to Sir Guy," she said. "And, Vachel, do see that food is served now. I warrant that there are hungry men among the returned hunters."

As they scurried to do her bidding, Annice allowed herself to be taken to Guy in a nearby chamber. The binding and sewing of wounds was a familiar task, and one she could competently manage with little thought. She had been used to doing such things in her own household. Hunts always saw a few injuries, usually minor. A long gash such as the one Sir Guy suffered was common enough.

"There," she said when she had cleaned and tended his wound, " 'tis nasty enough to keep you laid low for a few days. I see that I shall not be dancing with you at my wedding." She gave him a cheerful smile as she held out a cup holding a draft of herbs, but he caught at her sleeve.

"Nay, I do not wish to drink it." Grimacing, he tried to sit up, but she put a hand upon his chest to hold him down. Guy flicked her a rueful smile. His eyelids were heavy. "I am weak as a day-old kitten. 'Tis my own fault. If I had not interfered . . . my actions almost cost my lord's life as well as my own. But I pray you, believe me when I saw 'twas only my fear for him that bade me act unwisely."

Annice stared down at the wounded knight. "You must drink this, then tell me what you mean, sir."

Despite his gray pallor and loss of blood, Guy's voice was rich with vigor when he said, "I heard them talking! 'Tis being said that I almost caused Lord Rolf to be killed by not coming a'twixt him and the wounded boar." He sipped reluctantly at the cup she insistently held to his lips, making a face at the bitter brew. "Milady, I beseech thee," he said in rough English, "not to believe such false tales. When my liege's lance snapped in twain from the force of impact with the boar, he was in danger of being gored. In the struggle I could not be certain my aim would be true. . . ."

"Yea, I believe thee, Sir Guy," Annice soothed him. She understood his distress then. Some of the others—no doubt dull-witted huntsmen seeking to gain their lord's favor—had blamed Rolf's close mishap upon his knight. 'Twould not have to be true to be harmful to him. She managed a smile. "Rest now, and all will be well. I am certain thy lord does not hold thee to blame."

Guy turned his face toward the wall. "Nay, but he doth hold me full responsible," he said in a bleak tone. " 'Tis in his eyes when he looks upon me."

She said nothing, recalling the fire of suspicion she'd seen in Rolf's eyes. He might well think Sir Guy had meant him harm. And if he had— She drew in a deep breath.

There had been strain between the lord and his knight of late. P'raps events had come about that she did not know.

Rising, Annice murmured that she would return to observe him later and see that his wounds did not fester. Guy made a murmur of assent, drowsy from the mandragora she had given him. The herb should make him sleep heavily.

When she returned to the hall, she saw that Rolf's wound had been tended. A clean bandage wound around his left hand, and the dirt and leaves had been brushed from his hair. He wore a clean surcoat and appeared relaxed, sprawled in his chair behind the high table. Food had been hastily brought to the returned men, along with spiced wine that made them more affable. Laughter resounded from the beams overhead.

It appeared that her own vassals had decided to accept the Lord of Dragonwyck as their new overlord, for they jested with him as if long acquainted. Times were uneasy in the north, with some men openly proclaiming rebellion against the king, and others swearing fealty one moment, vacillating the next. Annice was far from secure that these barons would remain sworn to Rolf as long as he made it so obvious he meant to keep his oath to the king.

But for now she was glad they had come, was relieved that there would be no attempt made to force them to swear an oath they would not keep. For now a tenuous truce had been declared.

As she approached her chair, Rolf's gaze slid toward her, and she saw in the gilt-green of his eyes that the truce between them was just as tenuous, just as fragile as that of the king's barons. Yet it would suffice until their marriage.

And then, she knew, the real contest of wills would begin.

CHAPTER 10

𝕿he rising sun gilded the fertile fields below Dragonwyck with pale gold light. A faint mist rose above furrowed hills greening with new life. Standing at his opened window, Rolf stared across fields, forests, and fens without really seeing them. Below, in the village, there would be the bustle of preparations for the wedding to be held in the huge church that morning. Curling drifts of smoke already wafted on the breeze, drifting from thatched roofs.

When he'd first built Dragonwyck Castle, he'd had the fanciful thought that if he gazed long and hard enough, he would see the spires of Lincoln Cathedral in the distance. A fantasy only, of course. 'Twas too far away to be seen, even from the topmost battlement. But in that distant past he'd been more given to fancy than he was now.

Now the harsh realities of life were too often thrust upon him, will he nill he. Now he understood what it meant to see one's life shattered into fragments almost too tiny to perceive. He'd overcome disaster after a long struggle. Could he do so again?

He wasn't certain. He was older now, wearied of the constant solitary struggle. It had been overlong since he'd felt that singular emotion he'd once felt for a woman. Then he had still been naive and trusting. Margerie had shown him the folly of his beliefs in a single stroke.

His hand closed into a fist upon the stone sill of the latticed window. Slanted glass panes reflected the growing light in diffused colors, splintering into shards when he turned his head ever so slightly, rainbow hues dissipating like mist before his eyes. Just so, he had once held happiness in his hand and found it to be a mirage, a mythical collusion of false beliefs. He dared not risk such annihilating discovery again.

Yea, though he was to wed the beauteous lady Annice, he would not make that mistake again. He would not yield his heart to her, would not yield his manhood to the castrating hand of a woman. It had cost him dear the first time. He had yet to recover that which he held most dear in his life, and the bitterness of his defeat still pained him.

In just a few hours a priest sent by Peter des Roches, the justiciar of England and Bishop of Winchester, would bind him to Lady Annice d'Arcy in marriage. His vows were not lightly given. Once he swore to be her lawful wedded husband, he would keep that oath. Though this marriage was not of his choice, he would stay by his vows. Would she do the same?

The royal court was filled with wives who felt no compunction to be loyal to their husbands. They betrayed them in mind, body, and heart with a willingness that always amazed him. Aye, as husbands also betrayed their wives without thought. No hint of scandal had ever been attached to Lady Annice. Apparently she had not betrayed her husband.

Rolf's throat tightened. Luc d'Arcy's memory was still sharp in his widow's mind. She must have loved him a great deal. 'Twas rare in these times to find a husband and wife who cleaved to each other in love as well as loyalty. Yea, as rare as a unicorn. A faint smile tugged at the corners of his mouth. Just so had he described it to Edmund, and his master-at-arms had been highly indignant.

'Twas sad that he was not there this day. How the old man would have enjoyed seeing his lord brought to the altar in marriage! Long had Edmund insisted that 'twas what Rolf needed: a wife. A wife to hold on the long winter nights, to share tidings good and ill with—a wife to love. . . .

A knock upon his chamber door jerked Rolf from his musings, and he saw with some surprise that the sun had well cleared the horizon and was bright upon the land. No rain again today.

He called permission to enter, turning away from the window as Vachel's dark head peered around the edge of the partially open door. "Milord, Sir Simon wishes to speak with you in the hall."

"Sir Simon?" Rolf was vaguely surprised. Though the baron had made no sign of satisfaction at this wedding, neither had he demurred. Instead he had kept his own counsel. "Tell him I will join him shortly, Vachel. As you can see, I am not yet properly garbed for my wedding."

"Aye, milord. He awaits near the fire." Vachel hesitated, then added, "He seems most distraught."

Rolf's brow rose. Simon de Roget was the baron he watched most carefully. The others would follow where he led, he was certain. If he could convince that wary baron to keep his pledge to his king, then p'raps open rebellion would be avoided. Times were perilous, indeed, with so many avowed rebels who had once been loyal to John. The great rebel lords were usually followed almost to a man by men whom they regarded as their particular tenants, though there were exceptions. Knights' fees were certainly collected from many of them, thus leaving them in precarious positions should they attempt to remain loyal to the king. Their feudal lords would most definitely expect succor and aid as their just due. If those lords were rebels—aye, times were most perilous for all men these days.

With that in mind Rolf met the baron below in the hall. Sir Simon paced back and forth before the dais, while servants scurried about him placing benches under trestle tables; silver nefs holding spices and honey were set next to huge silver saltcellars. Wooden trenchers with carved handles shaped like dragons were stacked and waiting.

"Is there a more private site where we may converse?" Simon asked abruptly, and Rolf nodded.

"Aye." When they stood beneath the curved arch of an alcove that looked out over the courtyard, hidden from view of any who might chance past, Rolf turned to Sir Simon and said, "Speak freely, sir."

Frowning, Sir Simon looked down at his feet for a moment, then up into Rolf's eyes. "Cleit of Wulfcot believes that you have an enemy who would see you slain, milord."

Rolf smiled slightly. "Yea, I have many enemies who would see me dead. Is that what troubles you, sir?"

Already shaking his head impatiently, Sir Simon growled, "Nay. Any man in these chancy times has enemies. I meant that perchance the boar that almost caught you yesterday was no accident. Sir Cleit was there. 'Twas told to me that the beaters had turned the beast, but one man directed the path it would take."

Silent, Rolf gazed at the troubled face of Sir Simon. To come into a man's keep and accuse another of treachery was dangerous, indeed. Sir Simon must believe what he was saying.

Closing his hand into a fist, Rolf rested it against the stone arch and gazed past Sir Simon at a rearing dragon carved into the window ledge. Flames shot from the creature's open mouth, and its fangs were long and wicked. It towered over a carved knight on horseback.

"What man directed the path?" he asked as if the answer did not matter. The reply was not the shock it might once have been.

" 'Twas told to me that Sir Guy FitzHugh directed the path. As he was the first man to come upon you, and was wounded in your stead, I know not what to make of it." Sir Simon stood stiffly. "I felt it my obligation to inform you, milord."

Yea, he would. Sir Simon's forthright nature would demand it of him. Most like, he would have felt himself derelict in his duty if he had not come forth.

"My thanks, Sir Simon," Rolf said softly. "Your warning will be well heeded."

Slightly inclining his head, Sir Simon still hesitated a

moment before leaving. Rolf lifted a brow, and the baron said slowly, "I find you an honorable man, when I had been told you were less than so." A wry smile twisted Sir Simon's mouth. "I should not listen to rumors but am too old to change my ways. 'Tis not the first time I have been wrong, but I am glad to find that the lady you intend to wed is in good hands with you. It relieves me of an onerous task—but that no longer matters."

"God's mercy for your opinion," Rolf said politely, and Sir Simon put up a hand.

"Wait, milord. I mislike me to say this, but it seems that Sir Guy gazes too often and fondly upon the lady. I marked it last eve, and again today when he was brought into the hall on a litter."

After Sir Simon took his leave, Rolf leaned back against the cold stone of the alcove. Aye, he had marked it as well. Guy's gaze oft lingered upon Annice, and there was a light in his eyes that was only for the lady. Yea, he had seen it. And now he knew that 'twas not just his imagination. Others had marked it as well.

Passing a hand over his eyes, Rolf winced slightly at a twinge of pain. When he had gone to one knee in the forest, bringing up his lance and bracing himself for the boar's rush, he'd barely enough time to hold it ready. The lance had been at an awkward angle, so that when he'd turned it to spear the charging boar, the shaft had splintered in his hand. A long, jagged piece of wood had pierced his palm, and it was still sore. It might have been worse.

Though lanced, the boar had not been mortally wounded. Furious and in pain, it had charged Rolf again, tusks thrusting viciously at him. He'd barely managed to avoid the charge, using the broken shaft of the lance as a weapon by hitting the boar on the snout. Fiercely concentrating on the danger in front of him, Rolf had not seen Guy's arrival until the knight had cried out. Distracted, he'd looked away at the wrong instant and barely missed being gored. Only the boar's enraged squeal had given him warning of its next assault.

Before he could prepare, the animal was upon him. Its heavy weight had pinned him down, but the tusks had only grazed him. The hot, foul breath had come within inches of his face. Struggling, Rolf had tried to wedge the broken shaft against the beast's neck to push it off, but it had been too heavy. Squealing with hate and outrage, the boar had thrust again and again, the tusks narrowly missing Rolf's body. As the struggle had spun out in what seemed an eternity of time, he'd shouted for Guy to come to his aid.

Yet it was only when others had drawn near that Rolf's demand had been answered. Guy had plunged a lance into the animal but not escaped before it turned on him, gashing his leg in its death spasm. Panting for breath and sore, Rolf had stared at his knight across the still-twitching body for several moments as others came into the clearing, hounds barking and men shouting. He had not asked for and not received an explanation for Guy's delay. It could have cost him his life, and he had been too stunned to confront his sworn knight.

Now he wished he had done so. Any reply would have given him a sign of Guy's true intent. Did his favored knight delay because he wanted his lord dead? It had been Guy who had suggested hunting boars instead of geese. It had been Guy who had seen him lose his lance and then left him behind to follow the others. . . .

A bitter taste rose in the back of his throat, and Rolf swallowed heavily. P'raps this betrayal was his punishment for taking the lady against her will. There was a price for everything, 'twas said. He'd thought his penance was his being forced to wed when he had not intended to marry again. Now he knew better.

He'd lain awake so many nights thinking of the lady in the west wing that it had become almost an obsession. Only iron control had kept him from going to her chamber and claiming marital rights before they were wed.

Jésu, but he actually dreamed of her. It was appalling, that she invaded even his slumber with her fair face and russet hair, the soft curves beneath her gown that had almost made him forget himself. She was a fire in his blood now, and he was impatient for the wedding to be done.

And he did not know if she schemed with Sir Guy to rid herself of a husband she did not want. Were her shy smiles and soft words only a disguise for her true feelings? He had the bitter thought that it hardly mattered to him. Even if she wished him dead, if she wished to poison him or slide a dagger between his ribs, he still wanted her. Yea, that was the harshest realization—it did not matter to him if she hated him. He wanted her. He wanted to feel her soft curves beneath him and taste her lips again, slide his hands into her woman's warmth, and then his body—he was bewitched, ensorcelled, utterly in her thrall.

And there was naught he could do about it. He was to wed her in a few hours' time, and they would be bound for eternity.

Closing his eyes, Rolf had the bleak thought that he was truly damned.

Kneeling at the altar, Annice had the fleeting thought that she was making a dreadful mistake. Rolf knelt beside her, his body tense, his replies given in a rough voice that made her heart sink. There had been no admiration in his eyes when he'd first seen her, only a chill gleam of icy green before he turned away.

Heartsick, she'd clasped her hands tightly together and looked down at her clenched fingers. Rolf, resplendent in his gold-and-sable tunic, a scarlet mantle draped over broad shoulders—tall and handsome and splendidly golden—dismissing her as he had the first time she'd seen him, with an indifferent glance. All the pains she had taken to look her best were for naught.

Clad in the amber tunic of silk and a cloth-of-gold cotte, she looked like a living flame. Belle had been awed as she'd placed a heavy necklace around Annice's throat and told her how beautiful she was, but it had taken a glance in a polished silver mirror to convince her. Embroidered in gilt threads, the amber silk flowed over her body in graceful folds. Long sleeves edged in more intricate embroidery trailed to the ground; they were kept from dragging by thin, beaten gold chains fastened to a gold girdle worn around her hips over the cotte. Slender threads of gold had been woven into her loose hair, glittering in the light. A circlet of dainty, fragile blossoms lay atop her crown, the tiny yellow and white flowers delicately beautiful.

But it was the necklace that commanded the greatest attention, jewels of gold and garnet lying like fire upon her breast. Matching earrings dangled from her earlobes, flashing fire each time she moved. Rolf had sent them to her chamber as a wedding gift early that morning. She had wanted to thank him for the unusual gift and smiled up at him when they stood before the altar.

But the cold, frigid gaze turned on her had frozen her in place and made her heart sink. He resented this marriage, she knew, but she had thought he'd grown warmer toward her. His thoughtfulness in displaying her father's colors, and the soft words at the evening meal, had given her hope.

That hope was dashed now, and she bent her head and dutifully made the proper responses as the priest clad in richly embroidered vestments conducted the ceremony. Candles flickered in tall branches, reflecting from gilded statues and embroidered altar cloths. The smell of incense was strong, the rustle and murmurs overly loud in the crowded chapel of the village church. People spilled from the chapel onto the front steps, and all the way to the town square. This was an occasion for the villagers, and all had turned out. Not just to see their liege lord wed, but because after, at the castle, they would be given food and drink, and there would be entertainment for those fortunate enough to find a place to stand in the hall. Others would wait outside, craning their necks to see, drinking wine and ignoring the admonitions of the priests to be abstinent.

Most of the ceremony passed for Annice in a daze. Despite the stuffiness inside the crowded chapel, she was shivering by the time the priest finished his benediction and told Rolf to kiss his wife. After a fleeting brush of his lips against hers, Rolf took her hand and helped her to her feet. She turned blindly toward the sea of strange faces.

If this had been a normal wedding, there would be loved ones there to smile at her, to come forward and kiss her cheek and wish her well. But there was only Belle, smiling tremulously at her from the side, eyes aglow with romantic dreams. Poor girl. She thought her lord in love, when in truth he was only obeying his king.

Stepping down from the altar railing, Annice focused on where to put her feet instead of on her husband. He still held her arm, his fingers warm around her wrist, steadying her. She spared a prayer of gratitude that he held her up, for she could not have traversed the length of the chapel without support. She had a vague impression of vaulted ceilings and hundreds of candles, strange faces lining the chapel aisles. Then, as they passed through the tall doors to go outside, she saw her vassals standing attendance. They watched gravely, witnesses to their old lord's daughter and their new overlord's union.

Cleit of Wulfcot and Sir Simon stood nearest, and they dropped to one knee as she passed. Then she was gone, out on the front steps of the church, sunlight in her eyes and a soft breeze cooling her face. Rolf lifted her, both hands around her waist, and set her upon a dainty snow-white palfrey caparisoned in flowing silks and wreaths of flowers. They rode through the village streets at a slow pace, flowers strewn before them and grains tossed at them to bless their union with fertility.

Annice suppressed the urge to break into laughter. It seemed a masquerade to her, a mummer's play to entertain bored guests. Even when they were finally back in the great hall at Dragonwyck and she was seated at the high table, nothing seemed real. There was the element of a dream to it, all hazy passages of images before her eyes that would vanish when she awoke.

Time dragged past in an agony for her. She sat stiffly, the smile feeling frozen upon her face as course after course was proudly brought out and presented by the cooks. Servants bore heavy platters to the tables, jellied eels, baked salmon, stewed eels, boiled porpoise and herring—lamprey, pike, and cod—so many fish dishes swam before her gaze that she began to feel slightly seasick. That thought provoked a spasm of laughter that stuck in her throat, and she managed a cough to cover her distress.

"Milady," Sir Simon said, leaning close to her, "art thou well?"

She lifted her gaze to his face and saw concern there. Should she admit her fears? Nay, she knew she could not.

Managing a smile, she murmured, "Yea, Sir Simon. I am quite well, only a bit bemused by all the dishes being served. Is that a swan I see being brought in?"

Sir Simon turned slightly to look at the squires bearing a huge, heavy platter to the high table to present. A swan had been roasted, its feathers replaced, and the entire bird displayed upon a lake of blue pastry as if swimming. Jellied trees and bushes shivered with each step the squires took. Behind those came another magnificent dish, this time a roast peacock, feathers replaced as the swan's, the fanned tail resplendent with brilliant plumage.

As was his duty, Rolf rose to his feet and solemnly pronounced the dishes most beautiful and the cooks most imaginative. With his benediction the dishes were taken away to be properly carved.

Though the musicians had been playing throughout the meal, they struck up a livelier melody as these platters were removed to the kitchens. Now would come dancing before the next course was served, and Annice's throat tightened. She would be expected to dance with Rolf, of course, but had not thought about it. Nothing had been on her mind but the wedding and her husband's mercurial moods.

Fortunately, there were scores of willing dancers to disguise her stiffness from any who were watching. Rolf's hand on hers was warm and his grip light, as if he were not her lawful wedded husband but a remote stranger. When she dared a glance upward, even his eyes were those of a stranger, distant and cool, regarding her through the dark bristle of his lashes with indifference. She looked away, dismay clouding her vision.

Rolf's hand tightened on hers. "Do not pretend coyness where it does not exist, lady wife," he murmured, and when her glance shot to his face, a mocking smile curled his mouth. "Ah, I see that you are aware of my meaning."

"On the contrary," she snapped as anger scattered the cloud of dismay, "I have no idea what you are talking about. Pray, explain."

"Later." His fingers slid from the cup of her palm to her wrist in a light clasp. "When we are alone."

Though she would have liked to demand that he answer her at once, she knew that there were those present who would love nothing better than a reason to gossip. Nay, there would be no titillating pieces of gossip to take to Seabrook's willing ear, or even to the king's. Not if she could prevent it.

Her mouth tightened, lips pressed close together to hold back an angry retort. When they returned to their chairs, impatiently waiting servants began bringing in more courses for the tables. Intricate subtleties made of cake and jellies in the form of hunting scenes, castles, and even a man and woman, were brought in to mark the end of each course. Wine flowed freely, and there was a seemingly endless procession of peas, relishes, and greens.

After those courses were removed, there was more dancing. This time Annice was claimed by Sir Simon, and then Cleit of Wulfcot, followed by Rannulf of Melton Mowbray and Richard de Whitby. After dancing with her vassals, she found herself partner to a loyal agent of the king's, Robert de Vieuxpont.

Smiling down at her, Lord Robert said pleasantly, "I recall your father well, milady. 'Tis glad I am to see his daughter wedded to the king's man. Your recent . . . misfortune . . . has now been remedied."

Uncomfortable at his steady regard, Annice managed a smile. "Yea, milord, I pray that all misfortunes may be so alleviated. 'Twas kind of the king to remember me in my distress."

Lord Robert's brow rose slightly. Her reply could be taken in any manner he wished, and after a moment he apparently chose to regard it as favorable. He smiled.

"Though the king may at times appear to forget his loyal subjects, I assure you he does not. Many rebel barons will find to their sorrow that neither does he forget disloyal subjects. John has a long memory, it is said."

Annice looked down, and when the steps of the dance brought them close again, she murmured, "I pray that the king has a long memory indeed, for if he does, he will not forget that my father loved him."

" 'Tis obvious that he has not forgotten, or your misfortune with Luc d'Arcy could have seen you imprisoned." Lord Robert smiled and said softly, "I am well pleased that you have made the right choice, milady. You will not regret it."

Glancing toward Rolf, who was dancing with one of his vassals' wives, she murmured, "I pray that you are right, Lord Robert."

As if sensing her gaze, Rolf chose that moment to look up. Their eyes met briefly, and her heart lurched. Aye, he was fair to look upon, but what was in his heart? Would she regret this union even more than she regretted her marriage to Luc? She prayed not. Holy Mary, but she prayed that the man she had wed would not destroy her.

She barely realized when the dance ended and she was claimed as partner by another loyal vassal. Names crowded her head, and she struggled to sort through them properly, greeting each man by his correct title. It seemed strange to her that tenants of rebel lords could be loyalists, and conversely, that loyalist barons might tenure lands to avowed rebels. In Lincolnshire alone, it was said, over a hundred writs of seisin had been addressed. Eustace de Vesci owned vast Lincolnshire estates, with many tenants. Rebels crowded loyalists in this more densely populated shire and were conspicuously absent.

There would be a civil conflict, she was certain. Who would win? And what would it mean to her? Mary and Joseph, but she dared not admit that she cared not which side won, as long as she was left to her own. She was sick of war, sick of political strife, sick to death of watching every word spoken, every glance misconstrued.

Even worse was not knowing if she could speak frankly to her own husband, who was the most puzzling of all. The Dragon's fierce loyalty was well-known to all, but he would not be the first man who spoke loudly of loyalty while wreaking treachery in secret.

There was no one she could trust, no one she could turn

to in this chaotic world of politics and change. Least of all the man she had just wed.

Seated again, she took a deep breath. Her head pounded, and the music seemed overloud. She wished she could flee to her chambers and have this day over with. But it was still day, with light streaming in through the scraped hides stretched over high windows. No glass filled these tall windows, as in the luxury of the bedchambers. Candles gave off spears of light from a heavy candelabra swung from the high ceiling in the middle of the hall, and torches sputtered in metal holders along the walls. Even with the windows, light could not reach the darker corners and beneath the arches.

Boar and venison were served in another wave of courses, some in rich sauces, some roasted. Wild ducks and herons were brought in also, along with other game courses. Pies were cut and small birds flew out, soaring toward the vaulted ceiling in a flurry of feathers. The smell of the food began to nauseate her. People were louder with the passage of time and freely imbibed wine, and she longed for fresh air.

Annice's hand closed upon the stem of her goblet and she shut her eyes for a brief moment. At her side she could hear Rolf's deep murmur as he talked with the baron on his left. When night fell, they would be escorted to the bridal chamber, there to be shut in together until morning. With the unusual circumstances of the marriage and her being a widow, there was to be no bedding ceremony, and she was grateful. She could not have borne being undressed and examined before the assemblage, standing in gooseflesh and shivering while all remarked upon the fairness of the bride and the sturdiness of the groom. In this instance it would have been obscene.

"Milady," a voice at her shoulder murmured, and she turned to see Sir Guy. A faint smile curved his mouth, and he was propped with a crutch. Gesturing to it, he said ruefully, "I cannot ask you to dance, but I want to impart my best wishes for your happiness."

She smiled at him. "Your wishes are most appreciated,

Sir Knight. Should you be up and about? Your wound will not mend easily if you exert yourself."

A boyish grin squared his mouth, making him look much younger than she'd supposed him to be. " 'Tis worth a slow mending just to look upon your fair face, milady."

Annice felt Rolf shift beside her, heard his low voice say in an amused tone, "You do not seem overly injured, Sir Guy. It seems that your tongue is just as facile. I had thought you on your deathbed, if I were to believe some of the maids frantic at your condition."

Guy managed a stiff bow. "Some women are prone to hysteria, my liege. As you can see, I am not so maimed I cannot get about."

"Yea, God's mercy for that. It could have been much worse for you. Or me."

Annice did not miss the odd note in Rolf's voice, and 'twas obvious that Guy did not either. He grew even stiffer, his jaw set as he said between his teeth, "I would risk injury again under the same circumstances, milord."

For a long moment Rolf said nothing. Then he said slowly, "I believe you would, Guy. I have not thanked you for coming to my aid yesterday. Forgive me."

Some of the tension eased from Guy's tautly held frame, and he nodded. "Yea, lord. I need no gratitude. I am your sworn knight. 'Tis my duty to come to your aid."

Their gazes met and held, and Annice had the impression that she was missing something important. Then she thought she must be mistaken, for Rolf gave a barely perceptible nod and turned back to the man on his left.

Sir Guy looked down at her again. "Milady," he said softly in English, "do not look so a'frighted. Thou will be well this eve. Believe me when I tell thee that I will do all in my power to see thee kept safely. Thou hast a good husband in yon lord, though he oft be quick of temper."

Puzzled, Annice started to speak, but Guy shook his head. "Nay, not now, milady. I am weary, and maun return to my straw pallet before I fall and make a fool of myself. God be with thee."

A spate of laughter drowned out her murmur of protest, and Annice watched as Guy made his way clumsily through the crowd. Jugglers and acrobats careened over the rushes in agile antics, and a troupe of small trained dogs leaped through hoops and scaled tiny ladders for the crowd's approval. One of the castle hounds apparently took offense at the presence of these intruders in his domain and made a mad rush toward a black-and-white spotted terrier. Shrieks of laughter greeted the owner's efforts to retrieve his trained dog from the gaping maws of the huge brindle hound, but 'twas only when Rolf gave a short, loud whistle that the guilty dog left off his pursuit and trotted obediently to his master.

Laying a hand upon the dog's massive head, Rolf commanded him to lie at his feet, and the brindle hound obeyed. Annice gazed down at the dog staring adoringly up at his master.

Was that how she would appear? Enthralled and obedient, a dog to be whistled near or shoved indifferently aside? Nay, she would not. With every breath in her body she would resist being as Rolf had once suggested—a bitch brought to heel.

When she glanced up from the dog, her eyes met Rolf's. He was gazing at her steadily, an enigmatic light in his eyes that made her throat tighten. Did he expect it of her—that blind obedience? Then he would be sorely disappointed to find that his new wife had no intention of being crushed by him. A faint, mocking smile touched the corners of his mouth, and she wondered if he mocked her growing apprehension of the night.

'Twould be much too soon for her when they were escorted to the bridal chamber. She knew her duty well, and knew that to stay his marital rights could invalidate the marriage. If she did so, it could also cause a conflict between her vassals and his—loyalists against suspected rebels—'twould be a disaster.

But to yield to him would mean the shattering of her resistance and any hope she had of surviving, soul intact. And she did not know what she would do when the moment came. . . .

CHAPTER 11

Only Belle attended her mistress in the shadowed bridal chamber lit by several branches of candles. Fitful light flickered over her as she gave a final, nervous touch to the embroidered silk bed curtains. Guests crowded into the chamber, laughing merrily and making ofttimes crude jests as they escorted the bridal pair inside.

Moving to stand stiffly in the center of the chamber by a table laden with wine and a platter of cold meat and other tidbits, Annice glanced toward her husband when Belle murmured that the bed was made ready. Rolf stood nearby, silent and withdrawn, drinking wine from a cup. One of the guests jostled his elbow, entreating his lord to be more forward or else he chanced losing his bride to another.

Rolf set down his cup and managed a smile that felt more like a grimace. "Such as you, Sir Ralf? As a sheriff in Lincolnshire, you must be used to making terms of unequal surrender."

That jest produced general laughter and a flush from Sir Ralf Ridel, who was in charge of wresting taxes from the shires and tenants of Lincolnshire. He had much trouble with some baronies, who rebelled, and even those loyal to the king ofttimes protested his harshness.

A sly smile curved Sir Ralf's mouth. "Yea, milord, but I have had the most effort claiming your taxes. 'Tis well-known that you are close-fisted and miserly with what is yours. I would not dare to make free with your money—or your wife."

Laughter greeted that sally, and even Rolf smiled. He glanced at Annice and saw that she was pale and trembling. 'Twas best to end this play, before she swooned and he was the butt of even cruder jests.

"As you have so strongly suggested, Sir Ralf," he said loudly enough to be heard by all, " 'tis time I was alone with my bride. We are no novices to be lessoned on the coming joys of marriage, and lest some of you wish to feel the prick of my sword, you will depart swiftly."

"Aye," Sir Ralf retorted, " 'tis time for your bride to feel the prick of your nether blade, I think!"

Raucous laughter and ribald jests accompanied this reply. Finally, at the insistence of Rolf and some of his strongest vassals, the guests were firmly removed from the chamber. Vachel went with them, and loud merriment could be heard in the wide corridors as they returned to the hall to continue the feasting.

Watching as Belle murmured softly to her mistress and began helping her disrobe, Rolf felt a growing disquiet. The moment he had anticipated since first bringing her to Dragonwyck was at hand, yet he could feel no joy in it. There was only an overpowering sense of emptiness.

She would be his before the night ended, yet what would he possess? Certainly, the lady's body. But more? Nay, there was no love in the eyes she turned on him of late, only a growing apprehension. He had seen that look turned on him before, with his first bride. But Margerie had been a maid still; Annice was no virgin and would know well what was about.

Chiding himself for being a romantic fool, Rolf still longed for more than just physical release. He longed for what Edmund had talked of, of soft whispers in the night, an intimacy between man and woman that kept them close in spirit if not distance. There had been little enough of love in his life, 'twas true, and he had thought he had not missed it, save for the love of his son, an entirely different matter.

But this—yea, this weighed on him heavily, for he realized that some small kernel of need in him desired the emotion that Edmund had spoken of so often. He'd seen it before in others and had known instantly what existed between them. In these times love between a husband and wife was rare, and to be more greatly treasured for that fact.

A soft murmur distracted him from his thoughts, and Rolf looked up to see that the maidservant had finished disrobing her mistress. There was a swift glimpse of ivory skin and glorious, unbound hair streaming in heavy russet waves before Belle held up a voluminous robe to drape over Annice's shoulders.

Pulling aside the filmy curtains enveloping the bed, Belle assisted her mistress, holding tight to the ermine-trimmed robe to shield her from his eyes. Rolf smothered a smile at this last defense and reached for his cup of wine. Lady Annice commanded swift loyalty from those around her, 'twas apparent. She had certainly gained Belle's love and respect in the few weeks she had been at Dragonwyck, though young Belle had long been a serf of these lands.

When Annice was hidden behind the silk bed hangings and between the sheets with the coverlets pulled up over her, Belle took a moment to straighten the curtains hanging about the bed, then draped the discarded robe over a stool at the bed's side. There was still a chill in the air despite the woven wall coverings to prevent drafts; a coal-filled brazier emanated heat and the smell of smoldering spices from the center of the chamber.

A slight current of air made the gauzy bed hangings flutter gently, allowing Rolf a glimpse of Annice propped upon the goose-feather pillows. In the gloom of candlelight and shadowed bed, her face glowed pale and ethereal. He had a brief impression of wide, haunted eyes and bare shoulders before the bed hangings drifted closed again. His grip tightened on the cup of wine.

Jésu, but she looked like a lamb led to the slaughter. Did she fear his touch so greatly? Or did she fear that he would ravish her like a predatory beast, without thought of her feelings?

Rolf took an involuntary step toward the bed, his intention as yet unformed, but a discreet knock on the chamber door made him pause. Corbet, his squire, entered hard upon the echoes of the sound, face carefully composed. Obviously someone had been tutoring him on proper behavior, for his usual feckless gaiety was much subdued.

Irritated and grateful at the same time at the interruption, Rolf bade him enter and suffered the young man to begin undressing him. 'Twas part of the squire's duty to tend his lord in all things, dressing and undressing, the tending of his armor, weapons, and most important—his person. Never before had it chafed Rolf to be tended, but this eve he bore it with barely concealed impatience.

Corbet of Warrington had been sent to Dragonwyck several years before as page and only recently earned his silver spurs. The importance of his rank weighed heavily upon him, being so recently acquired, and he tended to take longer than usual in performing his duties.

Unclasping the ornate gold pin formed like a dragon's head that held Rolf's scarlet mantle of light wool, Corbet removed the garment and draped it carefully over a chair. Then he reached for the sable tunic emblazoned with a gold dragon, the beast formed of tiny squares of gold sewn one atop the other. Ornate braid edged the neck and sleeves, glittering as he pulled it over Rolf's head.

"A truly magnificent tunic, milord," Corbet murmured admiringly, and Rolf shot him an impatient glance.

"Yea, Corbet, but I would have this done quickly. I am in no mood to suffer compliments or delay."

After giving his lord a startled glance of comprehension, Corbet more hastily relieved Rolf of the rest of his garments. Undertunic, belt, breeches, and soft calf-leather boots were quickly removed. With swift, efficient motions Corbet wrapped him in an ermine-trimmed robe before he bent to tend the discarded boots.

"Leave that," Rolf commanded. "There is the morrow for such tasks."

During the time it took Corbet to complete his duties, Rolf had managed to form his thoughts into a more coherent direction. He could not let his passion rule his actions.

Still, when the squire had finally quit the chamber and the echoes of the door's closing had faded, Rolf found himself moving toward the high, wide bed. It was deeply shadowed, fitful light reaching inside the bed curtains. He stood still a moment, holding back the curtain, his eyes resting on his wife's face.

She stared silently up at him, her hair spread in a glowing mass upon the pillows and over her shoulders. Rolf took a deep breath, unprepared for the rush of emotion that swept through him. Yea, she was truly beautiful, this changeling wife of his. From haughty hostage to frightened maid to seductive siren, she had captured his thoughts too often to be ignored now.

There was the creak of ropes holding the mattress when he lowered his weight to the bed, the sound overloud in the gloomy silence. He sat for a moment, not knowing what to say, searching his mind for a neutral topic that would put them both at ease.

Finally Annice spoke, her lips twitching slightly with humor as she asked, "Do you always wear your robe to bed, milord?"

Ermine tickled his bare skin as he shifted position and the robe slid over his thighs. "Nay, not always." He paused. "Only when I feel awkward."

"And do you? Feel awkward?" Her eyes were large and dark blue with surprise in the shadows, gazing steadily at him.

"Yea, wife, I do." A wry smile twisted his mouth. "For all that has gone before, I cannot say that I feel comfortable with you now."

After a moment's silence, when neither of them moved nor spoke, Annice slid a hand toward him, her fingertips brushing against the hand he had placed on the mattress to bear his weight. He looked down at her pale hand, so fair and fragile against his much darker skin. Compelled by some emotion he could not name, he moved his hand to curl his fingers around hers, holding tightly.

For long moments they sat that way, while candlelight flickering in erratic patterns and shadows wove in and out around them. The smell of spice was heavy in the air, emanating from the brazier. A faint drift of her perfume wafted toward him, teasing him with sweet suggestion.

Rolf inhaled sharply. Though he had no intention of allowing himself to be mired in a morass of emotions, neither did he intend to tarry like a green lad in the first flush of love. This was his lawful wedded wife, and he would take what was his by right. She offered it freely enough, with the gentle touch of her hand and steady regard. Yea, there would be no ghosts between them this night, nothing but the sweet pleasure he had anticipated for what had seemed like forever.

Standing, he shrugged free of his robe and let it fall to the floor. Annice turned her face away, hand still lying palm up on the coverlet. Modesty or distaste? he wondered. He'd rarely found disfavor in a woman's eyes. How did Annice view him? There was nothing in her demeanor to suggest revulsion, though on occasion she had resisted his embrace. He'd put that down to the situation, but he could not help a twinge of unease now.

There were scars aplenty upon his body, from wars and tourneys and conflicts. None too disfiguring, but a man could not be certain what would repulse a woman and what would not. Rolf lifted the edge of the coverings and slid beneath. Bed ropes creaked gently at his added weight. With the coverlet wadded into a knot in his lap, he turned to face Annice.

She had shifted to look at him, the sheets still clutched at her neck, bare shoulders pale in the ghostly light. A faint smile touched the corners of her mouth.

"You are most comely to look upon, milord," she said softly.

There was an odd tightening of the muscles in his chest, a spasm that briefly constricted his lungs. Then it eased, and he said, "I am pleased I find favor in your eyes, lady fair."

Silence spun between them again, humming with tension, the awareness of one another, and what would soon happen. Consummation was inevitable and necessary. An unconsummated marriage would be invalid. Yet there was more between them than that knowledge; there was the unspoken draw of breathless enticement that seemed to pull them close without touching. He felt it. And he felt the trembling of her body as she waited, silent and watching.

It was that involuntary reaction that broke the yoke of hesitation and made him move closer to her. Shivering, she did not protest when he put a hand upon her shoulder, caressing the soft skin beneath his rough palm with light strokes. Though she shivered as if chilled, her skin was warm to the touch. He let his palm drift downward, from the slope of her shoulder to the ripe fullness of her breast.

The back of his hand moved aside the coverlet, and he cupped her breast in his palm. He heard the quick inhalation of her breath, felt her shiver again. Looking up into her eyes, he felt suddenly as if he were falling headlong into a shadowed region from which he might not return. More than physical pleasure waited just beyond the night. But he would not retreat now, not when his quest was so near ended.

Slowly he drew his other hand along the delicate curve of her collarbone, then down. He could feel the rapid beat of her heart beneath his hand, and her breathing was shallow. As was his. Already his body tightened in expectation, full and heavy and aroused beneath the concealing coverlet. Bending, he replaced the caress of his hand with his mouth, tongue flicking out to tease the hardening peak of her breast. Annice gave a soft gasp, and then her hands moved to cup behind his neck, fingers lacing together to hold him closer. The coverlet fell away. Her body arched toward him, and he felt the silky fibers of her hair brush against his cheek.

This reaction was unexpected, and it had the effect of spurring his arousal. With a groan he closed his lips around her taut nipple and drew it deeply into his mouth. Ah, but she was sweet as honey, finer than any wine he'd ever tasted, her perfumed flesh seeming to melt beneath his tongue. When he finally lifted his head, he was panting for breath and struggling for control.

Annice's face was a pale oval in the shadows, head tilted

back and her hands still clasped upon his nape. Her fingers moved slightly to spread into his hair, a light caress that was tender and arousing at the same time. Her lashes were lowered, shadows spiky upon her cheeks, and her lips were parted and trembling. A shudder traversed her body, and she opened her eyes slowly to stare at him.

"Thou art wondrous," she whispered in English, and he stared at her. He didn't know what to say. Nothing would justify what he felt. In truth, he wasn't certain what he felt, beyond the driving need to possess her completely.

"My lady," he said finally, his voice harsh and breathless, as if he had run a mile in full armor. "Annice—thou art my wife."

It sounded nonsensical even to his ears, and he wished he could recall the words. But she was smiling as if she understood.

"Aye, Lord of Dragonwyck, I am thy wife. Thine to hold for as long as thou wish. . . ."

P'raps that was what he'd needed. For all the times he had already taken her in his mind, his day and night dreams, he had yet to possess her. Desire pricked him hard, and he strove to be gentle as he pulled her beneath him, hands stroking down the sides of her body to mold her to him.

She caught her breath, looking up, eyes wide when he pressed the full detail of his arousal against her belly. It slid, hot and aching, between them, tantalizing yet not quite enough to ease his torment. Arrows of pleasure shot through him at the friction. He closed his eyes for a moment, yielding to the sweet bliss of the motion.

Annice made a strangled sound. Bending, he kissed her again, her eyes and nose and the full curve of her lips, lingering there to drink deeply. His mouth moved from hers to travel up the sweet, curved slope of her jaw, pausing at the whorls of her ear, tongue exploring lightly.

Leisurely, enjoying every moment, Rolf dragged his tongue down and over her shoulder to the taut, beaded nipple again, pausing to savor it, then moving lower. He found the tiny dip of her navel, heard her soft gasp, and moved even lower. There, nestled amidst the red-gold thatch of her curls, lay the honeyed goal he pursued so intently.

Bending, he kissed her there, tongue making a brief foray into the cleft. Annice went rigid, her thighs quivering as she made a loud sound of shock and startlement.

"Nay, Rolf . . . Holy Mary—do not!"

Resting his cheek against her trembling thigh, he stroked her lightly with his fingers. With one hand he gently explored her, heated and damp, beckoning to him with luxurious sweetness. God's mercy, but he did not think he could subdue the urge to hold back, to give her the pleasure she should have. Her shuddering movements and the fluttering cries drove him almost to the brink.

"Rolf . . . what do thou . . . ah, I have never . . ."

Her last words drew his attention, and he looked up at her face, contorted in the pale light. Could it be? Was it possible that her first husband had never introduced her to the joys of intimacy? That would explain her gasp of shock when he had kissed the sweet nether lips that hid her femininity. Deliberately, he bent forward again, lightly touching the tip of his tongue to her.

Annice gasped, a quick, indrawn breath. Her hands clutched at him, fingers sliding over his bare skin with lingering strokes. His hands tightened on her hips to hold her as he tasted deeply, tongue washing over her until she was writhing and panting. Only when he heard her high, lilting cry did he pause. She was shaking, making tiny sounds in the back of her throat, and he knew she had reached that pinnacle of release.

Finally he moved upward again, tongue laving the sweet softness of her skin. She gave a soft, shuddering sigh. He lifted his head to look down at her, shadowed and pale against the sheets, her hair spread in glorious abandon over the pillows in a fiery mass. Long had he dreamed of having her thus, her thick waves of heavy hair beneath her and him over her. . . . Rolf's gaze met hers, and he saw the wonder in her eyes.

With a trembling hand she reached up to cradle his jaw in her palm. " 'Tis a sin to feel such pleasure," she said softly.

Rolf took her hand, pressing a kiss to her palm. "Nay, sweeting, 'tis God's gift."

She drew in a deep, shuddering breath. Was it so? Was it meant for a woman to feel such ecstasy? She had never thought so, had never dreamed that such pleasure could be found in coupling. Luc had never attempted to give her pleasure but had only taken his. How could she have known?

There was much more that she did not know—worlds of it. How could she pleasure him as he had her? She wanted to ask but found her tongue bound by shyness. An almost overpowering emotion swelled her heart and filled her throat, tightening it so that she could not speak even if she found the right words.

As if he understood her silence, Rolf moved over her again, murmuring soft words like caresses. He kissed her mouth, tasting of perfume and her own scent. Her hands caught him by the shoulders, fingers testing the hard muscles in light motions, sliding down his damp skin to the taut sinews of his arms. He shuddered slightly when her hands dropped to the narrow span of his waist, and she brought her fingers up through the thick mat of curls on his chest, letting the tiny hairs wind around her fingertips. It was all so new to her, so wondrous and sweet, that she did not want it to end too quickly. She wanted this moment to last forever, to spin out slowly.

Tilting back her head on the pillow, she gazed up at him with a faint smile. All her worries faded away, drifting into oblivion. There was only this moment, only this night, with Rolf a heavy pressure atop her and all else insignificant. On the morrow reality would intrude again, with all its attendant problems. There would be the constant threat of war, the conflict between rebel and loyalist, and the nagging worry that Rolf of Dragonwyck was not the man she hoped.

But now, with Rolf lying atop her and her body still aching for him, there was only this. The sweet pleasure that she'd never found before, never dreamed truly existed—aye, once she'd thought it a mere fantasy, put about by men to lure women. A legend, like unicorns and real dragons.

But her own dragon was very real and had taken her to heights she'd never dared hope to scale.

Lifting his body over hers, Rolf poised for a moment, his eager member rubbing against the aching moistness between her thighs. She looked up at him, drew in a shaky breath when his hips moved forward, spreading her slightly. A faint sense of regret filled her that it would be done so soon. Once he entered her, the closeness they were sharing would be over in a trice. That much she knew from her times with Luc. A few short thrusts, and his seed would be spent and he would fall asleep.

But Rolf had already given her a miracle this eve, and she would not deny him his own pleasure. Her arms rose to curl around his neck, holding him as he slowly thrust forward, sliding inside her with a burning stroke. Her body took him deeply, stretching and closing around him in a convulsive wave. Then he was moving against her, withdrawing almost completely free before thrusting forward again, filling her in shattering ecstasy. To her surprise he did not slow after a few thrusts, but continued. Again and again he filled her, withdrew, and plunged forward again, making her shudder with pleasure.

Annice was vaguely aware of her own cries, his breath against her ear a harsh sob. His hands closed around her upper arms as if he would hold her still, but she could not help the arching twist of her hips as she rose to meet him. It was age-old, primitive response, coming from deep within her, this need to meet his thrusts with her own. Fiercely, as if this moment would never happen again, Annice clung to him. She answered his hard stabs with her own, impaling herself on his body with a savage pleasure. Sweet, wild ecstasy, hot and melting her into him so that they were one, bound together as man and wife and lovers.

Plunging deeply, Rolf did not withdraw even when she collapsed into a spinning vortex of release, crying out and clinging to him with panting ecstasy. Barely had the shattering residue of her culmination faded when he began again, moving his body inside hers with deep, lingering strokes.

She whimpered, and he whispered softly in her ear, "Nay, chérie, 'tis too sweet to stop. . . ."

Candles burned down and guttered, light dying out as Rolf swept her again and again to that elusive peak. Time blurred into soft, heated whispers and trembling rapture. Nothing beyond the silk-hung bed existed for either of them.

And when, finally, Rolf allowed himself the luxury of his own release, his hard body throbbing inside her with shudders of bliss, Annice thought that she had never dreamed loving the dragon could be so sweet. . . .

CHAPTER 12

Waking slowly, Annice looked up at the swagged curtains of the bed. Pale light filtered through the bed hangings. It was early morn, and no one had yet come to wake the sleeping couple. Shadows slowly defined into sharper images beyond the curtains—table, chair, and stools. She turned her head to one side to study Rolf. Her entire body throbbed with the reminder of their consummation. He lay still, his long, muscular frame filling up an entire side of the bed. He was asleep, face turned toward her, one leg thrown possessively over her thighs.

She smiled slightly. In slumber he seemed like a small boy more than the fierce dragon of legend. Yea, save for his beard, he looked as youthful as his son. Long lashes shadowed his cheeks, and his lips were slightly parted, revealing the gleaming white of his teeth. His golden hair was tousled, falling over his forehead.

Resisting the urge to push it back, she gazed at him. Could it be that her feelings had undergone such a rapid transition? Where were the doubts, the lingering taints of suspicion with which she had long regarded him? Last night there had been none of the constraint between them that had so recently existed, just the arousing pleasures of the flesh.

But that changed nothing. She was only too aware that men could easily put behind them any softer emotions in the bright light of day. Yet she could not say what had touched her the last eve, save Rolf's admitted awkwardness. That he had not only been aware of the strain between them but didn't mind admitting it had intrigued her.

As light grew, reaching inside the shadowed bed, she studied him more closely. Aye, he was a well-made man, indeed. Broad, hard-muscled shoulders, thick arms, and a wide chest would fill out his armor even without padding. Ropes of taut muscle banded his abdomen, tapering to slim hips and long, lean legs. Silky dark hairs pelted his chest. Yea, comely he was, as she had long known.

Fool, she chided herself with faint derision, *to lie here admiring a man who holds thy fate in his hands. . . .*

It was true. For all that he was comely, and he showed her a few kindnesses, she had no notion of what was to come. Would he do as Luc had done and beat her now that she was his wife? 'Twould not be the only man in England to regard a wife as mere chattel. Now that her lands were his, the wedding done and consummated, her fate lay within his hands. She could only pray that he would not be the harsh husband or fool that Luc had been.

For long minutes she lay there, contemplating the events that had changed her life so drastically in but a short time. Rolf's slow, even breathing did not ease her fears. Would he wake with the light she had last seen in his eyes? Or would he regard her as he had done in the church and at the wedding feast—with a hostile, cold gaze?

She almost dreaded his waking. Soon she would be expected to call for her servant. That would bring a party of revelers from the wedding feast to their chamber, where there would be much jesting and teasing of the newly wedded pair. It was too soon. She could not bear the thought of curious eyes staring at her, people wondering and laughing, p'raps smirking behind their hands. An enforced marriage would be cause for ribald jests, indeed, and she didn't want to hear them.

A glance showed her the silk, ermine-trimmed robe draped over a stool near the bed. If she slid gently from the bed and into her robe, she could visit the garderobe without calling a servant. There should be a chamber pot nearby, but she did not wish to use it with Rolf so near. Modesty prevailed upon her to seek the privacy of the garderobe, cold though the stone privy would be.

But when she moved, she discovered that her hair was caught beneath Rolf's heavy shoulder. If she tried to work it free and slide out from under the weight of the leg he'd thrown over her thighs, she would wake him. Trapped, she lay there considering what to do.

"Chérie. . . ."

Startled, Annice shot him a glance and saw his eyes open, heavy-lidded and penetrating as he gazed at her. She flushed.

"I but sought the means to rise without waking you," she began, but he'd already begun to pull her toward him. His beard grazed the bare skin of her arm, rough and bristly.

Touching the chafed skin on her breasts, Rolf murmured, " 'Tis a sin that I have marked such beautiful flesh with my beard. Shall I shave it?"

She laughed softly and touched his dark beard. "Nay, lord. It gives you the look of a bear instead of a dragon. . . ."

Giving a mock growl, he shifted to lie atop her, gazing down at her with a glitter in his green eyes. "Is it better to be devoured by a bear than a dragon, *chérie*?"

"Nay," she said with a slight gasp when she felt him slide between her thighs, hot and heavy and insistent. "The dragon easily bests a poor bear."

He curled his fingers through hers and drew her arms up slowly above her head, pressing her down into the mattress. His face was over hers, blotting out light and silk hangings, eyes intent as he gazed down at her. He seemed to be searching for words, and she felt a growing disquiet.

A sudden flush heated her cheeks as she recalled her responses to his caresses. Did he think to chastise her for her wanton behavior of the previous night? Did he think her unchaste, perhaps, like so many of the court ladies he must have known?

"I would know," he said finally, his words deliberate and slow, "what you meant by your actions last eve."

"Last eve?" She stiffened. Yea, he thought her wanton and would now repudiate her.

Impatiently, Rolf growled, "In the hall, when you pranced and minced about, pretending coyness where there was none."

Her mind went blank, and she struggled to decipher his meaning. "I do not know. . . ."

His hands tightened. "Yea, you know well what I mean. Your pretense at coyness—was it for me? Or someone else?"

Startled, Annice could only gaze up at him. She tried to imagine another meaning but could not. Her chief recollection was of his glare and terse comment that he would speak to her later in privacy. Did he think she had eyes for another man, p'raps? Was that the cause of his hostile stares?

A faint smile curved her mouth. Jealous? Rolf of Dragonwyck? Could it be that she had misread him after all? Yea, 'twas growing more apparent that she had. 'Twas not hostility that drove him, but the tiny seeds of jealousy that had been inadvertently planted.

Drawing in a deep breath, she murmured, "Since I first set eyes upon you at Stoneham, I have thought of no other man, milord. 'Tis you who have governed my thoughts, whether I willed it or no."

It was true. As much as she might dislike the capitulation of her heart, somehow this fierce warlord had taken it. 'Twas not just his actions of the night before, but other, small things, that had slowly turned her mind away from fear and hatred to admiration of him. For all that he was rumored to be such a brutal man, his servants loved him. The people of Dragonwyck were fiercely loyal, men and women. He did not mistreat them but gave freely of his time and possessions. Autocratic? Yea, at times, p'raps, but no more so than most men.

There were times he could have dealt most harshly with her. In the same circumstances another man might well have done so. She was his hostage but had remained defiant, and openly insulting. Yet he had done no more than lash out at her with words. If she had so defied Luc—yea, she would have borne the bruises for many weeks after. Rolf of Dragonwyck had not lifted a heavy hand to her.

But it was the small gesture of displaying her father's colors and device that had meant the most to her. Of all things he might have done—gentle wooing, expensive gifts, even promises—he had given her the greatest gift of understanding her heart.

Worming her arm free of his tight grasp, she lifted her hand to cradle his jaw. His beard tickled her palm, and there was a wary set to his mouth and eyes as he gazed down at her.

"My lord and husband," she said softly, "I have no explanation for what I did not do. Thou hast misread me, I fear."

Rolf sat back, hands resting on his thighs as he gazed down at her with a bemused expression. Then he smiled faintly. "Yea, p'raps I have. When first I saw you, I knew you a woman of honor. Your dealings with me and my son were admirable."

"And have I changed so greatly?"

"Nay," he said, shaking his golden head. " 'Tis only your circumstances that have changed." He paused, then added softly, "I should not have yielded to the temptation to abduct you. I did you a great disservice, I fear."

She reached up to stroke the thick pelt of curls on his chest and felt his muscles contract beneath her fingertips. "Nay, lord," she murmured, "no disservice that has not been rectified a hundredfold."

He caught her hand and held it tight in his, pressed against the taut band of muscles on his abdomen. She could feel the quick intake of his breath, the slight quiver beneath her palm. Looking up, she saw an odd expression on his face, half torment, half pleasure. His lips crooked in a rueful smile.

"My good fortune cannot last forever. Wilt though now tell me thou art a sorceress, mayhap? A changeling sent to bedevil me?"

"Yea, lord," she said, her breath catching slightly in the

back of her throat, "I am sent to plague thee with vows of loyalty and love. . . ."

The green of his eyes grew deeper, and he bent slowly to brush his mouth across her lips. That action drove everything from her mind but the need to feel his arms around her, and she reached up to pull him to her.

Before she succeeded, there was a loud knocking upon the chamber door. A voice shouted outside, filled with urgency. Rolf's head jerked around and he swore softly, bemoaning the lack of his weapon.

Hard upon the knocking, the door opened, and it was Vachel who stood framed in the entrance. He paused, barely visible through the silk bed hangings. "Milord," he said abruptly, "there is trouble afoot."

Rolf had already swung his body to the side of the bed and was rising. Without regard for his nudity he strode toward his steward. "What kind of trouble?"

"A traitor in our midst."

"Traitor?" Rolf reached for his discarded clothes, ignoring Vachel's effort to assist him.

Annice sat up in bed. She clutched the coverlet to her chin and listened with growing horror as Vachel informed his lord that the keep was under assault.

"Someone opened the east postern gate," he said grimly. "It had to be done from inside. No man could have managed to get in without aid."

"What is the damage?" Rolf's voice was muffled as he dragged his tunic over his head. "Has Sir Guy formed a defense?"

Vachel hesitated, then said gravely, "Sir Guy is still wounded, milord, and was given a strong draft to ease his pain. His mind is fogged."

A vile curse emanated from inside the tunic, followed by Rolf's head as he pulled down the tunic over his shoulders. "Then who is in charge? God's teeth, but Edmund's loss is sore grievous. None can match him in the mustering of soldiers—what of Gareth of Kesteven?"

" 'Tis he who is attempting to rally our men. So many are disabled from too much wine last eve. . . . Whoever planned this knew well that all our men would celebrate too heartily, milord."

Rolf turned to look hard at Vachel. "I gave the command that not all were to take part. Who countermanded my order?"

Giving a helpless shrug, Vachel murmured, "I do not know the answer, milord. But only a few men are clear-headed. . . ."

"By the bones of St. Jerome, there will be many more clear heads once I lay about me with the flat of my sword," Rolf said through his clenched teeth. "What of the sheriff? Has he rallied his men to fight?"

Looking downcast, Vachel murmured, "Those men are also wine-fuddled, milord, as is the sheriff himself."

Gritting his teeth, Rolf swore viciously as he stamped his feet into his boots. Annice lifted her voice to be heard above his growling oaths. "Vachel—tell me, where are my vassals?"

"Sir Simon is below cursing and trying to rally his men, as well as Sir Cleit. I do not know of the others."

"And Robert de Vieuxpont?" Rolf snapped. "Where is the king's agent?"

"I have sent servants to fetch him to the guardroom." Vachel handed Rolf his sword, then stepped back to clear his passage to the half-open door. Flicking Annice a glance, the steward said, " 'Tis best that you remain here, milady."

Halfway through the door, Rolf paused and turned back. "Aye. Do not think to flee unaided, for you will only be in danger. Linger here until I send a man to tell you differently. And bar the door once we are gone."

Then he departed, with Vachel close behind. Annice slid from the bed and reached blindly for her robe, heart hammering fearfully against her ribs. Holy Mary, but an assault! Enemies inside the well-fortified walls of Dragonwyck . . . aye, she was of Vachel's opinion. A traitor must have opened the castle gates. This keep was far too strong to be taken in the normal course.

After she lowered the bar over the door, wrestling the weighty oak with panting breaths, she rushed to the window that looked out over the inner bailey. It took her a moment to unfasten the latch and push open the heavy latticed glass and wood frame. When she leaned out, palms down on the rough stone ledge, she caught her breath in dismay.

Men battled fiercely across the stone ward and parapets. Shouts rose above the din of clanging swords and battle-axes. Some men wore only breeches and tunics, obviously unprepared for the assault that had come with the rising of the sun. A pile of straw in one corner of the bailey smoldered, tiny flames licking a path closer to a wooden out-building. If the fire took hold, the entire keep stood in danger of being burned out.

Annice whirled away from that window to the next, where the same scene met her eyes. In the chaos she could not identify Rolf. Most of the men wore steel helmets. She put a hand over her mouth as she struggled for composure. She must think, must not panic. First she would tend her body's needs, then garb herself so that whatever came, she would be ready.

As she did so, she blessed the absent Belle and murmured a prayer for her safety. Belle had taken great care to place suitable garments in the bridal chamber, along with Annice's own comb, brush, and other personal items. Through the open windows she could hear the shouts and clash of weapons, spurring her to action. It took only a short time to make herself ready; then she returned to a window.

The battle raged even more fiercely now. She leaned farther out, peering anxiously at the gate opposite. The portcullis was lowered, trapping men of both sides in the bailey. Though she could not see over the peak of the facing roof into the outer bailey, there was the distant sound of swords and battle there, too. The entire castle was under attack, and she could not tell which side was winning.

Closing her eyes, Annice tried to recall the design of Dragonwyck. She had been out but little since her arrival, and that always with a guard close on her heels. The walks in the gardens had been few. Her farthest foray from the hall had been to the village for her wedding, and that only the day before. Struggling, she searched her memory to sort out the maze of hallways and chambers that made up the living quarters of the castle.

The bridal chamber looked out over the inner ward from between a set of four bastions in the main tower. A series of parapets and guard towers rimmed the main building, with a long curtained wall enclosing the whole. The living quarters at the far end of the complex perched atop a high cliff on one side, with the rest of the castle sprawling out in front, guarded by gates, moats, and portcullises.

It was virtually impregnable. That the enemy had managed to penetrate this deeply to the doors of the living quarters was a dire catastrophe.

And it seemed as if the battle would not end soon, for as she watched, more men poured out from doorways, ranging over the ward and up stone steps into guard towers. Arrows flew thick and fast, and the clang of swords was pierced by the roars from men's throats. Flames had engulfed an outbuilding, raging unchecked. Yea, 'twas a fierce battle in troth, and she could do naught to aid them.

Not even during the siege at Montmorency those many years ago had she felt as close to peril. That now, when she was in the stronghold of the fiercest warrior in the land, she should be so endangered was astonishing. Only vile treachery could have wrought such a feat, and Annice shuddered to think who amongst them might betray his lord.

From below came a deep, echoing rattle. It sounded again, then again, measured and slow, as if a storm raged in the distance. Annice could not see directly below her windows to the doors that led inside but did see men fighting just beyond. Even as she frowned, it struck her as to the cause—a battering ram would make that sound as it pounded the doors. Holy Mary and all the saints—the enemy were storming the very doors that would allow them inside.

Jerking away from the window, she snatched up a decorative dagger with jeweled hilt, thrusting it into the links of her girdle. Then she changed shoes, putting on the soft leather ankle boots that Belle had included with her wardrobe. A chest brought from Stoneham had been placed in the chamber, holding necessities she might use during the days after her wedding. She knelt beside it, throwing back the heavy lid with some difficulty. A brief exploration yielded her another poniard, this more utilitarian in appearance and function. That one she tucked into the garter holding up her hose.

Heart pounding, she rose slowly from beside the chest and lowered the lid. God's grace, but that the enemy would be stopped before reaching the inner sanctuary of the hall. Where was Rolf? Was he unharmed? If he had been wounded, she would see his attackers dragged before the king and condemned to death . . . yea, would gladly lift the executioner's axe herself to send their heads flying!

It could only be rebels storming the castle of John's loyal baron. That she knew well. The king would not have sent men to take a well-situated keep such as Dragonwyck, especially when its lord had sworn fealty to him. Aye, only rebels would be this reckless, not caring if they incurred the king's wrath.

Time dragged, and Annice wore a path between windows, peering from one, then the other, trying to see. If only someone would bring word—surely it had been hours, and still the battle raged. Was she to remain there indefinitely? Had they forgotten her in all the excitement?

Flinching as a spate of fighting grew louder, she drifted to the east window again and leaned out. Her breath caught, and her hands curled tightly around the stone ledge. She recognized the colors of the men below—the house of Mowbray. They were fighting furiously, and 'twas not for Dragonwyck's cause.

Weak with despair, she lowered her head, cupping her forehead in a palm. William of Mowbray was a most outspoken rebel. Sir Rannulf had left his service, she'd thought, to come join the loyalist cause. Could she be mistaken? Could Sir Rannulf—a former vassal of Beauchamp—be the traitor among them? Pray God she was wrong. That one of her vassals should be accused . . .

A loud pounding on the chamber door jerked her upright, and she turned from the window, heart in her throat. It sounded again, a harsh rattle that portended a foe on the other side. But then she heard, loud and sweet, a familiar voice.

"Milady! 'Tis Belle! I beg of thee, let me in. . . ."

Annice was already running toward the door, grateful to hear Belle's voice. She was alive, and now there would be two of them to watch and wait. P'raps she bore news, or had been sent from Rolf to fetch her.

It took her a moment to lift the heavy bar sealing the door, but with a loud scraping it was shoved aside. As she tugged at the door's handle, it was roughly pushed from outside, almost knocking her down. Staggering slightly, Annice's heart plummeted to her toes.

Belle did, indeed, stand in the doorway. But 'twas with a dagger poised at her throat, wielded by a man-at-arms in Mowbray colors. He grinned at her. "Very wise, milady. Bid us well come. . . ."

Hard on the echo of his words, three men rushed into the chamber, grabbing Annice by both arms to hold her.

Weeping, Belle wailed, "I did not want to betray thee, milady! But they would kill me ere I did naught do what they said. . . ."

"I do not blame thee," Annice said, glaring at the soldiers crowding into the chamber. "I blame craven men who would hide behind a woman's skirts to gain false entry."

"False entry it may be," one of the men-at-arms said shortly, "but we were bade to bring thee to our lord by any means. And that we shall do."

Aghast, Annice began to struggle, realizing even as she did so that 'twas useless. She could only pray that Rolf would rescue her. And that he was still alive and unharmed.

Sir Guy painfully dragged himself from his cot, sword clutched tightly in one hand. It took him several minutes to reach the gallery overlooking the hall. One hand propped against the floor to hold himself up, he grasped one of the wood spindles with the other and pressed his face against it. Panting, he surveyed the scene below with horrified eyes. One of the huge doors leading into the hall hung askew, swinging slightly from a broken hinge. Daylight streaked inside, a hazy shaft spilling across the hall's floor. Armed men fought furiously, swords clanging and glittering as they battled across the rushes.

The screams of serving wenches caught between oppos-
ing forces only added to the chaos. The excited baying of
hounds clashed with the angry shouts of struggling men. A
table toppled over into the rushes with a loud crash, sending up a geyser of straw and chaff. One of the wall hangings
tumbled down atop two of the combatants. They struggled
to free themselves, looking for all the world like the
humped back of a dragon thrashing upon the floor.

"*Merde*," Guy muttered softly, teeth clenched against
pain, and the damnable fog still clouding his brain. He released the wood spindle and groped blindly for the hilt of
his sword. His first instinct upon recognizing the sounds of
battle had been to grab his weapon. He should have at least
paused for his crutch. There he lay, dragging one leg, unable
even to walk, he thought disgustedly. He should never have
taken the second draft of herbs. The first had been enough.
Now his mind was hazy with blurred images, coherent
thought flickering in and out like sunlight through dark
clouds.

Reaching up, Guy grasped the top post of the railing
that enclosed the musicians' gallery. He slowly pulled himself to his feet, using the hilt of his sword as a crutch. Then
he leaned against the railing to peer down into the hall.
Curse them . . . the rebels sought to cause trouble between
le Draca and the king. If they could take Dragonwyck, they
would have a key strategic position that commanded a
goodly portion of Lincolnshire. With other shire rebels, it
would be near impossible for John to conquer them.

And he would come once he heard, of that all could be
certain. Whatever else the king was, he was also tenacious
about those lands he considered his. He would promptly set
out to subdue the rebels. The offensive would divide his
forces in half, weakening him, but he would not care for
that. Nay, the king was not as cagey as Richard had been
when it came to strategy. That character flaw had most like
prompted these rebels to attempt Dragonwyck.

Divide and conquer. Yea, ages old, the ploy still worked
more often than not.

Guy breathed heavily with the effort to stand. Disabled
as he was, to enter the fray would mean certain death. But

to hang back and watch was torment. He was no archer, but even a bow and quiver full of arrows would be better than helplessly watching slaughter.

And that was what the fray appeared to be. Caught by surprise and still wine-fogged, Dragonwyck men-at-arms fought valiantly but ineffectually. Few had managed to rally. But where was Rolf? The Lord of Dragonwyck should be amongst those below, defending the inner sanctum of the hall.

Guy searched the combatants but did not see him. Though it seemed like hours, the fighting had spanned only a brief time. Was Rolf even down from his chamber yet? Had no one thought to inform the lord of the assault? It was inconceivable that he had not heard the din of battle, even besotted as he might be with his new wife.

But Guy determined to investigate, to ascertain himself that Rolf was awake and aware.

It took him thrice the normal time to traverse the winding steps that led upward. By the time he reached the top, his leg was dragging even more painfully. He ignored it as best he could. Still, he was forced to pause for a rest, leaning back against the wall, dragging in deep gulps of air.

His sword clanged lightly against the stones, and he shifted it to the front, resting both hands on the cross hilt. God's mercy, but the drug in his body still raged, making his ears ring and his head buzz as if filled with straw dust. He shook his head slightly to clear it, then went still.

Voices drifted down to him from the upper hallway. A woman's voice was sharp and angry, and he recognized Lady Annice. Was she with Rolf? Ever was she annoyed with him, it seemed, but he did not think she would be speaking to him with that particular tone. There was contempt in her words, though he could not make out the content.

Cautiously, he withdrew in a stumbling gait toward a curtained alcove. Barely had the curtain shifted to hide him than the voices came into close proximity.

"You will ever regret this, you ignorant fool," Annice said sharply. "When my lord hears what you have done, you will have scant time to bemoan your hasty actions."

"When your lord hears of this," a man's voice snarled,

"he will most likely do exactly what is expected. 'Tis not my concern who he belabors for this deed, for he will naught have long to think on't."

There was a brief silence, and Guy could hear the stomp of boots and scuffle of feet over the stones. Weapons clinked softly. His fist curled in impotent rage over his sword's hilt. There were several of them. If he tried to intervene, he would only be killed. If the attempt would save the lady, he would gladly die. But he knew that his death would not aid her. Any information he learned might.

Scarcely daring to breathe, Guy strained to listen.

"What of your lord!" Annice was saying scornfully. "He is aught but a peacock stuffed with conceit if he thinks to best Rolf of Dragonwyck. Do you think Sir Rannulf capable of meeting the Dragon in a fair fight?"

"Rannulf?" The man-at-arms laughed harshly. " 'Tis not Sir Rannulf who is clever enough to concoct such a scheme as this. Nay, milady, you credit that cackling peahen with far too much intelligence."

"If not Sir Rannulf," Annice asked, her voice fading as they passed by the alcove and began to descend the stairs, "then 'tis the Earl of Mowbray who dares commit such folly?"

Another laugh greeted this question. "Thou art fool indeed to think that William of Mowbray would have the courage to dare such as this, milady."

"Then who?" Annice demanded, her words hardly audible as they descended the curving staircase.

Almost stumbling in his eagerness to hear, Guy clutched at the curtain with a quick hand as he leaned closer. Barely drifting back to him on an errant current came the word, "Seabrook . . ."

Guy muttered a soft oath, fist tangling in the heavy material of the curtain. Thurston! Aye, that wily earl had intruded where he should not, for when Rolf discovered the truth, he would raze Stoneham Castle to the ground. Nothing but smoking rubble would be left.

Footsteps and voices faded away. Guy stepped cautiously from behind the curtain and glanced around. No one was in sight. Pricked with urgency, he started forward in a hobbling gait, using his sword as a crutch. The tip dug into the stone with a scratching rasp, and he almost slid before he caught his balance. Then he moved to the wall, sliding his hands over the stones to support himself, grimly determined to reach Rolf.

He had to get to him, had to inform Rolf of the true identity of their attackers. With the invaders clad in the disguising colors of Mowbray, it was a certainty that the innocent William would be blamed. Anxious that Rolf quickly learn the truth lest he send out forces in the wrong direction, Guy began a cautious descent down the stairs. He was forced to go slowly, fighting the almost overpowering urge to rush.

Focused on his goal, he did not see the man behind him until too late. It was only the slight sound of a step and the casting of a shadow that gave him warning enough to lurch sideways, and the blow struck him on the side of his head. Pain blinded him, swooping over him with dark wings to usher him into oblivion. As he fell headlong down the stone steps, the anguished thought occurred to him that it would be too late to retrieve Annice from Thurston's hands. Then all went black.

CHAPTER 13

Darkness slowly shrouded the inner ward of Dragonwyck. Shadows stole over stones slick with blood and scattered with bodies. The grating creak of the portcullis rising mixed with the sounds of groaning men and the clank of weapons.

Grimly, Rolf surveyed the carnage. Many of his men were dead. Of all the invaders only a few remained alive. Those who could had managed escape. The others had been taken below to await questioning in the dungeons. The colors of Mowbray were almost obscured with blood and sweat now, but he could find little satisfaction. Long had he abided close to William of Mowbray, and though they did not agree on John's rule, both men had kept a cautious truce. 'Twould weaken their forces were they to come to battle, and he could not understand Mowbray's sudden decision to end that unwritten pact. Yea, these were perilous times indeed, when men would rend asunder beneficial truces.

Rolf had entered the bailey with his armor still unbuckled in places, using his sword to cleave a path to the guardhouse and his groggy men-at-arms. He'd rallied them with curses and blows, spurring them to battle Mowbray's forces. It had taken great effort, and at times he'd thought the contest lost, but at last they had prevailed.

Weary, he lifted an arm to remove his helm. Sweat banded his forehead and stung his eyes. His armor had been hastily if not properly donned and had shifted, cutting into unprotected skin in places. Corbet would be horrified by such carelessness. If he had survived, Rolf amended silently. The young squire had not been seen since early morn, when the battle had raged so fiercely inside the hall. The last he'd seen of him, Corbet had been herding hysterical serving wenches to the comparative safety of the kitchens.

With the approach of sunset and the battle done, servants were emerging from their hiding places. Most knew better than to intrude in the midst of warfare, risking injury or death from even their own should they be in the way. It was one of his strictest rules, that should the castle ever be attacked, noncombative residents were to seek shelter as best they could. Long had it been since Dragonwyck had suffered a direct assault. Not since the early days—when scaffolding still clung to half-finished walls and men still dug the inner moat—had any dared invade his keep.

Now, surveying the damage wrought by Mowbray's forces, Rolf fought a rising surge of fury. Yea, he would muster his men and retaliate, and Mowbray would ever be sorry that he had begun this conflict. Not even the king would dare interfere.

With his helmet tucked beneath his arm, Rolf strode toward the ruined doors leading into the great hall. He had best send word to Annice, lest she fear the worst. He was faintly surprised not to have seen her, as the battle had ended an hour before.

The sight that met his eyes when he entered the hall again was hardly surprising, but he still felt a tremor of shock. Hangings had been pulled from walls and shredded. Tables were overturned, some now fit only as firewood, and benches were scattered. Candle stands had been knocked over, and there was a huge charred circle in the rushes where a fire had ignited and been put out. Bodies were being removed and the wounded cared for, and he walked among them offering comfort where he could.

Even his dog, Bordet, had been wounded. As Rolf approached, thinking the dog dead, it lifted its great head and whined, tail thumping against bloodstained rushes. Rolf knelt beside the faithful animal, anger filling him anew.

"Ho, my loyal servant," he said through a tight throat, and the dog dragged its tongue over his hand as if offering comfort. A deep gash had been cut into his ribs, bone showing a dull white through the blood-matted skin. He fondled the dog's ears gently.

"Milord," a soft voice said, and he looked up. Belle stood in trembling uncertainty, but he saw no sign of Annice.

"Yea, girl," he said roughly, and gestured to the injured dog. "See that Bordet is cared for as well as the others. He has long served me faithfully, and I would see him cared for, too."

After a brief hesitation Belle nodded. "Aye, milord, I will tend him myself. 'Tis said that I have a gift of healing and have long studied the ways of herbs and poultices."

She paused again, hands twisting in agitation, and he frowned. "Is there more you wish to say? Tell me, and then take word to your mistress that she is needed here."

"But, milord," Belle blurted, breaking into sobs, "that is what I maun tell ye!"

Rolf rose slowly. Impending doom hovered, and he sensed that he would mislike hearing what she would say. "What? What wouldst thou tell me?" he demanded in English.

Gesturing to the dog, Belle said between shaking sobs, "It was hurt trying to protect thy lady. I could do naught, though I tried, my lord, I swear I did!"

By now Rolf had grabbed her by the shoulders, cold seeping into his very bones as he tried to make sense of the girl's babbling. He gave her a harsh shake.

"Where is she? Where is Lady Annice?"

"Gone . . . they took her . . . soldiers . . . and Sir Guy is missing—"

Releasing her with a shove, Rolf stared incredulously at

the girl as she gestured toward the stairs leading upward. Sir Guy? Was he involved? Was it he who had taken Annice?

Already striding toward the stone steps, Rolf did not at first see the limp form lying at the foot of the stairwell. It was Belle's cry that alerted him, and he paused and looked down.

Guy FitzHugh lay still and pale upon the stones, leg twisted at an awkward angle beneath him. Kneeling, Rolf stripped off a gauntlet and placed his hand upon Guy's throat, fingers back-curled into his palm as he felt for a pulse. It was there, thready and weak, but a definite sign of life. Still kneeling, Rolf pivoted to scowl at Belle.

"Has no one seen to him? Would you have let him lie here until he died? Here—come with me."

Scooping Guy up in his arms, Rolf carried him into a chamber. It had seen fighting also, and furniture was overturned and shattered. He kicked a broken chair from his path and moved to a corner to place Guy gently on a pile of torn-down hangings. They cushioned him, and he motioned for Belle to come forward.

"Stop that foolish wailing and see to his hurts. I will find a man to come help."

Tears wet her cheeks, and Belle mumbled, "I did naught see him until thou almost trod upon him, milord, I swear it. . . ."

"Silly wench. Isn't there enough to think about without trying to explain?" Rolf glanced down at Guy. He'd been struck upon his head. A bloody gash still oozed, but it was shallow and only appeared mortal. "He'll come round soon. Ask him what he knows," Rolf directed, then left the chamber.

Within minutes he had a squire tending Guy's hurts as well as the dog's, while he took the steps two at a time. He knew what he would find when he reached the bridal chamber, but the sight still took him aback when he stood in the doorway.

The door had been left ajar, creaking slightly when he pushed at it with one hand. Bed hangings were shredded, torn down or left hanging by barely a thread from the bedposts. Annice's trunk had been opened, and its contents were strewn about the floor. Broken shards of glass were scattered on the carpet. The table that had been burdened with wine and food was broken, one leg snapped in two, the food dumped onto the floor. A pile of silk caught his attention, and he shoved away from the door frame and crossed the chamber.

Amber silk and cloth-of-gold lay in a tangled heap. He knelt slowly and lifted the silk, remembering Annice clad in the beautiful gown, her face hopeful as she'd looked up at him before the church altar. God's teeth, but he was an utter fool at times. He'd hardly been able to look at her, so full of misgiving he'd been. Being too close to her, too caught up in emotion, was a new sensation for him. A dangerous one.

Wadding the silk in one fist, he knew now why he'd resisted any tender emotions. 'Twas much safer to feel only lust. Anything more was a risk he'd not been prepared to take.

Shadows crept across the chamber, and the light through the open windows grew fainter and fainter, until he was left kneeling in the dark. When he finally lifted his head, it seemed to him that he had knelt there on the littered carpet, with the remains of Annice's garments, for an eternity.

Shreds of daylight barely lightened the sky outside the window, and he stood slowly. His legs were cramped, and he suddenly felt all the aches and hurts of the day. In the thick of battle a man learned to disregard the sting of sword cuts and the impact of weapons. Once the battle was ended all his wounds tended to hurt at once.

He frowned down at the colors he held in his hand, the amber and gold. A nagging memory pricked him, and he thought again of the invaders. They had worn the colors of Mowbray, but there had been no rallying cry to that standard. Now that he pondered on it, there had been a furtiveness about the soldiers that smacked of more than treachery.

Releasing the amber silk, he let it drift slowly to the floor and turned to the door. Vachel stood there, a dark shadow against light from wall torches in the corridor. A familiar voice in the night.

"Milord . . . Sir Guy is awake and asking for you. He says it is urgent he speak with you."

Rolf nodded stiffly. "Yea, Vachel. I begin to think I know what he might say."

The chamber where he'd left Guy now had several more occupants, all being tended. Even the dog lay stretched upon a pallet of blankets, bandaged and sleeping. Rolf crossed to Guy's pallet and sat down on a stool at his side. The wounded knight's head was wrapped in linen; his voice was slurred but amazingly vigorous.

It came as no surprise that Thurston of Seabrook was behind the unexpected assault. Rolf was vaguely surprised that the earl had been able to accomplish his ends so easily. Rolf had the bitter thought that had he not been so intent upon the lady, he would have paid greater attention to his instincts and taken better precautions.

As if reading his mind, Sir Guy said hoarsely, "No man could have known what he was about, milord. To put a traitor in our midst and use Mowbray's colors—even the king should condemn him for this."

"But will he?" Rolf's smile was mirthless. "And even more, will the lady wish it? She left so quietly, with none to mark her passage, that I begin to wonder if p'raps she did not encourage Seabrook to rescue her. It would not be impossible to annul our vows, though all in the village were witness to the lady's oaths."

"Nay, milord," Guy protested, trying to sit up. He stared at Rolf for a moment, then said, "You foully misjudge your lady."

"Do I?" Rolf shrugged. "Mayhap. But recall, Sir Guy, that she was abducted against her will. The vows were spoken against her will, even though in front of the king's men as well as mine. It is not impossible that she made a pretense of accepting John's edict to catch me off guard."

"Not impossible," Guy snapped with remarkable vigor, "but highly unlikely! She is a woman of honor, and you do her a great disservice by thinking otherwise."

Looking away, Rolf muttered, "I hope so. Yea, I pray that I am wrong." His hands curled into fists on his bent knees. He felt helpless and wanted to mount an entire troop and follow the intruders without waiting for light. Unfortunately, the men were exhausted, those who had not already been injured, and there would be little light to show them which direction had been taken. Patience had never been one of Rolf's greatest virtues, and it was even more chafing now.

A wall torch sputtered loudly, and sparks shot out in a sizzling arc to shower down. Rolf reached out to brush a glowing ember from his arm. He still wore his mail. He'd left his helmet somewhere but did not know where. P'raps by the dog, when he'd knelt in the rushes to see to it. Or even by Guy as he'd knelt to feel for a pulse, or in the wrecked bridal chamber.

"Milord." Looking up, Rolf saw Vachel hovering nearby, a silver cup of wine in his hand and an anxious expression on his face. "Fortify yourself with this, milord. I have seen to the comforts of your chamber and sent Corbet to ready your weapons for the morrow."

"Corbet." Rolf drew a weary hand across his eyes. "He is safe, then. I wondered. Gareth of Kesteven will go with me. We leave at first light. See that the men are well provisioned and rested. I will not return to Dragonwyck without her."

"Aye, milord." Vachel held the wine closer. "Sir Rannulf and Sir Cleit beg leave to speak with you. As does Robert de Vieuxpont."

Rolf frowned. "What of Sir Simon and Sir Richard?"

Vachel hesitated, then said, "They have not been found, milord. I do not think they are among the dead or wounded."

Glancing at Guy, Rolf said slowly, "If they are not found, I will assume them guilty of treachery. Do their men stay?"

"They brought only a few men with them, and some of those serving Sir Simon are still here. They do not know where their lord has gone. Whitby's men are disappeared."

After a moment Rolf said, "Have Sir Rannulf and Sir Cleit meet me in my chambers. And send Corbet to me, if he is not already there."

"Milord," Guy said with a troubled frown, and Rolf looked back at him. "There is something I should have mentioned, but it did not seem important at the time . . . Sir Simon. During the hunt he was not with us. When I found you, I could have sworn I saw him in the trees just beyond the clearing. But then everything happened so quickly, and when I was gored—"

Rolf put up a hand to stop him. "Do not think on't now. First I must go after Annice. Sir Simon will turn up soon, most like."

Rising, Rolf met Guy's gaze. His earlier suspicions were not entirely eased by his knight's injuries, or his protests. Sir Simon had said Guy had driven the boar toward him. It would be reasonable for a man to attempt to place a seed of doubt in his mind—but was it Guy? Or Sir Simon? Rolf sensed Guy was still holding something back, though he did not know what it could be, if not his guilt.

Guy cleared his throat and gestured to his injured leg. His voice was helpless and frustrated. "I could not go to the lady's aid, milord. If I could have done so, I would have. My first thought was to warn you, so that you could halt them. . . ."

Rolf put up a hand. "Nay, Sir Guy. Whatever else I might think, I know you would not willingly allow harm to come to my lady."

"Would that I were riding with you on the morrow," Guy muttered in frustration.

"I need all my knights, but only those able to ride," Rolf replied with a faint smile. "Tarry here and heal. As I am taking every man who can still ride with me, I leave the keep in your hands." His voice hardened slightly. "Do not fail me, Sir Guy."

After an instant's silence when the only sounds in the chamber were the sputtering of torches and the dog's labored breathing, Guy said clearly, "I will die ere I fail you or your lady, milord."

"Should you fail me, you may wish for death long before it comes," Rolf said slowly, and saw that Guy understood.

CHAPTER 14

_____

𝕴t was raining. Miserable, Annice huddled in her hooded cloak and prayed for deliverance, as she had done since being taken from Dragonwyck. The first day had been a blur of fear and fury, hours of hard riding, furtive paths, and a long night spent under a hayrick. At first light the men had split up into different routes.

Annice despaired. Rolf would never know which path to follow, which group of men-at-arms had her. And she would soon be at Stoneham, and far removed from his reach. How Thurston must have cackled with glee while planning this! 'Twas no wonder he had agreed so mildly to the wedding. He'd known she would not be at Dragonwyck for long. Her only prayer was that the king did not know of his intention and would disapprove. John could force him to release her.

Closing her eyes, Annice clung to the high bow of her saddle. Her horse was being led by a mailed soldier at a swift pace over the muddy track. Rain had swollen streams to overflow banks, and on two occasions they'd been forced to ford dangerously swift currents. The steady beat of rain would obliterate any tracks, making it virtually impossible for Rolf to follow.

If, indeed, he even attempted pursuit.

Would he? Their marriage vows had been spoken, the documents signed before witnesses, and the union consummated. Her dower lands were now in Rolf's possession. It would be easy enough for him to relinquish his wife and still retain control of her lands. The king's agent would validate their wedding. God's grace, the vows had been spoken in front of vassals and villeins alike. It could not be disputed, and she had not disavowed him. Yea, 'twas legal and binding, and she caught as neatly as a hare in a trap.

Grabbing at the saddlebow as the horse slid into a muddy rut, Annice struggled to keep her balance. Rain slashed down in an increasing tide, and she glared at the man leading her horse.

"Does your leader intend that we drown ere we reach our destination?" she snapped, and the soldier flicked her a sodden glance.

"When we halt, ask him yourself," was his sullen reply. 'Twas plain he was no more pleased by the weather and arduous pace than she. His helm was wet with rain, huge drops trickling down the noseguard to drip into his beard. The tunic he wore over his mail was drenched. Every time his horse shook its head, rain flew out in all directions, spraying the soldier. None of the others seemed to be faring any better.

Trees crowded close to the roadside, leaves dripping with rain. Branches were slick and wet, and the steady sound of driving rain spattering on ground and leaves grew louder. It threatened to be a torrential downpour. Thunder rumbled and growled, a low, ominous accompaniment to a wretched day. Horses trembled, some snorting nervously.

Finally the leader of the small group called a halt. A thick row of tall hedges formed a shelter of sorts, scratchy and dark, but at least providing some respite from the rain. Staggered at intervals, they huddled beneath sheltering branches to wait out the worst of the storm.

The sharp scent of wet horsehide, wool, and earth surrounded them, mingling with the brisk fragrance of hawthorn. Shiny dark-green leaves with jagged edges like teeth trembled in the wind. Thorns scraped over her arm, snagging the cloth of her cloak when Annice pulled it closer around her. Tiny flowers the color of a blush clustered on the branches, the new buds shuddering under the steady beat of rain.

Breaking apart a crust of bread, the soldier leading her horse held it out wordlessly to Annice. She took it. There might be no more food offered until they halted at dark.

"God's mercy," she murmured, and he nodded shortly. The bread was damp and stale but filled her rumbling stomach. She chewed slowly to make it last. After several minutes, when it seemed as if the rain would continue, she glanced at her guard. Still chewing, he stared straight ahead, eyes fixed on the muddy mire of the road.

"Are we near our destination?" she asked without any real hope he would reply.

Leather creaked as he shifted position in his saddle. "We do not travel straightly," he answered. "We go a roundabout way."

"To discourage pursuit, I presume," she observed, and the guard nodded.

"Aye," he said. " 'Twould not be safe to risk the Dragon's wrath."

Annice stared at him. "Do you think you have not already done so? Holy Mary, but when le Draca discovers us, you may well wish that you had not been unwise enough to join this doomed band, Sir Fool!"

The soldier turned his head to glare at her. "You may jape, my fine lady, but 'tis not I who am a hostage. Does it matter so muchly to you which man be your master? Truly, you are as much a pawn as any serf of my acquaintance."

There was too much truth in his statement to deny, and Annice shrugged. "Mayhap, but you are a free man. You have leave to choose the manner of your life—and your death. It seems that you have done both already."

For a moment there was only the sound of rain, restless horses, and the murmur of the other men under the trees. Then the guard said harshly, "My lot in life was chosen at my birth. I but fulfill my destiny, as have scores of other men born free in principle but bound by poverty. My father was a soldier, and his father before him, back to the time of William the First. 'Tis all we know."

Annice was silent. This nameless soldier embodied most of England. All were caught up in the steel links of destiny, it seemed, save for those strong and ruthless enough to break the chains that bound them, to embark on new lives. She counted herself among the former. She, too, was caught in a web she could not escape. Her circumstances might differ, her prison be made of silk and velvet instead of mud and wattle, but 'twas a prison nonetheless. Rules were strict, the bars invisible, and stronger for all that they could not be seen. Even serfs enjoyed more freedom than she.

If Rolf came for her, would her life be any different from before? Nay, she would still be bound by social strictures, her life at the whim of another. Not just her husband, but her king held her pinioned.

Hail began to fall. Pea-sized pellets bounced in the rutted road and off tree branches, occasionally penetrating the dense hedges to pelt those huddled beneath. Annice watched as hailstones cluttered the wagon ruts cut deep into the road, some disappearing in small mud puddles, others bouncing from the ruts' edges into hummocks of grass.

A horse blew nervously, and one of the soldiers coughed. Her guard sat still and quiet, face stony in the gloom of hawthorn branches. For several moments the hail crashed down in a noisy rattle that shredded leaves and pinged against metal helmets. Then it quit as suddenly as it had begun, leaving hailstones like bits of marble strewn across road and grass. Clouds blew past in a race against the wind, and sunlight peeked through in erratic patches. The tiny stones began to melt, reflecting light in icy sparkles.

They rode out from under the trees and into the road again, hooves sliding and squelching in mud and sodden leaves. Annice curled her fingers around the high bow of her saddle and tried to pray. No words would come; only the overwhelming press of hope filled her mind and soul.

The road curved ahead, disappearing into a shadowed line of trees. Light shone in silvery ribbons of water filling the ruts. Across a vale of jeweled green, a rainbow arched in iridescent color. 'Twas said to be God's promise to the world that he would not destroy it with flood again. Annice's father had once jested that it left Him with a vast array of disasters to ruin the world. There were those men who garbed themselves in robes of fustian and intoned the End was at hand, but they were generally considered to be heretics.

Sometimes she wondered if they meant 'twas each person's own world that was jeopardized by disaster. If so, hers was in grave danger now of being destroyed.

As they passed into the trees again, leaves blotted out the sunlight. The road was not so muddy there, as branches laced overhead to form a latticed roof of leaves. All was hushed, soft sound seeming to echo from each side of the densely wooded road.

Her horse's pace quickened suddenly, and its ears pricked forward. Annice turned to see that her guard had straightened in his saddle and put one hand upon the hilt of his sword. Her heart thumped hard against her ribs. The six men that accompanied them had already drawn their weapons in a rasping slide of steel. Her hand went to her waist before she remembered that her dagger had been taken from her.

Before she could ask what was afoot, a deep-throated bellow rang from just ahead. Startled, she thumped her heels against her mount's sides even as her guard was jerking on the lead rope. It had the effect of sending her horse plunging forward in a series of bucking motions that almost unseated her.

Then everything became chaotic, with shouts and bellows and the clang of swords. Annice clung to the high saddle bow with both hands while her guard managed to shorten her plunging mount's rope so that it could not rear. After a few more energetic hops, the horse settled into a brisk trot.

The hood of Annice's cloak jostled lower over her head, half blinding her as they galloped along the narrow dirt track. She had vague glimpses of her guard and a blur of trees and wet earth. Glancing back at her, the man growled a command to hold tightly. His mouth set in a taut line, and chinks of sunlight glittered on his helm and sword.

"You are to stay close to me, milady, no matter what happens," he ordered tersely. "I will let no harm come to you."

"Are they outlaws?" she gasped out, clawing at the edges of her hood with one hand.

Outlaws were the scourge of the forests, hiding in thick trees to wait for their victims. They didn't just rob travelers, they slew them so that there would be no witnesses against them. Those outlaws who were caught were quickly hanged, sometimes after having limbs and eyes removed, but it did not seem to be much of a deterrent.

Annice knew that 'twas unlikely outlaws would attack an armed band of obvious soldiers. Even in a caravan it was unlikely that she would be slain. Her ermine-lined cloak and elegant garments would convince any outlaw to hold her for ransom. Yea, her fate would be the same, whether she was taken by outlaws or carried safely to Thurston of Seabrook. It was not as comforting a thought as it might have been. Ever had she been a pawn, ever would she be one, a source of profit for men.

Her guard increased his speed. The others were left far behind. Chunks of mud flew from their horses' hooves, spattering the dragging hem of her cloak and gown with streaks of brown. Sounds of fighting still echoed behind them. The clang of swords and shouts were distant now, muffled by trees and the labored pace of their mounts. Annice leaned forward to duck a low-hanging branch, looking up as she did. Shadows dappled the ground, light flickering over the road and a dark form in the midst of it. Then a bright wash of sunlight broke through the clouds and leaves overhead, illuminating the form.

Catching her breath, she barely managed to choke back a scream at the apparition blocking the middle of the road. Huge and fearsome, with smoke seeming to coil all around it, a glittering beast that shimmered green and gold and black barred their progress. Silhouetted against ghostly light, it appeared to be aflame. For a moment her heart stood still, and she heard her guard cry out a prayer for mercy.

Annice felt faint. Holy Mary and Joseph! A dragon—all smoke and hellfire, giving a loud roar of rage to make the trees shake. In the deep gloom of shadow and misty sunlight, it pranced forward. No clumsy lurch of scaled beast this, but a graceful turn of legs and body.

Then she realized that it was a destrier bearing a rider in full armor. The smoke was only hazy streams of sunlight filtering through moisture-laden air, eerily lighting the knight's colors and sending up misty vapors from the ground. Her guard had checked his horse's pace with a sharp tug on the reins. The animal reared back on its haunches, front hooves flailing, and Annice's horse careened to the side to barely miss a collision.

She almost slid off but managed to cling to the saddle, heart pounding with fear. Her breath came in short pants. Through the tangle of her loose hair and disheveled hood, she saw the knight ride close and challenge her guard. Though the voice was muffled by the loud rush of blood in her ears, she knew him.

"Rolf," she breathed softly. Her guard had lifted his weapon and backed his horse next to hers, intent upon remaining between them.

"The Dragon," he muttered, and there was fear in his voice. Then he straightened in the saddle, and she heard him say, "I am sworn to guard this lady with my life."

Before she could stop him, tell him that 'twas her husband who had come to her rescue, Rolf had spurred his destrier forward to meet the defiant soldier. Sunlight skittered along his uplifted blade, gleaming bright and lethal along the edge. Wulfsige's great hooves churned furiously in the wet road, and the ground shook from the force of his heavy gallop.

To meet this challenge, her guard turned his mount to take the brunt of the impact, his own sword and shield held at the ready to parry the thrust. Annice closed her eyes and shuddered. She heard the first clash of swords, the horses' grunts of effort, and the rasping breaths of the two men. She could not bear it.

Opening her eyes, she saw that Rolf's attack had carried him past them, and he was already turning Wulfsige. The well-trained destrier positioned himself for the next assault, while Rolf tightened his grip on sword and shield.

"Nay!" Annice shouted, spurred into action by the sight of her guard's bloodied arm. "Do not, my lord!"

She tried to kick her mount forward, but the horse only snorted and backed into a hedge. Desperate, she flung herself from its back and into the road, stumbling to her hands and knees before regaining her balance. Hands outspread, she staggered to the middle of the road.

"Nay, milord," she panted, "do naught!"

The destrier pranced impatiently, chafing at the bit, nostrils flared and pink. Annice saw Rolf's eyes beneath the helm glitter at her with icy green fury.

"Move from the path," he snapped, but she shook her head.

"Nay. But listen. . . ."

Her guard growled something she didn't understand, riding close enough to her to yank at her hood. "Milady, I repeat that you are in danger!" he said more loudly.

She glanced over her shoulder at him. " 'Tis le Draca—'tis you who are in the greatest danger," she shot back.

Her guard glanced toward Rolf, and his jaw clenched. "I was sworn to see you safely to Stoneham," he said stubbornly.

Though she couldn't have said why—p'raps 'twas because he had said what he had about being born to his station in life—she felt an obligation to keep him from harm if possible. He had not been unkind to her, for all that he had intended to return her to Thurston.

"Surrender or he'll kill you for certes," she retorted. There was not enough time to be tactful and spare words. "Is Seabrook worth your death? I think not. I know him, and he will not thank you for risking your life, nor even for losing it."

The man hesitated, eyes flicking toward Rolf. His grip tightened on his sword hilt. "I swore an oath."

"To see me safe? Then release me to my husband."

"The Dragon?" Uncertainty tinged his voice. His mount shifted restlessly beneath him. "I was told that you were abducted and in danger."

"Yea, that I was, but we are now wed." She glanced at Rolf, who sat silent and furious, watching them with narrowed eyes. Taking a deep breath, she looked back at her guard. "Only yesterday we swore our vows before a priest and half of Lincolnshire. Would you steal a wife from her lawful husband?"

His sword wavered, and he shifted his shield slightly. After a moment he shook his head. "Nay. But you were forced to wed."

"Nay, lower your weapon, brave knight. I wed him most willingly. Be certain there is no shame in yielding what you have sworn to protect to the man who first swore to keep it safe. . . ."

After a moment he slowly lowered his sword, though he kept his shield at the ready. Rolf did not move but sat his destrier in tense silence, and Annice began to think he would not accept surrender. There was a fierce light in his eyes, and his huge mailed fist still held tightly to his sword.

Then, finally, he bent his arm to touch the flat of his sword against his helm in a salute. Wulfsige pranced forward, snorting and shaking his great head with a flurry of his long black mane.

Riding to where she stood in the center of the muddy road, Rolf bent slightly to lift her. His arm curved around her waist, and he held her suspended for a moment, staring into her face. Then he placed her in front of him so that the high bow of the saddle dug almost painfully into her thigh. She ignored the discomfort. Relief flooded her. He had come for her, when he could so easily have let Thurston reclaim her.

"Give me your name," Rolf said past her to the knight.

After a brief hesitation the man replied, "I am Sigehere, milord. In service to the Lady of Seabrook."

"You are a courageous and loyal protector, Sigehere. There is always a place in my keep for men of your stature, should you ever decide to leave your overlord. But hear me well—I will not suffer more attempts made upon my lands or my lady. If not for her interference, you might well have earned your death this day."

"If not for her interference," Sigehere replied, "I would not have yielded."

Rolf nodded. "I hope that if we meet again, it is not on the field of battle."

Glancing behind him down the empty road, Sigehere apparently decided that his companions were not able to join him. He looked back at Rolf and nodded slowly.

"Yea, lord, as do I."

"Go, and tell Lord Thurston that you succeeded in your mission. The lady is safe—with her husband."

A faint grin split Sigehere's face, and he shook his head. "I do not relish the reaction to my message, milord."

"I regret that I cannot deliver it myself." Rolf's arm tightened around Annice's waist, and he kept a steady hand on the reins to calm Wulfsige. The destrier was restive. "My advice is to ride to the east, then circle back. My troops are much about, and they are not in a pleasant mood of late."

Reining his mount around, Sigehere nodded. "God's mercy, my lord of Dragonwyck."

"Is it true?" Annice asked when Sigehere had gone. She twisted to look at Rolf. "Are your troops spread about to search for me?"

Rolf's gaze was icy. "What was that man to you?" he asked abruptly. "Did you know him at Seabrook's keep?"

Annice stared at him. "Nothing more than my guard. I have ne'er set eyes on him before yesterday," she replied.

Some of the tension in Rolf's arms eased, and she realized that he had thought the man a favorite of hers. Irritated, she gave him an exasperated look. It was not the time to explore the subject, but when he was calmer and they were rested, she intended that he not view every man she met as a possible suitor for her hand. Did he think her so ignorant of her station in life that she would dally with a soldier?

Easing her arm around his lean waist, she murmured with a sigh, "I thought you would never arrive, my lord. I had begun to suspect that you wanted Thurston to take me back. Has marriage palled upon you already?"

She had meant to tease him gently, to ease him from his sullen mood, but from the sudden flare in his eyes she knew she had erred.

In scant moments Rolf had swung down from his horse

and taken Annice with him. She was crushed against his chest, her cloak dragging in the mud of the road as he crossed to a copse of dense brush and trees. Without a word he snatched her cloak from around her shoulders and flung it to the ground atop a layer of leaves and grass. Then he pushed her downward with one hand, kneeling to loom over her.

For a moment she thought he meant to take her, there by the road upon a bed of cloak and leaves, but he only put both hands on each side of her so that his face was almost touching hers.

"Do not," he bit out through clenched teeth, "ever come between me and another enemy. Not all men would be so easily checked as Sigehere. If he had chosen to fight, you would have been wounded, yea, and possibly killed." He paused to draw in a breath between his teeth. "And do not think I would allow Thurston to take one more bit of my life from me. He has all he will take from me, and if I have to tear all of England apart to retrieve it, I shall do so."

"Yea, lord," she managed to say softly.

Rolf's nostrils were flared, his eyes a hard, glittering green beneath the curve of his lashes. Even his mouth was hard, set into a taut line as he stared down at her. He sat back a little and worked at one of his gauntlets, removing it. Then he touched her face, her brow, cheek, and lips, before he lifted a free coil of her hair in his fist. His eyes closed, and he held her hair to his mouth and breathed deeply. She did not move or speak, did not dare to while he slowly let the tension in him fade. For long moments they sat there beneath the wet leaves of the thicket.

When he looked at her again, the fire was gone from his eyes and his mouth had eased into a faint smile. "I feared I would not be able to overtake you before Stoneham," he said simply. "The delay was so long, and I was not certain which band of soldiers had you."

She rested her palm against his bearded jaw. "I prayed you would come for me. How did you find me?"

"Sir Simon." When her brows lifted in astonishment, he said, "He saw some of the men take you and recognized one of them from Seabrook's keep. Taking only a few men, he was able to follow without being seen. 'Twas Sir Simon who intercepted us with the direction."

"What of my other vassals? Do they live?"

Rolf looked down at the loop of her hair he held in his hand and frowned. "Yea, as far as I am aware. Sir Simon and Sir Cleit rode with us until we split into different bands. 'Twas Sir Simon who bade me take this road, thinking that the abductors would go this way."

"And Sir Richard de Whitby?"

Rolf's frown deepened. "He nor his men remained at Dragonwyck when the fighting was done. I know not which side they chose."

She expelled a long breath of disappointment. Sir Richard had long been a vassal of Beauchamp. That he had obviously chosen to side with Thurston was discouraging, but not unexpected. She studied Rolf's face for a moment.

"You do not suspect him of being the traitor, do you?"

He flicked her a glance and shrugged. "I do not know. Someone opened the postern gate to allow in the enemy. If not Sir Richard, then it must be someone else we did not suspect."

"To have a traitor in our midst, supping at the table, drinking wine with us—milord, he must be found and hanged."

A faint smile curved his lips. "Vicious little countess. Yea, I do agree. Or best, his identity must be discovered without his being made aware of our knowledge."

"What? You would let a traitor live?"

Rolf shrugged. " 'Tis always wise to keep one's friends close, and one's enemies closer yet. If we do not kill the traitor, then he will be much more valuable."

Straightening, he held out a hand to her to pull her to her feet. "Come, wife. We shall return to Dragonwyck and prepare a warm welcome for the viper in our midst. Pray he returns."

"But how will we know?"

" 'Twill be simple. The traitor will be the man with the most charming smile and facile explanation for his absence from the hall."

It was not a very comforting thought.

CHAPTER 15

Dragonwyck torches had already been lit, though night was yet a vague blur of shadows hovering over the forest spires beyond the village. The portcullis lifted with a scraping of chains and loud rattle to allow the returning troops and their lord passage inside. Hoofbeats echoed forlornly on the stones of the outer bailey as they crossed the drawbridge and entered.

An eerie silence pervaded the castle. Rolf glanced up uneasily at the murder holes pocking the walls overhead, half expecting to see a flurry of enemy arrows descend upon them.

But nothing moved there. Beyond the distant clatter of the guards in the barbican, he had seen no signs of familiar life. His hand tightened upon the hilt of his sword. Had the invaders returned in his absence? Sir Simon, riding behind him and abreast with Annice, muttered a soft oath, and it was echoed by another man.

It was Sir Rannulf who voiced aloud his fears. "Milord," he said, spurring his mount next to Rolf in the narrow passage, " 'tis dismal and quiet for a keep of such size. Is't always this way upon thy return?"

"Nay." Rolf's short answer did not satisfy Sir Rannulf, who kept his eyes shifting from wall to wall as if expecting men to leap out at any moment. After a moment Rolf added, "No doubt Sir Guy has given orders to watch us closely. The traitor has yet to be caught."

Rather taken aback, Sir Rannulf protested, "But he would hardly ride with you, milord!"

Rolf slid him an amused glance. "How not? He sat at my table, ate of my meat, and drank of my wine—would he not be bold enough to ride at my side disguised as friend rather than foe?"

Sir Rannulf's mouth opened, but no sound came out. Then he gave a shrug. "Yea, I see the sense in it. Yet it leaves us all as suspect, to my mind."

"Yea, Sir Rannulf. That is quite true."

Whatever Sir Rannulf would have replied remained unspoken, for at that moment the small band of men passed under the arch and into the inner bailey. Remnants of the battle were evident there. Workers had cleared most of the mess of shattered furniture and charred rushes from the hall, and there were piles of wreckage scattered about waiting to be carted away. Puddles of rainwater dotted the stones in places, reflecting towers, walls, and torchlight in undulating images. The smell of roasted meat teased him, and a fire burned against a far wall.

Armed men lounged about amidst the ruins of a burned-out stable, wearing the king's colors. *Peste!* Rolf thought grimly. Just what he needed at the moment, an envoy from John. He reined to a halt near the guardhouse steps. Echoes from Wulfsige's hooves had barely faded into the deepening shadows before Vachel rushed down the guardhouse steps to greet his lord. Close behind him came squires and servants, quickly filling the bailey with noise and laughter. Wary knights relaxed at the return of normalcy and began to dismount.

"Milord. You were successful in retrieving your lady, I see."

Rolf glanced at Vachel and smiled. "Yea. Did you doubt it?"

Already shaking his head, Vachel looked around and motioned for Corbet to assist the lady from her mount while he stood by Rolf's stirrup. The steward knew better than to attempt to hold the destrier's head, for the testy stallion would have more than like taken a hefty bite from whatever portion of Vachel he could reach first. Vachel was understandably skittish around the animal, though as long as Rolf was present, he suffered the close proximity quietly.

Dismounting, Rolf held the reins in one hand. He waited for Corbet to assist Annice and come for the stallion. Weariness rode him hard, and he suppressed the urge to relinquish his horse to Vachel without waiting for his squire. Since well before first light, he had been up. Plans had been made far into the night, and he'd snatched a few hours' rest before rising. A sense of urgency had pricked him into wakefulness, so now that he knew Annice was safe, exhaustion tugged hard.

Vachel kept a wary eye on Rolf's destrier as he quickly informed his lord of arrangements for castle security. "Sir Guy awaits in the hall, milord. As you must have noted, there are guests," he added, taking Rolf's shield. He beckoned to Corbet, who escorted Annice past Wulfsige. Thrusting the shield into the squire's willing hands, Vachel stepped back to allow the squire to take Rolf's weapons.

Rolf put a hand upon the hilt of his sword when Corbet reached for it, shaking his head. He did not yet feel comfortable without a weapon, king's men or no. Nor did most of the knights who had ridden with him feel at ease, for they held to their weapons also. The bailey was astir with squires and knights and weary horses. Stone archways provided shelter for some; for others, closely woven hemp stretched over poles. A metal spit and sizzling meat hung over a fire. The tantalizing smell of roasting duck mingled with the odors of wet horse and burning wood.

With Wulfsige in Corbet's capable hands, Rolf escorted Annice into the hall. There order had been restored. Tables were being set up for the evening meal, servants bustling about as normal. Torchlight and a fire cast a cheery glow over the scene. At the far end, sitting with his leg propped upon a low stool, Sir Guy waited. With him were two of the king's men in full armor, neither of whom Rolf recognized.

His hand went to the hilt of his sword as he strode forward, leaving Annice with Vachel. Both men turned to face him warily.

Struggling to stand, Sir Guy's face contorted in pain, and Rolf waved him back down. "Stay seated, Sir Guy. And present these visitors to me, if you will."

Both of the armored men exchanged quick glances, but it was Guy who said, "They come on the king's business, milord. Lord Henry of Bartelow, and Sir Francis of Epworth. 'Tis said the king wishes—"

"Lord Dragonwyck," the taller of the two men interposed, "allow me to explain. I am Lord Henry. The king has asked that we bring word to you of his pleasure with your recent marriage. Also, we are empowered to present to you an invitation to meet him and his royal entourage in Poitou with all due and seemly haste." Lord Henry smiled, but his eyes were cool and watchful as he regarded Rolf.

Rolf did not return his smile. He recognized a royal ploy when he saw one and knew well what was afoot. "I am honored, but as you can surely see," he said, waving a hand to indicate the bailey beyond the double doors, "we have had trouble of late. 'Twill be impossible to leave my lands at this time. Tender my regrets to the king."

"That is not possible, milord." Lord Henry stiffened. "Even now King John journeys between Niort and La Rochelle. He expects to see you with him again."

Tired and impatient, Rolf glared at Bartelow until that man dropped his gaze. "I have paid my scutage," he ground out slowly, "as well as given knights and vassals in service. I have fought in every war but am absolved from fighting Philip in a foreign war. Surely the king does not wish for me to risk my lands to an invader to fulfill a whim."

"A whim?" Sir Francis frowned. "I would not deem a command from the king a mere whim, my lord. Nor is this struggle with Philip to be deemed a foreign war. John seeks to regain lands that rightfully belong to England. I do not view it as fighting on foreign land."

"Nay, p'raps you would not, but in this circumstance I view it in that manner. I have been loyal, and I am holding my lands from those who would be disloyal to the king. Does he wish to risk more men and money in the hands of the rebels?"

Glancing about at the evidence of recent fighting, Lord Henry said, "What say you—that this conflict is the result of barons rebelling against John? I thought it a mere quarrel between neighbors."

" 'Tis much more than that." Rolf drew in a deep breath. "If you wish to learn more, please yourself by asking Robert de Vieuxpont or the sheriff of Lincolnshire. Both were here, and both are men astute enough to see the reason behind the taking of my wife."

Lord Henry looked uncertain. "I was not told your wife had been taken."

"Yea, and taken back," Rolf growled. He half turned and indicated Annice and Vachel at the other end of the hall. He beckoned them to depart with a flick of his hand. "See you that she is with me again. And so shall she stay, whether any man wills it or no. That she was abducted from me is a flagrant defiance of the king's command. The act smacks of treason, do you not think?"

Without waiting for a reply, Rolf demanded the latest news from France. After a brief hesitation Sir Francis revealed knowledge that was already common, and Rolf smiled slightly. He saw Guy shift uneasily in his chair. 'Twas obvious the king's men did not trust him. He supposed it was just as obvious that he did not care if they did not. Weariness pressed hard on him, and finally he abruptly took his leave.

"Sir Guy will see to your needs, and I will speak with you further on the morrow," he added, then quit the hall. He could feel the glares directed toward his back but ignored them. His leaving was a direct insult, but he was too weary to concern himself.

Annice was swift and efficient when he gained their bedchamber, directing servants in a soft voice to see to their lord's needs. Garbed in clean garments, her hair was still damp from her recent bath, waving down her back in shiny tendrils. Like a changeling, she'd transformed from untidy hostage to meticulous housewife.

Glancing around, Rolf saw that the chamber had been made orderly again, the mess wrought by Thurston's men cleaned up and removed. He sank to the hard comfort of a chair, his mind lingering on the summons of the king. 'Twas said that John's fight against Philip was going badly, and that the king was desperate for men and arms. John had turned his attention to La Marche, Count of Lusignan, after subduing Limousin and Gascony. Defeated nobles had either sworn fealty and given hostages, or been executed. 'Twas a simple enough process for John. But what did he want with Rolf? The scutage had been accepted readily enough. A number of Rolf's knights were still in France. Did he mean to levy more fines on him? Or did he simply mean to make it impossible for Rolf to refuse to fight?

Holy Mary, but he was weary of war, weary of the strife between king and barons. Would there never be peace in England? Was there always to be conflict? Yea, he answered his own questions, as long as John was king, there would be warfare. The monarch was possessed of a devil that would not rest, but ever made it impossible for men to subsist in peace.

"Husband," Annice said softly, and he looked up at her. A faint smile curved her lips, and she knelt beside his chair so that her face was level with his. "There is the morrow to deal with the king's business. This eve you should rest and gather your strength."

He gazed at her for a moment. Guileless blue eyes gazed back at him, and he felt a moment's shame for the doubts he'd had. Nay, she did not seek to deceive him. None of the recent events had been at her wish or of her blame.

Reaching out, he curved his palm beneath her chin, fingers gently cradling the smooth skin. "Sweet wife," he murmured. " 'Tis possible that I will be forced to join John in France. Will you suffer yourself to be left behind?"

"Am I being offered the choice of going with you?"

Startled, for he had meant only to learn if she would miss him, Rolf asked, "And would you go if that was my offer?"

"Yea, lord. Whither thou go, I will goest also." She smiled and lifted her hand to place it over his, holding it against her cheek. "I am sworn to be your wife, and would always be near you."

"Because of your vows?"

"Yea, and because I cannot bear to be apart from you."

Her simple words took his breath. He stared at her intently. Their silent communion was broken only by the entrance of a servant. Regretfully, he let his hand fall away from her face, and Annice rose to direct Belle and Corbet in the placement of a wooden tub.

Hot water was brought, along with scented soap and thick towels. Belle scattered spices in the bathwater, while Corbet struggled with the huge bucket of hot water. After filling the tub more than halfway, the young squire set down the bucket and turned to his lord.

"Shall I ready you for your bath, milord?" he asked as was his wont, but Annice intervened.

"I shall tend him," she said, and from the tone of her voice it was plain she desired no assistance.

Corbet withdrew gracefully, taking the bucket and exchanging a quick glance of amusement with Belle as he did so. The young maid opened the pot of soap and set it on a table near the tub, then stood uncertainly for a moment.

"That is all I require for now, Belle," Annice said pleasantly, and the girl dropped a slight courtesy with an expression of relief before retreating. Annice stood still a moment, then turned to Rolf.

Sprawled in his chair with legs thrust out in front of him, he cocked a questioning brow at her. "Am I to await your pleasure also, *milady*?"

Annice moved to the door and, with an effort, lowered the bar. Then she turned around and leaned against the closed door. Her heart was beating furiously. She was risking rebuke for acting without his knowledge, but she wanted him to herself. She did not want to sit and watch his squire bathe him, nor even wait impatiently until he was done. Nay, she wanted to touch him, to feel his skin beneath her fingertips and reassure herself that he was, indeed, there with her.

"Yea, lord," she only said demurely, and pushed away from the door. "Does it displease you that I wish to act as your squire this eve?"

Rolf grinned. Despite his obvious weariness, there was a gleam in his eyes. "Nay, lady fair. I believe I prefer it. Though you have not Corbet's dexterity, neither do you have his annoying habit of bouncing about like a loose hare in a wine barrel."

"Is that the only reason?"

" 'Tis but one of a dozen." He shifted in his chair, eying her with the grin still on his face.

Annice moved to him, eyes downcast as she knelt and began to unbuckle his belt. He held out his arms to allow her easy access. The sword clinked softly against the chair as she laid it down, arms straining from its great weight. It amazed her that Rolf wielded the weapon so easily, as if it were a feather. She was forced to use both hands to keep from dropping the heavy weapon.

When she turned back to him, he was gazing up at her with a speculative lift of his brow as if to ask what she wished next. First she pulled the coil of mail from over his head. It caught in a tangle of his hair, and she worked the tiny links free, then lay the mail hood aside.

"Please rise, milord," she murmured, and when he did, she tackled the buckle of his belt. It took her only a few moments to recall how difficult it could be to remove a man's armor. After removing the wide leather belt and surcoat, the close-knit links of chain mail resisted her efforts to unfasten the small buckles at the back. Rolf did not speak or help but stood quietly while she fumbled with them. At last she had them undone and helped him out of the hauberk. The thick aketon that formed his padding and kept the mail from chafing was much more easily removed. That left only his chausses, the mail leggings that were held up by straps to a waist belt.

Annice laid them aside also, then turned to eye him for a moment as he stood in his linen shirt, hose, and breeches.

"And 'tis said that women wear too many layers of clothing," she muttered, earning a laugh from him.

"Ah, wife," he said, reaching for her, "men only say that

because it takes us so long to attain the reward beneath infinite layers of silk and linen. A man must wear armor only to protect himself."

Allowing him to pull her close, Annice murmured, "And did you not think that a woman wears so many garments for the same reason? Ever are men eager to seek that elusive reward."

Rolf buried his face in the curve of her neck and shoulder, his words muffled in her damp hair. "Must it always be elusive?"

"Only to the wrong man, *beau* sire," she retorted, and pushed him away. She dared not let him see how easily he affected her, how he could make her yearn for him with the slightest touch, glance, or word. Shaking a finger at him in mock reproach, she said, "Thou stink of horse. Come, thy bath awaits, ere thou grow too amorous."

An amused smile touched his lips and eyes, and he said as she began to remove the rest of his garments, "I can wait a short time, *chérie*."

His husky words made her heart lurch, and she kept her gaze stubbornly lowered when he was naked. He laughed softly and stepped into the tub, sinking down with a grunt of pleasure.

Annice took up a pot of soap and began to lather it into a square of cloth, focusing on the soft, perfumed soap instead of on Rolf. It smelled musky, like sandalwood, and she breathed deeply of its spicy fragrance. When she looked up, Rolf's head was tilted back against the edge of the tub and his eyes closed. He'd rested his arms along the edge of the wooden tub. His hair was matted and dark where the mail hood had crushed it to his head.

Resisting the urge to run her fingers through the dark gold strands of hair, Annice knelt beside the tub and bent her attention to scrubbing his shoulder, then down the length of one arm. Tiny pale scars marred the smooth skin in places, white against the darker hue. She dragged the cloth over his forearm and down to his thick wrist. His hand was large and well shaped, the fingers long and blunt. The knuckles were knotty, and there were numerous scars etched into the skin.

Without opening his eyes, Rolf murmured, "Not a pretty sight, at best, eh, *chérie*?"

"I think your hands most marvelous and capable," she replied truthfully. " 'Tis these hands that brought me back to Dragonwyck."

He opened one eye to peer at her from beneath the bristle of his lashes. "Once you would have cursed me for that deed. What has changed?"

What, indeed? She looked at him helplessly for a moment, unable to say exactly what had changed. 'Twas obvious her feelings toward him had altered greatly, but she could not say what one thing had worked such magic. P'raps it was more than one thing. P'raps it was all that had transpired since he'd first brought her to Dragonwyck. The honor and gentleness she'd sensed in him had slowly become more evident, despite her worst fears. Yea, and the spark of attraction she'd first felt had ignited into a blaze. But to try to explain her emotions when she was so uncertain was more than she could do.

She smiled slightly. "I like your cooks."

A dark-blond brow lifted and both eyes opened. "My *cooks*?"

"Yea. Never have I enjoyed such culinary masterpieces as those served by your cooks." She drew the cloth through the water to rinse it, avoiding his gaze as long as possible. When she lifted the cloth, he caught her by the wrist, mouth twisted in a wry smile.

"If you do not wish to answer, just say so."

She lifted her brow to mock his gesture. "I thought I answered your question right fairly, milord." Waggling the dripping cloth, she said sweetly, "Now, shall I wash your hair next?"

As Luc's wife, she had been accustomed to seeing gentlemen bathed and tended and usually thought nothing of it. It was a wife's duty to see to the comfort of her guests. Never had she been the least tempted by any man's form or presence, nay, not even Luc's.

But 'twas not the same with Rolf.

As he stretched out, extending his long legs until his feet rested on the rim opposite his head, she felt an odd unsettling. A quickening of her breath, a faulty rhythm in her lungs and heart that made her hand shake. To oppose it, she set her hand diligently to the task, washing first his hair, then his broad chest, his other arm and hand, and then his legs and feet. There was only the nether region beneath the water that remained to be washed, and she delayed by paying special attention to his toes. By the time she finished, he was gazing at her with a faintly challenging smile.

"If you would attempt a task," he murmured, "do it well and thorough, *chérie*."

She met his gaze reluctantly. He must know that she was not accustomed to bathing a man in so intimate a manner. Never had she done so, not even for her late husband. Yet Rolf tested her, and she would answer that challenge boldly.

Deliberately, she dragged the soapy cloth down the contours of his chest and belly, then beneath the water. She felt his muscles tense with reaction, and his eyes were startled when she began to scrub most vigorously.

"Is that thorough enough, milord?" she asked when he jerked upright. Rolf grasped her arm. Water splashed upward in a tiny geyser, wetting the bodice of her gown and her face. She blinked away droplets clinging to her lashes.

"*Merde*," he muttered through clenched teeth, eyes like green flames as he stared at her. "I did not think—if you hope to dampen my ardor, this is not the way to accomplish that goal."

Her fingers moved boldly, though her arm was still gripped in his iron hold. His response leaped against her palm. A smile pressed at the corners of her mouth. "So I see."

Rolf's grip on her eased, though his fingers remained curled lightly around her arm. His lashes lowered over the gleaming green of his eyes, veiling them as he looked down toward her hand on him beneath the water. Slowly, deliberately, she drew her fingers up and down the length of him, the exploration more bold for all that it was being made blindly. The water was warm and scented, the sensation of his wet flesh under her inquiring touch mysterious and heady.

Rolf's lashes drifted closed, and he gripped one side of

the tub with a fist. His hold on her arm loosened, then fell away, and Annice struggled against an odd pressure in her chest. This was exotic, exciting, a unique experience . . . she wasn't certain what to do, how she should proceed. None of her past had quite prepared her for this, and she was amazed at her own daring. Her fingers and palm shaped him with even bolder explorations.

Rolf shifted, and water sloshed against the wooden sides of the tub, washing over the rim and wetting her. Even through the layers of her garments, she could feel its perfumed warmth. The moment was a vast contrast of sensations—the heavy fullness of him pressing into her palm, a contradiction of velvet and steel, and the scented heat of water dampening her skin and garments, making the silk cling to her in rapidly cooling folds. Exquisite. Arousing.

Lifting her gaze from the blur of water and skin, Annice met Rolf's eyes. They were narrowed and hot, blazing like dragon-fire. She caught her breath. As if in the dreams she'd had those many nights, he rose slowly from the tub, naked and powerful and awakening a fire in her that raged wildly. Once more she saw him as she had in those dreams, a golden dragon of might and myth, reaching for her.

The dreamlike quality persisted as he stepped out of the tub and took her in his arms, his body pressed in steaming heat against hers. She was standing but did not remember rising to her feet. Her arms moved around him. Bending his head, he kissed her, his mouth hot and urgent against her lips, forcing them open. Annice swayed slightly. Her fingers dug into the damp skin of his shoulders and slid downward, the wet muscles slippery and fragrant with sandalwood.

"Rolf," she got out in a tortured breath when his hand found the aching peak of her breast. He raked his thumb over the hard nub pressing against silk. Feeling helpless and swamped by emotions that swirled around her with dizzying speed, she clung to him fiercely.

Rolf's breathing quickened. Spreading his fingers over her hips, he slid his hands downward, bunching folds of her gown in his fists. Gathering it slowly upward, he drew it to her waist. Cool air whisked over her bare legs and hips, and she shivered, clinging to his neck with both hands.

Jésu, but it felt so right—so wonderful—to have him with her like this. The world that had tilted so awry righted itself again. The fear and uncertainty of the past two days vanished, melting into the warmth of his solid body against her. Giddy with heart-swelling joy, she writhed invitingly against him.

Rolf muttered something indistinguishable. Then he swept her into his arms and carried her across the chamber carpeted with thick Eastern rugs to the bed. The embroidered silk hangings that had once swathed the bed were gone, and light from branches of candles flooded the interior.

Hardly had she landed on the comforting cushion of the mattress than he was removing her gown, fingers tugging impatiently at laces and silk. She put her hand over his.

"Let me," she murmured, slanting him a rueful smile. "With your ardor I shall have few gowns left. . . ."

But in the end, laces were ripped and silk seams rent asunder. With barely contained ferocity, Rolf divested her of the garments with a muttered apology and a promise to purchase more. Caught up in his fervent passion, Annice could not even pretend to care.

His urgency mingled with hers. He was rough, jerking the silk remnants of her gown from beneath her body, then capturing her wrists in one of his hands to pull her arms over her head. Flickering rose and gold candle flame lit the heated intensity in his features. Angled planes of hard cheekbone and bearded jaw, glittering reflections in his green eyes—she caught her breath.

Her passion responded to his, urgent desire clamoring for the sweet release she knew would come. His mouth found first one breast, then the other, tongue washing over her with arousing diligence. The teasing, stimulating rhythm of his tongue made her moan with exquisite delight. Wordless and helpless in his tight hold, she curled her hands aimlessly into the pillows beneath her. Her body arched into the caress, aching and quivering with expectancy.

"Rolf," she murmured in a lingering sigh when he

moved to press his lips against the slope of her cheek, saying his name twice more before his mouth claimed hers in a deep kiss. He moved lower, his body shifting atop her thighs.

"Open for me, lady fair," he muttered, his words raspy and thick against her throat.

Before she could comply, his legs parted hers, insistent and demanding. Bare skin was a searing heat against her thighs, the force of his weight pressing her down. Annice made a sound in the back of her throat. She twisted, arms still held above her head, his grip pinioning her to the mattress.

Rolf looked up at her, dragon-fire in his eyes, sweet ecstasy in his hands. His lips moved to her throat, then to her mouth. Releasing her wrists, his hands swept down in a breathtaking caress over her body, then moved to cup her bottom and lift her against him.

The power of him pressed hard against her aching entrance, seeking admission with a slow thrust. She arched to receive him, shuddering with pleasure. Tilting back her head, she drew in a harsh breath that sounded like a sob.

Yea, 'twas this fulfillment that beckoned her to him, this consuming passion that drew her to him as a bee to nectar. Only one thing could compare to the exquisite delights he coaxed from her willing body. Moaning softly, she surrendered to the aggressive power of his invasion, the burning intrusion that filled her world. When they were one, inseparable in body, she felt as if nothing could ever separate them in spirit. He was hers. Her wedded husband. Her life. Her love.

Tears stung her eyes, and her throat ached with emotion. She loved him. Yea, loved him fiercely. Nothing would part them again.

Moaning and writhing beneath him, Annice lifted her legs to draw him even deeper into her. Breathless from the aching need that filled her, the release that waited just out of reach, she strained to grasp it. Rolf moved inside her with increasing strength, until the need melted into fiery culmination. She cried out, unable to still her singing sighs of ecstasy. Shaking, she clasped him to her with trembling arms, scarce able to breathe as he paused for only a moment.

Burying her face in his shoulder as he thrust slowly into her at first, then more strongly, she slid her hands blindly down the ridge of his ribs to his waist. Holding him, she shuddered under the fierce impact of his body deep within hers until she felt him quiver. His breath was a harsh sob in her ear, his muscles taut beneath her hands.

Then Rolf moved hard against her in a racking shudder. He clutched her fiercely to him, shuddering again, his body going rigid in her embrace. A long, low moan vibrated deeply in his throat, and she turned her cheek into the pelt of hair on his chest. Harsh breathing shook him, drifting warmly across her cheek.

Annice held him as he slowly relaxed and the candles burned down. Deep shadows claimed the bed and its occupants. With Rolf still hard within her, they slept.

PART II

Nature's enemy, John.

—Twelfth-century historian

CHAPTER 16

Summer waxed strong in Lincolnshire. Rainy days melded into sunny weather, and crops grew abundantly green in the fields beyond Dragonwyck's walls. Inside the walls of Dragonwyck, the residents existed in a state of uneasy peace.

Though commanded to rejoin the king in France, Rolf sent more fines in lieu of service. There was still Thurston to contend with, and he had no intention of leaving Dragonwyck vulnerable.

Lord Henry and Sir Francis were only slightly mollified by the additional monies Rolf paid. The king's men refused to leave Dragonwyck before securing a pledge from Rolf not to mount an assault on Seabrook until the king had been given the opportunity to review the events. Reluctantly, Rolf agreed.

Once the king's men left Dragonwyck, Rolf assuaged the worst of his restless energies by tending the affairs of his keep. Though no traitor had been found lurking in the castle corridors, Richard de Whitby's treachery was suspected.

Only Sir Simon defended him, arguing that Richard was an honorable man. Yet when word came back to Dragonwyck that Richard had met an untimely end in a squabble with a neighbor, there were those who said he'd earned his fate.

Then Thurston dealt another blow by refusing to turn over the keys to his former ward's keeps. Citing civil cases, the crafty earl filed claims against Annice for debts. Bound by his oath to the king's men not to assault Stoneham Castle, Rolf found himself in the untenable position of being forced to petition an absent king for justice. He knew, even when he wrote, that John would not stir himself to a swift reply. His only recourse would be to go to John, but that would leave Dragonwyck undefended for too long.

Caught between the devil at home and the devil in France, Rolf chose the former. This devil he could fight. The king was another matter.

Of late there was enough to do hearing cases brought before him to be judged. Mornings were spent in the hall, where claims and pleas were presented by the people of his land.

"Milord," Guy said wearily one afternoon when shadows finally fell on the last petitioner of the day, "times are even more perilous now than before."

"Aye." Rolf stared thoughtfully at Bordet as the dog sifted lazily through the rushes for any forgotten tidbits from a former meal. Though the mastiff still limped, he was regaining his strength rapidly, as was Sir Guy. He turned to look at his knight. "Matters worsen."

"Depredations by dishonest sheriffs have increased tenfold," Guy muttered. "Now convicted felons lose their land and chattels, not to the mesne lord to whom it ought to revert, but to the crown by office of the sheriff who collected it. Organized rule has all but unraveled."

"Free men are being arrested, ejected from their lands, imprisoned, and even exiled and outlawed without legal warrant or a fair trial," Rolf observed heavily. "At the mere whim of the king, men are forbidden to enter or leave the realm. Those barons he favors or wants to appease receive licenses to impose arbitrary taxes on their subtenants without regard to the limits imposed by feudal custom."

"Yet still you hold to your oath of fealty," Guy said after a long span of silence.

Rolf looked up with a scowl. "Yea, though 'tis not of my choosing. I have never betrayed an oath."

"P'raps God would forgive breaking this oath," Guy muttered, and Rolf surged to his feet.

"Are you saying I should join the rebels, Sir Guy?" Rolf demanded harshly. "Speak plainly. I would not have you serve a baron whose sworn oath repulses you."

Rising also, Guy faced him without flinching. "Nay. I would serve you whether you are with the king or against him. My faith is placed in you, milord."

"Then cease testing it," Rolf replied after a moment.

"Nay, lord, I do not mean to test your faith, only the man in whom it is placed. The king cannot continue, or the entire realm will be in revolt."

"Do you not think I know that?" Rolf moved to the high table to pour himself some wine. He waved away the ready hand of a squire and poured a liberal amount into his cup. "It weighs most heavily on me that our sworn king views all of England as an open coffer for greedy men and monarch." He drained his wine and poured another cup. "Yet I must remain sworn to him, in faith, though I detest the man as well as his rule."

The last was said softly, almost to himself, but Guy heard. He took a limping step toward Rolf. "Is there nothing we can do, save open rebellion?"

After a moment Rolf said slowly, "There is Stephen Langton."

"The Archbishop . . ."

"He met John at Winchester last July. Stephen seeks fulfillment of the promise John made as a condition of his absolution—that the rights of all men should be restored. Lesser men as well as higher would benefit." Rolf sighed heavily. "But Stephen knows that this aim can be gained only with the aid of the barons. Those men aloof from the northern rebels—the earls of Salisbury, Chester, Albemarle, Warren—would be the most logical choices. And the men of high standing in the official class, such as the heads of

Aubigny, Vipont, De Lucy, and Basset would be of great service also."

"Do not forget," Guy muttered dryly, "that two barons of secondary rank have already proved themselves traitors and cowards."

"Eustace de Vesci and Robert FitzWalter." Rolf nodded. "Nay, I have not forgot. Nor has the king, I am certain."

"Yet they have received pardon and restoration of their lands. Is John mad?"

"As a fox. They are barons, yea, but who among the lower classes would look to them for guidance?" Rolf frowned, his hand curling tightly around the stem of his wine cup. "Langton has brought into light an old forgotten charter of King Henry the First. He proposes that all the barons present it to John as a basis of action."

"A charter?" Guy's face lit with interest. "What charter is this, milord?"

Rolf hesitated. To reveal information might be dangerous should Guy be a traitor. Yet what better way to discover his true motives than to offer information that would not be fatal if it were known?

"A most interesting charter that regulates relations between tenants-in-chief and the crown. Langton believes that this charter may open the way to wider reforms and help abolish unjust oppression. It would affect the nation as a whole, not just the barons."

"A charter giving freedoms to all?" Guy repeated slowly. " 'Tis unheard of."

"Nay, Guy. King Henry swore to it, though in truth, he meant not the lower classes, but the higher. Yet it bears merit, I think. Why not? Free men are oppressed just as knights, and even earls. We are all repressed in these times. Would you not welcome a charter securing your rights before the king? It would render John powerless to steal." A satisfied smile curved Rolf's mouth at the mere thought. "Yea, and what a sight that would be, a king with limited powers. . . ."

"The king will never sign such a charter," Guy said flatly. "He would fight to the last breath."

Rolf stared down into his empty wine cup. "I fear the

same. Yet he is alienating even his loyal barons with this latest scutage he imposed."

In May, John had issued writs for the collection of a scutage of three marks per fee from all tenants-in-chief, royal demesnes, vacant bishoprics, lands in royal wardship, and escheats. For those fighting with him, the scutage, as normal, was ordered by royal warrant to be paid. The northern barons who had refused to serve John now refused to pay him, contending with some precedent that they were exempt. Because of their tenure, they would not fight on foreign soil; they then claimed that this tenure also absolved them from payment in lieu of service in John's army. It did not absolve them in John's eyes.

Nor did it endear the king to his barons.

A patch of sunlight streaming through the high window fell over Rolf's face, warming his cheek. He turned toward the light, blinking against the glare. Brisk summer days would soon wane, and in their aftermath would follow the cold winds of upheaval. He could feel it, as one felt the changing of the seasons.

Yet he could not break his oath, though it might yet cost him what he held most dear. Thurston of Seabrook still held Justin, and the king delayed negotiations for the boy's safe return. If he broke oath with John, he might lose Justin forever. Could he risk that? Nay, he knew even as the thought formed that he could not. 'Twas not just for the sake of his oath that he held to the king—'twas for the hope that he would someday retrieve his son.

It didn't help to realize that John was well aware of the powerful lure he held above Rolf's head. As long as Justin was held hostage, so was the Lord of Dragonwyck.

Annice came upon Rolf in the hall. He was seated on a stool near the fire, light from a high window dancing on the deft motion of his dagger moving over a length of wood. She stood there a moment, watching. The shape of a horse was clear, with flowing mane and tail, though the legs were yet to be defined. She did not have to ask for whom the figure was being carved.

He did not look up when she dragged a stool near but kept whittling at the wood. Tiny chips fell to a growing pile between his feet. Light gleamed in his thick blond hair as he kept his head bent to his task. Annice seated herself and put her hands on her knees.

"Do you put the Seabrook device on it for him?" she asked softly, and Rolf glanced up at her.

"Yea. 'Twas his request. He wishes his mother's arms as well as mine. If ever I see him again, he shall have both."

After several minutes of silent watching as he worked, Annice murmured, "I think you wise to heed the king's wishes in this. It would only be more trouble if you yielded to the impulse to storm Stoneham's walls."

Rolf flung her a bitter glance. "Yea, I am become most wise in my dotage, I think." He slashed at the wood with his dagger, gouging a deep gash in the horse's tail. Tightly gripping the wood figure, he took a quick breath. His knuckles were white; frustration carved deep furrows in his face. "Or p'raps I have only grown cowardly of late. Not long hence I would have done more than sit by a cozy fire and wait for permission from the king to act. Yea, I would have done as a man, and gathered my troops to assault Stoneham and take it apart stone by stone to retrieve my son." White lines formed around his mouth, and he took another harsh breath.

"You would do Justin little good hanging from the king's gibbet, I think," Annice said. "Nor would it aid him to have his birthright revert to the crown at John's pleasure. Is that what you wish?"

Flinging the wooden horse from him, Rolf surged to his feet. "Nay! What I wish is to *act,* not sit in my hall like a statue and wait for others to arrange my life." He turned abruptly away and raked a hand through his hair. Staring up at the zodiac signs painted on the high ceiling beams, he muttered, "Mayhap I will join the king in France. Fighting Philip would ease the tedium of waiting."

Standing to face him, Annice tried not to flinch from his rage. She understood it. Moreover, she felt the same frustration herself. But she knew—as he did—that to act foolishly would only undo all that they had tried to do.

After a moment she took a deep breath and said, "P'raps I should go to Thurston myself to negotiate for Justin's release. If I gave him some of the dower lands he covets, he might—"

Rolf whirled around. He grasped her by the shoulders. His fingers bit deeply into her skin until she gasped. "Do not even think it for an instant," he ground out between clenched teeth. "I will not risk you as well as my son with that viper!"

" 'Tis obvious John will not act," she said as she eased from his painful grip. "Our only recourse is to negotiate with Seabrook by offering a prize more tempting than your suffering."

Rolf's laugh was hollow. " 'Twould have to be all of England, France, and p'raps Spain to tempt Seabrook into yielding that pleasure."

He looked away from her, and light spangled his lashes like fine gold dust, making him blink. Annice lifted her hand to gently touch his cheek. His gaze shifted back to her, eyes an anguished green. It was like a dagger blade piercing her heart, to see his pain and not be able to alleviate it.

"My sweet love," she murmured as she stroked his bearded jaw, "if it were in my power, I would yield all of England to Thurston for your son. Yea, and heaven, too, if it would ease you."

He caught her hand and pressed a kiss into her palm. "If you wish to ease me, sweeting, do not even suggest risking yourself. I have enough to bear now without losing you as well."

It was the closest he had come to an open admission of love. Never had he said he loved her, though she thought he viewed her as more than a chattel. She took as evidence the sweet words he whispered in her ear, and the small kindnesses he gave without prompting. Gifts appeared as if by magic upon her chair, or wrapped in silk mantles draped on the bed. Thoughtful things—silver combs and brushes, a huge globe of amber with an insect trapped for all eternity in its translucent depths, silk ribbons for her hair, and even a necklace wrought of intricate gold with sapphire stones.

Yea, though he had not said the words, his actions bore

proof of his sentiments. There were moments, in the gray shadows of early morning, when she still faced her doubts, but those times were few.

Turning into his embrace, Annice drew a shaky breath as he held her close. It was too strangling, this love for a man. It washed over her in smothering folds at times, threatening to drown her common sense with fear for him. Yet she would not change it if she could. Instead, she clung to her love for him as if to ward off evil. Surely, nothing too fearful would happen to her once she had finally found true love.

Tears stung her eyes and filled her throat, but before she yielded to them, something cold and wet nudged her side. She jerked away from Rolf, gasping, then looked down and saw the source. Bordet nuzzled her again with his wet nose. She pulled away from Rolf and bent to pet the dog.

Rolf stared at them with a look of surprise. "He comes to you now?"

She looked up, smiling. "Yea. Since I cared for him while he was injured, he seems to have taken a liking to me." She stroked Bordet's silky ears. "After all," she murmured, "he was wounded in an attack on Thurston's men when they were abducting me."

For a moment Rolf was silent. Then he said, "I should not be surprised, I suppose. You have managed to enchant everyone else in my keep. Why not a poor dumb creature?"

"Are you angry with me?" Annice stood up to face him. "Would you prefer that the dog hate me?"

"Nay. Don't be foolish. It's just . . . he has never cared for any other person before." He smiled faintly. Then he put a hand out to touch her cheek in a light caress. "It never occurred to me that even a dog would fall under your spell, sweet enchantress."

Annice said, "More like the dog was attempting to bite the intruders, not save me in particular. I just happened to be there when he went for the throat of one of my captors."

"And he missed?" Rolf looked down at the huge mastiff. "I've never known him to fail before."

"Nay, I did not say he missed. If another had not used his sword, the man would have had his throat torn out. Bordet failed only because of greater force."

As if sensing they were discussing him, the dog looked from one to the other, ears pricked forward. Then he yawned hugely and ambled away, his gait still slightly askew. Rolf laughed.

"I think we bored him."

"No doubt." Annice snared Rolf's attention by the simple expedient of turning his face toward her with a finger against his jaw. His eyes registered faint surprise, and she smiled. "Milord, if I displease you in some manner, tell me. But do not think I will scurry to do your bidding as if a common serf. I am your wife. I belong to you, but so also do you belong to me. I am respected here because I am your wife, and because I command respect. I am not an enchantress, nor a sorceress, nor a witch. I am a woman. I have but simple means to gain my ends." She paused to take a deep breath, then said, "All I do, I do because of you. I share my burdens with you, and I expect you to share yours with me. I want to help you retrieve your son. If I can do even a little, you should allow me that much. Would you not battle for me and my interests?"

"Yea." Rolf's smile was crooked. "I would have gone to battle for your lands before now, if not for the king's denial. It would be treason if I were to—"

"Rolf, oh, sweet lord, I did not mean . . ." Annice faltered to a halt and stared at him helplessly. He had missed the point of her words, but without saying it plainly, she could not make him understand that she was willing to share the burden of his son's loss. How did she tell him that she had suffered such losses also, and that he was no less of a man if he eased his pain by talking to her of it? Her dower lands meant much less to her than his son did to him, though in truth, she did want to regain what was rightfully hers. But they were of far less worth than one small boy, and she would never equate the two.

When Rolf pulled her to him, arms folding around her, she rested her face against his broad chest. His heartbeat was strong and steady beneath her cheek. She closed her eyes, consumed with fear for him. He would not oppose John, not even for that which he most desired. Yet if he would not defy the king, she had no hesitation about doing so. She had sworn no oath. There were ways to accomplish her ends that had nothing to do with treason. Or with sorcery. She smiled against his velvet tunic. Yea, she knew a method that might regain all and confound Thurston of Seabrook and King John at the same time. But it would take infinite planning and all her courage to manage it.

CHAPTER 17

ⓄOctober winds blew strong around Dragonwyck's turrets. An uneasy peace lay on the land, after a summer of strife. When the days grew shorter, easing into the chill winds of autumn, corn and wheat were gathered and meat salted for the approaching winter. Now that John was back in England, all waited uneasily for his next move.

In July, John had suffered humiliation and a setback in his struggle to defeat King Philip. Though John's siege of La Roche-au-Moine was on the verge of success, Philip's son Louis advanced from Chinon to relieve the garrison. With English troops swollen in number by mercenaries and newly conquered barons from Poitou and Anjou, John was poised and ready to fall upon Louis. The prince issued a public challenge, which John eagerly accepted, having the greater number of forces. Then treachery fell upon the English in the form of the Poiteven barons, who refused to fight against their overlord's son.

Instead of attempting to reason with the Poiteven barons, John burst into an insulting tirade, and the barons deserted. The king was forced into retreat, fearing Prince Louis on one side, risking defeat if he lingered in Anjou. From La Rochelle a week later, John wrote to England and asked that all who had not accompanied him over the sea come to his aid, unless their presence at home was especially required by his representatives in government. He added the inducement with all its sinister undertones, "And if any one of you should think that we have been displeased with him, his surest way to set that matter right is by coming at our call."

Even Rolf could not ignore that underlying threat. He prepared to rejoin the king, calling vassals and knights still in England to arms. Yet before he could complete the muster of his men, word came that the king's forces had been completely routed at the bridge of Bouvines on Sunday, July 27. John's plans were shattered in a single stroke. To the consternation of his loyal barons, John refused to admit total defeat. Ever eager to defeat Philip, the king ordered three hundred Welshmen to join him over the sea before the end of August.

Then the pope interceded with a plea for peace between the warring kings, threatening ecclesiastical censures. Rolf delayed his departure, certain that John would now retreat. In mid-September, a truce was signed by Philip and John, proposed to last for five years from the following Easter, of 1215. In mid-October, John returned to England, smarting from defeat.

Now, to add to already overburdened tax collectors, John added new fines to pay the cost of the war. Loyal and rebel barons alike groaned under this new burden. Men spoke openly of rebellion, and the realm seethed with civil unrest.

"If not for those treacherous Poitevens," Sir Guy muttered to Rolf as they lingered in the hall after the evening meal, "western France would now belong to John. Instead, our troops came home beaten by the French. And to what reward? A new scutage."

"Yea, though 'tis true he is owed the fees." Rolf frowned into the fire. "Three marks is a lot to pay—he must be maddened by his defeat to risk open rebellion."

Guy sat forward, his gaze fixed on Rolf. "Do you think there will be open war now?"

After a moment's delay Rolf said slowly, "Not yet. Most have grown too wary, and to that end I credit Stephen Langton's fine hand. Now the archbishop has called a meeting of the barons." He lifted his gaze to meet Guy's stare. " 'Tis to be held the first week of next month at St. Edmunds abbey. The pretext is to discuss this new scutage. And to pray."

The fire popped and crackled, an ember flying out to land at Guy's feet. Idly, he pushed it back toward the hearth with the toe of his boot. "And the real reason? What other things will be discussed, do you think?"

"Of that, Guy," Rolf said heavily, "I mean to find out."

"Do you go, milord?"

"Yea." Rolf dragged a hand over his beard. "I like what I have heard about this charter Langton has dredged up from old kings. It might be the saving of the realm if John should be persuaded to sign this charter."

"And if he does not?"

"I dread to think." Rolf turned to look into the leaping flames. "All of England will be consumed by the conflagration that will be inevitable. . . ."

Leaving Annice in the capable hands of Gareth of Kesteven as temporary castellan of Dragonwyck, Rolf also left behind most of his men as a deterrent should Thurston learn of his absence. He took Sir Guy and a small body of men-at-arms with him to Bury St. Edmunds. He was greeted there enthusiastically by open rebels hoping to draw him to their cause, but none publicly questioned which side he would choose. There were many others there like him, cautious and curious. Even his brother Geoffrey was present, having traveled from his lands in Cheshire to the meeting. They met gravely, under the circumstances both wary of the other's intent. All listened attentively to the archbishop's plan, then left quietly and separately to consider what they'd heard.

On the forty-mile journey back to Dragonwyck, Rolf

pondered aloud his brother's presence there, discussing it with Guy as they sat close by the campfire that night.

" 'Tis said that some of Geoffrey's lands have been deseisened of late by the king. He protested but recovered only partially."

"Why were they taken?" Guy asked. He'd met Geoffrey of Hawkhurst before, and liked him. He was open and brash, more prone to levity than his younger brother, but with the same leonine look about him.

"Most like," Rolf said dryly, "because Geoffrey did not stop to think before he spoke out against the sheriff. He is quick of temper and action, only later suffering the outcome with regret."

Guy grinned. "It must be a family trait."

Snorting, Rolf muttered, "At least I do not have cause to regret losing my lands because my tongue was too quick. If anything, I have been much too temperate of late. I should have done as Geoffrey would have done and razed Stoneham to the ground when first Thurston took my son from me."

Guy was quiet for a moment, pondering the truth in that statement. Then he sought to change the subject, seeking to draw Rolf's mind from his own problems to the one facing all of them.

"Do you think the king will seriously consider the charter?" he asked as he huddled deep into his mantle and held his hands out to the blaze. Wind howled like demons in the trees surrounding them, making the fire dance and the men-at-arms shift uneasily.

Rolf stared into the yellow-and-orange flames as if they held the answer, then shrugged. "If the barons present the charter to the king calmly, he will at least read it without tearing it to shreds first."

"That is no answer," Guy complained with a sigh.

Rolf smiled slightly. "Nay, but 'tis the only reply I can give at this moment."

"Do you not have your own opinion?"

"Yea," he said after a moment, "but it may not be what you wish to hear."

Guy shivered, and not from the cold. His leg ached from

the raw weather they endured, throbbing where he had been wounded. He shifted his position, easing his still tender leg to a more comfortable posture while he studied Rolf.

"Tell me," he persisted.

Rolf's gaze shifted from his contemplation of the fire to his knight, and Guy had the uneasy feeling that his lord still regarded him with mistrust. There was constraint between them now, where once there had been none.

"I think there were barons present at this meeting who *want* rebellion and strife—those who hope the king will not calmly regard this charter but fly into one of his Angevin rages and provoke the few faithful barons he has left."

Guy lapsed into thoughtful silence. He feared there was much truth in what Rolf said. He stared beyond his liege to the shadows in the night, the huge gnarled oaks with winter-bare branches thrust starkly into the sky. His breath formed frost clouds. Rain was in the air. By morn it would be upon them, flooding the roads and slowing their return home. It would be a miserable ride.

But at the end of their journey would be Dragonwyck, with its steep stone towers and battlements gnashing like dragon teeth against the sky, promising sanctuary and welcome to weary men. Lady Annice would greet them in the bailey upon their return, her beautiful face concerned for their safety, eyes lighting when she saw Rolf.

Did Rolf even know what a rare treasure he held in his grasp? Never had Guy seen his lord betray by word or gesture any love toward his lady, though there were moments when his gaze rested upon her with obvious desire, and he did not mistreat her.

Thinking to remark in some fashion upon the lady, but not wishing to arouse Rolf's suspicions about his feelings for Annice, Guy said casually after a moment, "Has the king replied to your petition to him against Seabrook?"

"Nay." Rolf tossed another stick into the fire, scowling. "Nor has he replied to my appeal for the transferral of Annice's lands to me, as set out in the marriage contract. Thurston refuses to open the gates to any of her keeps, and I am constrained against assault until John gives permission." Another stick landed in the fire, this one thrown with enough force to send up a shower of sparks. Rolf looked up at Guy. "My last petition stated my intention to lay siege and take possession, as is my right."

Guy stared at him. The fire cast light and shadow over his face in wavering patterns. "And did the king respond to that?" he asked when Rolf said nothing else.

"Yea. He forbid it." Rolf rose to his feet, staring into the dark shadows beyond the fire. "But I intend to ride upon Chesterton."

"Chesterton . . . milord, that is the strongest of the Beauchamp fortresses."

"Yea, and sworn by law and king to my lady. Once Chesterton falls, the others will hear of our strength and yield more easily."

Aghast at the implications, Guy floundered for words. To ride against a keep the king had expressly forbidden his sworn baron to assault—'twould be almost open treason. Did Rolf not realize that? Or was he so wearied of waiting for John to act that he did not care?

Guy opened his mouth to attempt to reason with his lord. Then he realized that Rolf was studying him closely from the folds of the hood, his face shielded.

"You do not approve of my decision, Sir Guy? Or do you have a better plan, mayhap, that will retrieve my son and heir and my lady's dower lands? If so, speak. I would hear it. I welcome any words of wisdom that might accomplish what I have not."

There was, of course, nothing Guy could suggest. Everything that could be conceived of had already been tried. Gentle persuasion, official petitions, even bribes.

Guy shook his head slowly. "Nay, lord. I know of nothing you can do."

Annice gave her escort an impatient glance. "Do you think we ride for pleasure?" she snapped. "Must you tarry?"

Rain misted the air and dampened his cloak as Gowain gave a mournful shake of his head. "Nay, milady. I know well this is no pleasure ride. I shall lose my head for this," he added in a gloomy mumble. "The Dragon will ne'er believe I did not want to go."

"If you don't cease your whining, I shall behead you myself." Annice spurred her horse into a faster pace. She must hurry. If Rolf returned from his journey to Bury St. Edmunds and found her gone, he would be on her trail at once. If she was still on the road when he overtook her, she would never accomplish her mission.

Behind her and astride a destrier that had seen more youthful days, Gowain gave an audible groan. Not wanting to attract attention, she had set out clad in a rough wool cloak that few serfs would deign to wear, bringing only one man. No baggage had been brought, and beneath his equally shabby cloak, Gowain carried only a sword. She prayed no outlaws would give them even a glance. Even her horse was scruffy, with a swayed back and long teeth. The poor creatures had been put out to pasture and resisted Gowain's halfhearted efforts to capture and saddle them. Only Annice's dire threats had spurred him on.

She was still surprised at how easily she had stolen away from Dragonwyck. Her plans had been carefully laid months before and waited only upon the opportunity. At first she had thought it would be soon, as Rolf would be joining John in France. But then, when the king's defeat had brought him slinking back to England, she had been forced to change her plans.

If not for this meeting in Bury St. Edmunds, she might have waited much longer. But now that she was on her way, she began to have doubts about her chances of success. That it was daring was obvious. That it would work—she prayed that God was with her. And that He would forgive her for what she had been forced to do.

It had been necessary to drug her guard, Tostig, before slipping from the castle. A liberal amount of mandragora such as she had given Sir Guy had been easy to slip into Tostig's wine. He'd gone to sleep quite heavily and, when she had last seen him, was snoring loudly on his straw pallet outside her bedchamber door. Regrettably, she'd feared taking Belle into her confidence, and she, too, was sleeping quite peacefully.

Poor Gowain was simple enough for her to bully into doing her will, though she experienced a twinge of guilt at his dismay. The rest had been even easier. Annice had simply commanded the guards to open the postern gate. They had been surprised but were now used to her as the lord's wife. Gowain, all bundled in his hooded cloak, was assumed to be Tostig, and they were waved through with good cheer and a few idle jests.

What she had not expected was how difficult a journey it would be. Two days, and she was only halfway there. The supply of coins she had brought with her were few, as she did not want to risk being robbed and killed. Doling out a small amount at a time to Gowain, she remained silent with her hood over her face when he bartered the coins for food. At night they sheltered under hayricks on remote farms or took refuge in a monastery. They meant to appear as a simple peasant couple traveling to a distant village.

"Milady," Gowain had said frankly when she'd suggested they take lodging in an inn, "any innkeeper would recognize at once that you are no peasant. Your speech and manner cannot be disguised, even by a rough wool cloak and scruffy nag. This is madness. Let us return to Dragonwyck, and mayhap my lord will ne'er know we were gone."

Of course, she had no intention of taking that bit of advice, though she did relinquish with regret the notion of warm, dry lodging. Occasionally she had flashes of panic at the possible dangers, but she thrust them firmly from her mind. Her father had been one of King Richard's finest warriors, and her mother's family had distant connections to Harold Godwinson—the last Saxon king before the Normans had conquered England. Courage was hereditary, and she would not retreat without a fight.

But, still, when night shadows enveloped them and the wind made mournful sounds whistling through bare tree branches, she shivered and prayed for guidance. It did not help when she heard Gowain doing the same.

On the third day Gowain huddled miserably in his cloak and pointed to a road that was obviously well traveled. "I think this is the right road, milady."

She shot him a withering glance. "You said that earlier today, and we spent half our time mired in a cow pasture."

Gowain shrugged. "I thought 'twas a road. How was I to know it was only a cow track?"

"You swore to me you knew the way, that you'd been there." She paused to inhale deeply, curbing her impatience. Gowain was staring at her with a pitiful, shamefaced expression that she had come to recognize.

"I have been there," he admitted, "but 'twas long ago, and I was too young to pay much attention to how we traveled."

"If I had the energy," Annice muttered, kicking her tired horse into a trot, "I would take my whip to you. You deserve it."

"Yea, milady."

Being right was not much of a comfort when they still had a distance to journey. Annice concentrated on what she would say when she arrived and tried not to think about what Rolf would say when next he saw her.

Staring in disbelief at Gareth of Kesteven, Rolf repeated slowly, "Lady Annice is gone?" He put a hand out to still Bordet as the dog leaped and cavorted about him.

Gareth swallowed heavily and nodded. "Yea, lord. I did not discover it until the next morning. She drugged Tostig and her maid. Gowain, the huntsman, is with her, but I cannot ascertain if there are others."

"God's teeth—" Rolf started forward, but Guy put a restraining hand upon his arm.

"Wait, milord," Guy said. "Do not assault Gareth until we have learned if he has sent out patrols to find her."

Guy's dry tone infuriated him but brought Rolf to his senses. Assaulting Gareth would gain him nothing.

"Of course I sent out patrols," Gareth said. "As soon as I discovered the lady missing. But no one has seen them. Lady Annice's cloak was discovered in a hedgerow just beyond the village, as were the two horses they were mounted on when they left." He paused, frowning. "No other horses are missing, though one of the ostlers swears he cannot find two of the old horses no longer fit for riding. They may have wandered into the woods to die, though, as horses often do."

Rolf stared at Gareth thoughtfully. "How do you know Tostig was drugged by Lady Annice? Did he take the drug willingly?"

"Nay, lord. It must have been given to him in his wine." Gareth coughed slightly, and Rolf understood. Annice would know that Tostig slept outside her door, and she would know his habits. A bit of wine to ease a chill night was a favored method of guarding a doorway.

He didn't wait to hear more. Later he would ask details. Now he intended to follow Annice. Snapping out pertinent questions as he strode toward the stables and demanded a fresh horse, Rolf learned that the patrols had found no sign of her other than the cloak and horses. They had ranged as far as Crowland to the south, Grantham to the north, and Leicester to the west before coming back to report.

"I think," Rolf said as he stepped into his saddle, "that she has gone in another direction."

Guy frowned up at him. His breath frosted the air in front of him. "Do you know where she might have gone?"

"Yea." Rolf inhaled deeply, recalling their conversation a few weeks before. "She once suggested that she go to Thurston and negotiate for the release of my son and return of her lands. 'Tis there she is headed, I believe."

"But that would be mad! She has no guarantee he won't hold her for ransom . . . nay, lord, surely she has not been so foolish."

"Reason and women are never steady companions," Rolf said shortly, and wheeled his horse around without waiting to see if Sir Guy followed. Bordet raced alongside, his nose to the ground, occasionally uttering a short, sharp bay of excitement.

When Rolf reined his lathered mount to a halt a bit later, the dog barked excitedly. At first Rolf thought there would be some sign of her presence, but Bordet backed away when he approached him. Barking again, the dog turned and ran down the road in the opposite direction, then paused to look back at his master.

Impatiently, Rolf said, "Come here. Stupid dog, Seabrook's lair is this way."

Sir Guy was staring at the dog. A strange expression crossed his face. "Milord, if Lady Annice did not go to Seabrook, where would she have gone?"

Rolf turned to glare at Guy. "Where else would she go? She went to Seabrook, I vow, and when I see her again, I'll—"

He broke off. It hit him with all the force of an anvil that 'twas entirely possible he would not see her again. People had been known to disappear and never be seen again. The king's nephew was an excellent example, as well as Lady Maud de Braose, who had been foolish enough to chide the king for Arthur's disappearance.

Rolf broke out into a cold sweat despite the wet, chill weather. Where else would she go? Aye, where else but to the man who held all their lives hostage?

He turned abruptly, startling Sir Guy and Gareth. "I have been a fool. You were right, Guy. She would not go to Thurston."

"Then where—?" Guy began.

Rolf reined his horse around to follow the dog. "London. She has gone to see the king."

CHAPTER 18

Half-timbered buildings hunched over narrowly winding streets choked with people, horses, and burdened carts. London was a city of burghers and tradesmen. Shop signs depicting the goods inside swung over streets so cramped, sunlight had little chance to pierce the gloomy shadows but shone instead upon rooftops and church spires.

Annice and Gowain were barely noticed as they made their way through the crowded streets. When they reached the king's residence, Annice felt the pangs of misgiving grow stronger. No guard would do more than make sly suggestions or shove her roughly aside, much less give credence to her request to have an audience with the king. She should have anticipated this.

It wasn't until she chanced to see an old friend of her father's that she was able to circumvent the guards and gain entrance. Sir Robert was astonished to see Hugh of Beauchamp's daughter garbed in rags and attended by only one ragged servant, but he manfully swallowed his surprise and escorted her into the castle grounds.

"In these dark times, milady," Sir Robert said sorrowfully, "a lone woman should not roam England without her husband."

"Yea, Sir Robert, and I would not if my husband were able to attend me. However, he is on business for the king, and I had urgent news to impart to King John."

" 'Tis fortunate that I chanced upon you, then," Sir Robert said gallantly. "Come, I will give you into the care of my daughter, who is a lady-in-waiting for the queen. She will see to your needs and get you decently garbed for an audience with the king."

In much shorter time than she'd thought possible, Annice was being granted an audience with the king. He studied her with dark interest, his eyes flicking over her figure with an expression that made Annice uncomfortable. Still, she did not look away, but met John's gaze with a lifted chin and steady gaze.

"I am grateful to you for granting me permission to enter, sire," she said in reply to John's greeting.

"Beautiful women should always have entrance to my court," John said easily. His steady gaze made her think of a hawk. "Sir Robert was wise to bring you to me."

Annice did not correct his impression that she had journeyed to London with Sir Robert. Instead she inclined her head, lowering her eyes with a modest smile. "Yea, sire, Sir Robert is the kindest of men. My father was always fond of him."

"Ah, Hugh of Beauchamp was a good man. I miss his wise counsel." John leaned forward slightly. "And what brings you to seek me out, Lady Annice? Where is your husband?"

She anticipated this question and answered immediately. "My lord and husband was taken away on business, and I have come in his stead to beg a boon of Your Majesty."

"A boon." John sat back in his chair, drumming his fingers atop the curved armrest with a steady beat. "And what would that be, my fair Lady Annice? Lord Rolf must be busy indeed to send his wife to me to plead for some cause."

Meeting the king's dark gaze, Annice said before she lost her nerve, "I would ask that you bestow upon my husband the custody of his son, who has long been held by Thurston of Seabrook. I fear that my cousin's husband holds the boy for reasons not favorable to my husband or to you, sire. In return for your approval, I would agree to sign over my dower lands for the benefit of the crown."

"Really." After a tense silence John smiled, his lips curving wickedly. "Come, fair lady, and sit up here beside me. I would hear more of this claim that my loyal subject has shameful intentions."

As Annice mounted the dais and took a chair near the king, she had the thought that Rolf would be furious with her if she did not succeed. Nay, even if she did succeed, he would most like be angry that she had not consulted him before acting. But if she could get the king to grant him custody of Justin, surely that would ease the sting of her disobedience to his wishes. . . .

Cursing, London citizens moved aside sullenly for the armed troop of men that jostled them aside. The gold and black of Rolf's livery was a bright counterpoint to the thick gloom beneath the overhangs. Filth was thick in the gutters, and with a sense of relief they emerged from the close streets into a wider avenue.

Rolf drew in a breath of fresher air and glanced at Sir Guy. That knight was frowning, looking around him at the citizenry.

"Milord," Guy said, turning to Rolf, "it is worrisome to think of your lady riding unguarded through these streets."

"Yea." Rolf had not allowed himself to think of all the fates she might have met on the road to London. In truth, she might yet be far afield, set upon by brigands far more foul than those in London.

Save for King John, he thought harshly. The king was the foulest robber of them all, robbing not only goods and monies, but lives.

"Plague take the woman," he muttered. On the swift ride through the muddy shires, he had pleasantly envisioned beating her most energetically for this escapade.

Guy nudged his mount closer and leaned near to say

anxiously, "You mean her no harm for this, do you, milord? She came to London only to ease your burdens, I am certain."

"Are you?" Rolf shot at him. He gazed at Guy with narrowed eyes. "You take her part most readily, I see. Did you know of her intent before we left Dragonwyck for Saint Edmunds?"

Startled, Guy shook his head. "Nay, lord! She would not tell me for fear I would divulge the truth to you. The lady must know that I consider her safety above all else and would not allow her to endanger herself."

At last they reached court. Rolf asked for entrance to the king, but it was several hours before he was granted an audience. By then his already strained temper was beginning to fray, despite Sir Guy's urgent pleas to remain calm.

Finally, Rolf was shown into the king's court. His eyes fell first on the king, who sat leisurely upon a tall chair on a dais raised from the floor to a height of almost a foot. It gave John the illusion of being taller, more powerful, than the men ranging below him, a masquerade the king promoted with casual serenity. The chamber was crowded with court followers; some Rolf recognized and others he didn't.

Straightening from his obeisance to the king, Rolf's eyes fell on a woman seated near John. His mouth tightened. Annice. Garbed in elegant garments of silk and ermine, with a circlet of gold around her lovely throat, she sat with her hands folded demurely in her lap. He wanted to choke her.

Abruptly, he said, "I have come for Lady Annice, sire."

His short words stilled the hum of conversation, and people turned to stare. Rolf ignored them, his gaze trained on Annice, who had grown pale but for two bright spots of color on her cheeks.

John drawled with open amusement, "Ah, so you have only come to retrieve your lovely wife from our court, Lord Rolf? It has been some time since we have seen you here."

Rolf forced a smile. "Yea, sire, to my regret. England's business has kept us apart for far too long."

John smiled with his lips, but his eyes were wary. "Ever the facile tongue, as had your father. His presence is sorely missed in our court also."

"Yea, sire, as everywhere else. My father was a wise and just man." Rolf met the king's narrowed gaze steadily. This was not about his father, who had been dead these seven years past. There was an elusive point the king was certain to make at his leisure.

Waving indolently toward the ladies assembled on each side of him, John said, "You are acquainted with most of these ladies, I believe. And, of course, your wife is one of the brightest blossoms in our royal garden. It was very politic of you to allow her to visit us in your absence from home."

Rolf's gaze flickered to Annice and back to the king. What in the name of all that was holy had she really said? If John knew of his absence from Dragonwyck, then he most likely knew of the barons' meeting at Bury Saint Edmunds.

"Nay, sire," Rolf said steadily, ignoring the undertones of John's comment. "My wife seems to take pleasure in gamboling about the countryside unchaperoned."

"Oho." John's brow lifted with genuine amusement. "Do I detect dissension, Lord Rolf? 'Twas my understanding that your lady was given permission to visit us. Has she earned your displeasure with disobedience?"

"I am afraid that she has, sire." Rolf was aware of Annice's high color and angry blue eyes but kept his gaze on the king. He managed a light shrug of his shoulders. "She seems a bit willful, does she not? What, sire, do you think I should do with a wife who will not obey?"

John stroked his dark beard thoughtfully, eyes alight. "She should be rebuked, of course," he said, and several of the ladies tittered. "Unless, mayhap, the lady is indeed obeying her lord and husband in coming to our court in secrecy."

An ugly insinuation surrounded his outwardly idle comment, the hint that Rolf would send his wife to spy upon the king for the rebel barons. If 'twere any other man who had voiced such a clearly treasonous suspicion, Rolf would have rammed the words back down the culprit's throat. But it was not any other man. It was the king. He cleared his throat and smiled slightly.

"Nay, sire, I fear I have been wed to a rebellious woman

who insists upon her own way. She is ever taking vague notions and pursuing them despite my forbidding it."

"Does she?" John laughed softly, and there was a touch of malice in the amusement. "Then I chose the Dragon a fit mate, I think. Ah, I see you agree." He paused, pondering for a moment, then leaned forward in his chair, looking directly at Rolf. "But do you agree that those who rebel should be punished? Even when provoked, those loyal subjects who run astray must suffer the consequences of their actions. 'Tis said that only through penance can one gain redemption and absolution. Do you not agree, Lord Rolf?"

"With all my heart, *beau* sire." Rolf took a deep breath. The double-edged conversation had snared the attention of all those near enough to hear, and the hall had grown quiet and still. It was no longer just a discussion about Lady Annice, but covertly, the northern barons who were in rebellion. He met John's gaze steadily. "All men fall short of perfection and should subjugate themselves voluntarily to divine justice. Because I am the lady's lord and master, and only mortal, I will seek guidance and wisdom from others before I mete out my justice, however."

Silence lay thickly. There was the rustling of silk and shuffle of feet as those nearby waited to see if the king would take offense at Rolf's reply. It was well-known that John avoided the Church, and it had been many years since he had accepted the holy sacrament of Communion. There were those who whispered John considered himself above God, and that was the reason he refused. Some whispered that the king was so evil, touching the holy sacrament would cause him to turn into a puff of smoke and disappear.

It did not, however, surprise Rolf when John nodded and decreed that he not be too harsh with the lady. "Well said, Lord Rolf. I commend the lady to your care, with the remonstration that she not be unduly harmed. Do not bruise her too greatly."

Rolf bowed his head, outwardly humble, but inwardly seething at the king's arrogance in believing that Rolf referred to him for wise counsel instead of to God. "My thanks for your benevolence, *beau* sire," he said. "I am certain my lady wife is appreciative."

"And so should you be. She has, after all, pleaded most prettily for your cause as well as hers."

"Has she." Rolf did not dare look at Annice. If she so much as mouthed a single protest, he was not at all certain he could contain his anger with her until they were alone. So she had come to plead his case before the king? When she knew he did not wish it?

"Yea, she has indeed," John said with a sly glance toward Annice. " 'Tis our hope that you will linger here with us for a time. A chamber has been prepared for your visit, as we were certain you would soon join us. We have much yet to discuss, and I look forward to a long interview in private."

"As do I, sire," Rolf said, helpless to refuse. It was a thinly veiled command, and he knew it well. He was trapped. John would keep him in the royal court indefinitely, as assurance against his joining the rebel barons, and as retribution for his demands for justice. That would leave Dragonwyck defended only by its castellan.

Stepping forward, he held out his hand to Annice. After a brief hesitation she rose from her chair and put her hand in his open palm. Her fingers trembled in his clasp as his hand closed around hers, but he felt little sympathy. What he did feel was an increasing desire to fall to his knees with relief that she was well, mingled with the consuming urge to shake her until her teeth rattled as "prettily" as her tongue.

Neither of them spoke as they quit the hall and the king's presence, and Rolf was relieved that at least she had sense enough not to provoke him further. That situation, he discovered immediately upon closing the chamber door behind them, was not to last.

Turning on him, Annice lashed out, "How dare you humiliate me that way! Do you think me so big a fool to take a risk such as this one when I wasn't certain of my success? John would not harm me, nor turn me over to Seabrook when 'twas he who was responsible for our marriage. Whatever else he may be, the king is crafty enough to see the advantages to keeping you on his side, though he may still wish to keep you leashed. And I have all but secured his promise for the return of your son, but you talk about me as if I'm some unruly child run amok through England without my nurse!"

Grabbing her before she could continue her tirade, Rolf said through clenched teeth, "Bide your tongue, my lady, or you may swiftly wish you had."

Annice gaped up at him and lapsed into silence. He released her as if stung, and he wondered what she had seen in his face to silence her so swiftly. Rage? Yea, that and more.

Rolf drew in a deep breath and turned away from her. He stalked to a window that looked out onto the courtyard. In spring, roses would climb the walls to fill the air with fragrance. Now there were only stiff, empty vines that looked forlorn without the blossoms. He closed his eyes, recalling John's emphasis as he'd said Annice was one of the brightest blossoms in his garden. 'Twas no secret that the king was a lecher. More than one man had seen his wife attempted by the king, and there was little that could prevent him. He wanted to ask Annice but dared not. If John had so much as . . .

His hands curled into fists on the stone ledge of the window.

"Milord?" Annice came up behind him, stopping a few feet away. "I know you have cause to be angry with me."

He turned and leaned his hip against the ledge. "Do you? Not from the evidence of my ears."

She flushed. "I was angry and embarrassed and spoke unwisely. You are right. I should not have attempted this alone. I but hoped to convince the king to allow you to regain your son."

"So you rode out of my secure keep to brave the elements and outlaws just for me. I'm impressed, milady, with your courage and selflessness for my cause."

The flush faded from her face to leave it pale, but he continued ruthlessly, his voice flaying her. "Obviously, not once did you halt to consider that I might not wish to request personally the king's aid, for with aid comes indebtedness. Being indebted to a king is like borrowing from the moneylenders—there is always a balance left on the loan.

Never is there enough payment to the king, whether it be money or time or men. John will not allow me my son until forced to it—or until I yield him a greater prize."

Turning away from her again, he looked out into the bleak winter courtyard that was distorted by glass window-panes, scraping his hand over the stone ledge. His breath blew harshly between his teeth as he struggled for control, focusing on the hard edge of the stone rather than on the perilous future yawning before him.

"You don't know what you've done," he whispered into the heavy silence. His breath frosted the glass windowpane. He dragged his thumb across the mist, leaving a clear swipe. Behind him he could hear the slight scuff of Annice's silk shoes over the stones. Then her hand touched his shoulder. It may have been a firmer touch than it felt, for he still wore his harness of mail, and over it a thick surcoat and mantle for warmth. He looked down at his feet, muscles tensing, and in a moment her hand lifted from his shoulder.

There was mud on the hem of his mantle. It clung in streaks and clumps, breaking loose as it dried to litter the floor at his boots. So much mud smeared his boots that his spurs no longer clinked, as they were too clogged with it.

"Milord," Annice said in a choked voice, and he turned finally, feeling suddenly weary. Her face bore traces of tears, and she was staring at him with a look in her eyes that transfixed him. He'd seen that look before, yea, too many times. It had stared at him from eyes in France, Ireland, Wales, and England. It was the empty look of a child who has lost everything that gave stability to his world. It was the look of widows who have seen their husbands slain, mothers who have lost their children—there were times he even saw the soulless reflection of those empty eyes in his sleep.

His throat tight, Rolf reached out and drew her to him. "I feared I had lost you," he said roughly, and rubbed his jaw against the neat coil of hair she'd twisted atop her head. "I looked in hedgerows, monasteries, ditches, hayricks—in burned-out hovels where you might have taken refuge."

She twisted to look up at him. Putting a finger over his

lips, she whispered, "I was desperate to aid you, milord. I acted unwisely. Please forgive me."

Some of the tension eased from him. He sighed and took her hand in his, kissing her fingertips. "Perhaps you acted as I should have done. With John, one never knows. I had hoped he would view the return of your lands and my son as only what is my legal right, which is why I appealed to the justiciar for redress."

"But John has already agreed to negotiate the reversion of my lands." Annice curled her fingers into the edges of his mantle. "We spoke of it yesterday, and he set his scribes to writing the proper letters to Thurston."

Shaking his head, Rolf muttered, "John writes many letters as a matter of form."

"But he has promised to set his seal upon them—do you truly think them worthless?"

"Do you truly think Thurston of Seabrook will be moved by letters?"

"Yea, if the king threatens fines and reprisal." Her eyes searched his face anxiously. "Do you not believe the king will do it?"

"I don't know." He took another deep breath and looked around him. For the first time since entering, he studied the chamber they had been given. It was not large, but elegantly appointed. In a castle filled to the bursting with retainers, it struck him as unusual that Annice would have a chamber of her own. "This is the chamber where you've stayed?" he asked in surprise.

She shook her head. "Nay, I stayed in the women's quarters. I suppose the king means for us to be alone to—talk." Her last word was said wryly, for 'twas apparent that John had been delighted at the prospect that Rolf might lesson his wife with a belt or a harsh hand. If she was as some other women he'd known, she would then have turned to the king begging sympathy. Which John would have been only too glad to offer if it meant the lady yielding to him.

Rolf held her hands and continued his appraisal of the room. There was a bed hung with thick curtains bearing the royal emblem, a table, stools, candle stands, and carpets. The walls were ornate with carvings and embroidered tapestries that shifted slightly in errant drafts. Suddenly he frowned.

There was something out of place. Something a little bit different that had caught his eye, yet he could not immediately place it. His gaze raked the chamber again, while Annice pressed close to him with her face against his chest. Then he saw it, and knew.

He warned her to silence with a shake of his head, then led her to the bed across the room. Heedless of his muddy garments, he sat down heavily. When she turned to him, mouth open to speak, he shook his head and pointed. She turned slowly to see where he indicated.

Square wood medallions decorated one wall, some painted and some varnished. The painted squares had starburst centers, and in the center of one of them, a tiny hole glimmered with a different sheen. 'Twas a spy hole. Rolf had recognized it, for he was familiar with John's methods.

While seated beneath the bed's silk hangings, the angle would be difficult for anyone at the hole to see them, but they would be easily heard. If there was one spy hole, he reasoned, there would be more.

Annice looked at him uncertainly; then her face flushed with indignation. He smiled slightly as he saw she understood. Leaning close to press his lips against her ear, he murmured, "We must watch what we say. Speak in English, but even then be careful, for there are those in John's court who have a command of both languages. I trust no one, and neither must you. Later, when there are no ears about to hear, I will explain more fully."

He drew back. A faint smile curved her mouth, and her eyes began to take on the gleam he had seen before and knew to presage some mischief. Before he could protest, she drew his head back down and said against his ear, "Since the king expects you to be angry with me—and in truth, I know you have a right to be—p'raps we should do what is expected. It may take him off guard and would explain our lack of easy conversation with each other. How better to draw those eager to divide us even more? There would be whispers in your ear and mine, and if thought to fall on fertile ground, many seeds may be sown that would not normally be. . . ."

He saw the sense in it immediately. If they appeared estranged, it might serve their cause better. It would certainly serve to explain his failure to be drawn eagerly into the king's camp, and might even be seen as cause to leave court as soon as possible. A smile tugged at his mouth and he nodded slowly.

"Yea," he whispered, "I take your meaning. But are you not afeared that I will grow overfond of the notion and truly beat you most heartily?"

Her hands curled around his arms, and she said simply, "I trust you to do what is right, milord."

That simple statement made him almost ashamed of the suspicions he'd felt earlier. He looked away, then back at her. After a moment he rose to his feet and began to unbuckle his belt. Annice smothered a laugh with one hand and reached for a cushioning pillow to hold over her body with the other. Then she scooted deep into the shadowed folds of the curtained bed and he followed, uttering reprimands and loud threats that he would beat her until she was black-and-blue.

The sounds of blows falling against the pillow were loud and satisfactory, and in truth, released much of his anger toward her. Anyone listening outside the chamber would certainly report to the king and all who were curious that the Lord of Dragonwyck had beat his errant wife most harshly.

In the following days Annice found it quite easy to play the part of the chastised wife. She kept her head bent and her eyes lowered, and was relieved that after only a few murmurs of sympathy, the king left her quite alone.

For a short time it seemed as if their ploy had worked. Gossip was whispered in their ears most willingly, telling tales of the king's activities and suspicions. Few were not suspect of treason. John sent letters to the pope, it was said, and gathered money to hire mercenaries, as he did not trust his barons to provide loyal men. And the barons, it was also said, armed themselves in their distant keeps with men and horses.

Rolf held himself aloof from those who would seek to draw him into intrigues. He glowered savagely, snarling at any who dared speak, save, of course, the king.

Meanwhile John watched them thoughtfully, and Annice wondered just how much of their masquerade he truly believed. Enough, she discovered, for John to offer a return of her dower lands from Lord Thurston. Casting a sly glance toward Rolf, the king murmured that he could not accept so grand a gift from the lady as her lands, even though they were freely offered.

Stiffening, Rolf gave her a quick, narrowed glance that made her wish she'd told him of it before the king had. He gave no outward sign, however, but smoothly voiced his acceptance of the king's generosity. No mention was made of Justin, and Annice worried that the king would refuse her petition for the boy's return.

"Is there anything else you haven't told me?" Rolf demanded when they were alone, and Annice drew in a deep breath.

"Nay, lord. 'Tis true that I offered to exchange my dower lands for your son, but I feared you would not allow it if I told you."

"You were right." Curling his hand into a fist, Rolf raked his knuckles over a rough stone with frustration. "There is a limit to what I will use to bargain with John." He turned on her, eyes a hot, glittering green in the wash of sunlight through a high window. "Do not think to offer the king another *gift*, milady. Not even for my son. Not even for my life. Do you mark me?"

"Yea, lord," she whispered. "I mark you well."

Time passed swiftly, and the proper documents were written, signed, and sealed, then sent to Seabrook with a small contingent of men-at-arms.

Yet still John continued to delay ordering the return of Rolf's son. That, the king said smoothly, was still under consideration.

Rolf sent home most of his men to protect Dragonwyck, anticipating Thurston's reaction after receiving the king's letters. Sir Guy was sent to warn the castellans of Rolf's other holdings as well.

Christmas was spent with the king at Worcester. Still there was no sign of their being allowed to return to Dragonwyck. John delayed, asking Rolf's advice on military matters and repeating his pleasure in having him near.

"We never know when we may need our loyal barons close," John said, and his dark gaze fixed on Rolf's face so intently that Annice felt a spur of fear. Did he think Rolf would betray him? Or did he mean to ask something dreadful of him? Either was likely.

Yet the king did not, but merely continued to keep those around him in a terror of suspense throughout the Christmas season. If the king knew of the charter being proposed by the barons, he did not reveal it. But it became known that John had been at Bury Saint Edmunds on November 4, only a short time before the barons' meeting. It seemed very likely that the king was aware of everything, including the names of the men who had attended.

That fact became evident two days after Christmas, when the king moved from Worcester to Tewkesbury. He planned to stay there only a few days, then move on to Geddington and back to London by Epiphany. Rolf was invited to remain with the king. This time Rolf refused.

Annice listened fearfully as the king inquired icily why his loyal baron did not wish to remain with him.

"*Beau* sire," Rolf said slowly, eyes fixed steadily on the king's sullen, suspicious face, "my main keep is long overdue my presence. I have been at court too long, and my castellan sends urgent messages for my return. And at your good grace, I have been seisined of more properties that require my earnest attention. While I am most grateful for your kindness, and humbled by your royal regard in wishing me near, I beg leave to see to my necessary business. Should I be gone too long, it leaves my keeps in danger of being overtaken by rebels. Lincolnshire is in a most uncertain state, as you are fully aware, sire, and I would not wish to have to beg for relief from assault."

"Well-spoken, Lord Dragonwyck." John gave him a petulant stare that belied his compliment. " 'Twould seem that you have prepared your plea most thoroughly."

Rolf bowed his head, and Annice saw the muscles in his jaw tense. He dared not reply hastily, for the wrong word risked John's erratic Angevin temper. After a moment Rolf looked up at his king, green eyes veiled by his lashes, a faint smile curving his mouth.

"A man should never be unprepared when dealing with a royal monarch of your considerable perception, *beau* sire. I would be a fool indeed were I to ask anything of you without due thought."

"Yea, but men are still fools enough to think I am dull-witted," John replied shortly. He toyed with the gold-encrusted trim on his robe, then smiled slightly. "Tell me, dread knight, of what do you hear from your brother in Cheshire?"

Here it was. Rolf had told her not to dismiss any chance word of the king's, and John's referral to Rolf's father and family loyalties the first day had finally borne fruit. Now the king was questioning the loyalty of his brothers.

Shrugging, Rolf said calmly, "My brother Geoffrey has always been the king's man. As you must know, sire, we do not communicate frequently, though if I summoned him, he would come to my aid."

"Would he?" John shifted slightly, eyes narrowing at his liege man. "And would he come to mine, do you think?"

"Has he given any sign that he would not?"

"Nay, but his lands closely border Wales. Word has come to me that the Welsh chieftain Griffyn ap Llewelyn traffics with barons known to be loyal to me."

"As Llewelyn traffics with you also, sire. He is crafty, as are most of the Welsh, but has given you his oath of loyalty."

"So you swear that your brother Geoffrey is loyal to me?"

Rolf hesitated. If he said yea, he might be held accountable for his brother if Geoffrey joined the rebels; but if he said nay, then he might be held responsible for the king's anger toward his brother.

"Sire," he said firmly, "I can swear to no man's loyalty but my own. Each man is accountable for his own oaths, and I would not presume to know another man's heart."

After a moment John snorted and said nastily, "Ever a facile tongue, Lord Rolf. You remind me more of your father with every passing day."

Rolf made no reply. After a moment of tense silence the king dismissed him with a wave of one hand. "Go now to your lands, but we shall expect your estates to be honestly levied and those fines remitted promptly."

Annice released the breath she had been holding, her lungs aching from the strain. They were free to go, though John was making Rolf pay dearly for the privilege.

She took another deep breath and stepped forward before she lost her courage. "Sire, I beg an answer to the request I first made when I arrived at your court. If you would be so good as to grant my plea to have my husband's son returned to us, God would surely smile upon you with His greatest favor."

Rolf made a muffled sound, but she kept her gaze trained on the king. John was regarding her with a dark, lifted brow, his eyes cold and narrowed. He drummed his fingertips against the carved arm of his throne for a moment, then leaned forward.

"Do you not think I am already blessed, Lady Annice? Surely, no other man in the realm has as much as do I. Loyal barons and lovely ladies surround me at all times. My children are strong and healthy, and my kingdom tended by wise and noble men." His mouth curled in a malicious smile. "Save for those barons who tend to desert me when most needed, I am the most fortunate of men in England."

"Yea, sire," she managed to say in a voice that did not betray her tension. "And as you have just said—your children are strong and healthy. My husband—who has proved himself loyal to you—does not have the same assurance. He but wishes to ascertain himself of his son's safety and good health. In Lord Seabrook's care, that is not a definite state."

"Are you suggesting that Seabrook would defy me so openly?" John lifted a hand in a languid motion. "Lord Thurston is not brave enough to dare that. I have written him, as I promised you I would. You have your dower lands, and the monies that come with them. Go now, before my patience wears thin. All of England stands in danger,

which is more important to me than the fate of a small boy."
He paused when Rolf took a step forward, then shrugged.
"Your son is well, Lord of Dragonwyck. You must accept my
assurances on that score for now. He will continue to be
well as long as you are my loyal baron."

Crushed with disappointment, Annice barely heard
Rolf's reply to the king. All for naught. Her frightening journey, the weeks spent dancing attendance on the king—all
for naught. She had failed, when she had been so certain of
victory.

"Chérie," Rolf murmured when they were alone in the
corridor, "do not despair. In truth, I did not expect much
from John. He holds my loyalty by holding Justin, with
Thurston as the guardian. It binds both Seabrook and myself to John. I do not blame you and am proud of you for
your attempt."

Though appreciative of his comfort, and grateful that he
did not hold her responsible for the king's refusal, Annice's
dark mood remained with her. It wasn't until they were finally within sight of Dragonwyck that her spirits began to
lift. It would be so good to get home and have her own
things around her again, her own garments and brushes,
and familiar surroundings. It would be a pleasure to see
Belle, and pet Bordet, since he had been sent back to
Dragonwyck with Rolf's men-at-arms. And Sir Guy—she
had missed him also, his pleasant countenance and quick
humor always uplifting. Even the sight of the tall, crenellated battlements stark against the sky, with Rolf's banner
flying from the highest tower of the keep, gave her a great
deal of pleasure.

With a slight shock she realized that Dragonwyck had
truly become her home.

CHAPTER 19

May 1215

"Are you going?" Annice asked anxiously. Rolf looked up from his cup of wine and nodded. Night shadows filled Dragonwyck's great hall, and the fire had burned low. Bordet lay asleep on the floor between master and mistress, nose almost touching the feet of Sir Guy, who sat across from them. In the four months since they had left the king, much had happened.

"Yea," Rolf said. "The king has called for a muster of those loyal to him, and some are already in Gloucester. They have been commanded to proceed with horses and arms, taking all men who will answer his call. The fortifications of London, Oxford, Salisbury, and others are being strengthened and manned, and help has been summoned from Flanders and Poitou. The king is returning to London and is now at Windsor. I am to meet him."

Annice sank slowly to the hard comfort of a stool, staring at Rolf's grave expression. War. Utter civil war had come, when she had hoped to avoid it. Already a huge body of men-at-arms were in Dragonwyck's bailey, waiting for word from their liege to go to John.

"What shall we do?" she whispered, and Rolf smiled faintly.

"War may yet be avoided," he soothed. "If John signs the charter, mayhap—"

"If John *keeps* the charter," Sir Guy interrupted bitterly. They both turned to look at him, and he shrugged. "Even if he signs it, he has a bad habit of refusing to honor his oaths."

"But surely the pope will intervene—" Annice began, and this time it was Rolf who interrupted.

"The pope is furious with Langton. Do you not recall his actions of a few months past? When he ordered the bishops to quash all the barons' 'conspiracies,' he admonished the king to treat his nobles graciously. It had little effect," Rolf said bitterly.

"I cannot blame the king for his reaction," Guy replied. "He was given the choice between signing the charter willingly or being compelled by force. 'Tis said that John wondered scornfully why the barons did not ask for his kingdom at once."

" 'Their demands are idle dreams, without a shadow of reason,' " Rolf quoted heavily. "Yea, John told Langton outright that he would never grant the barons liberties which would make himself a slave. The past months since the barons presented the charter to John and renounced their homage have been most crucial. I know the king will not swallow the insults they propose to feed him in a revised charter, either."

"I thought the proposed charter was to limit the king's power, not insult him," Annice said miserably.

"And do you think John wants his power limited?" Rolf shook his head. "Nay. Guy is right. Even if he signs the new charter being negotiated, 'tis doubtful that he will keep it."

"Not since he has the pope on his side," Guy muttered, dragging a hand over his face. "Innocent has suggested that an impartial legate arbitrate the differences between king and barons."

"Matters have gone too far," Rolf said. "Many barons

have refused to mediate, proposing harsh new demands that no king would honor. If they can take enough of the king's castles, the barons can force him to come to terms."

Annice swallowed her pleas that Rolf not join the king. The entire country was in a state of unrest, with barons raging over Lincolnshire like wolves. So many neighboring keeps had fallen to them—or been gladly yielded—that Dragonwyck was almost surrounded by the rebels. Even Lincoln Cathedral was said to be occupied by the rebels, though it was a sanctuary. She was afraid, yet did not dare admit it.

Only recently had Rolf returned from defending one of their own beleaguered keeps, eyes alight with pleasure as he'd described to her how they had stormed the small donjon and taken it back.

"The castellan I set there—Sir Robert of Houghton—is a good man. He held it even though outnumbered, yet I could see he would not be able to hold it much longer," Rolf had said, then gone on to tell how he and his men-at-arms had managed to come upon the besiegers in the night and overrun them. The fighting had been fierce and bloody, and he had sustained an injury to his thigh from a lance.

Though she had listened quietly while tending his wound, his account had struck fear deep into Annice's heart. He could so easily have been slain. Must he speak as if battle were a pleasure?

Now, when Rolf and Guy began to discuss weapons, and troops, and plans for the coming struggle almost with eagerness, Annice's fear began to turn into anger as she listened to them.

Finally she exploded, "You sound as if you look forward to this! Are you so filled with blood lust and joy of battle that you don't mind the death that goes with it?" Surging to her feet, she stared down at their surprised faces for a moment before fleeing from the hall.

Racing up the stairs, she heard Rolf call to her but ignored him. She would lose him. The fear pricked her into almost mindless terror, and she ran blindly, as if she could escape it. Dragons leered at her from doorways and window ledges, carved into stone and wood and ranging fiercely through Dragonwyck's torch-lit corridors and chambers. Holy Mary and Joseph, if only those stone dragons could be depended upon to keep them all safe. . . .

Breathless, she reached her chamber and flung herself inside, startling Belle, who was kneeling before a chest. "Milady!" Belle struggled to her feet. "Art thou unwell?"

Annice knew she must look as if hellhounds were after her, and paused to lean against the high back of a chair for support. Her fingers curved into the carved wood, and she managed a smile.

"Sick of war talk, 'tis all," she said with a little catch in her breath. "Rolf and Sir Guy speak as if eager for it. Do they not realize—?"

She broke off, seeing Belle's eyes widen with alarm. There was no point in terrorizing the girl. The fear would come soon enough, and for good reason. Drawing in a deep breath to calm her turmoil, she said easily, "Wouldst thou fetch some spiced wine, Belle? I have need of something to clear these cobwebs from my brain."

Belle scurried to obey. Annice went to the window to stare out over the surrounding countryside. Far into the distance, beyond the security of Dragonwyck's thick walls, ranged men who would take the castle apart stone by stone if they could. The rebel barons would show no mercy to any man who supported the hated king. Only Rolf stood between her and disaster, and though she knew that he was more than capable of keeping them safe, she feared for him. It was more than fear for herself, which she had felt when married to Luc. This was a quivering, helpless emotion that threatened to consume her at times. If Rolf was killed, she would die also. Life without him would be pointless. Unendurable.

She buried her face in her hands. There were moments she resented feeling this deeply for a man. Men were prone to dying in war, or in a useless quarrel with one another. *Men!* Quick-tempered, proud creatures with little thought of how their deaths might affect those who loved them . . . yet she would not regret one instant of the days she had spent with Rolf, even knowing that they might all be snatched away in the blink of an eye.

When she heard the door opening, she turned away

from the window, knowing instinctively whom she would see. Rolf stood framed in the opening, a faint frown marking his handsome face. Her heart leaped, and she thought herself foolish for still reacting that way after a year of marriage. Yea, her pulses still raced, her heart lurched, and all her senses came alive when he was near. She had thought time would ease those reactions, but it had only increased them.

Striding toward her, Rolf said, "It seems that you are not as resigned to the inevitable as I had thought."

She smiled slightly. "Nay, lord. I am not."

He took her into his arms and held her, one hand pressing against the back of her head, his fingers drawing down the length of her heavy hair in a casually affectionate gesture. "Do not worry unduly, *chérie*. P'raps John will sign the charter and keep it, and all this conjecture is for naught."

"But you don't really think so," she said into his tunic, her words muffled by velvet and fear. His embrace tightened. That was answer enough, and she slid her arms around his waist and gripped him tightly. "Can you not stay?" she asked, the words tumbling from her though she knew 'twas useless to ask. He would not stay, and in truth, she would not want him to go against his oath. 'Twas that loyalty of heart and mind that had made her fall in love with him, knowing that here was a man who would always keep his sworn oaths.

After a moment, during which Rolf still stroked her hair with gentle caresses, he said, "I finally managed to wring an agreement from the king that he would review my claims to retrieve Justin from Thurston. Of course, 'twas only after Seabrook foolishly ordered the castellan of one of his larger keeps to resist the king's troops. John will have to choose one of us soon and cease playing his barons one against the other."

She drew back a little and looked up at him. During the long winter months, almost an entire troop of small wooden horses and men-at-arms had been carved, each lovingly detailed. She had watched silently, knowing his heart must ache with longing for his son. Yea, he was right. The king would have to choose which of his barons to alienate soon, and she did not think it would be Thurston.

"Soon," she said tremulously, unable to stop the slight shaking of her voice, "all will be well. Justin will be with us here at Dragonwyck, and the king will allow peace to settle upon the land."

Amused, Rolf flicked her under the chin with an affectionate gesture. "Are you a sorceress, that you have cast a spell upon the king and all the barons?" he teased. " 'Twill take magic to set all aright in England."

Fiercely, she said, "Nay, not magic, milord, but an appeal to God."

Rolf's expression grew solemn. "God must be wearied of hearing all the prayers that have been sent heavenward these last fifteen years," he muttered. Raking a hand through his hair so that the thick gold strands bore darker streaks, he turned away from her and went to the open window. A brisk breeze that smelled of rain and fresh-turned earth filtered into the chamber. The raspy serenade of frogs below in the moat could be heard, familiar sounds that carried no hint of disaster.

Coming up behind him, Annice slid her arms around his waist and pressed her cheek against his back. She wanted to hold him close, cling to him as if her love would protect him from all harm.

Rolf put his hands atop hers where they met at his belt buckle and, holding them, loosened her embrace and turned around to face her. There was a gleam in his green eyes that she recognized, a heated glow that brightened the green to almost gold, and her heart fluttered. He glanced toward the bed, then back to her, and grinned.

"The nights will be long without you, and cold," he murmured.

"Even in June?" she asked with a laugh.

"Yea, 'tis always cold when you are not near to warm me, chérie."

Most willingly, Annice allowed Rolf to draw her with him to the wide shadows of the bed. Parting the hanging silk curtains, he lifted her to the high mattress and followed. He lay down beside her, one hand leisurely exploring the length of her leg, then stroking upward to the flat mound of her belly. Annice put her hand atop his.

"Once I was glad to be barren," she murmured regretfully. "Now I pray for your child."

He stared down at her stomach, then looked up into her eyes. "Let us recover the child already here before we think about praying for another to be pawn to John's whims," he said slowly. "I cannot share your desire for a babe. I miss Justin too greatly to risk another child. Times are too uncertain, and it pains me to know that I cannot keep what is mine because my king is dishonorable."

Annice put up a hand to stroke his bearded jaw, throat tight with painful emotion. Though she saw his reason, it still grieved her that he did not want a child from her. Long had she yearned for a babe, then resigned herself to being barren. Only since coming to love this fierce warrior had she again desired a child of her own to nurture. If she had a child . . . if she had Rolf's child, she would always have part of him with her. There would be the reminder of her love for him in a child with golden hair and green eyes, created of their love.

But now she clung to Rolf with an aching heart, fearing to lose him, fearing to hold too tightly. Rolf's caresses grew bolder, the hunger always in him growing hot and urgent. His mouth moved to take hers. The familiar surge of pleasure blossomed between her thighs when his hand moved lower, seeking her through the silk and linen of her garments. She tingled in delicious agonies, ached to feel his bare skin against hers.

Impatiently, urgently, they removed each other's garments, flinging them to the floor and over the bed, careless of laces and flimsy material. At the core of their urgency was the silent knowledge that their time together was short. The future yawned uncertainly before them, with all its implied disasters.

But here and now there were sweet pleasures to be found in the coupling of their bodies. Flesh against flesh, united in form and heart, seeking and giving delight. It mattered not to her that he did not speak of love; he gave evidence of it in his gentle caresses, then in the growing ferocity of his touch as he ranged over her.

When she was at a fever pitch of excitement, lifting her

hips to urge him enter her, he parted her thighs roughly and thrust inside. The movement took her breath away, and she clung to him with arms and legs twined round about him like a summer vine, offering body and heart and soul. He drove into her with shattering motions that swept her to the height of suspense and held her there.

Moaning, she met his fierce thrusts with her own, hands caressing him and wresting ragged gasps from him as she touched him intimately. She cupped him in her palm, hand reaching between their bodies to caress him, and felt his shudder. His breath was hot against her cheek, his body hard within her as he checked his movements. With his forehead resting on hers, his lips traced light kisses over her nose and mouth. Then he shifted, easing his body away a bit to look down at her.

With light from candles silhouetting his broad frame, he gazed down at her, his hair a muted gold in the shadows, his features dark against the candle glow. "Promise me," he rasped, "that you will obey me without question in the coming days."

She stared up at him. There was an urgency in his tone that compelled her to agree. "Yea, Rolf. I will obey what is asked of me."

He did not have to explain. She knew that she must yield to him in matters of warfare. The slightest delay could mean death.

And knowing the possibilities that loomed ahead of them, she drew him down to her again, fiercely resisting the intrusion of anything between them now. Rolf's breath came harsh between his teeth as she lifted against him to take him more fully inside her. Braced over her with a hand on each side of her head, he drove his body into hers with a feral sound of pleasure. Again and again he penetrated to the very core of her, sending shuddering waves of bliss through her until finally she poised on the brink of release.

Clutching him to her as if drowning, she sobbed against him, "I love you," then yielded to the shattering ecstasy he gave her. It was a surrender and a victory at once, and she held him to her long after he had reached his own release, hands stroking down his misted skin with tender caresses of love.

Thick mist shrouded the turrets towering over them, and damp shadows crawled over the stones of the bailey as Rolf mounted his destrier. He looked down at Annice, a tightening in his throat. She had wept most of the night, turned away from him in their bed as if she could hide her sorrow. He had not let her know he heard but, when she had finally subsided, had pulled her to him and held her through the night.

Women were ever fearful when men rode off to war, and he could not reassure her that he would come back. Even the stalwart King Richard had been slain by a chance arrow that had fallen from the sky. Rolf thought it a celestial error. Richard had been amusing himself by watching an enterprising Frenchman use a frying pan to catch the stones catapulted toward their fortress; those stones had then been used as ammunition against the English who had launched them. Then had come the arrow that struck Richard in the shoulder, and he'd broken the shaft attempting to pull it out. It had taken the king twelve days to die from the festering wound. No leech had been able to save him.

Nay, he would not promise Annice that he would return. He would not give her hope that might prove false

Tidings were grim. London had been taken by the rebels, and the city prepared to defend herself against Salisbury's Flemish troops. But it would demand enormous siege machines and an endless supply of ammunition to break the city, as the river alone made it nigh impossible to broach, so the Earl of Salisbury withdrew. That left the very core of John's resources in the hands of the rebels, gold and goods held hostage by his enemies.

Now the rebels were locked inside the city, unable to leave, but fortified against the king's efforts to enter. In the game of chess the situation would be called a stalemate.

Messengers between Windsor and London were wearing new ruts in the road as the king attempted to negotiate with his barons. Rolf was called to the king's aid, and now he answered with his troops, leaving Gareth of Kesteven as able castellan for Dragonwyck.

"I have given Gareth his orders," he said to Annice. "Do you obey whatever message I send. I have made arrangements for you to go to the nunnery near Gedney should the rebels turn to Dragonwyck. Though I do not believe it would fall easily, I dare not risk your safety. Take Belle with you should this come about, and flee for your own safety."

"Yea, lord," Annice replied, though 'twas obvious she only half attended his words.

He smiled slightly and leaned from his saddle to draw her near. Wulfsige snorted his displeasure at having anyone close to his head, and Rolf quieted the destrier with a firm hand as he held Annice in a fierce grasp.

"I will come back for you," he said softly. "Whatever I must do, I will see you safe from harm. Do not fear for me, but mind your own danger. The rebels are in foul moods and will not barter."

Heedless of those watching, Rolf spread his fingers in the hair at the nape of her neck and kissed her fiercely. His mouth ground into her soft lips as if he would never taste them again; then he released her abruptly. She stumbled back several steps, blue eyes wide with anguish and tears.

Unable to bear it a moment longer, he wrenched Wulfsige's head around and spurred him forward. The thunder of shod hooves against stone filled the air as they rode out of the bailey and over the drawbridge. They were just cleared of the bridge when he heard it being raised. Gareth would not allow any man to enter once the castle was closed.

Rolf did not look back.

By the time he reached Windsor, negotiations were all but ended between the king and his barons. Strife had raged back and forth, messengers wearing roads and metal horseshoes thin as powerful men bartered critical issues. Finally, sixty-one articles of the charter were decided upon.

It was the last that drew Rolf's attention and dismay.

"Why in the name of all that's holy," he muttered to Guy, "does anyone think twenty-five men will ever agree on what is just cause for rebellion? These barons named as mediators will think only of their own interests, not those of the country or the king."

"Yea," Sir Guy agreed tonelessly. He looked past Rolf to the broad meadow stretching beyond their camp. They had been ordered to make camp there, in this meadow between Staines and Windsor. It was called Runnymede, and 'twas there that a meeting had been placed between king and barons on this morning of June 15. The long reach of level grassland stretched along the banks of the river, and the rebel barons had also made camp. They had come with a multitude of illustrious knights, all armed to the teeth. It looked as if the whole of the nobility of England faced the king, while John had many less.

The archbishops of Canterbury and Dublin were there for the king, as well as the master of the English Templars, and the earls of Pembroke, Warren, Salisbury, and Arundel. About a dozen barons of lesser degree were among their number.

It was to those men that the king finally capitulated, signing the document known as the Magna Carta with dignity and all the decorum usually assigned to his rank as king. With sunlight gilding grass, trees, and the glitter of the king's litter, the great charter was signed. It proposed to grant equal rights to every class and every individual in the nation, but held far more implications than those.

The twenty-five barons chosen to "observe, keep, and cause to be observed with all their might" the provisions of the charter were present at Runnymede and triumphantly accepted the king's signed document. King and barons all swore to keep all the provisions of the charter "in good faith and without deceit."

John also promised that he would not procure from anyone anything whereby his concessions might be revoked or diminished, but few placed much faith in the king's promises. Why else would John have hired so many foreign mercenaries?

"England is merely exchanging one king for five-and-twenty overkings," Rolf observed bitterly when it was over and John had retired to Windsor. The noise of celebration and feasting was a muted rumble in the distant meadow littered with tents and rebel barons.

Guy turned away from the open window. " 'Tis whispered that once in privacy, John treated his steward to the sight of Angevin temper at its worst. He snarled blasphemous oaths, gnashed his teeth, rolled his eyes, and snatched up sticks and even straws from the floor, gnawing them like a madman. Shredded wood and embroidered hangings litter his chamber, I am told, and none dare go near him till his temper is lessened." He paused, then added softly, " 'Tis said that the king frothed at the mouth like a rabid dog, foam flying about and covering his garments. He is mad. We are lost."

"But the king is not mad." Rolf drank from his cup, the wine doing nothing to ease his own disquiet. He lifted his eyes to look at Guy. "Mark me, this is only the beginning. When John recovers from his tantrum, he will set about to undo what has been done this day, and all of England will suffer for it."

Four days after the signing, all the barons of England, rebel and loyalist, repeated their oath of homage to the king. During the next seven days the king dispatched copies of the charter to the sheriffs, foresters, and royal bailiffs in every shire, with letters ordering them to make the men under their jurisdiction swear obedience to the twenty-five named barons in whatever form they might request. He caused twelve sworn knights to be elected in the next county court to inquire into the evil customs that were part of the grievances listed, promising their extirpation. To the outside world John showed a calm, smiling countenance, conversing gaily and familiarly with those he met, declaring himself satisfied with the settlement of affairs and peace.

Hubert de Burgh, a loyalist of John's, had been appointed new chief justiciar. He ordered the sheriffs and knights of every shire to punish any person who refused to swear an oath of obedience to the twenty-five barons.

When the king left Windsor ten days after the signing of the charter, unable to move earlier because of a severe attack of gout, Rolf and his men went with him to Winchester. For a brief time it seemed as if the king meant to keep the charter, and the barons would keep the peace.

But the hard core of rebel barons openly insulted John and refused to relinquish the city of London to him. July and August passed in a haze of sultry weather and a flurry of letters between England and the pope. The pope sternly instructed the barons to obey John and pay him homage in any matter which he required of them.

Then it was widely learned that even before the signing of the Magna Carta, John had entreated the pope to annul the hateful agreement forced upon him by disloyal rebel subjects. Stephen Langton, traveling to Rome to entreat the pope to allow king and vassals to work the charter into a peaceful solution, was intercepted by the pope's letter disavowing the Magna Carta as well as the archbishop.

Caught between unconditional surrender by order of the pope or open war to the bitter end, the rebel barons flew into revolt. They were not ready for war, however, and the king was. John had been gathering men and arms, and Poitevens, Gascons, Brabantines, and Flemings flocked to his cause from over the sea. The Earl of Salisbury visited ten royal castles and selected from their garrisons troops for John's service. The king issued a general safe-conduct to "all who may wish to return to our fealty and service," then toward the end of September advanced as far inland as Malling.

Rolf and Sir Guy camped their men outside London with increasing disquiet. News had come that Seabrook was wavering between open rebellion and homage to the king. Justin, Rolf worried, was in grave danger. He intensified his efforts to retrieve the boy and finally wrested from John a promise to send royal troops for him should Seabrook rebel. But that did not seem likely to happen soon. He was still left to wait and wonder and watch.

Rolf wrote careful letters to Annice, keeping back the worst news. He did not mention that the rebels had appealed to King Philip of France to join their cause and depose John.

"What do they expect?" he snarled in frustration to Guy. "That King Philip will help them wrest England from John's grasp and then go quietly back to France? Nay, if we lose, England will be part of France. Philip will give England to Prince Louis to rule, and Louis will pay his knights with the English lands belonging to those foolish barons who summoned him."

After a moment of taut silence Guy murmured, "Now that the rebels have renewed the siege of Northampton Castle and laid siege to Oxford, John's efforts to induce the archbishop into yielding Rochester Castle to him have failed."

Sensing undercurrents in Guy's remarks, Rolf looked up at him. "Yea, 'tis well-known. What of it?"

Guy took a deep breath and said, "Your brother Geoffrey has sided with the rebels." He held out a letter, and after a moment Rolf reached out for it.

It was short and had been sent first to Dragonwyck. Gareth of Kesteven had forwarded it by messenger to Rolf, but that man had not been able to find him at first, and thus had the letter fallen into Guy's hands. It was a guarded appeal from Geoffrey to his brother to join the rebel forces.

The wind blew steadily and harshly against the walls of the tent, and he listened to it for a long minute before folding the parchment in half. His brother was just across the river from him. He found it vaguely entertaining that the letter had followed him about England for near a month before ending up in his hands only a few miles from his brother.

"What will you do, lord?" Guy asked when Rolf remained lost in silent thought.

"What would you have me do?" Rolf snapped. "Geoffrey is my brother, and though I will not join him, neither will I betray him."

Rather stiffly, Guy said, "I never thought you would. But you must know that the king intends to take Rochester from the rebels, and your brother is one of its defenders. We will be called to arms against them."

"Yea, but I cannot do other than serve where I am called." Rolf raked a hand through his hair, feeling utterly weary. "I can only pray I do not have to face Geoffrey at the end of my sword."

In the middle of October the king drew near the gates of Rochester. When they arrived on the banks of the Medway River that separated them from Rochester, the king gave his orders. Sir Guy and a party of men went upriver to fire the bridge from beneath, thus cutting off communications between Rochester and London. Robert FitzWalter and a picked body of knights and men-at-arms were guarding the bridge and managed to drive off the assailants and extinguish the blaze. But then FitzWalter and his men returned to London, and Rolf led the second attack on the bridge. This effort was successful and the bridge was destroyed, opening the way to Rochester Castle and the assault of the town.

At first town citizens manned the battlements and walls with a great show. But when they saw the king and his men, they fled. John's forces entered through the gates and chased the citizens through the city toward the bridge so determinedly that all the defending knights were forced into the castle. Now the castle was defended by ninety-five knights and forty-five men-at-arms.

A siege was laid that lasted over a month. No reinforcements came to the aid of the beleaguered men inside Rochester Castle, and every possible mode of attack was attempted by John's forces. Mining, battery, assaults, and siege engines were plied day and night against the mighty walls. Nothing worked. The brave men barricaded inside the castle walls with little food expected no mercy from the king, nor were they of a mind to yield.

Rolf knew Geoffrey to be inside, but there was nothing he could do. His brother, like himself, had chosen his side.

On November 25 John ordered the justiciar to send him forty fat bacon-pigs. These were used to set fire to the stuff that was bundled together beneath the tower. A blaze was kindled beneath the square tower which destroyed it and rendered vulnerable those inside the castle. Still, they did not surrender until St. Andrew's Day, five days later.

Gallows were set up, and the king declared that he would hang the defenders, one and all, including Geoffrey. Only the pleas by Rolf and Savaric de Mauléon swayed him, as they pointed out that if the king hanged brave knights such as these, the rebels would surely do the like to any loyalists who might fall into their hands. Then no man would be likely to remain in the king's service. So the knights were sent to prison, Geoffrey among them, and the men-at-arms were left to be ransomed. John's only vengeance was the hanging of a crossbowman whom he had had in his service since boyhood.

Now the king's attention turned in another direction. He

marched through Essex and Surrey into Hampshire and thence proceeded to Windsor. On the twentieth of December he held a council at St. Albans, and this led to the division of his army into two bodies.

Rolf fretted at the king's actions. Another Christmas season would pass in John's company, but this year he had not even Annice with him to soften the tension. It would be months before he saw her again, though he wrote her letters almost daily.

News had come about Seabrook, and as Rolf had half expected, the wily earl had sworn homage to the king. That meant that Justin would remain at Stoneham Castle, with his uncle as his guardian unless the king could be persuaded to relent. But with so much turmoil in the kingdom, the private moments with John were rare. Even when he managed to confront the king, John was—as usual—reluctant.

"I see no need to change matters at this time," John said coolly when Rolf pressed him for a decision. "Really, Dragonwyck, you begin to chafe me with your constant badgering about your son. He is well, and much safer in Seabrook's keep than he would be ranging the countryside on his way to your keep in Lincolnshire. French mercenaries would be only too glad to have such a valuable pawn in their hands, and then where would we both be? Nay, 'tis too risky, even if I was inclined to grant your request right now."

It had taken all Rolf's self-control not to fling the king's half promises and threats back into his teeth. If not for the knowledge that it would only endanger Justin more, as well as Annice, Rolf might have quit the king in disgust at that moment. He'd left the royal chambers with a heavy heart and heaving stomach.

Then came even worse news. Rolf and Sir Guy were commanded to join the king in his sweep through the northern provinces of England. They were to destroy with fire and sword everything in their path—human, animal, and habitat. Nothing was to be spared.

Sickened, Rolf reluctantly ordered his men forward.

CHAPTER 20

It was late spring when word came from the highest battlement that a body of troops had been sighted in the distance. Annice remained outwardly calm, though inside she was aquiver with fear. She had heard the reports coming in from the patrols Gareth had sent out and waited with terrified resignation for either rebel forces or loyalist forces to lay siege to Dragonwyck. All around the countryside, villages had been burned, muddy fields trampled, inhabitants slaughtered.

Rolf's orders to Gareth had been to send Lady Annice to safety at once if enemy troops came too close. But was the king's army their enemy? Though she had heard of the destruction of northern provinces by John, she did not know how widespread it was, or how close. No one would tell her. If she chanced upon Gareth or any other knights deep in discussion of the king's advance, they immediately ceased talking.

Preparations were made, though Gareth explained the preparations for war or possible siege as mere precautions.

Steadily, while trembling serfs in the village attempted to plow muddy spring fields, Dragonwyck men-at-arms gathered pitch, tar, and oil for the walls, stones and leathers and wood for the catapults, and shafts and feathers for arrows. Armor was patched and mended, blacksmiths hammered steel into swords day and night on their anvils, and hides were fashioned into shields and padded gambesons to fit under mail. These detailed preparations boded ill, but no man would admit it to their lady.

Sometimes, Annice thought fretfully, not knowing was worse than knowing the truth.

But when the armed troops approached and the sentries posted in the barbican sent down word that 'twas the Lord of Dragonwyck who drew near, Annice soon discovered that knowledge could be a two-edged sword.

Running down the stairwell toward the entry where they would soon come, she paused on a flat landing to catch her breath. Hope spurred her forward but dread held her back. What if he had come home because he was injured? The country was in such turmoil that 'twas possible no messenger could have got to Dragonwyck with the news. She uttered a short prayer.

The prayer was interrupted by the sound of Rolf's voice in the hall, and she took a deep breath and gathered her courage. He sounded hale and uninjured, though infinite weariness tinged the usual resonance of his voice. When she rounded the last curve of the winding stairwell, she saw him. He stood sturdily enough, and there was no sign of a wound or bandage.

Relief flooded her, and she moved toward him. He turned as if sensing her approach, and she stopped in shock. It was Rolf, but it was as if he had been carved from a block of stone. The features were the same—firm mouth, straight nose, large eyes beneath dark-blond brows—but there was a carefully tense set to his face that struck her with all the force of a broad plank. It was as if he were afraid to show any sign of life.

"Milord," she said finally, moving forward when he just stood motionless, "I am relieved to have you home safely."

"And I am relieved to be here."

Disquieted by his flat tone, Annice managed a trembling smile of welcome and went to him. She glanced at Sir Guy and received another shock. His face bore the same expression, one of intense suffering and strain. Where there had always been a smile for her, or a jest, there was only a polite murmur of greeting that chilled her more than the winds of winter could do.

Gathering herself, Annice quietly bade servants to fetch wine for their lord and set stools near the fire. Neither Rolf nor Guy made protest but accompanied her to the hearth to be seated. No one spoke, and even after the servants brought wine to them and departed, the silence remained.

At her feet the dog Bordet looked from her to his master and whined. Rolf turned then and put a hand upon the mastiff's great head. The dog wriggled with joy, and Annice felt a spurt of jealousy that she quickly extinguished. At least Rolf was reacting to something, even if 'twas to the dog instead of to her. Not even Vachel had been able to draw him out, and that was unusual.

Drawing in a deep breath, Annice asked, "Tell me, milord—how goes the king's struggle?"

Guy muttered something beneath his breath and tilted back his head to drain the wine in his cup, startling her. Rolf said nothing, but his knuckles were white where he gripped the stem of his goblet.

Terrified now that all was lost, Annice could not still the fear in her voice as she pressed, "Are we undone? Has all been lost?"

Rolf gave a harsh laugh. "Lost? That depends on if you consider charred fields, burned keeps, and slaughtered women and babies as necessary chattels of England."

Confused, Annice looked from one man to the other. Her nerves were stretched tautly, and she bit her lip to silence an outburst. Finally Rolf took another sip of wine and cleared his throat.

"We took Rochester, but I wrote you of that. My brother was there, fighting with the rebels. John imprisoned him, but at least he is still alive."

He paused, frowning at the goblet he held, and Annice refilled it for him and sat back down. She put her hands in her lap and waited, sensing that it was not that which so disturbed him. An awful premonition stirred in her, and she fixed her gaze on Rolf's face as if to lend him strength. He looked up at her, and she smothered a gasp. It was the first time he had made direct eye contact with her since he'd returned, and she was shocked by the haunted, dead eyes that gazed at her.

"I used to enjoy war," he said in a soft, thoughtful murmur, as if he were speaking to himself. "There was pleasure in storming castle walls, engaging a worthy enemy in combat, and emerging victorious. There was honor in it. A sense of purpose." His voice changed, becoming harsher. "There is no honor in what the king has set us to do. 'Tis more like shutting horses up in a stable and setting it afire, than warfare."

Annice shivered with a sudden chill. She looked at Sir Guy, and his gaze was as lifeless; his dark eyes that usually danced with mischief had turned old and dull.

"The entire east has been retaken by the king," Guy said, his voice strained. The words sounded as if they were pulled from him. "Everywhere you look there are corpses. Piles of them. After Rochester fell, the king commanded that our troops go with him because our men are well trained and have good leaders. I was glad at first to go . . . glad!" The last word was a mixture of pain and revulsion, and he paused to pour more wine into his goblet. His hand shook, and Annice shivered again.

Turning agonized eyes to her, Sir Guy whispered, "We were ordered to burn everything, kill everyone. Old women and men. Mothers. Babies. We could control our men, but those bloody French mercenaries of the king's—!" He swallowed heavily. "They enjoyed it. John loosed them on England like ravening wolves, and they devoured all they could. Babies spit on pikes—Holy Mary, but I hope never to see such again."

Guy's shudder of horror made Annice's stomach clench. Rolf was still staring into his goblet of wine, his mouth set in a taut slash of pale color.

"Is this John's vengeance?" she asked in a faint whisper. "Does he intend to give England over to the mercenaries?"

Rolf stirred. "Nay. Not even John is that mad. If offered

a large enough bribe, he will most gladly spare an enemy. Our troops were bade to defend those who yielded."

After a moment Annice asked, "Can you not remove your men and come home?" It was a futile request, she knew, but from the look in Rolf's eyes, she held a faint hope he would agree.

But Rolf laughed bitterly. "Yea, I believe I would do so, oath or no, but I cannot."

"Why?"

Lifting his eyes to her, he said tonelessly, "My brother Geoffrey is in the king's hands. If I do not obey his orders, my brother will die. While I might reason that Geoffrey is a man and made his own choice, I must also recall who has my son in his hold. Seabrook is safe, but Thurston is eager to keep the king's grace after being rumored to traffic with the rebels. He would gladly hand Justin over to John for hostage at the merest suggestion." He looked down at his wine again and said hoarsely, "I will not risk my son."

A single candle pierced the darkness smothering them in soft folds. The bed was shadowed, the light beyond a small pinpoint. Rolf removed the last of his garments and hung them on the bed pole, then slipped beneath the sheets and turned to Annice. She did not resist him but enveloped him in her embrace as if she wished to hold him forever.

For several minutes he lay there without moving. There had been so much death, so much anguish—how could he bear to lose her? Yet how could he keep her safe when he must join his king?

Rolf slid one hand from her shoulder down the slope of her breast, cupping it in his palm. She shuddered beneath his caress and moved closer. He felt her soft skin against him, breast to breast, her hips a gentle urgency against his loins. Yet he felt nothing else. No passion, no life. Only a great, overpowering sadness that threatened to consume him.

After a moment she drew back slightly. "My lord? Have I displeased you? Or are you too weary for other than rest?"

"Why must women always think themselves at fault?" he muttered, and felt her stiffen against him. He sighed. "Nay, sweeting, I did not mean it thus. 'Tis not you. 'Tis me, and what I have seen of late. I feel as if I reek of death."

She was still again, then said softly, "Let me warm you. You are chilled. Turn over onto your stomach and try to sleep."

Lifting to her knees beneath the bed linens, she began to massage him, a gentle kneading up and down his aching muscles, from shoulders to ankle and back. Slowly, his tension eased with her ministrations. He began to relax. Annice's fingers moved up to his neck, rubbing in small circles, then up into his hair.

Finally Rolf turned onto his back and reached for her, this time eagerly. He pulled her astride him, thrusting up into her with a hunger he had almost forgotten. There was a ferocity to it, a mixture of rage and need and passion that shook him deeply. With his hands at her waist, he held her, thrusting strongly until he heard her cry out, felt the deep, racking shudders that marked her release.

When he would have slowed, she gripped him fiercely, urging him on. 'Twas as if they battled rather than loved, their bodies straining against each other like two combatants. Limbs entwined, they turned and twisted on the bed until the sheets were in a hopeless, damp tangle. Finally, when the candle across the chamber had guttered and pale shadows gleamed at the window cracks, they collapsed in sated exhaustion. Holding tight to each other, bodies damp with effort and release, they fell asleep at last.

"I have been here near four mouths. 'Tis time for me to join John, and for you to go to safety." Rolf looked away from Annice's distress. He could not bear leaving her behind, but he could not keep her safe if she was with him. If he could not see to Justin's safety, he could at least do whatever was possible to keep his wife safe.

"But why must I leave here?" Annice asked softly. Her voice shook slightly, and she glanced around the chamber as if to imprint it upon her mind. "Dragonwyck is the strongest castle I know of."

"Yea, but too great a temptation to Louis's French

knights. It was almost taken by Thurston and a single traitor just last year. I will not risk you in my absence."

"And so you send me away to a nunnery?" Annice cried. "Do you think I shall be so much safer there?"

He looked down into her eyes, unwilling to describe to her the atrocities he had seen committed upon the women in the keeps that had fallen to John. The French would hardly be more merciful were they to take Dragonwyck, a rich prize coveted by Louis even more for the fact that it belonged to John's baron.

"If I did not think you would be safer, I would not send you there," he said slowly. " 'Tis a small nunnery, and worth nothing to greedy predators. I doubt the French would bother with it."

So as not to frighten her even more, he did not tell her of his precautions; the force of men who were to guard the nunnery would take her to safety should it appear to be endangered. There was little enough safety anywhere in England. Prince Louis of France had invaded England in May. His troops had met little resistance, save for those keeps strong enough to thwart him. But those were few. Keep after keep fell to the invaders, until by August nearly two thirds of the barons had yielded. Now it was early September. Dragonwyck's walls were strained with refugees from the surrounding countryside, and all of Lincolnshire was in turmoil.

Turning away from Annice, Rolf went to the window and stared out into the bailey below. "Many of the rebel barons are changing sides again. They see what Louis is doing, and they are returning to John's cause, bitter but wiser. Better the devil we know than the devil we don't. I am to meet John to aid in the relief of Lincoln keep. 'Tis being held by Nicolaa de Hay, but 'tis not known how much longer she can resist the besiegers."

He turned back to Annice, who was staring at him with fearful blue eyes. His throat tightened against a surge of emotion. How did he admit that he feared more for her than for his own life? How would he put into words such a weakness? He could not. He could only do what little was possible to safeguard her, and pray that it would suffice.

"Do you think me less brave than Nicolaa de Hay?"

Annice asked after a moment. "Do you not think I would hold out against besiegers as well as she?" She gestured to the bailey below the window. "You have an able castellan here, and I am not so foolish as to allow the gates to be opened to any man."

Dragging a hand over his eyes, Rolf said heavily, "Why do you think the French besiege Lincoln? Because they know 'tis being held by a woman. They believe it to be weaker and so set to bring it down that much quicker."

"Then they are learning the errors of their thoughts," she said sharply.

He smiled grimly. "Yea, but if Lincoln should fall, Lady Nicolaa will be most fearfully slain for her defiance. I will not risk you."

Annice drew in a deep breath. "I yield to your persuasion, milord, but I cannot say I like it."

Reaching out, he drew her close to him. "My fierce little wife. I know you are brave, and that you would fight to the very last to hold Dragonwyck. But 'tis only a pile of stones, and you are much more than that. I must join the king and could not feel easy thinking you in danger."

She looked up. Her eyes searched his face as if waiting for something, and he stared down at her. It was not easy, leaving her behind. But he could do no more to keep her safe. Yea, 'twas difficult enough knowing that he could not safeguard his son. Must he risk all that he loved?

Jésu, but he wished he had the words to ease her, to assure her that all would be well. But nothing he said would assuage her fears, and in truth, he could not say that all would be well. He could only hope and pray that fate would not wrest her from him.

"I will go as you ask," Annice said softly, "but I shall pray for you daily."

He closed his hand around the one she put upon his chest. "Yea, and pray also for Justin. These are dangerous times for us, and even more so for a small boy."

Annice leaned her head on his chest, her lips moving against his velvet surcoat as she whispered, "Justin is a brave lad, like his father. He will survive this, as will all of us. God could not be so cruel as to separate us now."

"I hope you are right, *chérie*. I hope you are right." He tilted her face up to his and gave her a swift, fierce kiss. "You will be safe at the nunnery, with the good sisters to care for you and God to watch over all."

But still, when they had traveled to the small nunnery near Gedney and he left her standing at the gates, he had to fight the urge to go back. After learning of John's actions against the abbey church and village in Crowland, how the king had set to flame the harvest fields of St. Guthlac with his own hands, he did not know if Annice would be safe even in God's house.

"I think she will be much safer here, milord," Sir Guy said when they rode away from Gedney. " 'Tis a poor nunnery, with nothing to recommend it as worthy of destruction." There was a pause; then he added, "And the men-at-arms set to guard it know their duty well. At the first sign of approaching troops, Lady Annice will be escorted to safety."

Rolf didn't reply. Nothing in England was safe these days, and he could only put his faith in a swift end to the rebels' revolt. Surely, when they saw that John was so determined, they would yield. Even now 'twas said that Louis's partisans were slowly retreating. The long siege Louis had laid at Dover was not yet successful, with Hubert de Burgh holding out against it most stubbornly. Even a Flemish adventurer had spent the summer with a thousand bowmen hiding in the wilderness, coming out only to harass the French with deadly arrows that were rumored to have killed thousands of the invaders. Louis was growing disheartened and weary.

The relief of Lincoln was swift, for the French there must have learned of John's savage advance and ruthless disposal of English rebels. They fled before the king's advance, retreating to the Isle of Axholme. With his troops, Rolf accompanied the king's grim pursuit of the invaders to Barton, Scotter, and then Stowe. Mercenaries were sent across the Trent to ravage the isle with fire and sword; then John marched back to Lincoln.

Rolf resisted the urge to visit Annice at the nunnery. He would draw no attention to the tiny sanctuary, for fear John might choose to make an example of it, as he had St.

Guthlac. Nor could he aid his neighbors but could only watch silently when Lincolnshire fields, heavy and ready for harvest, were put to the torch. Houses and farm buildings were sacked and destroyed, with John an eager witness. It sickened Rolf to see the destruction, but he knew that if the king was to be victorious, he must leave no forage for his enemies. Despite those who would lay the sins of sloth and cowardice upon John's shoulders, the king was possessed of a crafty strategic nature. His blunders were not those most oft attributed to him, but were of innate moral evil. It had been said by a historian twenty years before, "Nature's enemy, John," and Rolf knew it to be true.

In early October they arrived at Lynn, where the townsfolk greeted them joyously. John, pleased with the generous monies given to him, graciously set about fortifying the town. A feast was arranged, with the wealthy burghers of Lynn giving John his royal due. He feasted greedily, but the excesses for which he was so notorious undid him.

Ill, racked with a violent attack of dysentery brought on by his excesses, the king seemed to be dying. Uncharacteristically, he granted to Lady Margaret de Lacy some land so that she might build a religious house in memory of the souls of her father, brother, and mother—who had died of starvation in John's dungeons. Her mother had been Lady Maud de Braose who had defied the king's demand of her son as hostage, saying that she would not yield a child of hers to a king who had murdered his own nephew.

" 'Tis fitting that the king feel some remorse at last," Sir Guy remarked.

Rolf turned to stare at him. "Yea, but it bodes ill. For John to do such a gracious thing, he must feel the wind of death upon him."

"But if the king dies . . ." Guy broke off, and both men looked at one another. The implications were overwhelming.

"We can only," Rolf said slowly, "pray for the best." He did not say aloud what was in his thoughts but saw from Guy's face that his knight must know.

It was in every man's face in the following days, that awareness of the approaching end. It would be the end to many of their troubles should the king die, yet no man dared say aloud what all thought.

Ill as he was, the king insisted upon leaving Lynn and moving to Wisbeach. The king swept northward as if fleeing death's demons, listening to no one in his haste. Impatience cost him dearly. With all his newly gathered loot, as well as England's treasure and crown jewels in his caravan, they came to the banks of the Welland River. When they paused at the mouth of the river, John gave orders to cross the Wash without waiting for the ebb of the tide.

"Sire," Rolf was moved to protest in alarm, "the soil is treacherous here. See the brackish water that covers it. We will not have secure footing and must wait until the tide is out to see where 'tis safe to progress."

Snarling, John spat, "Craven coward, I will cross now, and you will do what you are told."

Rolf stiffened. "Yea, *beau* sire," he choked out past the rage clogging his throat. He withdrew and quietly ordered his men to cross at a certain point.

They started across, Rolf silently cursing both the waves lapping about the legs of the terrified horses and the king, with impartial and equal fervor. Then the ground opened up beneath them. Men and horses drowned, and the wooden carts overturned to spill out everything of value. The gold was heavy and sunk quickly.

Rolf managed to get the king and some of the troops to the opposite shore, but most of the baggage train slowly disappeared into the boggy ground. The water was icy, and the wind blew sharply across the marshlands. Men who managed to remain dry removed their clothing to give to the king, while others went back into the water to attempt to retrieve some of the king's treasure. Even John threw himself into the effort but was barely saved from being drowned when his horse became mired.

It was useless. The mire had quickly claimed it all, save for some plates and a few small trinkets. The crown jewels, Eleanor of Aquitaine's fabulous treasure, were lost forever.

Admitting defeat, the wet, shivering troops went on to Swineshead abbey, where the king—in fevered rage and grief—consoled himself with peaches and new cider. This only aggravated his already deteriorating condition, so that when they moved on to Sleaford two days later and a messenger brought disastrous news from besieged Hubert de Burgh at Dover, John was forced to send for a leech to ease his suffering. The physician was unsuccessful.

Through gritted teeth the king announced his plans to set out for Newark the following day. "Hubert de Burgh has written for permission to surrender, or for aid," he added furiously. "Dover is lost."

Rain poured from the sky and the wind howled around the thick walls of the Sleaford keep, but John still persisted in his determination to leave. To Rolf's dismay, the king was able to ride only a few miles before he collapsed, panting and groaning. A crude litter was fashioned for him, formed of willow boughs cut from the roadside with the knight's swords and knives, then woven together. A horse cloth was thrown over the woven branches, but there was no cushion nor straw to relieve its hardness. At first the litter was slung between some of the knights' destriers, but those high-mettled creatures made it too difficult to progress. The litter was then carried on the shoulders of the men, but the jolting of it proved to be intolerable for the king.

At last John was placed atop a horse to finish his journey to Newark, finally reaching the bishop of Lincoln's castle on the banks of the Trent. The abbot of Croxton rushed to his side to minister to his body and soul, for it was plain the king was close to death.

Numb by this time from all the disasters, Rolf could only wait for the inevitable. During the next three days John declared his eldest son, nine-year-old Henry, as his heir and commanded all those with him to swear fealty to the boy. Letters were sent out to the sheriffs and constables of royal castles, bidding them accept Henry as their lord and king. After appointing a guardian of his younger son, Richard, the king entrusted the guardianship of Henry to William the Marshal, Earl of Pembroke.

It was, Rolf thought wearily, the best possible choice. William was known to be fair and just.

At midnight of October 18, 1216, a whirlwind swept through Newark with such force that houses shook like dry leaves. People cried out that the devil had come for the king, and indeed, in that terrifying hour, John died.

Rolf learned of it from John of Savigny, a monk who had kept watch beside the king's body on the morning after his death. Having gone to deliver a letter to one of the sheriffs and only just returned, Rolf was angered to hear that the servants of the royal household had fled with everything of value they could carry.

Rolf formed a guard to escort the king's funeral procession from Newark to Worcester, where John had requested that he be laid to rest in the Church of the Blessed Mary and St. Wulfstan. They passed unhindered across England, Rolf's troops and a large band of foreign mercenaries escorting the king's body to its final resting place. Rolf had the morbid thought that it was fitting that the escort should be composed mostly of the foreign mercenaries who had been brought to England at John's command to fight against English rebels.

After the king's interment Guy turned to Rolf and asked, "What do we now, milord? Prince Louis will continue to fight."

Rolf stared past him into the rain. "Fight for what? He can no longer pretend that he is aiding England's deliverance from a tyrant. The tyrant is dead. No Englishman will fight to seek bondage under a foreign conqueror."

"Then we may return to Dragonwyck." Hope sprang into Guy's eyes, and a smile touched his lips. "We may retrieve Lady Annice, and peace will come to England at last." He took a step toward the door, then turned back impatiently. "Are we for Gedney and the lady?"

Rolf leaned a shoulder against the stone wall and gazed steadily at Guy. "I would know," he said bluntly, "of your sentiments toward my wife. You speak of her frequently, and 'tis always with just such a light in your eyes. Did you have ought to do with her abduction after our wedding? Was it at your word that she was taken to be returned to Thurston?"

Guy stared back at him. Gloomy light filtered through the open door smelling of rain and smoke from coal fires. A heavy silence lengthened, until finally Rolf shifted slightly and his sword clanked against the stone wall.

"Well?" he demanded. "I would hear what defense you may have to offer."

Lifting his shoulders in a shrug, Guy said, "I have no defense, milord. 'Tis true that I gaze fondly at your lady, but 'tis not for the reason you might think." He paused and turned his face slightly toward the open door. Rain swept in on a gust of wind, misting his face as he stared out past the church steps, his gaze fixed on some distant point. "Whatever you may think of me, I would not betray you. I have not done so, nor will I." He looked back at Rolf, and there was a bleak light in his eyes. "If I am guilty of anything, 'tis of not being honest with you about my reasons for caring so steadfastly for Lady Annice."

Rolf's hand went to the hilt of his sword, and his gaze narrowed. "Then pray, be honest now, for it may well save us a battle inside the church."

Throwing up a hand, Guy said, "Nay, lord. I cannot fight you. Not even when your assumption that I would dishonor either you or your lady rakes sharply on my temper."

"You'd best explain," Rolf growled, "ere I spit you where you stand. . . ." He drew in a deep breath to calm his raging temper. Filled with the residue of frustration and tension from the past months, he realized that he was releasing the pressure by attacking his knight. That he might or might not have just cause ceased to be important, and he slowly released the hilt of his sword and shook his head.

"Sir Guy, though I cannot say that I have trusted you fully this past year, I have no evidence that you would betray me in any way. Before, I would have trusted you with my life, and in truth, you always proved worthy of that trust."

Guy smiled faintly, and some of his tension eased visibly. He put out his right hand to show it free of a weapon, and after a pause Rolf reached to take it, their clasp sealing an unspoken pledge not to fight. They stood for a moment while the wind blew rain in on them and tugged at the folds of their cloaks.

"Perhaps," Guy said, " 'Tis time to share a confidence with you, milord. It may explain a lot of your concerns."

"Yea," Rolf replied. "Mayhap it will. Let us go seek a

warm fire and wine, and if you wish to unburden yourself, I will listen."

Taking a deep breath, Guy said quickly as if he would lose his courage, "Your lady is my half sister, milord. Hugh de Beauchamp was my father, and I am his bastard son." He put up a quick hand when Rolf's eyes narrowed with sudden suspicion and said hastily, "Lady Annice does not know. I had never met her before the road from Stoneham, though I knew of her, of course. I—thought it best—that she know nothing of me. In truth, until you revealed that her father was Beauchamp, I did not know she was my sister."

For a moment Rolf stared at him in the scented candle-gloom of the church; then he nodded slowly. Yea, that explained much. He smiled and put a hand upon Guy's shoulder.

"You can tell me of it while we sup, Sir Guy. I would be interested to learn why Annice still does not know of it."

Guy's smile was thin, but there was a relieved light in his eyes. "Aye, lord. I will be glad to tell it all over a cup of wine."

As they left the church and their dead king, Rolf had the fleeting thought that there would be more war, but it didn't matter. The battles to come would be to insure the little Prince Henry—nay, now King Henry III—his rightful place as heir. But Louis would be turned back, and England would once more belong to them. Yea, out of evil had finally come good, and with able counsel the new king might bring peace at last to England's shores. It was long past due.

Pulling his hood over his head to shelter it from the rain, Rolf said aloud, "I go first to seek my lady, then to retrieve my son from Thurston of Seabrook. With John dead, only Seabrook stands between me and Justin. I intend to dispose of him swiftly. As a family member, do you go with me, Sir Guy?"

Guy flung him a broad smile. "Yea, lord, I go most willingly on both quests."

CHAPTER 21

─────────────

Just before dusk, when the vespers bells began to ring, Annice heard a voice call to her from the bushes edging the small garden of the nunnery. She rose and turned toward the sound, giving a start of surprise and pleasure when she recognized Gowain.

"Gowain. Come in at once—let me unfasten the gate for you. Will you stay to break bread—?"

"There is no time for questions, milady. I have come to warn you. The French are near. You must flee at once."

"The French?" Cold dread chilled her spine, and she forced herself to remain calm. "Of course. I shall fetch Belle and the others. We must hurry."

"Nay, milady. Take no time for others." Gowain put a hand upon her arm. "Gareth of Kesteven bade me see to you, and I dare not tarry. Your escort awaits in yon grove."

"I understand," she said firmly, "but I am not leaving without Belle. And the abbess must be warned. Mother Sarah will want to get the others to safety."

A note of panic crept into Gowain's insistent words.

"Nay! I cannot allow it . . . I will warn them. You must flee, milady, ere the French come upon you too swiftly."

Despite her protests, Gowain pulled her firmly with him and into the grove behind the small wooden quarters that housed the nuns. Neat gardens lay sleeping in the autumn sun, and birds called in the trees as if the entire world were at peace. It was hard to believe that danger was close.

"Really," Annice protested as she was shoved into the waiting arms of a captain and mounted atop a horse, "if the French are so near, why can we not hear them?"

The captain of the guards said grimly, "They are storming the walls of Dragonwyck, my lady. Patrols range nearby. I am to take you elsewhere for safety's sake."

Dragonwyck. Annice clutched at the high saddle bow and glanced down at Gowain. His face was worried, and he gave a short bob of his head. " 'Tis true, milady. Dragonwyck is besieged. I used the secret gate to slip out and bring you warning."

"And these men—?"

"Have been here as long as you have," the captain replied shortly. "The Dragon set us to guard you from the first night." He bent to grab up her reins, but Annice snatched them away.

"I am fully capable of riding alone, Captain," she said. "I will not be a burden. But I do insist upon bringing along my maid. Gowain, go fetch Belle to me at once."

Obviously caught between Annice's determination and his orders from Gareth, Gowain hesitated an instant too long. Annice dug her heels into the horse's sides, and it bounded forward toward the line of buildings dozing behind walls in the late-afternoon sun.

Cursing, the captain gave chase, barely catching her as she reached the high wooden fence surrounding the nunnery. He signaled to Gowain impatiently. "Go inside to fetch her maid and be quick about it. I have no desire to meet up with the French in such an unprotected place."

"Captain," came the urgent call from one of the soldiers, and they turned. In the distance, down the winding curve of narrow road that led from the nunnery to a cleared patch of field, could clearly be seen the unmistakable glint of sunlight from knights' armor and weapons.

"Too late," muttered the captain, and without regard for her protests, yanked Annice's horse into a run. She clung to the saddle as her mount was pulled along, racing down the narrow twist of road and barely managing to duck tree branches dangling dangerously low. Fear struck her deeply as she heard the shouts of the soldiers in the rear, and then the sound of battle being engaged. The captain pulling her horse had drawn his sword and was obviously searching for a safe spot for his charge.

A faint whistling sound captured Annice's attention, and she looked up just in time to see an arrow descending from the sky. It plummeted in a swift, accurate strike like that of a hawk, piercing the captain's chain mail and striking him from his saddle. With only a faint, choked cry, he fell to the ground. His riderless horse swerved wildly, while Annice's horse ran amok.

Leaning over the lathered neck, she strained to reach the dangling reins before the horse could trip and send her sprawling. It took much effort, but finally she caught them up and straightened in the saddle. Then her heart flipped. There, in the road before her, waited several armed men. She reined her mount to a halt and dared a backward glance. None of her guard was in sight.

And in the distance, rising above the burnished September leaves of gold and brown, rose a thick black cloud of smoke. It came from the direction of the nunnery.

Sir Guy stared at the ruins with helpless rage and grief. It was obvious that the little nunnery had been ravaged weeks before. A raven sat atop a blackened stone, head tilted to one side as it eyed the intruders with dislike. Spreading its wings, the bird let out a raucous screech of defiance, then lifted into the air. The sound of its wings flapping against the wind faded into the gray sky.

Rolf turned to Guy slowly, as if dazed. "There is no sign of the abbess or any inhabitants." His hand curled into a fist on his saddle bow. Fire-blackened timbers stuck out at odd angles, pointing accusing fingers to the sky. Tangles of brush and uprooted trees indicated a fierce struggle.

Clearing his throat, Guy said in a strangled tone, "There should be some sign of the men you left behind as her guard. No doubt, they got her to safety ere the nunnery was overrun."

"God's grace, I hope so."

Guy recognized the fear and strain in his lord's tone. He was afraid for her, also. There were too many dangers about in this land still beleaguered with battle and death. Too many mercenaries still roamed forests and fens, and they had witnessed too much destruction on their journey to Gedney. All of Lincolnshire was a wasteland. Here and there could be seen small signs of recovery, but they were too few. They were almost home when they learned that Dragonwyck was under assault.

Though under siege for a time, the keep still stood. One of the towers had crumbled from the onslaught of the siege engines. The fighting had been fierce, and the castle balanced on the brink of falling when word came of the Dragon's approach. Knowing of le Draca's ruthless reputation, the French disappeared in the night. Gareth of Kesteven, castellan in Rolf's absence, met his lord at the smoldering gates and gave them the first indication that more disaster loomed.

Hesitantly, Gareth informed Rolf that one of the men he'd sent as messenger to warn the nunnery of approaching troops had been found mortally wounded and died before anything useful could be learned. He had been found south of Dragonwyck, whereas Gedney lay to the east, near the rocky coast and several leagues from the castle. It was unknown whether he had succeeded in warning those in the nunnery.

Now, with the evidence of the nunnery's destruction, Guy was forced to agree with Rolf's earlier prediction that forces had ranged toward the south and west. This would indicate that if Annice had been abducted, she was being taken into the midlands of England. If, in truth, she was still alive.

"She is highborn, milord," Guy said, and knew from the

sharp turn of Rolf's head that he was thinking the same thing. "If taken, she would not be slain, but held for ransom."

"Yea. And who would pay the most for her, do you think?" Rolf's fist moved from his saddle to take up his reins. His mouth set into a straight slash, and fierce anger sparked his eyes to an unholy green. Guy was not at all surprised to hear him say through clenched teeth, "No ransom demands have been sent to me. I vow that Thurston of Seabrook has her."

It was, Guy thought, highly probable.

" 'Tis just as well," Rolf growled. "I will take back what is mine, both my son and my wife, and Thurston will rue the day he ever dared keep Justin from me. Nothing will keep me from him now."

Shivering, Annice huddled in a corner of the damp cell into which she'd been thrust. Straw littered the floor at her feet, and she heard the furtive noises of rats in the shadows. Occasionally one of them would grow bold enough to slink out from the shadows and approach, red eyes gleaming dully. Using her boot as a weapon, she had killed two before they grew more cautious.

Though she'd been given little enough to eat, fierce hatred and defiance fueled her determination to survive. Thurston had been most pleased to see her again. His smirk of pleasure when she had been brought before him had sparked the dislike she'd always felt for him into a towering blaze of hatred.

"Ah, now I have both of you," Thurston had crowed with glee as she'd stood in his hall with her chin tilted defiantly. "I have the Dragon's mate as well as his get. Yea, this will bring him to his end swiftly."

"More like," she'd retorted, "he will slay you outright this time. With the king dead and no man to stay le Draca's sword, you will soon meet your own justice, Lord Thurston. Why do you think he has not slain you before now? Because he is afraid? Because he cannot? Nay, 'twas only John who held him in thrall, and that thralldom is ended with the king's death."

At her husband's side Alais had made a sound of dismay and fear, turning to Thurston. "She is right! My lord, we are undone if the Dragon comes. . . . Release her to him, and do not risk our lives for the sake of vengeance."

Even her cousin's pleas had not swayed Thurston, and Annice had been imprisoned below the keep in a damp, foul cell. She prayed for strength to last until Rolf could come for her, and prayed for the safety of his son. Thurston's triumph had been dimmed by her refusal to cower or show fear, and she had recognized that beneath his sneering facade lay a man who had come to the realization that he might well have courted death with his rash acts.

Closing her eyes, she tucked her hands into the folds of her gown to warm them. The rough wool of a novice nun was not as soft, but much warmer than her silk gowns would have been. She was glad the abbess had insisted upon her wearing it. The abbess—were they all slain? And sweet Belle, too? She didn't know. Things had happened so swiftly, and there had been so much chaos. She uttered a prayer.

Her stomach rumbled, and the sound drew a rat closer. She could hear its feet scrabbling on stone and straw and opened her eyes a slit to see. The glitter from beady eyes warned her, and when it drew close, she aimed a lethal boot heel at the rodent. She missed, and it scurried away with angry squeaks of alarm.

Jésu, now it was still alive to come again. She settled her shoulder blades back against the damp stone wall and waited. If not for her continual battle with the rats, she might have gone mad with fear and worry. This battle of wits was a distraction and kept her from dwelling too long on her possible fate. Rolf would come. She held tight to that certainty, for to despair would mean death.

The Dragon would come—and with him, her liberation, life, and love. Yea, he had never failed her, and he would not fail now. He would come to Stoneham Castle to take his wife and his son, and they would all go safely home to Dragonwyck.

With that hope steady in her mind and heart, Annice gradually succumbed to uneasy slumber. She slept in only fits and spurts now, ever wary of the rats who would nibble her feet and arms if she slept too deeply.

Dream fragments haunted her at times, visions of the past days of terror jerking her awake. Images swam before her, flashes of people and events—Rolf, Sir Guy, Belle, and even Gowain, the huntsman, appeared at times. In the ensuing chaos she hoped the huntsman had slipped away into the woods. She could only pray that Gowain had got through safely and managed to tell Gareth of her straits.

Deeper into the dungeons, she heard a muffled scream, and shuddered. Thurston had many people imprisoned within his keep. She caught glimpses of them on the brief occasions when she was taken from her cell, and heard moans and sobs in the murky gloom. Yet even with the chilling sounds of other tormented souls, she felt as isolated as if totally alone. Her brief attempts to communicate with others in the cells had been futile. No one dared reply, and a burly guard had come along to kick the door of her cell and bellow threats of violence should she not be quiet. The occasional shriek of agony that she heard was evidence enough against foolish defiance, and so she'd crept back to her corner to wait for the rats.

Hugging her knees close to her body, she thought now of all the days she had spent in the comfortable chambers above. Padded bolsters for the chairs, plush eastern carpets, embroidered silk hangings, and long tables burdened with tempting food that she had usually scorned. She recalled Thurston's hearty morning meals. Hunger gnawed her stomach daily, when once she had spurned the platters of white bread, broken meats, and fresh vegetables and fruit. Now an apple would have made her weak with delight.

A loud scratching jerked her from her dreams of food, and she tensed. A rat. And this one must be huge, for it sounded as if it had long claws like a cat. She reached down, fumbling for her boot.

Then a hiss sounded, unlike any rat she had yet heard. She froze, hand still on the buckle of her boot. The sound was louder, and this time she heard it distinctly.

"Cousin! Annice. . . ."

Alais.

Scrambling to her feet, Annice stumbled to the door and peered through the tiny barred opening. Feeble light from a wall torch glowed on pale hair, and she recognized her cousin's features. She curled her hands around the slender bars and pressed close to the grate.

"Alais—have you come to free me?"

"I cannot," Alais said, her voice a helpless, frightened gasp. She glanced around her wildly. "If Thurston discovers that I have even been down here . . . I had to bribe the guard with my favorite gold clasp. I also told him that if he said I was here, I would call him a liar and have his eyes removed." She stepped closer to the grating, peering inside. Her nose wrinkled with disgust. "*Jésu*—how do you stand it in there? It smells foul."

"Yea, and so it is," Annice said sharply. Exasperation battled with common sense. She could not alienate her best hope for assistance. "What news have you, Alais? Has my lord sent word?"

Alais shook her head. "Nay. Which is rather a relief, as I greatly fear le Draca."

"Rolf would not harm you, unless, of course, you were to harm me or his son." Annice paused to allow that to sink in, then said, "He will come for me. The Dragon would never allow Thurston to keep us now. Is it true? About the king?"

"Being dead? Yea, 'tis true." Alais sounded petulant. "John's death has certainly ended my husband's plans. He intended to sway his forces to the king's side, you know."

Annice did not point out that Alais's admission was made easily enough now, when the king was dead. She rose to her toes to whisper, "Alais, you must get a message to Rolf. He must know where I am. Please. You are my cousin, my blood."

Alarm creased Alais's perfect features. "But if Thurston was to find out, he would beat me! Or lock me away. Nay, 'tis too dangerous. Besides, what assurance would I have that your beast of a husband would not slay me once he arrived? None."

Taking a deep breath, Annice said calmly, "Rolf is no beast. He is a fair, just lord, and his people all love and respect him. None have cause for complaint. The only men in his dungeons are felons who belong there."

Alais frowned. "I do not care about the people on his lands. And the people imprisoned here are debtors for the most part, who refuse to pay their rightful taxes." She paused thoughtfully. "I did try to help you."

"Oh? And what did Lord Thurston say to freeing me?"

"Thurston? Oh, I didn't mean now. I meant last year, when you had been forced into marriage with the Dragon. I sent men to your rescue, but they were unsuccessful. I am sorry. I tried to aid you, but the men were incompetent fools. They waited until after the wedding, and then . . . well, it's of no consequence now." She leaned closer. "I just wanted to tell you that I do care about you, and I did try to help."

Startled by her revelation, Annice could not respond for a moment. Then she asked, "Who did you send to my aid?"

"Oh, Sir Simon de Roget. I always thought him to be honorable, but I vow, I think the man bungled it a'purpose. He claims 'twas others who erred. Something about not getting his orders right. And I paid him most handsomely aforehand to secure your safety." She looked down with a frown and made a face. "Holy Mary—there is some kind of noxious sludge soiling my shoes. . . . How do you stand it down here?"

" 'Tis not easy." Annice smothered an exclamation with no small effort. "Alais—if you cannot aid me, at least send word to Rolf where I am. He must know."

Dismay clouded Alais's face. "I will do what I can. I make no promises." Her wide eyes narrowed slightly. "If the Dragon comes for you, you will not allow him to harm me?"

Ever-selfish Alais, thinking of her own plight—though she did manage small kindnesses, at times, with a casually generous hand and indifferent heart. Annice shook her head.

"No harm will come to you at le Draca's hand, that I vow. He has never lifted a hand to me, though he has had cause several times."

Alais widened her eyes. "He has never beat you?"

"Nay. Though betimes he has threatened it."

Alais shook her head doubtfully. "I will do what I can," she repeated after a moment. Then her eyes brightened. "I almost forgot."

Reaching into the folds of her cloak, she brought out a small cloth bag and held it up. It was too large to fit through the grating, so she tugged open the drawstring securing the neck.

"I brought you a few things from the table. The food in here cannot be very pleasant."

"Almost nonexistent," Annice agreed dryly. Her mouth watered, and her stomach rumbled loudly as she detected the odors of roast meat and bread. Alais had brought cheese, also, and two oranges. These she stuffed through the bars of the grating, muttering imprecations at the thoughtlessness of men who would form a grate too small.

Immediately stuffing a chunk of bread into her mouth, Annice vowed she would never again take food for granted. She ate several bites, then asked, "What of Justin?"

"Who?"

"The Dragon's son." She swallowed a sliver of cheese and tucked the rest of the food into the cloth bag Alais shoved through the bars for her. If she could keep it from the rats, she would have food for later. "Justin, Alais—what news of him?"

Shrugging, Alais said, "He is still in the nursery, I suppose. I saw him when I went to visit—oh, p'raps you do not know. I have another child. A boy, finally. Thurston was most pleased and gave me a snow-white palfrey and an emerald necklace when he was born. It's really beautiful, with huge stones and an ornate setting."

Annice opened her mouth, then shut it again. Alais would never change. Wondering how many bastards Thurston had from his legion of willing and unwilling mistresses, Annice murmured her congratulations to her poor cousin.

Then she said, "Alais, you must do something for me. Wait before you say me nay, it is vital that you listen. Justin. He is just an innocent child. You must promise me that no matter what happens with me, you will see that Justin is taken to his father. Do that for me, Alais."

"What is he to you?" Alais countered with a frown. "The boy belongs to the Dragon. What do you care about his fate?"

"I love Rolf. And I felt great affection for his son even before I felt love for my husband. I know you are in an awkward position, but you will find a way to do it. You are clever, far more clever than Thurston knows. You try to hide it with your gossip and overweening vanity, but I know that there is much more to you than you show the world, Alais. Care for Justin. Keep him safe from Thurston, and I will see to it that Rolf rewards you for it."

Alais fiddled with the gold-encrusted threads of embroidery edging her sleeves, frowning. Then she looked up, and Annice saw a flash of something in her eyes as she said, "Very well. I will do what I can."

Before she could ask more questions, the guard intervened, stepping up to inform Alais that she must go before the other guards came on duty. He glanced inside at Annice, then back to his lady, twirling the ring of keys on one finger as he waited.

Alais whispered a swift farewell, then lifted the hem of her gown with a mutter of disgust as she followed the guard. Annice could hear her remonstrating with him on the foul condition of the stones as they traversed the long, dim hallway to the far door. She smiled faintly. Would Alais even remember her promise? Or would she think it too risky and decide to stay safely uninvolved? There was always the chance she would be too afraid. But it was more than Annice had expected even to find her cousin at the cell door, and at least she had a bag of food to lessen the aching pains of hunger.

Turning around, Annice put her back against the door and studied the shadows for a place to put her bag, to keep it safe from the rats.

War had ravaged the lands around Stoneham Castle. The woods had been largely burned, the fields destroyed. The pinched faces and haunted eyes of the villagers told a story of hunger and suffering.

"They slink away like curs," Sir Guy remarked as they passed a cottage.

"Yea, they have much cause if the tales are to be believed," Rolf responded. A man here or there had told of Thurston's reaction to the invading troops, how he had shut up the keep and refused to give shelter to any of his people, and how the French armies had devastated the countryside in vengeance when their siege had failed.

"If Stoneham can resist a French army, how is it that you think we can take it?" Guy asked when they reined their horses to a halt on a hilltop in view of Stoneham.

Rolf looked around him, remembering the last time he had paused atop this hill. Sunlight had glittered brightly then, reflected from the helmet of the knight who held Justin. His son's face still haunted him, the lingering echo of his cries a painful memory.

"Because," Rolf replied after a moment, "I intend to use my wits. The French depended upon their strength. I have both."

Guy glanced around, and grinned as a mail-clad knight rode toward them. "Yea, I recognize yon knight as a most energetic warrior, though I cannot recommend his wit to be as sharp."

Turning to see whom he meant, Rolf grinned, too. "My brother may not be clever enough to avoid capture and imprisonment, but he has a most novel method of escape, I think."

Geoffrey of Hawkhurst rode toward them at a swift pace, light reflecting from his helmet in blinding splinters. When he reached them, he jerked his mount to a halt, remonstrating, "If you want me to help you assault Stoneham, you'd best give the right direction. We went due south as you said, and—"

"West, Geoffrey," Rolf interrupted. "I told your man to ride west. Do you assign as messenger the most witless man in your service? Or just the deafest?"

Glaring, Geoffrey reached up to remove his helmet. He

tucked it under his arm. "If the knights in my service are so witless, then why did you beg my assistance?"

Shrugging, Rolf glanced toward Stoneham and said, "As targets for Seabrook's archers, of course. I need a distraction while my men form an assault."

Guy laughed aloud, and even Geoffrey grinned. "What is your plan, milord?" Guy asked, sobering.

"First we will surround the keep, and open negotiations. I expect Thurston to refuse to surrender, of course, and have already instructed my men on the building of siege engines. Yet I don't think that will be necessary but for a showy spectacle to keep Seabrook busy."

Surprise was evident on Guy's face, but Geoffrey began to grin. "Ah," he said with satisfaction, "you know a way inside."

"Yea," Rolf said softly, "I do." He took a deep breath and looked toward Stoneham. The drawbridge was up, and there was no sign of life. But he knew Thurston was aware of their arrival. With the countryside bare, he would be able to see for leagues, and Rolf had been deliberately visible. He wanted Thurston to know he was there, and to be waiting and watching. Yea, he would soon repay that base knight in kind for all that he had done the past seven years.

Wheeling his destrier about, he rode down the hill to make camp and detail his plans.

As the fire flickered brightly that night, Rolf huddled near it with his most trusted knights and captains. Using a stick, he drew a plan of the castle, pointing out its weaknesses.

Sir Guy frowned, then burst out, "But how do you know this man can be trusted, milord? He is Thurston's knight, and one of the men who abducted Lady Annice. . . ."

Rolf glanced from Guy to Sigehere, who returned his stare steadily. He was taking a chance, he well knew, but when the man had come to him, he had remembered him. There had been no subterfuge in Sigehere's eyes that foul day on the muddy road leading from Dragonwyck, and Annice had told how he'd done his best to protect her. Now he had come to protect her again, swearing that he had been sent by Lady Alais with a message for the Dragon.

Reluctant at first to believe him, Rolf had slowly been convinced when Sigehere had produced a diamond-and-sapphire ring that he knew to be Annice's. He'd seen it on her hand the day he had taken her from Seabrook and recognized it now. With the ring was the plea to rescue Annice but to do no harm to Thurston's wife.

Sigehere had flatly stated that he would not help le Draca if he did not receive an oath to absolve Lady Alais. "I care not for Thurston of Seabrook," he'd said firmly. "But for the lady's welfare I would have left his service long ago. I mislike serving a dishonorable man, and I know you to keep your oaths, milord. If you would have my help, you must swear to me that you will do no harm to the innocent."

"You have my oath and more, Sir Sigehere," Rolf had promised. He had been surrounded by too many dishonest men not to be able to recognize one who was honorable.

Now, in the face of Guy's concern, Rolf said, "Sir Sigehere will not betray us, for he would also be betraying one he has sworn to keep safe." He smiled faintly. "He is an honorable man, just as you are, Sir Guy."

After a moment Guy looked down at the ground and muttered, "I pray you are right, milord." He looked up to give Sigehere a fierce stare. "If we are betrayed, I will see the man responsible in too many different pieces for even the kites to notice."

Sir Sigehere did not look away from Guy's glare. "If we lose, 'twill not be for my treachery."

Silence fell, and some of the sergeants-at-arms exchanged uneasy glances. It was Geoffrey who broke the tension, saying dryly that if they lost, Thurston would no doubt see them all dead anyway. "And I, for one," he added, "do not intend that a craven coward such as Seabrook will find reason to gloat over my poor bones. Better to die a fool than a coward."

"That's easy for you to say," Rolf commented, and some of the men laughed. Taking up his stick again, Rolf dug the point into the dirt and said, "This door will be opened to us. . . ."

• • •

Dimly at first, Annice heard the shouts. They melded into the usual mutter of moanings that she'd grown accustomed to hearing, but in a short time became more distinct. She pushed herself to a sitting position. A wave of dizziness shook her.

Was it her imagination? She had dreamed of hearing sounds she'd once dreaded for so long . . . nay, 'twas no dream. Men were shouting, and there was the definite racket of battle drifting down through stone shafts from above. The clang of steel swords was unmistakable. Her cell was situated near the shaft built into the castle walls for the disposal of waste, and though the smell was foul, it allowed her to catch certain sounds at times. The garderobe shaft emptied into the moat, but her cell was above the water level, and so the opening carried the clamor of battle to her.

Sliding up the wall, Annice wished the food Alais had brought had lasted longer. She was so weak. Holy Mary and Joseph, mayhap it was Rolf come for her. She prayed that it was. Days had drifted into one another for so long, with little means of telling day from night save for the tiny opening high above her head, that she had no idea how long it had been since she'd been imprisoned. Time had ceased to exist. Even the rats were familiar to her now, and for a way to pass the time, she'd begun to name them.

Bent Back—from a firm strike of her boot—stared at her with a malevolent red gaze, tail twitching against the straw. Annice returned its gaze and pushed away from the wall, stumbling toward the door. She curled her fingers into the metal bars of the grating and clung there, holding tight for support. Closing her eyes, she prayed that Rolf had come for her.

How long she hung there she did not know. A lifetime. An eternity. When, finally, she heard the heavy door far down the narrow corridor open with a crash, she lifted her head hopefully.

"Rolf," she whispered in a faint sob.

Footsteps swiftly approached, and she loosened her grip on the metal grating and stepped back, fear surging upward to choke her. She had expected to hear Rolf call out for her, but whoever it was knew which cell she occupied.

A flash of premonition was her only warning before keys turned harshly in the lock and the door swung open. Light fell in a wavering path over the fouled straw of her cell, and Thurston of Seabrook stood in the opening.

He reached for her, then paused a handsbreadth away. A sneer crossed his face. Turning to the guard, he motioned him forward with the comment, "She reeks too badly for me to touch. Take her to the hall. Ah, I think a bracelet of chains would be a nice touch, don't you, milady?"

Annice just stared at him silently, conserving her energy. There would be time aplenty to bandy about insults, she thought with a sinking heart as the guard locked her into heavy iron shackles and jerked her forward. Blinking against the unaccustomed glare of light from the torches lining the corridors, Annice was led through an endless maze. Everything was a blur, and she held desperately to her resolve not to show Thurston how weak she'd grown.

That resolve was tested strenuously when they entered the hall. She stumbled slightly over her tattered hem and tried to hold her chin high as she felt the stares turned toward her. People whom she had once supped with eyed her with obvious horror, and she knew that her days in the dingy cell had taken their toll. She'd attended her daily functions as best as possible, but having no comb, and the only water that in a fouled bucket, she was well aware of how she must look. Still, she stiffened her spine and kept her eyes forward, striving to walk without falling in the heavy shackles that dangled from her wrists.

As her gaze shifted over the faces turned toward her, she saw her cousin. Alais was ashen-faced, brown eyes wide and muddy as she stared back at her with a strained expression. She sat in a chair next to her husband's, her hands curled into claws on the arms.

In a high, unnatural voice Alais said loudly, "Bring her closer, Thurston. I would speak with my cousin to see if she is penitent for her transgressions against you."

Annice was tugged forward, stumbling slightly. She met Alais's eyes and understood. It was only knowing that her cousin was as trapped as she that kept her silent when she was forced to her knees in the rushes before Seabrook's chair. He did not sit down but stood only a short distance away. Despite his casual, almost lighthearted, manner, there was a tension about him that finally penetrated Annice's haze. She turned her head to look at him.

Now she saw what she had not noticed in the gloomy light of the dungeon. His eyes were fever-bright, taut lines scoring deeply into each side of his mouth. Though he had always been arrow thin, there was a sparse, vibrating intensity to him now that she'd not seen before. It struck her that he was afraid. Deathly afraid, and the glitter in his eyes was terror of the Dragon.

She smiled, and his dark eyes sharpened. "For what reason do you smile, my lady of Dragonwyck?" he snarled. "Your husband will die before the day is done. Does that amuse you?"

"If, indeed, t'was true, t'would not amuse me. But I think, Lord Thurston, that 'tis you who will die ere this day is done."

Alais drew in a sharp breath, which was scant warning for the blow Thurston gave Annice across her face. It sent her reeling backward, and bound by the chains, she sprawled on the floor. Black dots danced before her eyes, and there was a roaring in her ears that drowned out all else. She clung fiercely to the shreds of images that whirled about her head.

I will not swoon, she told herself over and over. She was vaguely aware of Thurston towering over her, of his voice shouting and people running. The noise changed subtly, from a loud roar to a chaotic blend of different sounds. Metallic clangs, wrenching cries, piercing screams, all fused into a chain of discord that made her shut her eyes. She was falling into the black void that waited to claim her, all the dots merging into one velvety abyss yawning hungrily just ahead.

Alais screamed, and Annice tried to focus on her cousin. She was standing, mouth open in a terrified wail as she stared at the far end of the hall. Annice turned slightly, but the throbbing noise in her head allowed only the barest motion. She shut her eyes again, then opened them.

And then she saw him. His helmet was gone, and the golden hair blazed brightly. But even if he were in full armor, she would know him anywhere. Fighting ferociously, Rolf le Draca battled his way toward her through Thurston's knights, his sword cleaving and slicing with swift, lethal strokes. Men fell as if grass mowed down by a scythe, and Annice had the eerie impression that she was in one of her dreams again. She must be, for she saw two of Rolf. Two blond giants side by side, swords flashing with deadly accuracy.

And then she was slipping into the abyss, though she tried desperately to hold on. The black void claimed her in one single gulp like a devouring beast. Like a dragon. . . .

CHAPTER 22

Bursting into the hall, Rolf saw Thurston strike a thin, pale ghost of a woman with dark, matted hair. She sprawled on the floor in a dazed heap, and he felt a surge of fury wash over him. To strike a helpless woman bound in chains—yea, death for a man such as that could not come too quickly.

"Thurston!" he bellowed, and held up his sword. The blade was slick with blood, shining silver and crimson in the light of torches. His helmet had been lost in a fierce skirmish in the outer bailey, and he had not paused to grab another. Now he reached for one, wrenching it from a fallen knight near his feet. Seabrook made it quickly obvious he had no intention of personal combat and snapped out orders to his knights.

They moved toward him in a single wave, and Rolf tensed for battle. When he felt Guy and his brother at his side, he smiled grimly, and they began working their way forward. Thrusting and slashing, they quickly cleared the hall of knights able to fight. But by the time they reached the dais where Seabrook had been, he was gone.

Furious, Rolf looked at Seabrook's wife, who stood as if frozen behind the high back of her chair. She lifted an arm and pointed with a shaking hand to the figure still sprawled on the floor. He glanced down, then stiffened. Nay, it could not be. . . .

"*Jésu*," he groaned, and knelt beside her, pulling off the helmet to see her better. A red mark swelled one side of Annice's face. Her eyes were closed, and her beautiful dark-red hair was dull and tangled. He lifted her gently. She moaned pitifully. She felt like a sack of dry bones with no substance. He looked up at Lady Alais with a fierce glare. "You allowed this?"

In a quavering voice she said, "Annice promised you would not hurt me. . . ."

Rolf swallowed his angry words. And he had given his oath to Sir Sigehere that he would not harm Lady Alais. Despite her selfishness, he was bound by that oath.

"Nay," he said harshly. "I will not harm you."

Rising to his feet with Annice in his arms, he turned to his brother. Geoffrey waited with a frown, his bloody sword clutched in one hand, his helmet in the other.

"Guard her," Rolf said quietly, and moved to place Annice upon a pile of chair bolsters that had tumbled to the floor. He turned to Lady Alais and bade her stay with her cousin until his return.

"Do you go after my husband?" she asked, staring at him with wide brown eyes. At his short nod she took a deep breath. "You had best go swiftly, my lord. Thurston has gone to the nursery to fetch your son. . . ."

Time was his enemy, for he knew as he raced down torch-lit hallways that Thurston would not hesitate to take his vengeance with great satisfaction upon a small boy.

Rolf was barely aware of Sir Guy behind him, running to keep up with his swift pace. They ranged like wild beasts through the halls until they came upon a cowering maid-servant, who told them shakily where to find the children.

"But, milord," she added fearfully, "if you seek the lord of the keep, he has gone above to the battlements."

"Alone?" Rolf demanded, and saw from the widening of her eyes the answer. He did not need to linger to hear that Thurston had Justin with him.

"He means to barter for his life," Guy muttered.

"If he has harmed one hair on Justin's head . . ."

When they reached the top, a small knot of men-at-arms barred their way. Guy and Rolf fought furiously and dispatched them with little trouble. Squinting against the glare of a winter sun, Rolf paused, breathing hard through his teeth as he looked about for Thurston.

A large bastion dominated the far end, its curved walls rising high above the crenellated walls of the other battlements. A banner bearing Seabrook's emblem snapped loudly in the wind atop a slender pole. One of the doors leading upward to the very top was open and swung back and forth with a sharp, banging noise.

"He has gone to the very top," Guy said, but Rolf was already striding toward the door and commanding him to stand guard.

It was close inside, the narrow steps allowing only one man at a time to ascend, curving in a tight spiral. He took the steps two at a time. His sword scraped against the stone walls when he held it in front of him at the ready, so tight was the passage. It was quiet in the stairwell, noise from the battle below muffled by space and thick stones.

When he stepped warily outside the passage, howling wind and light burst onto his senses. He saw Thurston at once. He was leaning against the far curve of wall, Justin held in front of him. The boy was rigid and still, fear widening his eyes as his uncle held a dagger to his throat.

Rolf swallowed heavily. Sunlight glittered along the blade of Thurston's dagger, and slid in silvery runnels from the edge of Rolf's sword when he held it high.

" 'Tis over, Thurston," he said loudly, but the wind whipped his words away so they sounded distant and weak. He stepped closer.

"Nay," Thurston said with a sneer. His dark eyes gleamed with hatred as he pressed the dagger's edge harder against Justin's throat. " 'Tis time to slay the Dragon. But first, his get."

Rolf held up his free hand. "You have children of your own. Would you see them die?"

"They will die anyway, whether I allow your whelp to live or no. Do you think me fool enough to believe what you might say to save your son? I am not. I have not lived so long by trusting in other men to keep their oaths."

Wind whipped at Thurston's tunic and hair, and caught the hem of Justin's short tunic. The boy had a hand curved over his uncle's wrist as if to stay his movements, and his lips were taut with his fear. Rolf met the boy's eyes for an instant, and his throat tightened at the pleading trust he saw registered in them.

Taking a deep breath, Rolf looked back at Thurston and said, "I am a man who keeps my sworn oaths. You know this. Never have I broken a bond. I give my oath that your children will not be harmed. But you must release my son to me, or I will give no such oath."

After a moment Thurston laughed harshly. "Release him? Yea, p'raps I will, after all. Lay down your weapon, and I will free the boy."

Rolf froze. He had no intention of allowing Thurston to escape. But neither did he want his son slain. He hesitated, and when Seabrook made a move with the dagger that brought a thin red stream of blood welling up on Justin's neck, he held up his sword.

"I yield my weapon," he said, thinking swiftly. Thurston would not hesitate to kill both of them once Rolf was unarmed, but he was much bigger than Seabrook. And he had his dagger still in his belt. Even without his sword he might be able to overpower him.

Taking a cautious step forward, Rolf bent and placed his sword on the sun-scoured stones between him and Thurston. He rose slowly and waited, with arms dangling at his sides.

Thurston laughed, and the wind carried his laughter from the tower top in a resounding wave. The sound echoed eerily from the ridged walls.

"Yea, Dragon," Seabrook sneered, "I will keep my oath to you. I shall free the boy as if he is a bird."

In a motion too swift for Rolf to predict or prevent,

Thurston swung Justin's small form to the ledge of the chest-high wall. Justin clutched frantically at his uncle's sleeve as he was held precariously near the edge.

"Father!" he screamed. "Help me!"

Rolf's instinctive reaction was to wrench his dagger from the sheath and fling it. The blade struck Thurston in his neck. He staggered back. Rolf was already throwing himself toward them, desperate to snatch Justin from the edge before he was shoved over.

But Thurston, even dying, was tenacious in his grip. Snarling through lips bubbling with bloody froth, he resisted Rolf's efforts with startling strength. Blood pumped from his throat as they struggled, and Justin slipped ever closer to the precipice.

Thurston's fist was wrapped in Justin's tunic, and he gave a mighty shove to send the boy over the edge. Rolf clamped a hand down on his arm with fierce strength and grabbed for his son with his other hand. But Justin was just beyond his reach, dangling precariously over the side of the tower. The boy's tunic had caught on a jutting stone corner.

Far below lay the jagged stone buttresses that supported Stoneham. The wind was fierce around them, cold and bitter despite the sunshine.

Rolf pressed against Thurston using his forearm as a wedge to drive him hard against the angle of the stone ledge. Still Thurston clung fiercely to life.

Slowly, Rolf was able to reach up and grasp the blood-slick hilt of the dagger jutting from Thurston's throat. He shoved fiercely. As Seabrook went limp, Rolf heard Justin's high scream.

Diving toward him, Rolf grasped the hem of the boy's tunic. They both hung perilously over the edge of the tower wall, while Rolf struggled to regain his footing.

For an instant Rolf thought they would both tumble over the edge. Then he felt a strong arm curve around him and heard with relief a familiar voice in his ear as Guy pulled them both back over the edge to safety.

Rolf slid down the wall to the stone floor with Justin in his lap, too weak with relief to do more than pant for breath. His son held tightly to Rolf, small limbs quaking with reaction. Shameless tears stung Rolf's eyes and slid down his cheeks as he drew Justin to his chest, holding him as if he would never let him go.

Guy knelt in front of them, his hazel eyes narrowed against the sun. "Seabrook fell over the side. Even if I'd wanted to, I couldn't have caught him in time." He looked away, then back. A faint smile curved his mouth as he met Rolf's gaze. "The castle is secured, and your brother is with Annice. Shall we join them, milord?"

"What," Rolf began, pushing painfully to his feet without loosening his grasp on Justin, "took you so bloody long to get here?"

Guy laughed. "I was ordered to stand guard, milord. I am but used to obeying your orders."

"I have trained you overwell," Rolf muttered, but his smile eased any sting from his weak jest.

"Holy Mother—you're mortal wounded," Annice cried, rising weakly from her pallet of cushions.

Before Rolf could reach her, Alais was there to push her gently back down. "Be still, or you will only swoon again. Ahh, I fear me I will not like what your lord will say. . . ."

Covered with blood and holding tight to Justin, Rolf paused a few feet from Annice. He set Justin gently on his feet, then straightened with the boy clinging to his side. Annice's fears slowly eased. He was not limping, nor favoring any part of his body. The wounds could not be too serious. And though Justin was bloody as well, he seemed whole save for an ugly scratch on his neck.

For a few moments Rolf spoke in a low tone to Sir Guy and the man whom he had set to guard his wife. This man seemed an older version of Rolf, save for the fact that he continually jested with those around him. Since she'd awakened, she'd heard him bedevil Alais most unmercifully, until Alais snapped at him to be quiet or she would gut him with her poniard. It had had no effect at all.

Now the man Rolf called Geoffrey turned toward Alais with a solemn countenance. "Milady," he said, "my brother brings grim tidings to you."

"Thurston is dead," Alais said flatly, and Geoffrey nodded.

Annice realized then that this was Rolf's brother and understood that they had joined forces to come to her aid. And now Thurston was dead, and her cousin a widow. She turned painfully to look at Alais, who stood still and quietly thoughtful for a long moment.

"I expected such. Am I to be imprisoned now?" Alais asked shortly, and Rolf shook his head.

"Nay, you are to be allowed to go wherever you wish, as long as you do not stay here. This keep is now mine, by right of force. Sir Sigehere will be your escort."

Annice watched as Rolf regarded Alais stonily. If he had expected hysterics or pleas, he was very much mistaken. Alais simply shrugged and stated her intention to go to her favorite dowry keep, which had much more pleasant weather and, though smaller, was more comfortable. She and her children would be happy there.

Turning to her cousin, Alais asked, "Am I expected to take with me Thurston's bastards? I would much rather leave them here, as they are too many to support and I do not care for them."

It was typical of Alais that she would be most concerned with her own welfare, but still Annice found it disquieting.

Before she could reply, Geoffrey laughed and said, "By all means, milady, leave them here. I fear for their welfare should you take them with you."

Alais knelt beside Annice and took her hand. The shackles had been removed, and Annice clasped her cousin's fingers weakly.

"I know," Alais said softly, "that you think me selfish. And you are right. But I could be little else and survive with a man like Thurston. 'Twas all he understood. This I will tell you, cousin—I have a great affection for you, and admiration for your courage. I wish you happiness with your lord, for I think you have found a man worthy of you at last."

Tears clogged Annice's throat, and she could not reply. In her weakened state, emotion swamped her too readily. Alais smiled and squeezed her hand, then bent to press a kiss upon her brow. "You should bathe as soon as possible," she whispered, then rose to her feet and announced her imminent departure. "Send Sir Sigehere to me at once," she said as she swept from the hall.

The easy tears slipped down Annice's cheeks, and she could no longer hold up her head. She pressed her face against the velvet softness of a cushion, exhausted. Around her she could hear men giving orders for the restoration of order and the security of the keep. Rolf still did not come to her but talked softly to Justin in a low tone she could not hear.

Did he no longer care about her? Was she, then, as she had always feared, just one of his possessions? She'd seen how fiercely he held to what was his, not releasing even a groat unwillingly. Never had he said he loved her, only that he feared for her. She had thought once he might say it, when he'd held her close and said he would come for her and would keep her safe from harm, but he had not. Nor later, when he had left her at the nunnery near Gedney, had he said the words she longed to hear.

Now, when he once more had his son, he had forgotten about her, and God grant her grace for it, but she felt a spurt of envy that the child held his love while she did not. Tears seeped from under her closed eyelids, and she choked back an anguished sob.

Though she had not heard him approach, Rolf's voice was close and gentle. "*Chérie,* do not weep. We are all safe now. My men have secured the castle, and we will remain here until you are well enough to travel." His hand touched her hair lightly, lifting a tangled strand to hold in his fist. "Are you strong enough to hear me?"

Opening her eyes, Annice turned her face to look up at him. There was no revulsion in his expression, though she knew how thin and dreadful she must appear. From some hidden resource deep inside her, she managed to dredge up a smile.

"I am only weary. It has been a long time—" She halted, then asked, "Belle? Did she make it back to Dragonwyck with Gowain?"

Rolf looked away, and Annice's heart sank. He said slowly, "Belle returned safely, though she is still recovering from her ordeal. But Gowain—he was mortal wounded, and survived only long enough to say you had been taken."

Annice's throat closed with grief for the gentle huntsman who had served her well, and she vowed to erect a cross in his memory. *Jésu,* so many had been lost in the past years. "How long have I been held prisoner?"

Rolf's hand moved to caress her cheek. " 'Tis now a sennight past All Saints' Day."

Annice's throat tightened. She had been held for close to two months. It was November, and she had last been at Dragonwyck in the middle of September. Helpless tears rolled down her cheeks, and she looked up at Rolf and whispered, "I want to go home. Rolf, take me home to Dragonwyck."

For a long moment he gazed at her, then said softly, "My love, I will take you wherever you wish to go. You are my life."

The last simple words made her catch her breath. She searched his face for a moment, then drew in a deep breath for courage and said, "I love you, Rolf of Dragonwyck."

"Yea, sweet wife, well I know it." His hand curved along the line of her cheek, and his green eyes were misted with a faint sheen of silver. "I think, mayhap, that you love me near as much as I love you. . . ."

Her heart lurched. She clung tightly to his hand, holding it to her face as she turned to press a kiss into his palm. Never had she thought to hear those words. She wanted to hear them again, but a surge of overpowering weakness left her too shaky to ask.

She need not have worried.

Bending close, Rolf grazed her mouth with his lips, whispering, "I will love you always, *chérie.* I swore to keep you safe and to see to your needs, and those I do to the best of my ability. I am not always successful. But the love I give you will never dim. 'Twill always be there, even when I am not. I pray that it is enough for you, and you will forgive me these past months."

Opening her eyes, Annice smiled. Her hand curled trustingly in his. "There is nothing to forgive. If I have your love, I have everything."

DRAGONWYCK CASTLE

May 1218

EPILOGUE

𝕵ustin looks much happier now."

Annice put a hand over her eyes to shade them from the sun, watching as Justin gamboled about the garden with Bordet. The huge mastiff was gentle and protective of the boy, eagerly fetching a tossed stick to bring it back.

Rolf followed her gaze and smiled. Yea, Justin was happy. He was still a bit thin but had grown much sturdier since being at Dragonwyck. The small garden within the castle walls was abloom with roses that nodded in a warm wind. For the first time it seemed like a true home to him rather than a military fortress. The transformation that had begun with Annice's arrival was completed. They were a family. He had his son and his wife, and God willing, the new babe she carried would be born healthy and strong.

"Milord," Annice said, and he turned to look where she indicated. Sir Guy approached, striding toward them across the small patch of grass. Rolf rose to his feet from the stone garden bench.

Grinning, Sir Guy first acknowledged his overlord, then

his lady, kneeling at her feet to take her hand. "Even fat you are beautiful," he said promptly, and laughed when indignant color flushed Annice's face. She put a hand upon the swell of her belly and glared at him.

"I am not *fat*." She paused. "Pleasantly round, mayhap."

Guy pressed a kiss to the back of her hand and rose to his feet, gazing fondly down at her. Annice looked up at him with a smile. "How fare the Beauchamp lands?"

"Excellent." Guy glanced at Rolf. "Chesterton prospers. With proper guidance I think the keep will be most profitable."

Rolf nodded. "Yea, with you as castellan, I expect it."

"It's fitting, I think," Annice said softly, "that the lands should be held by a man of Beauchamp blood."

There was a softening in Guy's eyes when he looked down at her, and he nodded. "Yea, though I never dreamed that one day I would be able to claim my heritage. It never occurred to me that you would not resent me."

"Resent you?" Annice echoed in surprise. "Nay, you are more my brother than Aubert ever was, for you bound yourself to me in love and loyalty as well as blood." She paused, then added, " 'Tis not the fault of an innocent babe that his parents were not wed. I am shamed that Aubert was cruel enough to deny you your heritage."

"I can understand it, I suppose," Guy said. "A brother, even a bastard, might lay claim to part of his inheritance. Aubert has been ever watchful over what is his."

"And what is not his," Annice said sharply. "My brother is greedy. Our father should have provided for you."

"If he had but known of my existence," Guy said slowly, "he most like would have done so. When my mother's father pressed Aubert to notify Lord Hugh of my birth, he said he had done so when in truth, he had not. 'Twas Aubert who sent me to the monastery in my early years and provided for my keep until I came of age. I owe him that much, I suppose."

Quiet until now, Rolf said, "Never fear about Aubert collecting his debts. Now that Louis has returned to France, he has found his subjects and neighbors most insistent upon recovering what is owed them. I understand that Aubert is besieging King Philip with demands for monies owed."

Annice and Guy laughed, and their amusement drew Justin to his elders. His green eyes were alight with pleasure as he leaned against the stone bench where Annice sat. She pulled him close and ruffled his pale hair with an affectionate hand.

"Have you tired out poor Bordet?" she teased, indicating the dog, who lay stretched out on the grass beneath the branches of an oak.

Justin smiled widely. "Not as much as I should have. He chewed up one of my wooden knights."

"One of those your father carved for you?"

"Yea, but it's all right. 'Twas the one I called Seabrook, and I shall not miss him." The last word was said with grim satisfaction.

Rolf stared down at his son and wondered if the painful memories of his early childhood would ever be eased. Since coming to Dragonwyck, Justin had slipped slowly into a more relaxed temperament, but at times he still woke at night from frightening dreams.

"I nearly forgot," Guy said after a moment, and held out his hand. "I bring news from your brother, milord."

Rolf lifted a brow when he saw the parchment. "Geoffrey must want something if he wrote a letter. I've never known him to bestir himself to actually write otherwise."

Anxiously, Annice asked, "Is all well in the land, Guy?"

Guy smiled down at her. "Yea, sweet sister. Though King Henry is young yet, he has able regents—and no uncles who might murder him for the throne."

Breaking the seal and unrolling the parchment, Rolf grumbled, "If his counselors would cease quarreling with one another, all of England would be at peace."

"Henry will grow up," Guy said. "And 'tis rumored that he is nothing like John. I think that he may prove to be an able ruler."

Rolf swore softly as he read Geoffrey's letter. Guy and Annice turned to stare at him.

"My energetic brother has decided to help Lady Alais regain some of her Welsh lands. The Welsh chieftain Griffyn ap Llewelyn has seized some of her dower estates. Geoffrey asks for my assistance."

Annice rose shakily to her feet, her voice much steadier than her trembling hands. "And will you go, milord?"

He met her gaze for a long moment, then smiled. "I have no interest in Welsh lands. I have been to Wales and would sooner fight demons. But there are those in my service who would leap eagerly at the chance to earn honors and lands for themselves. Gareth of Kesteven shall surely wish to go, and young Corbet has only recently won his knight's spurs. I shall send word to them and let them choose who among them would join my mad brother in his quest."

Rolf could see the relief in Annice's eyes. He pulled her to him, careful not to overset her balance. She'd grown clumsy with the coming child, and he was always at pains to make her comfortable.

Tilting her head back against his shoulder, she smiled up at him. "Shall we walk through the garden, my lord?" she murmured.

Guy said tactfully, "I think Justin and I will visit Belle. She always knows when the cooks have prepared tasty treats for dinner." He urged Justin with him, and they strolled toward the kitchens.

Rolf watched them go, his arm resting on Annice's shoulders in a loving clasp. Sunlight brightened the corners of the bailey and glittered on the turrets above. It seemed to him that all of England was alight now, where so recently there had been only the dark shadows of war and fear and desperation.

War might come again, as a few rebel barons still quarreled among themselves, but the Magna Carta that had caused so much strife and death had brought forth a new concept that all struggled to achieve. There was a new climate of understanding brewing among all men—kings, barons, and villeins alike.

"Are you content, sweet lord?" Annice asked.

He pressed his cheek against the top of her head.

"Nay." When she jerked to a halt and looked up at him with wide eyes, he smiled and said, " 'Blissful' would best describe how I feel, my love. Never did I think I would be so happy."

Annice's blue eyes filled with tears, and she managed a smile as she whispered, "And never did I think I would find such happiness loving a dragon. . . ."

To My Readers:

For those of you who may be confused by some of the references to the new year beginning in March, let me assure you that while doing my research, I was also confused at first. Then I discovered that the new Gregorian calendar was not proposed until the fifteenth century, at which time the new year began on January 1 instead of in March. I won't go into all the details—suffice it to say even back then they knew much more of mathematics than I still do—but will just say that when England adopted the new calendar in 1752, time leaped from September 2, 1752, to September 14, 1752. That canceled a few birthday celebrations, I'm certain, but got the lunar year back on track.

Also interesting is the fact that George Washington was born on February 11, 1732, but after the calendar change, his birthday became celebrated on February 22.

I tried to remain true to all historical events, as they are known for certain, but records dating from the medieval times are often scanty. Forgive me for any errors, but I took the liberty of choosing which version would best suit my story. I hope you enjoyed it.

Juliana Garnett

ABOUT THE AUTHOR

Juliana Garnett is a bestselling author writing under a new name to indulge her passion for medieval history. Always fascinated by the romance of *knights in shining armor*, this Southern writer is now at liberty to focus on the pageantry and allure of days when chivalry was expected and there were plenty of damsels in distress.

Ms. Garnett has won numerous awards for her previous works, and hopes to entertain new readers who share her passion for valorous heroes and strong, beautiful heroines.